# THE
# MacGuffin

NOVELS BY MICHAEL CRAFT

Rehearsing

Flight Dreams

Eye Contact

Body Language

Name Games

Boy Toy

Desert Autumn

Hot Spot

Desert Winter

Desert Spring

Bitch Slap

Desert Summer

The MacGuffin

STAGE PLAYS

Photo Flash

The Transit of Venus
with Burt Peachy
Pink Squirrels

WEBSITE

www.michaelcraft.com

THE
# MacGuffin

A MYSTERY

MICHAEL CRAFT

QUESTOVER
PRESS

Design and typography: M.C. Johnson
Front cover photo: Jim Harper
Author's photo: Questover Press

Library of Congress Cataloging-in-Publication Data

Craft, Michael, 1950–
  The MacGuffin / Michael Craft
  ISBN-10: 0615499716
  ISBN-13: 978-0615499710
  BISAC: Fiction / Mystery & Detective / General

First Questover Press paperback edition: August 2011
**Questover Press**
Rancho Mirage, California

ACKNOWLEDGMENTS

Although writing is a solitary pursuit, novels rarely materialize without some help along the way, and this effort was no exception. For their generous assistance with various plot details and technical issues, I extend deep gratitude to David Grey, Dan Hurley, Peter Springall, and Eddie Swaim. For their support and counsel relating to the words on the page, I am indebted to Eston Ellis, James McGuire, Barbara McReal, Leon Pascucci, Burt Peachy, and Mitchell Waters. Perhaps most important, I am grateful for the motivation supplied by the many past readers who kept asking, "When?" The answer, of course, is "Now." My heartfelt thanks to all of you.

— *Michael Craft*

# Contents

# Part One

## *Heat*

Energy can be neither created nor destroyed; it can only change forms. The total amount of energy in the universe remains constant. For a thermodynamic cylce, the net heat supplied to the system equals the net work done by the system.

— *The first law of thermodynamics*

# Chapter 1

**A** silky blond Yorkshire terrier—all fur and attitude, all of five or six pounds—sniffed in the grass near its master's feet and found something of interest, not in the turf, but crusted on the heel of the old man's spit-polished, fancy-tooled cowboy boots. The dog licked it.

The man didn't notice. He stood without stooping, cutting a fine figure in his dark blue suit, its jacket detailed with a Western-style yoke across the shoulders. Hat in one hand, a bunch of roses in the other, he peered down at the modest gravestone, a flat rectangle of granite and bronze resembling the hundreds of others, maybe thousands, that gridded the grounds of Desert Memorial Park. EMMA EMERY, said the burnished letters, glowing warm in the morning sun. DEVOTED WIFE, LOVING MOTHER. She had lived only six decades, that and some change, when, twenty years ago, she was first in the family to become one with the earth in California, just outside Palm Springs. Vacant plots—perpetually groomed, forever tidy—flanked her, awaiting the rest of the clan.

Her husband, well into his eighties, crouched to lay the flowers, all but one of them red, at the edge of her plaque. His boots squeaked under the weight of his haunches; the dog's tongue lapped the bottom of one heel. Locusts buzzed in the pines, the ficus, the towering border of tamarisks. A fountain petered from a nearby mausoleum wall, a great chevron of tiny crypts. Overhead, a jet whined, banking low toward the local airport at the foot of the San Jacinto Mountains.

He mumbled something—a prayer, a memory, an afterthought—then blessed himself with the sign of the cross, slapped the dove-gray Stetson onto the remains of his silvered hair, and pulled a solitary white rose from the bouquet. When he stood, the dog yapped, jumping clear of his feet.

"Quiet, Pyrite."

The Yorkie yapped again, prancing a few tentative, sidelong

steps toward the narrow roadway that wound through the cemetery. The widower checked his watch, a chunky Rolex, loose and heavy on his skinny wrist. "Wanna visit Frank?"

Pyrite led the way, crossing the asphalt drive to a neighboring section of plots where one of the flat headstones, otherwise indistinguishable from the surrounding rank and file, was decorated with a mishmash of faded American flags, wilted bouquets, tossed pennies, and offerings of cigarettes, some whole, others partly smoked. One of the longer butts, bearing a crimson lip-print on its filter, immediately drew Pyrite's attention. He nosed it and quivered.

The old man trudged after, joined the dog at the grave, and stared down at the stone, inscribed FRANCIS ALBERT SINATRA. Above the name: THE BEST IS YET TO COME. While Pyrite dirtied his beard with shreds of tobacco, the man leaned to drop his rose among the other memorials, then tapped his fingers to the brim of his hat, a jaunty salute to the late crooner. Standing erect again, he straightened a bolo that adorned the long-pointed collar of his satin shirt and slid the clasp, a sizable nugget of gold, tight to his throat.

Pyrite sneezed.

"Whatcha got, you little son f'bitch?"

The dog glanced up, a cigarette dangling from his mouth, looking a tad like Sinatra himself.

The man suppressed a laugh, commanding, "Pyrite. Drop it."

The dog stared him down, licking the butt farther into his mouth.

"*Drop* it."

The dog lowered his jaw and let the cigarette fall.

"Good baby. Good Pyrite. *Good* little son f'bitch." He squatted, picked up the dog, and fingered debris from its beard. "Got to look our best today. Somebody might want to take your picture." When he plopped the dog back on the ground, it gave a vigorous shake, primping its luxuriant coat, rattling the tags on a fierce studded collar, the sort more in vogue with pit bulls.

"Let's go, sweet pea." The man stood and walked across the grass, zigzagging between headstones toward the middle of the cemetery, where he had parked near a side entrance on Da Vall Drive. Pyrite trotted behind, beelining over anything in his path, skittering on the polished markers, deterred only by the occasional urge to sniff or pee. The sun had inched higher into a pristine October sky, shushing the locusts, now drowned out by the ecstatic trill of mockingbirds. A roadrunner darted past, about the size of Pyrite; it showed no fear of the dog, which halted wide-eyed to let the bird pass.

At the center of the grounds, an open-air chapel slouched among a few palms. Near it hulked the old man's Hummer, gun-metal gray, sporting an extra ton of chrome trim as well as vanity plates proclaiming BIX EMRY. He had tried pulling strings to get the second *e* in *Emery,* but even he hadn't the pull to exceed seven characters, a humbling reminder that power has its limits. He opened the door, telling the dog, "Well? Hop in."

Pyrite hunkered low to the pavement, preparing to spring, calculating the leap, at least a yard up to the driver's seat. But there was no way. He sat, flipped his tail, yapped.

"Pansy." Bix chortled, picked up the dog—"pansy pup"—and placed him gently on the seat. Pyrite scampered over to the passenger seat, where he curled into a doggy bed.

Bix hoisted himself into the Hummer and slammed the door; even with his Stetson, there was headroom to spare. He fired up the ignition, cranked up Frank wailing "My Way," drove past a low hedge of pink oleander, past the NO PETS ALLOWED sign, and through the gates to the street. Turning left, he goosed the accelerator and blasted northward out of town, then west toward open desert.

In the middle of nowhere, somewhere between the fields of giant wind turbines in the San Gorgonio Pass to the west and the solitude of Joshua Tree National Park to the east, somewhere in these wastelands north of Interstate 10, a stretch of sand, four square miles of it, now crackled with development. On this bright Thursday morning, however, construction had ceased—paused—for the formal dedication of Phase One.

The sign near the entrance, though nearly a block long, was designed with an eye toward sleek understatement and, above all, cleanliness. It announced, simply, crisply, in raised stainless steel letters on a wall of stacked stone, EMERY ENERGY. With a spray of gravel, Bix's Hummer sped past the sign and braked with a squeal to turn through the main gates. The visitors' parking area was already filled with at least a hundred dignitaries' cars, and near the front of the new corporate headquarters, a smattering of TV trucks had telescoped their antennas skyward. The broad front stairs of the building served as a provisional stage. An empty podium stood dead center, and behind it sat a few rows of VIPs, beginning to wilt in the full sun; though the event had been scheduled early to avoid the brunt of the desert's heat, the autumn morning was already nudging eighty degrees. In a dry breeze, a banner fluttered over the stage, summing up both the facility's purpose and the company's challenge: REPOWER OUR NATION!

Bix told Pyrite, "Looks like we're late."

The dog rose from his bed and reached his front paws on the door to snoop through the window. Assessing the situation, he gave an anxious little whimper.

"Nah"—Bix laughed—"they can't start without *us*."

Reassured, Pyrite sat, facing forward, though too short to see through the windshield.

Frank, winding into a frenzy, walloped some lyrics about "those little-town blues." Bix switched off the music. "Sorry," he said, perhaps to the dog, perhaps to the singer, "we've got work to do."

A security guard at the gate had radioed a pair of parking valets, who appeared in a golf cart, one to whisk away the Hummer, the other to shuttle Bix through the crowd to the stage. During his grand entrance, just late enough to have heightened the anticipation, he waved to the applauding assemblage with one arm, holding Pyrite in the other. When he alighted from the cart at the bottom step of the stage, a man in a black business suit and silver-striped tie rushed forward to meet him. Balding, in his fifties, he blotted sweat from his head with a white linen handkerchief. "Thank God," he said. "I can introduce you whenever you're ready."

Bix asked, "Did the governor make it?"

"Uh, wildfire upstate. But he sent the lieutenant governor."

Bix grumbled something; Pyrite gave a low growl.

"CNN is here. And the local and L.A. media."

"Let's go." Bix led the charge up the stairs, the man in black tailing him. More applause. Bix turned, waved, then sat in the chair reserved for him, front row center.

"Glad you could make it, Bix," the woman seated next to him said with good-natured sarcasm. Poised, sixty, still beautiful, and more than a little bored, she reached to pet Pyrite. A few tasteful platinum bracelets jangled on her wrist. Unlike the others seated onstage, she had yet to break a sweat.

"Had to visit your mother." Bix joined his daughter in mussing Pyrite's coat. "She needed fresh flowers, Stasia."

Born Anastasia, she had been Stasia since a toddler, Stasia Emery-Brant since her second marriage. In deference to her family's wealth and social standing, some were inclined to address her as *Stah*-cia, but she always reminded them, "I've been a California girl most of my life, and I was born in Oklahoma. It's Stasia—rhymes with 'Asia.'"

Bix reached across his daughter to clap a hand on his son-in-law's shoulder. "Well, Coops," he said, "today's your big day."

"I think today belongs to you, Bix." Cooper Brant pocketed his sunglasses and turned his attention to the podium, where someone—he wasn't sure who it was—stood at the microphone and said to the crowd, "Please welcome Emery Energy's chief financial officer and second-in-command, Austin Royce."

Royce, the balding man in the black suit, stepped forward to polite applause. "Before introducing our founder, I'd like to share with you the sense of honor I've felt working alongside so great a visionary for the past quarter century. Long before I arrived on the scene, Bix Emery was already a prime mover in the oil markets of Oklahoma and Texas, but his dreams were bigger. So he headquartered Emery Oil in Los Angeles, a strategic move that eventually awarded him market dominance of the entire West Coast . . ."

Cooper Brant watched the speaker but silently rehearsed the remarks he himself would make, hoping Bix would not refer to him publicly as Coops. Everyone else called him Cooper or Coop. Was the added s an expression of familial affection? Or a subtle goading, an emasculating affix?

". . . knew that the bold challenges of the twenty-first century require bold solutions. Then"—Royce paused for dramatic effect—"when the scope of the Gulf oil disaster became apparent, that's when Bix Emery made the decision to rebrand and redirect his entire life's work. That's why today Emery Oil becomes Emery Energy, committed to the research and development of alternative fuels and technologies. That's why he's picked up shop and moved the entire operation here to Palm Springs, an area already synonymous with wind, solar, and geothermal power . . ."

Cooper rested his hand on Stasia's knee; she placed her hand on his. They looked good together, he thought. He often wondered how it had happened. How had they managed to find each other, some ten years ago, after each had suffered the failure of a first marriage? Two years her junior, he used to call her a cradle robber, and they had laughed about it.

". . . my distinct privilege to introduce our founder, president, chairman, and chief executive officer, Bix Emery."

The entire crowd stood as Bix rose to approach the podium. Taking a step or two, he realized he still held Pyrite, so he turned and passed the dog to his daughter. When seated again, Stasia passed the dog to Cooper and plucked a few long golden Yorkie hairs from the skirt of her silver-gray silk suit. Pyrite nestled into the lap of Coop's bottle-green corduroys, oblivious to the fawning stares of several hundred onlookers.

When everyone was settled, Bix cleared his throat, then began, "Some folks talk about my background as a mineralogist. Others just call me a tycoon—and I don't think they mean it as a compliment, exactly. Truth is, I'm just an old oilman. Old enough, I've seen big changes in our industry, our thinking, and our climate. So I guess what they say about old dogs isn't true—we *can* learn new tricks. I'm no do-gooder, far from it, but I know an opportunity when I see it, and I see it now. In plain talk, now is the time to do the right thing for our country, our planet, *and* our business."

Plain talk, indeed, thought Coop as the crowd broke into earnest applause. That old guy can turn a phrase with the best of them. Don't be suckered by his cornpone jive.

". . . luck, fate, or the will of the Lord. For whatever reason, my wife, Emma, God rest her, wanted us to plant roots here in the desert. At first, it was a home away from our real home on the coast, but she was always raring to get back, and eventually, we just stayed. Can't beat the weather, and the golf's good, too. So here we are today—lock, stock, and barrel. Emma would've approved . . ."

Pyrite squirmed. Coop was starting to sweat, and his lap felt damp under the dog. Stasia had warned him that he might be "pushing the season" by wearing cords today, and now he conceded she was right. Another month, maybe, when the cooler weather would set it. But he *liked* corduroys—always had, ever since he was a kid—liked the way they looked, liked the way they felt on him. He had even worn cords, black ones, the day he married Stasia. Not a white-tie ceremony, obviously. Today he wore his green cords with a camel-hair blazer, checked shirt, and a cotton knit tie. A good look, he thought, for an architect at a construction site.

". . . so forgive me if I'm a little prejudiced." Bix laughed; the crowd joined him. "Who *else* would I turn to? My daughter, Stasia, just happens to be married to one of the finest architects in Southern California—the whole damn country, for that matter . . ."

Bix's hyperbole brought a knot to Coop's stomach. He'd *had* a reputation, once, but that was fifteen years ago, before everything fell apart. Now his career consisted solely of projects—big ones, thank God—tossed to him by his wife's wealthy family.

Pyrite reared up to smooch Coop, slurping his chin. He winced. The pooch's breath was never sweet, but today it was downright rancid. Had the little prankster been . . . *smoking*? It brought to mind those tacky paintings of dogs playing poker. Coop imagined Pyrite in a beret, *le chien qui fume*. He lifted the dog from his lap and set him at his feet. Leaning back in his chair again, he feigned a cough and wiped the Yorkie's spittle from his chin.

". . . no question, Cooper Brant was the man for this job. Not just because he's a hell of a designer, but because he knows our mission, he lives it. In fact, it's in his blood. Many of you might remember that his father, Ferris Brant, was a top-notch scholar . . ."

Don't go there, thought Coop. Don't remind them. Besides, that's *my* story.

". . . landed a goddamn Nobel Prize, no less, for his work in thermodynamics. Some say he was on the verge of cracking the secret to the holy grail of energy research, the legendary 'water engine.' Imagine that, using water as fuel. But his life was cut too short—fifteen years ago. We could sure use a mind like that *now*."

Was it possible, Coop wondered, to feel smaller, to feel more eclipsed by the long shadow of someone else's greatness? It was as if his dead father had conspired with his living father-in-law to calcify the generational divide and defend their legacy against all upstarts. Or was Coop being overly defensive? It was a big day for both Bix and him. Why not enjoy the flattery and forget the rest?

Coop reached for Stasia's hand. Her fingers felt cool and oddly reassuring in his clammy grasp.

". . . but I want to let you in on a little secret, a bit of forgotten Hollywood trivia . . ."

Coop mumbled, "God help me."

Stasia squeezed his hand tighter. With her free hand, she calmed a sputter of laughter.

Bix continued, "I never had the pleasure to meet Ferris Brant, but long before he scored that Nobel Prize, I used to see him all the time, and so did you, or at least your kids did—every Saturday morning, in the early days of TV. His stage name was Ferris Oxhide, better known to his young audience as Sheriff Rusty Oxhide."

With a gasp a recognition, the crowd broke into gentle laughter, then applause.

"Yep," Bix assured everyone, "when my son-in-law grew up, he used to watch his daddy on TV, dispensing justice the old-fashioned way—on a horse, with a six-shooter."

Coop leaned to tell his wife through a false, frozen smile, "If I don't make it through this alive, remember that I love you, okay?"

"You haven't said that in years."

"I'm sure that's an exaggeration."

"*I'm* not. But yes, I love you too."

Hearing the words from her, Coop realized they did sound foreign.

". . . haven't been on a horse in years," said Bix, "and I'm a lousy aim with a six-shooter, but I do carry my silver bullet." He patted his chest.

The crowd's only response was a confused rustling, but Coop understood the reference: In recent years, Bix had been having "incidents" with his heart, including one flat-out attack that nearly killed him. He was otherwise healthy for his age, but realistically—actuarially—how many CEOs could plan to celebrate a ninetieth birthday on the job? That was still some three years off for Bix, but that was the plan, and he had a talisman to help him achieve it. Under his shirt, he wore around his neck a locket, a silver bullet that screwed open, containing a nitroglycerin tablet that could be placed under the tongue to stave off an attack of angina. "If you carry an umbrella," he once said of it, "it never rains."

He told the crowd, "I've palavered long enough now. Coops? Come on up here, you handsome fella. Tell these fine folks what a pleasure it is to design a project like this for an old crank like me." Bix then led the applause in welcoming Coop to the podium.

Pyrite followed. Bix gave Coop a hug, slapping his back. As Coop arranged his notes and adjusted the microphone, Bix sweet-talked the dog, telling him, "Come here, you little son f'bitch," and carried him back to the seat next to Stasia.

Coop cleared his throat. "Architects d'don't—" He paused. The vestige of a stutter remained from childhood, and though long ago conquered, it could bubble to the surface now and again, typically at the most inopportune moment. He swallowed and focused. "Architects don't often get asked to make speeches, so forgive me if this isn't too polished. One of the best-known guidelines for the nervous toastmaster is to start with a joke. Unfortunately, my comedic talents are surpassed only by my abysmal public-speaking skills." He paused again, ran a finger under his collar, loosened his tie, and said, "You can laugh now."

And they *did*. "Okay. That's better. I do have a joke to share with you—just one, I promise, and it's relevant to our gathering. This goes back to my college days. There was a story told by architecture students about something once said by Frank Lloyd Wright. I don't know if it's accurate, but the quote went like this: 'The physician gets to bury his mistakes, but the architect can only advise his clients to plant vines.'"

They loved it. "Well," Coop continued, "ivy doesn't thrive in the desert, so there'll be no quick cover-up, and I'm glad, because *this* is no mistake." He made a broad gesture that encompassed the entire headquarters and sprawling research campus. "This is a project any architect dreams of designing maybe once in his career . . ."

As he spoke, his gaze drifted just above the faces in the crowd, a theatrical technique his father had taught him. "Never let anyone in the audience grab your eye," Ferris Brant had told his son. "It'll destroy your focus. Make them feel engaged without actually engaging them." Odd words, perhaps, from a thermodynamics wiz, but his first love had been the stage. "Life's richest lessons," he'd often said, "can be learned in the theater."

"This project," said Coop, "combines a strong social and practical purpose, as envisioned by Bix Emery, with a design vision that I hope, in all humility, may be judged equally strong. 'Form follows function,' the great Louis Sullivan told us . . ."

Coop turned a page of his notes. His left hand rested on the edge of the podium. Sunlight glinted from the wedding band—on his middle finger. His ring finger ended at the middle knuckle. Missing its two upper joints, the remaining stub measured little more than an inch. He had no recollection of the accident during his infancy, in his crib—the hinge, the pinch, the fall. He'd heard the grim details from his mother, later. "There wasn't much blood," she'd said, "and you barely cried, but *I* was hysterical."

". . . so I found that in searching for inspiration for these structures, I needed to look no further than their lofty purpose. If, to any degree, I have succeeded . . ."

His words, smooth and well cadenced, flowed. Coop made a point of looking up from his notes often, glancing at no one and at everyone, seducing the audience, the "many-headed mistress," as his father had referred to it.

And then the snag, the eye contact. He blinked.

". . . that s'success c'can only . . ." Pause. Focus. "That success can only be attributed to the quality of the inspiration . . ."

When he dared to look again, panning the crowd, he saw that all eyes were upon him—no surprise—but the intensity of a particular stare had an effect nothing short of magnetic. He stumbled on his words again, wondering, Who *is* that? Do I know her?

". . . my f'father's research . . . his research, so abruptly ended . . . its implications to the status quo were staggering. Sure, there were skeptics . . ."

Coop forced his eyes back to the page, forced the words to keep coming, reasoning that even a faulty delivery was preferable to none, to dumbstruck silence. Who *was* that woman? He blocked her from his mind and trudged through his rote narrative, but his thoughts hemorrhaged with another scene altogether, one that had played out fifteen years earlier:

Coop climbs the stairs to the second floor of the campus building in Riverside, having agreed to meet his father early, help him load the prototype into a van, and drive over to the lecture hall, where they would set up for the press conference and demonstration. As the event was planned on short notice, it was scheduled for a Sunday, when the hall would be available and a highly select audience, a consortium of automotive, oil, and government interests, could arrange to be there.

The second floor contains faculty offices, research labs, and a few small seminar rooms. Cool morning air—it is an early Easter in March—drifts through the length of the main hall, carrying with it the smells of floor wax, crab trees in blossom, and the distant, recollected whiff of a long-ago neighbor's toy chemistry set. Beyond the open windows at the end of the hall, birds twit and chatter. Nearby, a drinking fountain's condenser switches off with a thud. The only other sound is that of Coop's footfalls on the ancient, buckled linoleum.

When he turns into the side hall, he sees that the door to his father's office is open. Good, at least he's on time. After summoning a wary audience with his usual dramatic flair, at least he won't keep them waiting.

But entering the office, Coop is jolted by the discovery that Ferris Brant will indeed keep his audience waiting. His body slumps in the chair behind his desk, one leg kicked forward, arms drooping to either side, head lolled backward, mouth and eyes open. "Dad? Good God!" Coop rushes to his side.

Above the collar of Brant's white dress shirt, his neck is circled with scars of a violent strangulation. Oddly, these abrasions are marked at regular intervals by shallow punctures that have trickled blood, now black, into the shirt collar. Coop's first thought: a crown of thorns. His father's face has blanched; the dangling fingers are purple. No question, the man is dead, but Coop instinctively feels for a pulse beneath the chin, which has turned cool and rigid. Coop's hand withdraws as if burned. After collecting himself for a moment, he reaches for the desk phone, calls someone—anyone, not sure who—and sounds the alarm.

Only then does the rest of the scene begin to register. Desk drawers are on the floor, contents strewn about. File cabinets gape open, folders rifled, flung everywhere. The desktop computer is missing its guts, its CPU; Coop recalls that his father always worked simultaneously with a laptop, now vanished. A hefty bookcase is largely untouched, except for several shelves containing stacks of audio cassettes used by Brant to rehearse his lectures, hundreds of them, now scattered in piles. On top of the bookcase, some old, unused office equipment continues to collect dust—Dictaphone, Ditto machine, Selectric and Royal typewriters, jugs of duplicating fluid, a slide projector. The chalkboard spanning one wall is wiped clean; the bulletin board spanning another, where Brant tacked and organized his notes, is now covered with only the sun-bleached shadows where scraps of paper once tiled the cork.

Coop knows enough not to disturb the body, which is clearly beyond reviving, but the ransacked office screams to him a living, urgent concern: What did they take? Did they find the essence of his father's work? He had shared it with no one, preferring the theatrics of a surprise announcement and the literal unveiling of a promised prototype—the water engine, the MacGuffin, as he jokingly referred to it. Did they steal it? Or more important, the formula to build it? Did it even exist?

The need to answer these questions, the impulse to protect his father's legacy, the knowledge that stakes have suddenly been raised to the level of murder, all these forces, combined with sheer nosiness, prompt Coop to take action better left to others: he starts digging in the rubble. He's down on his knees, sitting on his heels, leafing through folders in the bottom drawer of a file cabinet, tossing pages aside, muttering nonsense, looking disheveled and possessed when the police he alerted rush into the room and promptly cuff him.

"Your housekeeping skills leave something to be desired," says Arcie Madera, a young detective with the Riverside County sheriff's department, newly promoted and assigned to the case. She's a hotshot, good looking, if a bit butch, and Coop knows he's in trouble.

And now, there she was again, fifteen years later, standing among the crowd at Emery Energy, listening to Coop's speech, catching his eye, shattering his attention. When at last Coop connected the dots, he gave up on his prepared text. "You know what?" he said. "It's getting hot. Enough of my pontificating. Let's get on with the program." Robust applause followed him back to his seat.

He steadied himself as he sat, feeling ashen, wondering if it showed.

"What happened?" asked Stasia, leaning close to speak in his ear.

Lame laugh. "Not sure. Touch of stage fright, maybe."

She eyed him askance. "Stage fright? Rusty Oxhide's son? I don't buy it."

The remaining speeches were brief but exuberant. The lieutenant governor, the congresswoman, the mayor, they prattled employment statistics, touted green technology, advocated LEED certification—that is, Leadership in Energy and Environmental Design—and all but called for the canonization of Bix Emery for dreaming up his new venture and building it in the desert. "This could be the biggest thing since the Silicon Valley," crowed a local commissioner.

When the speeches ended, a willowy man in his mid-thirties introduced himself as Kavanall Emery Follet, corporate vice president for communications. Bix's grandson, the sole offspring of Stasia's earlier marriage, dressed smartly that morning in cream-colored slacks, matching shirt, and a dusty-sage gabardine jacket of modified Eisenhower styling. He sported buttery brown crocodile loafers with no socks. His deep tan and sun-bleached hair suggested Kavanall spent more time on the golf course than in his office.

But today he was on duty and set about the task of arranging a group photo for the assembled press. He stationed Bix with the lieutenant governor in the middle of the front row; other dignitaries and corporate officers filled in the flanks. Kavanall asked a few people to switch places so their faces would show better. Then Bix stepped out of formation to review the lineup before proceeding with the pictures. He handed Pyrite to Kavanall; the dog nipped at the younger man's fingers.

"I want Coops in front," Bix said, then resumed his place in line.

Kavanall nodded without comment and, with a finger-wag, instructed Coop, his stepfather, to move forward.

Assuming his new position, Coop straightened his tie and buttoned his jacket. He wondered why so many of the others prepared to be photographed by clearing their throats, but they did. Most of the men in the front row, not knowing what to do with their hands, folded them modestly below the belt.

The phalanx of photographers huddled before them, preparing to shoot. "Gentlemen," one of them called, "can we drop the fig leafs? Looks a little prim." With uneasy laughter, they complied, dropping their hands to their sides.

Coop's left hand fidgeted near his pocket. He tried hooking the thumb inside—far too casual. So he let the fingers drop straight against his leg—accentuating the missing digit, he felt, though of course no one could see it. Then he balled his hand into a fist.

It was a habit, a reflex, dating back to his first day of kindergarten:

Coop's fifth birthday is only two months past, and he tries to be brave about spending a whole morning away from his mother. The other children, he has never seen them before, except for *that* girl, the snot who lives around the corner, but they all seem to know each other, and they *smell*. They smell like soap and crayons and vomit. The teacher, Mrs. Pease, seems nice enough, but she doesn't see the horsing around and the punching every time she turns away. She shows everybody that their names are spelled out on pieces of cardboard, and when they get to school each morning, they're supposed to find their name cards and put them in this pocket-thing on the wall, to show that they're there. She asks everybody to take turns saying their names out loud, and Coop feels like he can't breathe. "C'Cooper B'Brant."

"What, dear?" asks Mrs. Pease.

The girl, the snot, points and laughs. "He *always* does that." And then everybody else laughs with her.

The big bathroom smells funny, and then it's time to go outside for recess. Everybody's yelling, and the snot runs for the monkey bars, saying how she can do it best. She bets a million bucks there isn't a boy who can hang on longer or get to the other end faster. Nobody takes her up on the dare. She looks around, going from face to face to face, then says, kind of whiny, "How about you, C'Cooper?"

"I . . . c'can't."

"Why not—cuz you don't have all your *fingers*?"

Everybody looks at Coop, wide-eyed. "Huh?" they shout. "Show us!"

He balls his fist, but the snot and two of the boys push him to the ground and force his hand open for everybody to see. Boys and girls alike shriek in horror, but some of them are brave enough to reach and touch the nubbin before recoiling. "Creep!" "Freak show!" "Frankenstein!"

When they let him up, Coop is crying, and the snot says, "What's a matter, stubby?"

"Yeah, *stubby*," the others singsong, "what's a matter?"

He runs from the sand beneath the monkey bars, runs across the playground looking for Mrs. Pease, but his eyes are blurred with tears, and he falls, skinning both elbows on the asphalt and ripping the knee of his brand-new starchy brown corduroys.

His hand relaxed against the leg of his soft bottle-green corduroys as the strobe flashes ended and one of the photographers, the fig-leaf guy, shouted, "Thanks, that oughta do it."

**W**ith the scripted portion of the ceremony over, Kavanall invited those who could stay to tour the new headquarters. The lieutenant governor voiced regrets—he was needed upstate—but most of the others, including the press, were eager to look inside the buildings and walk through the connecting grounds, already adorned with an innovative "solar garden," which combined overscale sculpture with fountains, oasis landscaping, and photovoltaics.

Bix himself led a group of bigwigs, mostly investors, into the main office building. Though the company was publicly traded, he still held a majority of its stock, and business pundits often marveled at his mastery of the discrepant roles of absolute monarch over his domain and obliging servant to his shareholders. Austin Royce, his spaniel and second fiddle, scurried next to him, carrying Pyrite; the pooch had some difficulty traversing the feathered granite floors, and Bix didn't want him stepped on. Kavanall sidled through the clump of onlookers, handing out press kits. Coop and Stasia brought up the rear.

"Mr. Brant?" asked someone from behind.

Coop turned. "Yes?"

"Marc Gambill." He offered his hand and a business card. "I'm writing a piece for *Architectural Record*. Do you have a moment?"

Stasia squeezed her husband's forearm. "I'm sure you can handle this on your own. Catch up with me later?"

He kissed the corner of her mouth. "Thanks."

With a wink she told him, "Knock'm dead," then disappeared into the crowd.

Coop turned to Gambill. "Wow"—he shrugged—"the *Record*.

I'm surprised you guys noticed."

The reporter laughed. "Hard *not* to. Emery's P.R. machine has been in high gear. Besides, we haven't heard your name in a while. Looks like you're set for a big comeback." He gestured to their surroundings, nodding approval.

Coop thought of those tabloid stories about washed-up celebrities, headlined WHATEVER HAPPENED TO . . . ? He walked Gambill to a quieter corner of the main hall, where they sat on a leather-clad window seat beneath a soaring, angular slab of plate glass that admitted a view of sapphire skies, ruddy mountains, and the distant windmill fields. A chromed slot between the cushion and the window whispered cool air. Coop said, "I have to admit, the project scared me."

"Why?" The reporter opened his notebook, set it on his knee, and poised his pen.

"My prior practice was exclusively residential. I was the 'society architect' of Santa Barbara. In the eyes of some, I was a dilettante, all style and no substance."

"Don't sell yourself short. Most of the architectural giants considered residential work their highest calling."

Coop nodded. "*I've* always thought so. And here in Palm Springs—this area was a mecca for the development of residential modernism. Neutra, Schindler, Frey, Cody—they all left their marks here, and that's a tough act to follow."

With the trace of a grin, Gambill glanced about. "You've captured their influence. The allusions are subtle, but unmistakable. None of it's derivative, though. You've paid homage to the masters while reinterpreting their vision on an entirely different scale."

Coop said nothing, then chuckled.

"What?" asked Gambill.

"If you want to print that—be my guest."

When Coop and the reporter caught up with Stasia, she was chatting with Jay Pontarelli, one of the company's principal outside investors. The sight of him brought an acidic twinge to Coop's stomach. To the casual observer, Pontarelli projected the image of a harmless buffoon, a jokester, but Coop had seen through the act and come to understand that his clowning was typically more calculated than off-the-cuff. His wealth, which was considerable even by Emery standards, had not been amassed because he was stupid. And there he now stood, hanging near the back of the VIP tour as it ambled through corridors surrounding the executive offices.

The door to each suite abutted a glass wall that allowed a view into a reception area. Bix's was the largest of these. Gold-leaf lettering on the glass wall spelled out his name, followed by the litany of his titles. Toward the rear of this posh but starkly contemporary anteroom, a hall led past two secretaries' offices to the inner sanctum, off limits today.

Among the other—smaller—offices along this corridor were two identified in gold leaf as belonging to AUSTIN ROYCE, CHIEF FINANCIAL OFFICER and KAVANALL EMERY FOLLETT, VICE PRESIDENT, COMMUNICATIONS. Conspicuously, another office suite, a sizable one, bore no name, no title; its waiting room was dark and unfurnished. Noting this, the reporter said, "Odd use of space—in such a prime location."

Coop was about to speak, but Jay Pontarelli chimed in, "Why, that's the *president's* office, isn't it?"

The reporter glanced across the hall. "But 'president' is one of Bix Emery's titles."

"It is *now*." A big, vigorous back-slapping man in his fifties—an erstwhile frat jock clad in a business suit—Pontarelli explained with a laugh, "That's the bait." Then he gave a confidential wink.

Stasia crossed her arms. Coop studied the ceiling. The reporter looked confused.

Pontarelli continued, "My father was no different. That's how these good ol' boys tick. That's how Bix keeps his minions in line. He dangles the big promotion, and all the king's men jump for it."

With a crooked smile, Stasia asked, "Isn't that a tad undiplomatic, Jay?"

"It's just the barefaced truth." As if to prove his point, Austin Royce skittered by at that moment with Pyrite; the dog had piddled on his arm. Pontarelli stopped him with a huge mitt of a hand. "Hey, Royce, looks like you got some trouble there." He tweaked Pyrite's beard; the dog snarled. "We were just talking about this dark office here, the *president's* office—why isn't your name on it yet?"

The CFO, an eloquent man, a lawyer with a sharp acumen for big oil and big business, rarely at a loss for words, now sputtered, unable to respond.

Pontarelli snapped his fingers, feigning a lightbulb. "*That's* right. Kavanall wants that office, doesn't he? And his middle name *is* Emery."

Within a half hour, the tour had petered out. Pontarelli sauntered off to hobnob with Bix behind closed doors; Marc Gambill, the reporter, needed to leave. Stasia told Coop, "You were a hit. Congratulations."

"Thanks." Coop spoke the word without emotion.

"Something wrong?"

"Sorry. Distracted, I guess. Mind if I check my desk? Then I'll drive you home."

They walked over to the research facility, one of several that would eventually be built, where a substantial area of the ground floor served as an in-house design and construction headquarters. Upon completion of the project, still several years off, the architectural staff would surrender the space to the research team, a contingent of which had already moved in from Los Angeles.

Tessa Irwin, one of the lead research scientists, spotted Coop with Stasia in the hall and emerged from her office to greet them. Recently turned forty, she had begun her career at Emery straight out of grad school, so she had already accrued considerable seniority in her department. A natural charm and a youthful, pretty face were offset some by granny glasses, a pert little lab jacket, and an earnest manner that seemed more efficient than personable. Still, she was undeniably attractive—and single—making her a prime target for those in search of an office romance, though few were ever granted a first date, and even fewer could claim arriving safe at first base. "Maybe she's a lesbian," Coop had once speculated to Stasia. With a toss of her head, his wife had replied, *"Men.* You are *so* full of shit."

There in the hall, Tessa now asked Coop, "Can I bother you for a minute?"

"If it's about the ground plan for the new labs, can it wait till tomorrow? Things are sort of hectic today."

"Actually, that's not it." She hesitated. "And I'm glad Stasia's here too."

Stasia exchanged a quizzical look with Coop, then asked the younger woman, "What is it, Tessa?" The threesome stepped to a turn in the hall where a bank of offices was not yet occupied. Smells of new carpeting and fresh paint hung in the air.

Tessa said, "It's Kav."

Coop blew a low whistle, shaking his head. He asked Stasia, "Want me to bow out of this—*Mom."*

"We're in this together—*Dad."*

"Stepdad," he corrected her. Then he turned to Tessa. "What's Kav been up to?"

"More of the same, I'm afraid. Umpteen phone calls every day, lingering visits at my desk, suggestive e-mails. Yesterday he jangled something in his pocket and said he had the keys to the jet. Wanted to 'do dinner' in New York. I've done nothing to encourage him, but he won't take no for an answer. He's acting very"—Tessa whirled a hand, searching for the right word—"privileged."

Well, he *is,* thought Coop, but didn't say it. Instead, he told his wife, "Some might dismiss Kavanall's come-ons as the antics of a pampered playboy. Others might call it harassment."

"I know, I know." She tossed her hands in disgust. "I thought he'd grow out of this, but Jesus Christ, he's thirty-six." She guided Tessa a few steps away, huddling for some sympathetic she-chat. Coop heard only *"Men,"* punctuated with another toss of Stasia's hands. Her bracelets rattled in the harsh acoustics of the empty hall.

"Mr. Brant?" a woman asked Coop from behind.

He turned, expecting someone from the construction office who might need his signature on a materials list, a shipping manifest, a revised work order. But it was Arcie Madera, the face in the audience that had brought his speech to a stuttering halt.

"Remember me?" she asked, turning the lapel of her jacket to reveal a badge clipped inside. She wore a mannish gray suit, pin-striped, but tailored with sufficient flair to suggest a well-toned body, decidedly feminine. Her white blouse resembled a man's dress shirt, but with a hint of a ruffle adorning the placket and a row of pea-sized pearl buttons. Her piercing dark eyes hadn't changed in fifteen years, but her jet-black hair bore streaks of silver. Coop figured she was now in her late forties.

He asked, "Detective . . . Madera, is it?"

"Right." She crossed her arms and looked about, nodding but not smiling. "Big job here. Seems you've been busy."

He said nothing, cocking his head, as if to ask, Do you *like* it?

She continued to nod. "Very nice. Very arty."

Philistine, thought Coop. Arty, indeed. He was surprised she wasn't chewing a wad of gum. Even though she was far less eloquent than Marc Gambill had been, Coop recognized a compliment when he heard one, especially from a cop who had made no secret of her suspicion that Coop was guilty of patricide. After an uncomfortable pause—with Stasia and Tessa still buzzing in the background—he said, "I have a lot going on right now. Is there something I can help you with?"

Her gaze turned to the ceiling, following a long, serpentine sculpture of crushed glass that doubled as a chandelier, like a frozen riverbed suspended in midair. "You mean, why am I here?"

"I s'suppose that's what I meant. Yes."

She looked him in the eye. "I didn't realize you'd moved here from Santa Barbara. When did that happen?"

"Two or three years ago. I've divorced and remarried since we last talked."

"Yeah, I heard." The detective glanced over toward Stasia, making little effort to conceal a grin.

"We made a permanent move here because of the project. Plus, we like it."

She nodded without expression. "Beautiful place. Very pretty—hot, but pretty. See, the thing is, Mr. Brant, your father's case was one of my first assignments, and it's the only one that's ever gone cold. Still a black mark on my record. Then, lo and behold, with all the publicity, I realized that you've *moved* here, to Riverside County." She paused. "It got me thinking."

"Detective, the c'cold case bothers me as much as you. I wanted the facts of my father's murder cleared up all along, more than anyone."

"Yeah, I'll bet. Well, guess what. There's been a lot of advances in forensics over the last fifteen years. So I'm thinking it might be time to open this up and take a fresh look."

**W**ho was *that*?" asked Stasia.

Coop walked her out of the building through a rear entrance that led to the executive parking area, much of it shaded by a roof of solar panels. Near the door, a crew was waxing and buffing Bix's Hummer. Coop's Tesla roadster, basic black, was parked near the lot's perimeter. He explained to his wife, "That was a cop—the detective who originally investigated my father's death."

"Ugh. How dreary."

Coop waited for her to ask, What did she want? But Stasia must have had other things on her mind. She couldn't have known, perhaps didn't care, that Coop wanted nothing dredged up. Despite his claim to the detective that he shared her interest in discovering the truth, he feared that the process would only leave him floundering, once again, as the logical suspect. Once again, nothing would be proven, but he would be lanced by opinion and battered by innuendo. Last time, it had scuttled his career, snuffed his hobbling marriage, and made a stranger of his own daughter. He'd struggled to reinvent himself—*Architectural Record* took notice and seemed to approve, a first in itself, a landmark affirmation—but now he found himself, once again, staring straight into the depths of an abyss. He closed his eyes, overcome by a plunging sense of weightless free fall.

"Hidey ho, fellow green-freaks!" called Jay Pontarelli from behind. Coop and Stasia turned as he pumped his way across the parking lot.

Stasia asked, "How was your meeting with Bix?"

"Super." He paused to catch his breath. "Except the old guy seemed a little off with me, sort of 'guarded.' Guess he got wind of newco."

"What?" asked Coop.

"Just a term the accounting guys use for 'new company'—like when you're setting something up, maybe it's just exploratory, and the lawyers haven't crossed the *t*'s yet."

"Or dotted the *i*'s," said Stasia through a wary smile. "So it's true then?"

Pontarelli lifted both palms in a halting gesture. "Hate to be vague, but no comment. Tell you what, though. Why don't we have dinner Saturday? After a drink or two, who knows?"

"Can't," said Stasia. "Big opening at the museum that night. I'm on the board, so it's a must-attend." She turned to Coop. "You too."

"Yes, ma'am. I've got it in ink."

She turned back to Pontarelli. "But how about tomorrow, Jay?"

He thought for a moment. "Friday? Yeah, that works."

"Let's keep it simple. Our club at seven-thirty."

"Good deal—you're paying. And tell you what. If he's available, let's include Kav. He's . . . well, he might find this of interest."

Stasia asked, "What's *Kav* got to do with this?"

Pontarelli repeated the halting gesture. "Tomorrow, okay? Seven-thirty." Then he nodded, turned, and walked off to his car.

Under her breath, Stasia said, "Whatever Jay's up to, I'm worried about it." Coop didn't respond; his own thoughts were stuck on Arcie Madera.

High in a nearby palm, a raven broke the stillness and let out a loud, ugly caw.

Coop and Stasia exchanged a startled look, then laughed.

# Chapter 2

IronLand. The name belied the setting. Sure, there was iron galore—and plenty of pumped-up guys pumping it—but the biggest gym in Palm Springs had a mostly gay clientele, middle-aged and up, mostly up, whose workouts were interrupted by hoots of laughter, blown kisses, gossip breaks, and the occasional cat fight. The thundering dance beat was better suited to midnight than seven in the morning, when the early crowd did their duty before going to work. Suspended from the vast ceiling of the converted supermarket, flat-screen monitors, dozens of them, flashed music videos, CNN, weather maps, cooking shows, decorating makeovers, film noir, and Technicolor musicals—but no sports, not even golf. This was not your father's men's club.

If Cooper Brant felt ill at ease in IronLand on Friday morning, he didn't show it. He was there to tighten up some middle-age flab, and the gym was at the north end of town, a convenient stop along the drive to his office at Emery headquarters. Having grown up in the company of his father's many theater connections, he was unfazed by the gay vibe, which in fact had provided one of the few bright spots in a youth troubled by the usual insecurities of boyhood and the particular ignominy of a stutter. But he was ultimately sold on IronLand by his wife's recommendation of Teddy Duncan as "hands down, one of the best personal trainers in this whole damn valley. Just *look* at my ass. I mean it—just *feel* those glutes."

Stasia bragged not in vain. Her glutes rivaled those of any woman half her age, so when she tired of the gym routine and switched to tennis lessons, Coop snapped up her coveted early-morning slot with Teddy.

"Okay," said the trainer, checking his clipboard, "shoulders and biceps today."

Coop never paid much attention to which muscle groups they were working; he just did what he was told three mornings a week. Teddy started him with a basic dumbbell curl using a pair of thirty-pounders, a weight increase from the prior week. Coop winced at the first lift, grunted at the second repetition, and then settled into a steady, mechanical curl, stopping at twelve. "Good job," said Teddy, watching his form. The second set felt easier.

Having never set foot in a locker room since high school—bad memories—Coop thought of himself as supremely unathletic, even *dis*-athletic. Still, at fifty-eight, he was in better shape than most other men his age, and he had decided it was time to become proactive in preserving a cosmetic advantage that was little more than dumb luck in the gene pool. Though fitness would be its own reward, he wanted more; he wanted it to show. "I'd like to look more like you," he had told Teddy with a shrug when asked about his goals a year earlier, at the start of their first session.

Teddy had given a thoughtful nod, assessing the words of a new client who was twenty years his senior, whose expectations might be unrealistic. "You want to feel better about yourself."

"Doesn't everyone?"

With the passing of months, they had progressed far beyond the tentative dialogue of an older straight client with a younger gay trainer, of student and teacher. Now nothing was off limits as they gabbed during the brief rests between exercise sets. "Sometimes," said Coop, noting this evolution, "I think of you as others might think of a priest. Or psychiatrist."

"Or hairdresser," Teddy said with a smirk, sipping a protein shake that left a thin moustache of espresso-laced froth gracing his upper lip. He wiped it with a finger, prompting, "Last set. Ready?"

Though the gym was cool on that chilly morning, Coop broke a sweat while finishing the curls, and as he paused to blot his face with a towel, one of the other trainers gave him a thumbs-up, saying, "Looking good."

Before Coop could respond, Teddy squared his shoulders and through a chipper smile said, "Thank you."

They all laughed, and when the other trainer moved on, Teddy said, "Seriously, you're making great progress. Not everyone could wear that." He was referring to the second-skin style of sleeveless T-shirt that Coop had only recently mustered the confidence to pair with his baggy workout shorts—the same sort of training outfit worn by Teddy all the time. Teddy rarely offered such compliments, and when he did, they rang as genuine. He glanced across the main floor of the gym. "One of the cable machines is open. Let's grab it."

The machine stood along the inside perimeter of an oval running track that looped around the equipment. As they arrived and Teddy began adjusting the height of the cable, a sinewy guy in neon-hued spandex, one of the regulars, passed near them along the track, doing weighted lunges. Looking over, he said with exaggerated fatigue, "It's tough wearing flats—after spending the night in heels!" His sleek Pumas slapped the rubber surface of the track as he trudged on.

Dryly, Teddy told Coop, "Bet you've never heard *that* in a gym." Handing him the pair of ropes clipped low to the cable, he said, "Okay, upright row."

Coop whipped through the first set. Either he was getting stronger, or Teddy had backed off on the weight, which wasn't likely. "Piece of cake," said Coop.

"Good. We'll fix that." Teddy shifted the pin a notch heavier on the weight stack.

"You sound like Stasia."

"Really?" Teddy's brow wrinkled.

Coop paused. What, he wondered, had prompted him to say that? Stasia and Teddy sounded nothing alike; her patrician cadences were a far cry from his down-home style of understatement. Was it the hint of menace in his words? *Good. We'll fix that.*

"None of my business," said Teddy, "but is everything all right with you two?"

Was it? "I think so," said Coop. He did the second set of upright rows, which took longer than the first. After pausing to catch his breath, he asked, "You and Rob, how long have you been together—couple of years?"

"Closer to three."

Coop hesitated, then stepped near. "Is the sex still good?"

"Yeah. Fabulous." Reacting to something crestfallen in Coop's features, Teddy added, "Maybe it's different with guys."

"Maybe," Coop agreed with a halfhearted laugh. Maybe the mix of two guys' testosterone did guarantee an extended run of friskiness. Surely their relative youth was a factor. And their three years still qualified as something of a honeymoon, compared to Coop and Stasia's ten, a decade that had dulled the passions and reduced their intimacy to an occasional tumble, stiff and ritualized, every few months. Which left only love.

Coop began his third set of rows, yanking the ropes. *Which left only love.* Was it that, he wondered, jerking through the reps, or was it mere momentum, a known routine that offered a comfortable life and promised a secure future?

"Too heavy?" asked Teddy. "You were straining."

Coop was about to assure him that the weight was fine when a woman working out near them—one of the few on the premises that morning—tapped Coop's shoulder and asked, "Hey, is that you?" She motioned to one of the overhead monitors, tuned to CNN.

"Wow!" said Teddy, looking up. A report from Thursday's dedication ceremony showed Coop speaking from the podium.

"I've seen you here a lot," said the woman. "Are you a politician?"

"Just an architect."

"Cool." She nodded, then moved on.

There was no sound from the broadcast—electronica still pulsed through the cavernous room—but Coop saw himself stuttering as the camera made a slow zoom toward his face. Then, with a sinister will of its own, the camera traveled the contour of his shoulder, his arm, and down to his left hand on the side of the podium, where the wedding ring gleamed on his middle finger, next to the stub. Coop turned away from the screen, grabbed his towel, and swabbed sweat from his face.

"Is that Bix?" asked Teddy.

"Huh?"

Teddy squinted at the monitor. "The older guy sitting next to Stasia—is that Bix?"

Coop looked up again just as a caption appeared at the bottom of the screen: OIL GIANT BIX EMERY GOES GREEN. The caption covered the image of Coop's hand on the podium, and he realized the purpose of the shot was to focus not on his deformity, but on his father-in-law.

"Are you all right?" asked Teddy. Both his tone and his expression were laced with concern. "You look pale."

"Sorry," said Coop with an embarrassed smile. "I'm fine—paranoid sometimes, but otherwise just fine."

"Paranoid—about what?" Teddy glanced at the screen again, then back to his client.

"This." Coop splayed his left hand a few inches in front of Teddy's face. "I thought CNN was doing an exposé on nine-fingered architects."

Teddy scrunched his features. "You could see *that*? I didn't even notice."

"Exactly. Paranoia." They had discussed the crib accident during one of their early sessions—an innocent and appropriate question for a trainer to ask a client—and in the rest of the time they had worked together, it had never come up again.

But now Coop felt inclined to elaborate. "As a kid, it seemed huge. It wasn't till my college years that I could actually forget about it, even joke about it. But then it became an issue again—when I got married. I mean, there was a one-in-ten chance, and it *had* to be the ring finger, right? So when I married Cheryl—that was my first wife—I wore the ring on my right hand. And people, total strangers, used to *ask* me about it. I was stunned. They thought I was European."

"Either that," Teddy suggested, "or gay."

Coop wasn't expecting that. He gave his trainer a dumb look.

Teddy explained, "Back before the era of commitment ceremonies, let alone marriage, lots of gay couples wore their rings on the right hand."

"Why?" asked Coop, mystified.

Teddy shrugged. "Closeted? Coy? I dunno."

"So the second time around, I decided to wear it on the left hand—but on the wrong finger, of course. And I *still* get asked about it."

"And this is a problem? Get real. You lost half a finger, not an arm."

Coop paused to consider this, then told Teddy, "You're better than my shrink—and a hell of a lot cheaper. *She* said the missing finger represented castration issues."

"Ouch. I didn't know you had a shrink."

"I don't. I dropped her."

"Good. When?"

"About the time she started on castration. She was like a dog with a bone."

Teddy pondered his clipboard, then glanced about the gym, checking for open equipment. "Let's do the T-bar. It's been a while."

"Don't remind me. It's no accident you never have to wait in line for that one."

"Yep," Teddy agreed with a sardonic chuckle, "it's everyone's favorite."

A medieval-looking contraption of cold steel, hard rubber, and black leatherette, the T-bar resembled, in Coop's imagination, a catapult from days of yore. Teddy busied himself loading the long hinged arm with weights while Coop got in position, leaning butt-up over a chest pad, preparing to lift the weighted bar underneath him. It was an exercise that would call upon his entire body's strength, pushing him to the limit; invariably, it left him gasping.

"Oh," said Teddy, sliding an extra ten pounds onto the bar, "almost forgot—Rob wanted me to ask if you and Stasia would like to attend a gallery opening tomorrow night. He said it should be a good show."

"Can't, but thanks," said Coop, craning to look up at Teddy. "Stasia already has us booked with something, says it's a 'must-attend.' I'd like to meet Rob, though. She says he's a great guy."

"Trust me"—Teddy twitched his brows—"he is."

Coop wasn't sure if his wife had come to know Rob Pollard, who owned a small downtown gallery, during her training days with Teddy or if she had made her own connections with Rob through her board work with the art crowd. Either way, his name came up often at home, and Teddy constantly spoke of him in references to "we," so Coop had grown to think of him as a mysterious but benevolent unknown, a shadow force, like a rogue planet perceived only by its tug on other orbits.

"Have fun with that beast," someone told Coop while passing by the T-bar.

Mounted over the machine, Coop squirmed, wondering what sort of signals he might be sending with his ass in the air. He asked Teddy, "Who was that?"

"Don't know his name—just one of the regulars."

In his year at IronLand, Coop had noticed an odd phenomenon. The place was always busy, and most of its members followed schedules, many of which dovetailed with his. Working with a trainer, he did little socializing during his time there, but he absorbed a subliminal familiarity with the clientele. Away from the gym—in a crowded restaurant, for instance, or sitting in traffic—he now and then caught someone's eye with a flash of recognition but knew with certainty they had never met, leading him routinely to conclude, It's a face from the gym. At other times, however, the déjà vu would double back on itself, like a helix spinning in reverse, forcing him to wonder if someone working out at the next machine was known from somewhere else: Isn't he a waiter, a clerk, maybe a guy from the office? Regaining his bearings, Coop would then conclude, Nah, it is what it is—just another face from the gym.

These circular thoughts distracted Coop and fogged the pain as he grunted through his first set on the T-bar. "That's twelve," said Teddy, reminding him to stop.

Coop stood, feeling dizzy for a moment. "That doesn't get any easier."

"It would if I hadn't upped the weight." Teddy smiled while jotting a check mark on his clipboard.

Before Coop could think of a snappy reply, they were interrupted by voices raised in anger, several machines away. "What the hell's your *problem*?" said one of the men.

Coop asked, "Who's that?" It felt like one of his mind loops setting in.

"That's just Dennis." Teddy rolled his eyes. "Do you watch

much gay porn?"

"Well . . . *no*," said Coop, as if the answer should be obvious.

"Dennis Dill used to do lots of videos, but then he got too old for it, so he's in the escort biz." Teddy added, "He's not the only one at this gym."

Coop assumed Dennis was the bleached blond in tastefully coordinated workout wear—powder-blue muscle shirt, heather-gray shorts. He didn't look at all familiar, but the other guy did. He sported a no-nonsense butch cut and wore street clothes—khakis, white T-shirt, black shoes and belt, which looked conspicuously inappropriate to the setting. "The other one," said Coop. "Do you know him?"

Teddy studied him for a moment, shook his head. "I've never seen him before."

Then the guy in khaki shouted, full-throated, "Keep your faggot hands *off* me!"

A hush fell over the room. One of the managers, a beefy guy with a shaved head and a huge tattoo of a poodle prancing on one arm, darted out from behind the front desk and walked the track at a brisk clip, ready to referee. But by the time he arrived, Dennis Dill had backed off, raising his hands in mock horror, seeking refuge among a gaggle of laughing friends. The guy in the khakis pumped away at one of the chest-press machines, staring grimly into space.

With the commotion ended, conversations resumed, and the manager returned to the front desk. Teddy turned to Coop. "Ready? Second set."

Coop exhaled noisily, then hoisted himself into position, staring down at the weighted bar.

Unlike some of the trainers, Teddy never came across as a drill sergeant; it wasn't his style. But he couldn't help laughing at Coop's hesitation to begin. "You're really loving this, aren't you?"

"Ughhh." Coop twisted his neck, looking up over his shoulder. "I hate anything facing down."

Deadpan, Teddy said, "Tell *that* to your shrink."

**S**hortly before nine that morning, Coop arrived at Emery headquarters and pulled into his shaded spot in the executive parking lot. He locked his Tesla and plugged its recharging cable into a socket powered by photovoltaic panels forming a brise-soleil over the carport. Then he walked toward the main courtyard that connected a cluster of administration buildings.

Fountains pattered, birds chirped. From a distant quadrant of the campus, workmen hollered, muffled by the whir of cranes, the grinding of gears, the productive thrum of construction. Crystalline sunlight drenched the entire valley and chiseled the surrounding mountains with deep, sharp strokes of chiaroscuro.

Coop paused in the courtyard, invigorated by the surroundings, his early workout, and the unknowable promise of another new day. Every building in sight had sprung from his own mind, taken root in the sand, transformed a barren patch of desert into a gleaming model of environmentally responsible modernism, and had caught the eye of *Architectural Record*. Plus, it was Friday.

Coop instinctively turned in the direction of the research facility, which housed his design team, then reconsidered. He should at least show his face in the main office building, prove he was there, shuffle some paper, maybe enjoy a bit of backslapping after his appearance on CNN. So he turned on his heel, slalomed between the sculptures that sprouted like trees throughout the courtyard's solar garden, and entered the plush, hushed sanctuary of corporate headquarters.

He popped his head into the reception room of Bix's office suite and asked a matronly secretary, "Is he in yet, Connie?"

She glanced up from her typing, flashed Coop a demure grin, and gave the slightest shake of her head. "Not yet, Mr. Brant." Her helmet of spray-lacquered pewter-streaked hair wobbled over severely penciled brows.

Coop nodded his thanks and continued down the hallway toward Kavanall's office. Earlier that morning, Stasia had asked Coop to remind her son of their dinner plans that evening with Jay Pontarelli. There was no one in Kav's reception area, so Coop crossed the room toward the inner office, where he could hear his stepson conversing with someone: "Crazier things have happened—they elected Sonny Bono." Brays of laughter spilled through the doorway as Coop stepped into view.

"Hey, Pops"—Kav waved Coop into the office—"you remember Cliff Sloan."

"I ought to," said Coop, shaking hands with the other man, who stood. "He's my dentist."

"Some of us have to work for a living," said Clifford Sloan with a perfect smile, too white, jerking his head meaningfully toward Kav, who looked, as always, as if he'd just stepped off a golf course. Kav's outfit that morning included cream-and-oxblood saddle shoes. Cliff, who had known Kav since their college days together, wore basic "desert casual" business attire—nice slacks, dress shirt, no tie.

Coop hesitated. "I've been meaning to phone for that follow-up appointment, but things have been hectic here."

"That's right," said Cliff, recalling, "you're due for a deep scaling, correct?"

Kavanall murmured, "Ouch . . ."

Coop knew a euphemism when he heard one. Deep scaling, indeed—it was a sanitized way of saying that down in his gums, the roots of his teeth needed cleaning, a gruesome process he barely dared to imagine. He told Cliff, "No point in putting it off, I guess. Let's set it up."

Cliff patted a pants pocket. "We could schedule it right now, but I left my iPhone in the car; my appointments are on it. So just call the office, and we'll get you right in." He handed Coop one of his business cards.

Coop slipped the card into his pocket, asking, "Not working to-day?" Then he wished he hadn't said it—did it make him sound too eager?

"Had an early cancellation, so I decided to take a spin and check out Kav's new digs. Congratulations, Coop. Everything's, well . . . awesome."

Coop wondered if "awesome" would find its way into the headline in *Architectural Record*.

Kav sat on the corner of his desk, swinging one of his jaunty shoes; its yellow laces matched the pale hue of his polo shirt. Through a wry smile he told Coop, "It was more than mere curiosity that brought Cliff out here this morning. Our friendly local DDS has an agenda. It involves political ambitions."

"Guilty," said Cliff with a soft laugh. "We'll have an open seat in the state senate race next year, and I've been, well . . . exploring things. I was wondering if Kav thought I might get some early support from Bix. It would make a big difference."

Kav said, "Ask him yourself," and led Cliff's glance to the doorway, where Bix stood holding Pyrite. Austin Royce, the CFO, stood a respectful pace or two behind, wearing a dark three-piece suit, looking like an East Coast banker.

Both the dentist and the architect snapped to attention as if royalty had entered—a king shod with cowboy boots. During the fawning and the good-mornings, Bix passed Pyrite to his CFO, who bobbed his head and disappeared with the dog.

Dismissing the small talk, Bix asked, "So what's this about politics, Clifford?"

"Well, sir, due to term limits, there'll be an open contest—"

"Why," Bix interrupted, "would a smart young man like you—and a hell of a dentist, I hear—why would you want to get involved with such an iffy, dirty business as that?"

Flustered, Cliff explained, "I know a political career is iffy, but it needn't be dirty."

Bix grunted.

Cliff cleared his throat. "It's the right time for change, not only for the district, but for me. Since the divorce, I've started weighing options, wondering if I'm in a rut."

If you think you're in a rut now, thought Coop, just wait twenty years.

Cliff continued, "I've sat on some local boards and worked with a couple of county agencies, even chaired a few committees. I honestly think I have something to offer."

Bix studied Cliff for a moment, gave another grunt, then asked, "Busy Sunday?" Before Cliff could answer, Bix said, "Come on up to Questover. It should be a nice fall day up in Idyllwild. We'll get the whole family together, have dinner, talk about this." He paused, nodded approval of his own idea, turned, and left.

Plans would be changed, schedules rearranged. Bix had spoken.

**W**hile crossing the courtyard to the research facility, Coop phoned Stasia to let her know they'd been summoned for Sunday dinner at Questover, the family's alpine retreat, about an hour's drive up into the mountains surrounding the valley. "Crap"—her voice rattled the earpiece of the phone—"we've got that bash at the museum Saturday night."

Coop suggested, "We could leave early."

"Don't you wish." Her words sounded less like a question than a warning.

"Okay, we'll stay."

"And I *hate* that drive."

"I'll drive." Coop didn't like the narrow, twisting route either, but volunteering was easier than listening to Stasia grouse about it.

"Thank you, sweets." And they said their good-byes.

As Coop pocketed his phone, he noticed Tessa Irwin hustling from another building toward the research center, lugging a bundle of files. Her white lab coat flapped in the warm breeze. With a wave, Coop hailed her, "Got a moment?"

She turned, smiled, and waited near the entrance. "Good morning, Cooper," she said as he approached and opened the door for her.

Stepping into the quiet lobby with her, he asked, "How's it going—the situation with Kav—is he keeping his distance?"

"For the moment." She nudged her glasses higher on the bridge of her nose. "He was bugging me about going to dinner with him tonight, but then, late yesterday, 'something came up.'"

That, thought Coop, would be the dinner with Jay Pontarelli. He told Tessa, "And he has a fresh commitment to be in Idyllwild on Sunday, so I think you're in the clear for the weekend."

"Lucky me, a breather—but that doesn't exactly solve the problem." She shifted the weight of the folders from one arm to the other.

"Here," said Coop, "let me take those."

"Thanks." She handed them over. "You're a model of chivalry, Cooper—much more like your father than your stepson."

It often slipped Coop's mind that Tessa had known his father, who had been nearly forty years older than she. She was born too late to remember Ferris "Rusty" Oxhide, the TV cowboy, but she was old enough to have been mentored in her graduate studies by Dr. Ferris Brant, the Nobel Prize–winning professor of thermodynamics. In fact, it was his glowing recommendation of his star student that had landed Tessa a position on the lead research team at Emery Oil just a year before his death. Coop didn't know her then; he was settled in Santa Barbara and had no connection to his father's students in Riverside. But now? Here they were, Coop and Tessa, working in the same building, working on the same mission, energy independence, that had been championed by the elder Brant.

Standing in the hallway outside Tessa's lab, Coop asked her, "What was he like—as a teacher? I probably knew him as well as anyone, but I never knew him that way."

She closed her eyes. A smile warmed her face. "He was brilliant. And inspiring. What a mind." Opening her eyes, she added matter-of-factly, "What a loss."

They entered Tessa's office, and Coop set the stack of files on her desk. He said, "The water engine. How involved were you with that?"

"Very little, and only indirectly. I was in one of his seminars that devoted an entire semester to exploring the theoretical possibility of a water engine, and one by one, we 'proved' that such a construct would violate every known law of thermodynamics. Heat without fuel—perpetual motion—it's the stuff of dreams. And then . . . ," she trailed off.

"And then," Coop finished the thought, "he announced he'd found the secret."

Coop's corduroys whooshed as he crossed the lobby to the construction offices. An open space behind a glass wall contained a maze of cubicles devoted to scheduling, purchasing, accounting, and other backroom functions. Larger office suites housed the design, engineering, and drafting teams. Computer terminals glowed at every desk. Workers typed. Printers whirred. Phones warbled.

Opting to forgo the hubbub, Coop tapped his security code into a keypad and entered his own office through a side door at the rear of the hall. As he closed the door behind him, a gust of ventilation seemed to seal the room, dispelling the noise and clutter of an outside world that was all too often unruly. Though these quarters were temporary, they were already a tangible extension of their occupant's mind-set and bore his mark, bespeaking order and logic.

The desk, a heavy rectangle of plate glass supported by two chrome trestles, bore only a phone, date book, keyboard, and pencil tray, all arranged at right angles. Perpendicular to the desk sat a drafting table with T-square and triangles poised at the ready; though these tools were now relics of a precomputerized era, he respected the tradition, the roots of his craft, and still preferred the tactile feedback, the exactitude of graphite on vellum when designing residential projects. Across from the desk stood several high cabinets of flat-files for the storage of plans. Behind the desk, the wall above a long credenza displayed an arrangement of framed photos, mostly black-and-white studies of landmark modern houses designed not by himself, but by the masters he revered. Conspicuous among this gallery of greats was a color glossy of Sheriff Rusty Oxhide, iconically handsome in his mid-twenties, waving his white hat from the saddle of a rearing palomino.

Coop reached into his pocket, pulled out his keys and Cliff Sloan's business card, and set them on his desk. He thought of calling Cliff's receptionist and setting up the appointment for the deep scaling, which Cliff had been recommending—threatening—for over a year. What was the hurry? It could wait till Monday. Coop turned a page of his calendar to the next week and set the card there as a reminder.

A light winking on the phone signaled a waiting voice mail, so Coop sat, lifted the receiver, and punched in his code. He had one new message: "Hello, Mr. Brant. This is Detective Arcie Madera with the Riverside County sheriff's department." Coop pulled the phone from his ear as if it had stung him. He blinked, took a breath, then continued to listen: ". . . a matter of some importance pertaining to your father. Could you call me? At your earliest convenience, please. And, oh—almost forgot—saw you on TV this morning. Very nice. Very photogenic. Seems you're really making quite the name for yourself. Bye, now."

He replaced the receiver. That one could also wait till Monday.

In the early years of country club development in and around Palm Springs, a large swath of land in nearby Rancho Mirage, which was as yet unincorporated, was snapped up by two brothers intent on creating the valley's most desirable address. They named it Entrada al Infierno, thinking it sounded fancy and, with limited knowledge of Spanish, deducing a reference to heat. All Hades broke loose, however, when one of the first investors, a pale Methodist wintering from Detroit, was informed by his pool boy that he had just bought a stake in the Entrance to Hell.

The consequent uprising of early homeowners led not only to the brothers being banned from the grounds as personae non gratae, but also to something of a civil war within the HOA regarding what to call the damn place. The signs were already up, and in spite of its name, the club's reputation was growing, so while everyone clamored for change, there was also a consensus that any tinkering with the name should be more of a surgical correction than a clean sweep.

A vocal minority of homeowners embraced switching the name to Entrada di Paradiso, but others had no taste for the proposal, finding it too smarmy. As the battle waged on, the original name began to feel, for many, more palatable, and speaking at one of countless protracted meetings, a weary resident finally suggested, "Why don't we just run with it and call the place Hellsgate?" The idea drew moderate enthusiasm, but would require a complete change of existing signage. Ultimately, the compromise solution was to abbreviate the name of the whole development to, simply, Entrada. The clubhouse and its main dining room were named Hellsgate, and in an incongruous nod to the dissenting faction, its bar was called the Paradise Lounge. The restaurant was decorated in a fiery palette of reds; the bar, heavenly blues.

Oddly, it all seemed to work, and not even the club's clumsy nomenclature could diminish its appeal. Entrada's jaw-dropping views, world-class golf, and A-list membership roster were second to none. Though neither of the founding brothers lived to see it, they had indeed accomplished their objective of creating the valley's most coveted address. So when Bix and Emma Emery decided to escape from L.A. and find a desert retreat, where else would they choose to roost? Entrada had just opened a new phase of the development, another twenty acres, and claiming a need for elbow room, Bix bought it all.

Flash forward. Some four or five years prior to Thursday's dedication of Emery Energy's new headquarters, when it became apparent that the entire Emery clan would eventually make a permanent move to the desert, Bix offered his acreage at Entrada for the construction of homes for himself, for Stasia and Cooper, and for Kavanall and his future family. Since Emma was long gone, Bix razed the house he had built with her and told Coop to start from scratch on the design of three new homes, separate but related. His only instructions were "make it nice" and "be sure to save some room for any grandkids."

It was a plum assignment for an architect who had been longing to return to his residential roots, but the scale of the project quickly disabused him of any notion that he was designing "housing." No, this was a "compound" within the fully gated and guarded confines of Entrada, with expansive golf-course views seen by others only on television during the occasional tournaments held there. More often than not, going out to dinner meant taking a short walk to Hellsgate. Why go farther? It offered some of the finest dining in the valley.

Coop was proud of the compound—it embodied a mature articulation of the highest tenets of modernism, offering an elite lifestyle in an enviable setting—but in the final analysis, he was his own harshest critic and brooded that the structures looked more like a resort than a family's cluster of private homes.

Now, on a Friday evening in October, Coop and Stasia were in their bedroom suite, dressing for dinner at the club with Jay Pontarelli and Kavanall. Shortly after seven, a fading purple glow of twilight clung to the crests of the Santa Rosas, which pricked at the skyline beyond the terrace outside the bedroom windows. A double row of date palms, lit from beneath, formed a colonnade at the perimeter of the golf course, leading to Hellsgate, not visible from the house, shielded in the distance by berms and plantings.

Facing a mirror in the bedroom, Coop finished knotting his tie for the second time, getting it just right, with the tip centered on his belt buckle. He dimpled the knot with a masterful pinch and called to Stasia, "It's supposed to get chilly tonight." On the first night they had spent in the new house, they had laughed about needing to shout to each other while getting ready for bed. Though they shared the same bedroom, they had separate bathrooms, walk-in closets, and dressing rooms.

"Sounds wonderful," her voice wafted from afar. "Maybe we can light a fire later."

"I know a double entendre when I hear one."

"No," she assured him with a chortle, "you don't."

"Guess not," he mumbled, his tone colored by no hint of disappointment, merely resignation. He reached to the edge of the bed for a black cashmere blazer, slipped it on, and fastened one button.

Stasia strolled in from her dressing room in a pantsuit of nubby silk, warm-hued, verging on ochre, heralding the onset of autumnal evenings. A simple necklace and bracelet, both rose gold, completed her ensemble with an understated sparkle. She studied Coop for a moment, shaking her head. "Nix the tie, sweets—it's just the club."

With a shrug, he took off the jacket and began undoing the perfect Windsor knot of his necktie, a favorite old Armani that had followed him through two marriages and how many homes?

Stasia fussed with a handbag, removing a few items—breath spray, pillbox, reading glasses—then putting them back.

Coop asked, "Something on your mind?"

She tossed her hands. "Jay Pontarelli, of course. What's he up to? And what in God's name does Kav have to do with it?"

Stasia's son had Emery blood, but he'd evidenced not a jot of the family's resourcefulness, intelligence, or drive. To Coop's way of thinking, Kav simply didn't matter. What were he and Pontarelli up to? Coop wanted to ask Stasia, Who cares?

Instead he checked his watch and said, "We'll find out soon enough. Want to head over and have a quick drink first?"

"Good idea."

On Friday night at the height of the dinner hour, the club was bustling, but there were no lines, no waiting, not at Hellsgate. The clientele was members only, many of whom had standing reservations throughout "the season." The staff was drilled to know every member by name (how photos were collected for this purpose no one was quite sure), and a stroll through the dining room felt like a nightly reunion of friends and family.

"Christ," muttered Stasia as they walked through the main entrance, "don't you get sick of these tired old gasbags?"

"Isn't that a tad harsh?" Coop's wink conveyed that he couldn't agree more.

"Ah!" The tuxedoed maître d' glided toward them from behind an imposing podium of anguished wrought iron; it looked as if it could have been pilfered from Satan's cellar. "Good evening, Mr. and Mrs. Brant. So nice to see you, as always. Welcome." With a scrape and a flourish, he gestured toward the dining room.

"Thank you, Richard," said Coop, "but we're going to relax at the bar first. Maybe you could help our guests find us when they arrive."

With a knowing nod, Richard said, "A bit of heaven before the inferno—but of course. And I believe you'll find Mr. Emery at the bar already."

"Kavanall?" asked Stasia. Under her breath, she said to Coop, "He's *never* early."

"No, ma'am," said Richard. "Mr. Bix Emery."

Coop and Stasia crossed the lobby toward the Paradise Lounge. She said, "This could get awkward."

Coop asked, "Should we invite him to join us?"

"We'll have to. But if he accepts, Jay won't open up."

"He will if we get enough booze in him," said Coop, escorting Stasia into the dimly lit, bluish confines of the lounge. The cool air within carried the lilt of quiet, amiable conversations, punctuated by the clink of crystal and the rattle of purified ice. Live entertainment was provided by a harpist, who plucked her way through something genteel and French, perhaps Debussy.

"There he is," said Stasia, spotting her father at the far end of the bar. A tall brown cocktail, half finished, sat before him. On the stool next to him sat Pyrite, nibbling cubes of raw tenderloin that Bix slid from a bamboo appetizer skewer.

"Evening, Bix," said Coop as the couple drew near.

"Well, looky here," said Bix, breaking into a wide smile, standing to kiss his daughter, hug his son-in-law. Then he frowned. "Coops," he said, barely above a whisper, "where's your *tie*?" Bix tightened the clasp of his bolo.

Humiliated, Coop drew his hand to the open collar of his shirt.

"Hell, Coops"—Bix roared a laugh—"it's just the *club*!"

Coop allowed himself a feeble smile. "Maybe I need a drink."

Bix raised an arm and gave a loud finger-snap, but the bartender was a step ahead of him, shaking the bejesus out of two martinis, gin for Coop, vodka for Stasia, their usuals.

Pyrite coughed.

The others turned to see him, paws on the bar, chewing a large sprig of parsley he had snitched from the appetizer plate. A fist-size clump of frilly greens hung from his maw as he tried working the stem farther down his throat.

"Pyrite," said Bix, "drop it."

The dog froze for a moment, eyeing the old man, then resumed chewing.

"*Drop it!*" The entire lounge hushed and looked.

Pyrite's jaw sagged, and the parsley fell to the seat of the stool.

"Good Pyrite," cooed Bix, "*good* little son f'bitch." With one hand he patted the dog; with the other he returned the parsley to the plate. He explained to others seated nearby at the bar, "Only command the little fella seems to understand." With the drama ended, the lounge resumed its chatter.

Stasia asked him, "Have you had dinner yet? Care to join us?"

"Nah, thanks, other plans. Besides, I wouldn't want to intrude—on Jay Pontarelli."

Coop and Stasia glanced at each other.

"And Kavanall too." Bix slugged the remainder of his drink.

Stasia flashed him a sly grin. "You certainly keep your ear to the rail."

"That's my job." He grabbed his hat from the adjacent barstool, patted it onto his head, picked up the dog, and cradled it in one arm. "Come on, sweet pea. We'll be late." Before leaving, he pinched off a small sprig of the parsley and ate it, telling Coop, "It's good for the breath—case I get stopped on the way home," then let loose with another hearty laugh.

Coop and Stasia watched as he crossed the room. Near the door, the harpist had just reached a pause between selections. Bix told her, "I'll give you a smasher—a hundred bucks—to play 'Lady Is a Tramp.'"

She rolled her eyes; they'd been through this before. Sitting back, she leaned the harp against her shoulder, poised her fingers, and plucked into a lethargic rendition of "Clair de Lune."

**P**rawns diablo—an excellent choice, madam." The head waiter then clicked his pen and reviewed the entree orders of the three men at the table: "Deviled halibut, pollo alla diavola, and the bone-in rib eye, inferno-style. Very good. Please, enjoy your cocktails." With a deferential bob of his head, he retreated.

"When in Hellsgate . . . ," said Coop, lifting his martini glass.

The others joined in his toast, sipped their drinks, and paused before settling into a conversation that promised to be strained. Candles flickered through heavy red water goblets. The chitchat of other tables was muted by crimson velvet curtains that puddled luxuriantly on the rough-hewn stone floor. Though the clubhouse commanded postcard-perfect mountain views in all directions, the main dining room had no windows. Most critics of higher gastronomy lauded this feature, as it allowed diners to focus on the purity of the cuisine, free from other sensory distractions, but a younger wave of new members bitched that it was like eating in a cave, and a flat-out revolt was brewing over the no-jeans policy (*"everyone* in L.A. wears jeans—*everywhere"*). There was no music—another sensory distraction that had been banned—though a pipe organ's quavering pedal tones would have fit the setting to a tee.

Against this backdrop, Stasia said point-blank, "All right, Jay. Tell me about newco."

*"Yes,"* said Kavanall. "We're dying. What's up?" He leaned back in his chair, fluffed the silk pocket square that adorned his sport coat like a corsage, and traced a finger around the sugared rim of a concoction that passed as a martini. Wisps of steam rose from chunks of dry ice that drifted on the surface of the alcohol. He licked his finger.

Jay Pontarelli leaned forward, elbows on the table. The jacket of his dark business suit bunched at his shoulders; his arms filled the sleeves like plump, firm sausages. Massive gold cufflinks peeped from the sleeves and scraped the table linen. He grinned. "No small talk first?" He turned to Coop, asking, "Hey! How 'bout those Lakers?"

Coop responded with a vacant stare.

Jay nudged, "Looks like a good season, huh? They might go all the way this year."

Though Coop had spent most of his life in Southern California, he'd never paid much attention to this aspect of the local culture. With a squint of curiosity, he said to Jay, "You might know the answer to this. I've always been curious: Why are they called the Lakers? I mean, L.A. isn't on a lake."

Jay glanced at Kavanall. His expression asked, Where did you *find* this guy? Turning to Coop, he explained, "They moved here from Minneapolis in 1960. Lotsa lakes there."

"Oh."

Kav said, "Everyone knows *that,* Pops."

"No," Coop assured him, "not everyone."

"*I* didn't," said Stasia with a soft smile, patting Coop's hand. Then the smile dropped as she turned to Jay. "Enough small talk." With no inflection and a steady gaze, she added, "Newco?"

Jay tweaked the knot of his tie; other than the staff, he was the only man in the room wearing one. "Newco is still on the drawing board—in the organizational sense—but as you can probably guess, it's a new company devoted to the development of alternate energy supplies. On a global scale." Leaning back, he added, "Sound familiar?"

Stasia hadn't blinked. "How you gonna fund it, Jay? You're rich as Croesus, thanks in no small measure to your Emery stock, but you're not *that* rich—not on a global scale."

He whirled a hand vaguely, conceding, "It'll take a consortium, of course, an international team of heavy hitters, and trust me, they're lining up for this. But I'm the principal investor, which means failure is not an option. It *has* to succeed. Bottom line: I'll be selling off my interest in Emery Energy. I'll need the capital, and I can put it to better use—in PontaPower."

Stasia blinked. "Catchy name."

Jay Pontarelli continued, "The time is right for this. Your father proved it. If Bix Emery says the future's not in oil, I'm listening."

Stasia leaned toward Jay, stabbing the table with her index finger. "This is a natural evolution for Bix. He's been in oil all his life. He's uniquely qualified to make the next moves."

Jay shook his head. "You don't have to 'do oil' in order to *not* 'do oil.' To my way of thinking, the torch has been passed."

"Tell *Bix* that. He won't like this."

"He doesn't have to. This is business, Stasia. Consider this evening a courtesy call; I wanted you to hear it from me. I bear no ill will. In fact, I love you guys."

Coop winced.

Kav laughed. "Why, *thank* you, Jay. I never knew you cared."

Jay turned to Kav and studied him for a moment. "You're a bright young guy. You've been in the family business for years. Maybe bigger things lie ahead for you at Emery; maybe not. Ever been on an oil rig? Ever had the stuff under your fingernails?"

Kav shuddered. "God, no."

"I like that. A clean past. And yet, you carry the family name."

Stasia reminded Jay, "Emery is Kav's *middle* name. His father was a Follet."

Jay shrugged. "And his mother was an Emery. So what? Nobody knows the difference. Besides, we could fix it with a hyphen."

Again Coop winced. When Stasia had married her first husband, she had abandoned the pedigree of her maiden name and had become Anastasia Follet, but the second time around, she had chosen to become Anastasia Emery-Brant. "Do you mind?" she had asked as they planned their nuptials. "Of course not," he had assured her. "I'm not the sort of man who needs to *own* a woman. You're not my chattel—I'm a little more evolved than *that*." But now, as Jay pounced on the hyphen, Coop crossed his legs under the table as if fending off a kick to the groin.

Stasia eyed their dinner guest with the stern disapproval of a miffed nun. "Excuse me, please," she said quietly, barely parting her lips. Then she took her purse, pushed back her chair, and left the table.

"My, my, my," said Kav, watching his mother's retreat, pausing to sip his smoking martini. "What *exactly* are you driving at, Jay?"

Jay clapped a beefy paw on Kav's shoulder. "Do I have to spell it out? If you get frustrated with your prospects in the family biz, I could sure as hell put you to good use at PontaPower."

What, wondered Coop, could Kav possibly have to offer other than his name?

Kav weighed Jay's words, nodding. "Someone might consider that a declaration of war, but let me think about it. We'll talk."

At that moment, four dashing waiters appeared, bearing four silver-domed plates.

**W**hile walking home from the club, Stasia turned to Coop and said, "You don't like Kav, do you?"

The pollo alla diavola did a little dance in Coop's troubled stomach. He told his wife, "That's not a fair question."

"Perhaps." She stopped walking; Coop halted a step later and turned to face her in the dark. Crickets chirped. She continued, "I'm his mother; I *have* to love him, and I do. But *like* him? *You* don't have to. Sometimes, I'm not even sure I do."

"I respect him," Coop lied. "He was a grown man when I married you, so I've never thought of him as a son."

"And yet"—Stasia smirked—"he calls you Pops."

Coop returned her smirk. "He does that to annoy me—same as Bix, calling me Coops."

"Bix does *not* mean to annoy you. He's always been crazy about you."

"He's always been crazy about Kav, too—so much for Bix's judgment." Coop stopped himself. "Sorry. That came out all wrong."

Stasia laughed. "It *is* strange, isn't it, the way Bix seems to dote on Kav? They're not at all alike; in fact, they're polar opposites."

"Must be the bloodline, pure and simple."

Stasia began walking again, turning onto the path that led to the Emery compound. She asked Coop, strolling next to her, "What do you think are the chances Bix will name Kav president? I mean, honestly."

Honestly? Coop thought Austin Royce, the CFO, would be a far better choice, hands down. He told Stasia, "I think Bix should name *you* president."

*"Me?"* She stopped in her tracks.

"You're the smartest woman I know. Hell, you're the smartest *person* I know. You've seen that business from the inside out, and you've been part of the corporate culture all your life. You've got an MBA—"

She interrupted, "I went back to school because I was bored. Same thing with that stint as president of the chamber."

"Plus," he continued, "you're an Emery. Why not?"

"Why not?" she echoed with a laugh. "Because I've got tits."

"Yeah, baby," said Coop through a low growl. He mock-humped her hip.

Stasia's laughter rang in the chilly night air. The Milky Way swooped overhead, a dim blur through a cluster of palms, their fronds silhouetted black against the sky. Catching her breath, she elaborated, "Bix is a good ol' boy, he's pushing ninety, and he'll never change. End of argument."

Coop admitted, "The term 'glass ceiling' does spring to mind. I still cringe every time he calls one of his secretaries 'my girl.' I mean, jeez, they're both on Medicare."

"And here's a news flash," said Stasia. "Some of us now refer to secretaries as 'assistants.'"

"I'll make a note of that."

Although the grounds of Entrada were walled and gated, with a full-time security staff that rivaled any small-town police force, Coop and Stasia paused on their front stoop to unlock the door and to keypad an entry code, deactivating an alarm system. Property crime was unknown here—zero—but Bix fretted constantly about the welfare of his family, about the sinister capacities of the world's have-nots, so Coop and Stasia humored him, agreeing to the pointless ritual of the keypad whenever they left or returned to their house. Even Kavanall, who knew to curb his cynicism just short of crossing the old man, had agreed to play along, repeating the same drill at his own home, just beyond the next knoll.

Coop opened the door for Stasia and followed her into the foyer. "We're *ho*-ome!" he called to the phantom cutthroats and desperadoes lurking in the empty house.

"Stop that," she said with a laugh. "Night cap?"

"Sure. I just need a minute to look through some mail." He placed his keys on a shallow console table near the door, where he had left a small stack of envelopes brought home from the office.

"Think I'll light the fire," she said, stepping in the direction of the bedrooms.

"Nice."

"Bring cognac," she said.

"Will do." Listening to the peck of her heels retreat down the hall, he picked up the stack of mail and flipped through it. Conspicuous among the white business-size envelopes was a smaller one, baby blue, addressed to him by hand in the blue-black ink of a fountain pen. The script was a neat, well-practiced Palmer Method, but its loops and swirls bore the pained inconsistency of older, perhaps arthritic, fingers. The other envelopes had already been slit open for his perusal, some with memoranda attached, but this piece of mail was clearly personal, so his secretary—that is, his assistant—had left it sealed. Glancing at it earlier, he hadn't noticed a return address, but now he turned it over and saw two lines of script on the flap, an address in Pioneertown, California, a bohemian community with a colorful past, surrounded by the wilderness twenty-some miles north of Palm Springs. Coop muttered, "Jesus Christ."

He slid his finger under the flap, ripped the envelope lengthwise, and read the handwritten message on the tissue-thin pages within:

*Dear Cooper,*

*I doubt that you have been eager to hear from me, but I felt I must write. With all the publicity leading up to the opening of Emery Energy, I was so surprised to learn of your involvement with the project and so delighted to know that you have made a permanent move to the area. Yes, I am still in Pioneertown—some things never change.*

*Though I have not seen you in many years, I think of you often. You were such a beautiful child, and you grew into such an extraordinary man. Would it offend you if I confided that I sometimes dreamed you were my own son?*

*When your mother died, my heart bled for you. Can it possibly be eighteen years ago? It seems like yesterday, as does your father's death, only three years later. This is so difficult, but I need to tell you what I never had the courage to say before. I know you blame me that your mother took her own life, and I often fear you may be right—may God forgive me. I am so very sorry, dearest Cooper.*

*But please never doubt that I truly loved your father. For a woman of color, born in a time of segregated schools (and worse), it was a fantasy beyond imagining to move to California and to win a foothold in pictures, however small. To think back and know that I also won a small portion of Ferris Brant's heart . . . well, my life has been full beyond measure.*

*I am still in fair health, but nearly eighty now, so how many years can I have left? If there is any room in your heart for forgiveness, Cooper, I would welcome having you back in my life.*

*All my love, always,*
*Mimi*

Coop wadded the letter in his fist and shoved it deep into a pocket of his corduroys. Though he stood in the foyer of a house he'd designed for his second wife, his thoughts propelled him back to an incident that would eventually doom not only the home he'd made with his first wife, but a thriving career in Santa Barbara:

The ashes of Coop's mother, Peggy Brant, rest in an urn on a pedestal, surrounded by photos and flowers, at the front of the chapel. A Unitarian, clad in a starched white surplice and long floral-patterned stole, presides over a simple service, reading from the limp gilt-edged pages of a black leather-bound book.

Coop, recently turned forty, sits in the front row, feeling numb with the sudden loss of the woman who gave him life, who anguished over his lost finger, who lovingly helped him conquer a childhood stutter. At Coop's left sits his father, Ferris, a widower at sixty-two; he weeps openly, blotting tears with a damp linen handkerchief. At Coop's right sits his wife, Cheryl, and their daughter, Clio, barely in her teens.

Clio didn't want to attend, and her mother was inclined to let her stay home, but Coop insisted. So there she sits, slouched in her chair, watching her shoes with adolescent resolve. Clio is not in mourning; rather, she is mortified that Grandma Brant offed herself with an Osterizer one hot afternoon when she improvised a Slurpee consisting of ice, pills, and booze—with a double shot of antifreeze as a chaser. It's the talk of the town, and poor Clio has been unable to show her face at school since the story hit the papers.

In the second row, behind the immediate family, sits a select assemblage of Ferris's university colleagues from Riverside, where he maintains a second home for use while school is in session, weekending with his family in Santa Barbara.

During a lull in the service, Ferris reaches over to pat his son's knee. "Be strong, Coop." With a sob, he adds, "I know how hard it is."

Yanked from a thick stew of conflicting emotions, Coop turns to his father and tells him, in a strained whisper that carries farther than intended, "Well, it's your own d'damn fault—she c'couldn't handle it."

Ferris stares at his son bug-eyed. Cheryl digs her nails into her husband's wrist. Clio's gaze snaps from her shoes to her father; her eyes sparkle with delicious anticipation. Behind them, in unison, the academics lean an inch forward. Coop's heartbeat throbs in his temples as silence pricks the room like the sword of an avenging angel.

Then the Unitarian clears his throat. "Let us pause to meditate."

For the remainder of the service, Coop says not another word.

Afterward, in the parking lot, while walking to their cars, Ferris attempts a conciliatory pat of the hand on his son's shoulder.

Coop stops short, blocking his father as other mourners squeeze past. "I ought to fuckin' k'kill you," says Coop. "This never would've happened if you'd stopped playing house with that b'black bitch."

# Chapter 3

Parking valets sprinted to greet each vehicle arriving for Saturday's opening-night reception at the Palm Springs Art Institute and Museum. Huge vertical banners on the stone façade, as well as smaller ones on the streetlights, trumpeted BRUCE ROLLO: NEW EXPLORATIONS IN GLASS. A throng of cognoscenti, whose getups ranged from matronly to hip, climbed the grand staircase toward the main entrance, gushing about *the* big art event of the season. "It puts this valley on the *map*," said a dolly with a bad facelift, her brows frozen in perpetual surprise.

"Who *is* this guy?" Coop asked under his breath, plodding up the stairs with Stasia, feeling out of his element.

Stasia's expression asked if he'd been living under a rock. "Bruce Rollo," she said, "is only *the* biggest name in glass sculpture since Dale Chihuly."

"God, *yes*," said a woman standing within earshot, drawing near. She wore an extravagant silk tunic swirling with huge tangerine-and-peacock arabesques, a gauzy turban of emerald green that drifted over one shoulder to her knees, and armloads of noisy bracelets. "*Everyone's* got Chihuly now," she proclaimed with a bark of laughter. "Dora floats the stuff in her *swimming* pool!"

"Krystal," said Stasia, pecking the woman's cheek, "I was hoping to see you tonight. Have you met my husband, Cooper Brant?"

"At last—the *architect*." She extended her hand regally, as if expecting it to be kissed, causing a backup on the stairs. A man below grumbled to his companions.

Stasia told Coop, "This is Krystal Kaylee, who serves on the museum board with me. She's on the college faculty—professor of fashion design."

"Delighted to meet you, Professor," said Coop, shaking her hand.

"Oh, posh, dah-ling"—she tossed a shoulder—"it's *Krystal*."

He added, "Stasia's told me so many nice things about you," though he had never till that moment heard her name.

"Really?" she bubbled, clamping a hand to her bosom. With her other hand, she grabbed Coop's arm and yanked him close; he nearly lost his footing on the steps. "Your wife," she said in an exaggerated stage whisper intended to be heard by all, "is without question the most able and competent board member I've ever had the pleasure to work with. She's tireless, smart, and incisive. I tell you, this woman's talents are being wasted on volunteer work. She could do anything—*anything*!"

"I tend to agree with you, Krystal." Coop gave Stasia a wink.

"We're holding things up," said Stasia, as if she'd heard none of it. "We'd better get moving." And she led the way up the stairs to the entrance.

Inside, Coop encouraged Stasia to mingle while he waited in line at one of the bars to fetch cocktails. When he returned, bearing a measly shot of liquor on ice for each of them, he found Stasia gabbing with Garrick Bates, the software titan who, several years earlier, had moved to the area and built, from the sand up, the Bates School of the Art Institute—his way of "giving back" to society. Adjacent to the museum, there had been an abandoned shopping mall, an eyesore that had blighted the city's main drag for a decade. With a single stroke of his check-writing pen, Bates had bought and demolished the mall—problem solved— and with a second stroke of the same pen, he had built the arts college, staffing it with a top-notch faculty cherry-picked from prestigious old schools across the land. He greeted Coop with a few pleasantries, told Stasia, "Think about it," and then excused himself, disappearing into the crowd.

Coop clinked glasses with Stasia, but before drinking, asked, "Think about what?"

She rolled her eyes, sipped from the dainty ration of vodka, and swallowed. "He wants me on his board."

"The software biz? Or the college?"

"The college. I think he just wants the Emery name on the

letterhead."

"But you've been hyphenated."

"Stop that." She kissed his cheek.

Her lips felt icy against his skin. He asked, "What's the connection with the college—I mean here, tonight? Garrick Bates. That Krystal character."

"I'm sure they're *all* here tonight," said Stasia. "It's hardly a coincidence. Bruce Rollo is a visiting professor on the Bates School faculty. He's been exploring a major new direction in his work, so tonight's the unveiling."

Samples of Rollo's new work sparkled atop white rectangular pedestals throughout the main lobby and reception area. While his precursor, Chihuly, was known primarily for organic forms suggestive of gourds and exotic sea life, Rollo now made an abrupt departure by constructing elaborate, hard-edged geometric forms. While Chihuly favored a palette of brilliant jewel tones, Rollo's new work was exclusively black, white, or clear. An artist's quote in the show catalog referred to "the linearity of glass, the opacity of the transparent." Though the statement struck Coop as absurdly pedantic, the work itself enthralled him. "It's mesmerizing," he told Stasia.

"I knew you'd like it. It's so 'you,' so structured. Maybe you'll find one in your stocking, come Christmas." Easy for her to say—these stocking stuffers, according to a discreet listing at the back of the catalog, started in the tens of thousands. In deference to refined sensitivities, the list contained no dollar signs.

The main gallery had not yet been opened. Guards would ceremoniously fling the doors wide only at the conclusion of the artist's lecture, to be held in the museum auditorium. For now, arriving guests were confined to the reception area, already packed to capacity. The culture-hungry hordes milled and eddied; bartenders hustled to pour stingy refills; a battery of waiters plied the crowd, holding high their trays of crab cakes and brie tartlets; upbeat party music was drowned out by talk and laughter. In the midst of all this, the white pedestals rose like little islands of serenity, each in a safe zone cordoned off by velvet ropes on chrome stanchions. Still, thought Coop, *there's* an accident waiting to happen.

"*There,*" said Stasia, tugging Coop's sleeve.

"What? Where?"

"Bruce Rollo—over there, in black."

"*Everyone's* in black." Coop was exaggerating, but not much. With the exception of Krystal and a few other colorful types, it was a turtleneck-and-leotard sort of crowd, basic black. Coop wore the Armani tie that had been nixed the night before; silvery gray damask, paired with a charcoal silk shirt and his trusty black blazer, it looked both tasteful and inconspicuous among tonight's gathering.

"The *tall* one," said Stasia, "with the big hair."

"Ahhh," said Coop, spotting him. Rollo stood well over six feet, with his graying blond hair worn full and long, suggestive of a lion's mane; the image was made all the more striking by a neat goatee that enhanced a strong, square jaw. He appeared to be about fifty, a few years younger than Coop. Perfectly groomed and nattily dressed, he belied the popular notion of the starving artist, the iconoclast in the garret. He stood apart from the crowd, under the landing of an open staircase, huddled in cozy conversation with another man, dark-haired, younger, and very buff. Coop asked, "Is that his boy toy?"

"No," replied Stasia with a hint of strained patience, "Bruce Rollo is straight."

Metrosexual, thought Coop. I've never actually met one.

"Besides," Stasia continued, "the man he's talking to is already taken—by your trainer. That's Teddy's husband, Rob Pollard. Rob represents Bruce at his gallery on Palm Canyon."

Time stood still for a moment as the pieces fell together for Coop. Of course: when Teddy had extended the invitation to attend a Saturday opening, he'd been referring to *this* event, which was surely the only show in town tonight for the local art crowd. Coop asked Stasia, "Is Teddy here?"

"Probably, but I haven't—oh! Even as we speak." She gestured into the crowd just as Teddy emerged with a woman, crossing the lobby toward Rob and Bruce.

Coop had to laugh. He'd never expected to see Teddy with a

woman on his arm—and what a knockout. Though Coop's view of her was fragmented by the shifting crowd, he liked what he saw. Older than Teddy but younger than Coop himself, she wore a little black dress and spiked black heels, with her dark hair, almost black, slicked into a lovely chignon that bobbed against the nape of her firm but graceful neck. As she arrived under the landing, Bruce Rollo wrapped an arm around her waist and kissed the top of her head; even in heels, she was six inches shorter than he. Still, Coop noted with a tinge of disappointment and a soupçon of jealousy, they made an attractive-looking couple.

Stasia handed Coop her empty glass, saying, "Let's say hello," then took off in their direction.

Coop glanced about, but saw nowhere to put her glass—or his, also empty—so he loped after, wary of missing the round of introductions.

Stasia was already kissing cheeks with the men, shaking hands with the woman, when Coop arrived. "Ah," she said, spinning the woman in black toward him, "do meet my husband, Cooper Brant."

Coop's broad smile fell as her face came into full view and the two glasses slipped from his hand, crashing on the terrazzo floor.

"Cooper!" said Stasia. "What on Earth's the matter with you?"

The sound of breaking glass hushed the crowd as a trio of waiters converged near Coop's feet, picking up the splinters, sweeping the chips with folded cloth napkins. Shards scraped and hissed against the floor of the suddenly quiet room.

"Is this s'some kind of joke?" said Coop. "Are you s'stalking me, Detective?"

Arcie Madera countered, "Are you avoiding me, Mr. Brant? You haven't returned my calls."

"Could we, uh . . . ?" Coop gestured that they should step away from the others and talk privately.

Stasia went ashen with chagrin, Bruce Rollo seemed on the verge of laughter, Teddy's brow wrinkled with concern, and Rob Pollard looked flat-out confused. The hubbub and merriment resumed as Coop and the pretty cop moved out of earshot and took refuge in a corner of the lobby behind a towering potted palm.

Standing there, she crossed her arms and shifted her weight to one hip, looking Coop in the eye. "You haven't answered my question. Didn't you get my message?"

"It's the weekend," Coop snapped. "I planned to call you Monday."

"The law never rests, Mr. Brant." Her smug look was so ambiguous, Coop didn't know whether her clichéd words were meant to be intimidating or laughable.

He said, "You haven't answered *my* question. Are you stalking me?"

"No, Mr. Brant, I'm sleeping with Bruce Rollo. So he asked me to his little soirée." She pursed her lips and tilted her nose in a snooty expression.

Coop's curiosity outweighed his tact: "What are you doing with *him*?"

"I beg your pardon?"

"Sorry. I guess that was presumptuous."

"No, it was pompous and prying."

"Sorry," he said again. "It's just that, well . . . he doesn't seem your type. *You* don't seem *his* type. I mean, you're a cop." Aware that his rambling had dug him in too deep for redemption, he added lamely, "And we thank you for your service."

She eyed him for a long moment with a neutral expression that made him squirm. When at last she spoke, her tone was pensive, even wistful. "My mother was a cop. But my father was a sculptor—a metalsmith. He did these huge abstracted figures in raw, welded steel—people, horses—sometimes you couldn't tell which."

"Really?"

"Mm-hm." She nodded. "So . . . ever since I was a little girl, I've been attracted to creative men. Enter Bruce Rollo."

Coop mumbled, "He's awfully tall."

"What?"

"Nothing." Coop cleared his throat. "So tell me, Detective, what did you want me to phone you about?"

"About your father's case, obviously."

"Obviously." Though Coop now found himself on full alert,

he was momentarily distracted by someone in the crowd passing by the other side of the potted palm. It was a man with a familiar face, though he couldn't place it at first, which led him to assume it must be a face from the gym. Yes. Exactly. It was one of those faces that had remained in the background until only yesterday. It was the bleached-blond guy in the powder-blue muscle shirt who had gotten into the shouting match with the bruiser in khaki. Teddy had said his name was Dennis Dill, former porn star, currently an escort. And now, sure enough, there he was, parading past the potted palm with a *much* older man whose exuberant array of jewelry included a diamond pinkie ring mounted with a rock the size of a cocktail onion. Dennis was laughing at his every word. How much, wondered Coop, did the old guy pay for a night on the town? Was there more to follow? And what exactly, at his age, would he *do*? Just lie there?

Arcie Madera was saying, ". . . so I'm reopening the case."

Coop's attention snapped back to the moment.

She said, "You don't look pleased." Her voice was laced with irony. "On Thursday you told me you wanted this solved more than anyone else."

"I . . . d'do. Of course." He managed a stiff smile.

"Forensics has progressed by leaps and bounds since the murder. With recent developments in DNA analysis, we need to go back, review all the physical evidence, and see if there's something we missed."

"Great," he said. "That's encouraging. I recommend it." He wished she'd let it rest.

"Then help me out with this. Volunteer a sample of your DNA."

"Me? Why?"

"It could clear you," she said.

Or it could nail me, he thought. He hadn't killed his father, but he had touched the body and trashed the crime scene. Stupid, yes; culpable, no. Other than the killer and the police, he was the only one to witness the physical circumstances of Ferris Brant's murder. Had he sneezed on something? Had a fleck of dandruff drifted from his scalp to the crusted blood on his father's shirt? Just when he was reestablishing his career and growing bored with the comfort and security of a second marriage—such enviable boredom—just then, would his life fall apart again?

He struggled for an answer to give the detective, but she wasn't paying attention. She had stepped out from the cover of the potted palm to give a friendly little girlie-wave to a woman in a silk jumpsuit who was strolling through the lobby with a pleasant if dumpy middle-aged man in a tired-looking workaday business suit. They both waved back. "Isn't that Gretchen Wong?" asked Coop. "The filmmaker?" She was a prime example of the star-caliber faculty Garrick Bates had recruited for his school.

"Yeah."

Coop waited for some elaboration, but getting none, asked, "You *know* her?"

"Yeah. The man she's with, he's a colleague of mine, a sheriff's detective, Len Nolan. They've become quite . . . *involved.* Odd match, but it seems to be the real deal."

"How'd that happen?"

"Long story. But once Len got to know Gretchen and her college crowd, he thought I'd like to meet Bruce Rollo. So the four of us had dinner at Gretchen's place. She *cooked.* She's a doll."

And Rollo? wondered Coop. You're sleeping with him. Does *he* cook, too?

"So then," she said, "if you didn't kill your father—"

So much for social pleasantries, thought Coop.

"—if you didn't kill your father, you ought to be eager to volunteer the DNA and help us steer the investigation down another course."

"I, uh, should probably talk to a lawyer first."

She nodded. "Thought so."

With a trace of umbrage, he asked, "What do you mean, 'Thought so'?"

"Look. Several credible witnesses gave affidavits that you threatened your father's life—at your mother's funeral, no less. Then your dad turns up dead, and you're found at the crime scene destroying evidence. It doesn't take Sherlock Holmes to connect *those* dots. All that was missing was the hard proof. And now, maybe we'll get some."

"Detective"—Coop's head was spinning, this couldn't be happening, not again—"we've been through this before, how many times? At my mother's funeral I was crazy with grief and, I admit it, angry. But my father was killed three *years* later. That hardly qualifies as a crime of passion. I went to his office that morning at his request, to help him set up for the presentation."

"So you say. It would be handy if you could prove it."

"He was my *father*. He didn't send an engraved invitation. He just asked me. It was fifteen years ago; I didn't even *have* e-mail back then. So yes, you're correct, there's no paper trail."

"If you were there to help him, why were you destroying evidence?"

"I *wasn't*. The office was ransacked when I arrived. I was looking *for* evidence—of the prototype—or what might have happened to it."

She asked, "If there really was such a prototype, it would be fairly valuable, right?"

Coop tossed his arms. "Priceless."

She paused. Her wry smile said, Gotcha. Her steady gaze asked, Do *you* have it?

Coop struggled for words, but his thoughts were nipped by a commotion in the lobby—a loud thud, a collective gasp, and then, after a suspended millisecond of silence, the blistering explosion of a five-hundred-pound glass objet d'art as it met the rock-solid surface of a polished terrazzo floor.

Arcie Madera dashed from behind the palm to the crowded lobby; Coop followed. Throngs of guests, horror-struck, gaped at the fallen pedestal, at the waiter on the floor who was slimed by a heap of appetizers, and at the tangled velvet ropes that had caught him behind the knee when someone had turned too abruptly to pluck an extra canapé of salmon mousse from his overloaded tray. The artwork had wobbled before falling, and had it tipped in the opposite direction, the waiter would surely have been crushed.

The crowd parted, allowing the museum director, a dozen guards, and Bruce Rollo himself to approach the crash site. As they neared, shards of his new masterpiece crunched beneath their shoes. They tended to the waiter, who wept with embarrassment and the raw emotion of his brush with death, helping him to his feet. In the process, one of the guards, a portly one, slipped on a prosciutto-wrapped melon ball, landing on his polyester-clad keister; the others, in turn, assisted him.

Turning to the assembled onlookers, Rollo announced, "He seems to be okay, thank God. Everyone's okay."

The museum director mumbled to him, "But your piece, your magnificent piece, I'm sure the insurance . . ."

Cameras flashed.

With a flick of his hand, Rollo told everyone, "It's only glass."

Late Sunday morning, sitting in the passenger seat of Coop's open Tesla, Stasia donned her sunglasses and tightened the gold-hued Hermès scarf she'd fashioned into a head wrap. "Thanks for driving, sweets. I am *so* not up to this."

"That makes two of us." But in truth, Coop found himself looking forward to the outing. They weren't going far—the drive would take about an hour—but a jaunt to Idyllwild, regardless of how many times he'd been there, always felt like an adventure into uncharted territory, offering a complete change of scenery from the desert setting he had come to know as home. More to the point, he was so badly rattled by the previous night's encounter with Arcie Madera, he hoped the alpine excursion might help clear his mind and calm his foreboding.

In Palm Desert, Coop turned off the valley's main thoroughfare, Highway 111, and aimed the car up a long, continuous rise of Highway 74, heading out of town and into the foothills of the San Jacinto Mountains. A road sign bore the route's alternate name: PINES TO PALMS HIGHWAY. "How poetic," said Stasia, her voice tinged with sarcasm.

"Well, it *is* a beautiful drive." Coop gripped the wheel and accelerated.

Stasia touched her fingers to his knee and sounded a cautionary note: "Once we get beyond this straightaway, it's hairpin curves all the way up. Good luck."

Coop settled back, intent on enjoying the changing landscape, but as soon as they hit the curves, his spine stiffened. Stasia's knuckles blanched as she grasped the seat with her left hand, the door handle with her right. The valley floor descended, and with each switchback, her view from the side of the car was filled with alternating sights—a sheer wall of rocky rubble as the inner lane hugged the mountainside, then a panorama of the faraway San Bernardinos as the outer lane skirted the brink. On these outer swings, her position in the passenger seat was far more torturous than Coop's; from the middle of the road, he was not forced to look directly over the precipice, and all the while, he had the wheel to hang on to. Stasia could only claw the upholstery, grit her teeth, and try to sway the direction of the car with her own feeble body English. There was no slowing down for the turns. With cars ahead and behind—and no passing allowed—they had no choice but to stay with the flow as they zigzagged ever higher.

"Let's stop a minute," said Coop. "That scenic lookout is just ahead. We can let some of this traffic get ahead of us."

When they rounded the next turn, the two-lane road widened sufficiently to accommodate perhaps a dozen parked cars. A rustic sign touted the view and elevation. A smattering of tourists gathered near the edge of the observation area, separated from the sheer drop by only a split rail fence and a few pay telescopes. A car was just leaving, so Coop signaled and braked, then parked in the vacated space.

As he opened the door and stepped onto terra firma, he took some long, slow breaths and felt the racing of his heart begin to calm. Stasia hugged herself, warming her bare arms with her hands. It was a clear October morning under full sun, but compared to the desert below at sea level, the air at four thousand feet felt goose-bump brisk.

"I wonder what's going on," said Coop, pinching his brows as they walked to the lookout, where a gathering of people focused intently on something. They didn't mingle or meander, pointing this way and that. They didn't even peep through the telescopes. No one spoke. They stood as one, peering just beyond the fence. Coop quickened his pace; Stasia followed.

Joining the others, they saw, only a few feet away, on the other side of the fence, a hang glider preparing to thrust himself out over the valley.

A young man in spandex was outfitted with a harness beneath broad, brightly colored nylon wings—a human kite, sans tail. A steady breeze blew around the mountain from the west; an updraft rose with the warmer air from the desert below; the effect of both could be seen in the wings as they tipped and bulged. His shoes flexed on the pebbled surface of his granite perch as he studied an instrument that clicked and whirled, mounted in front of him on the harness. He stood in this manner for several minutes, eyes fixed on the meter. All was quiet, save for the whoosh of the wind, the clicking of the meter.

Then, when the instrument conveyed something apparent to no one else, he launched. He didn't leap or dive or even jump. Rather, his feet seemed to act as hands, gently pushing him forward. He disappeared from view for a horrifying moment, then rose on the updraft and soared like Icarus before the spectators. Coop felt a wave of vertigo plummet from his chest to his groin as the others joined in quiet, awed applause. The glider rose even higher, suspended by nothing. Far below, to the right, sparkled the surface of the Salton Sea; to the left were the gridded roadways of the desert cities; beyond it all was the San Bernardino range, rippling in the waves of heat.

Someone said, "He could ride those currents for hours, if he's lucky."

Stasia mumbled to Coop, "And what if he's not?"

The little crowd began to disperse.

Coop asked her, "Had enough excitement?"

"Are you referring to Bat Boy? Or the curves?"

He laughed. "Both, I guess." They began walking to the car. "Remember that old movie, *The Long, Long Trailer,* with Lucy and Desi?"

"Christ!" Stasia clapped both hands to her cheeks. "I think of that every time we make this damn drive. That scene where they're in the mountains, and they're *squeeeeeking* around the curves, and the rocks are falling off the edge, dropping so far you don't even hear them crash—I peed my pants when I first saw it as a kid, and I have to force myself not to think about it whenever we head up here." She paused before adding, "Thanks for reminding me."

"My pleasure." Coop opened the car door for her.

"Making it all the worse"—she got in, buckled up—"some of the locals insist it was filmed on this very road."

"It wasn't." Coop walked around to his side and got in. "Looks like this, but it was filmed on the road that leads up to Mount Whitney in the Sierra Nevadas."

She turned to him, looking skeptical. "How do you know that?"

"Let's just say I'm an exceptionally inquisitive man, a veritable font of trivia." He started the car and pulled out to the road. "Anyway, we're going up another two thousand feet, but most of the bad curves are behind us now."

As they journeyed along, not only did the road become flatter, but it began traveling over some low crests, rather than hugging the sides of the mountain. It was a different world, strewn with boulders and pines. While its beauty was distinct from that of the desert below, the high-altitude landscape was no less formidable, with few signs of habitation along the way.

This less-daunting portion of the trek proved more relaxing and enjoyable, and the couple in the open car soon found themselves gabbing like sightseers on a tour bus, except that their conversation centered not on the local flora and fauna, but on the hang glider. Stasia mused, "I wonder if he made it down in one piece."

Noting a glint in her eye, Coop teased, "You seem downright tantalized by the prospect of tragedy."

"Nonsense." She looked straight ahead, hands crossed on her knees. The wind whipped the tips of her scarf. A smile turned the corners of her mouth.

QUESTOVER, said the rough-hewn sign supported by two stone pylons flanking the driveway. Bix had chosen the name. Whether it alluded to a delayed retirement or to a life complete or to a perfect little acre of mountain land or, literally, to the end of some specific but unnamed quest—Coop never knew and was not inclined to ask. When his father-in-law had suggested building a family retreat near Idyllwild and had hired Coop to design it, his only stipulation, framed as a question, had been "Could you make it sort of woodsy?"

*Woodsy* was not part of the design vocabulary in which Coop had been trained, but his years of practice in Santa Barbara had taught him to set aside his own stylistic preferences and simply give the customer whatever sort of residence was desired. Rare was the client who could appreciate the intellectual purity of a glass and steel box, so he drew up façades ranging from Tudor to Tuscan, from Cotswold cottage to adobe hacienda, from a Greek revival plantation house to a particularly glamorous specimen he described as Frenchy Hollywood modern. What mattered was the plan—the organizational concept, the creation and ma-nipulation of space, the "bones"—and at this he excelled without compromise. The rest, he rationalized, was mere decorating.

So when Bix challenged him to create what amounted to a mountain cabin, pumped up on steroids, he leaned into the task and decided to have fun with it, asking himself, What would Ralph Lauren do? The result was a log-style home at one with its setting, its half dozen levels rising at offsets among the pines, its steep, complex, shake-shingled rooflines echoing the surround-ing slopes.

Inside, there were vaulted, timbered ceilings; lofts for read-ing or for the amusement of future great-grandkids; crude stone fireplaces big enough for roasting a stag, though this, of course, was never done; overscale kicked-back furniture, mostly leather, draped with red plaid throws; private bedroom wings for the family's three households; a sprawling, open kitchen for Bix to putter in; and in anticipation of his latter years, an elevator, though he had never set foot in it.

As the Tesla passed between the pylons, Stasia said, "Bix must've been up early this morning." His Hummer was already parked near the front door, which allowed entry to the house at its main level. Due to the pitch of the terrain, the area in front of the house could accommodate only one parking spot, and Bix had claimed it as his before the house was finished being built. He'd even posted a sign: DON'T EVEN *THINK* OF IT. All others were to park in an area excavated from behind the structure, accessible by a cobbled driveway that led to a back entrance on the bottom level.

Coop made the descent slowly, careful not to scrape the front bumper. When he muttered something, Stasia reminded him, "You designed it."

They got out of the car, retrieved a few shopping bags from the trunk, and paused to savor the setting. At six thousand feet, the air was clear, thin, and cool. The noontide sun shot from the crest of a nearby peak, casting short bluish shadows near their shoes. On the gravel, a mat of pine needles glistened with tiny, sticky manzanita berries dropped from the trees that seemed to thrive only here, their stunted, ruddy-barked trunks so gnarled and unearthly. The stillness was broken only by the drilling of woodpeckers, the fussing of jays, and the drifting of music from the house. Frank and Nancy Sinatra were "feelin' kinda Sunday," backed up by a cheery arrangement of church bells chiming in the Sabbath morn.

"I guess the party's started," said Coop.

"But we're the first to arrive." Stasia made a broad gesture indicating the parking court in which they stood. Theirs was the only car.

He shrugged. "Maybe the bar's open."

"The bar's *always* open." She led him to the back door and reached to open it, but found it locked. Grousing, she punched in a keypad code, then stepped indoors, calling, "Yoo-hoo. We're here, Bix!"

A moment later, the volume of the music dropped. Wild-eyed, Pyrite stuck his head through the rungs of a railing up on the main level, yapping at the intruders. Bix yapped back at the dog, "Quiet!" Then he sweet-talked, "It's just Coops and Stasia. You know how much they wuv you. Yes they do, you little son f'bitch."

Stasia led the way up the stairs. Coop followed, wondering how soon they would be able to leave.

Bix met them at the top of the stairs, wearing one oven mitt and a white but very sullied apron. He hugged them both, beaming.

"Guess what. I found a recipe in the local advertiser for manzanita jam."

"Is *that* what your cooking?" asked Stasia. The kitchen was a fright.

"*No*. I'm fixing Sunday dinner. But the recipe caught my eye. Always wondered if those puny berries were good for anything—other than gumming up your windshield."

Coop snooped in the kitchen, opening the oven door. A beef roast as big as a baby lolled in a baking pan and bubbled in its own juices. At Coop's feet, Pyrite sat at attention, brushing the floor with his tail, sniffing, quivering at the prospect of a week's worth of bloody-rare leftovers.

Bix asked, "Any signs of life from Kavanall this morning? I'm doing this for his friend—he'd better show up."

"I checked," said Stasia. "He'll be here. He was waiting for Cliff, who wanted to follow him. The directions can be pretty confusing, once you're off the highway."

Bix laughed, thinking aloud, "Kavanall—up, dressed, and on the road by Sunday noon—who'd've thought? I'm surprised he wasn't out all night."

"I've no idea," said Stasia, "but *we* had some excitement last night." She turned, adding, "Didn't we, Coop?"

Coop had learned to recognize her cues. She wasn't asking for a nod of agreement; she was telling him to chime in and help amuse her father. So Coop told the story of the waiter and the Bruce Rollo glass sculpture—"smashed to smithereens, crème fraîche *everywhere*"—but as he spoke, he marveled at his and his wife's differing perspectives on what had made the night memorable. For her, the main event had been the accident, while for him, the evening had climaxed moments earlier when he learned he was being drawn into another investigation of his father's murder, an investigation that threatened to change his life irreparably. He had somehow managed to pick up the pieces and start over—once—but he was certain he couldn't do it again. He had neither the emotional strength nor, most likely, sufficient years remaining to struggle back, once again, from ashes. Stasia had asked him about Arcie Madera in the car, riding home from the museum, but when she learned of the new investigation and the request for a DNA sample, her only comment had been "She certainly cleans up well, for a cop. But I can't imagine what Bruce Rollo sees in her."

Hearing about the museum guard slipping on the melon ball, Bix roared with laughter. Coop concluded, "It was like something out of a Marx Brothers farce."

"*Yes*," agreed Stasia, dabbing a tear of mannerly amusement from the corner of an eye. "I nearly died."

**W**hen Kavanall arrived a half hour later with Cliff Sloan, Pyrite went crazy again and wouldn't calm down until Bix lifted him to the stranger's face, advising, "Go ahead, Clifford—give this little pansy dog a nice little kiss."

With a stiff smile, Cliff inched in for the smooch, meeting Pyrite's long, warm tongue, which traced wet circles around the guest's lips, nose, and chin. Bix then set Pyrite on the floor. The dog gave a shake, jangling its collar, and strolled off to the kitchen to plop on the floor and mind the roast. As Bix's gaze turned to follow the dog, the visiting dentist wiped his hand across his mouth, staving off the urge to gag.

Kav leaned to tell him, "Goes with your new political territory, Cliffy boy—kissing babies."

Through a low laugh, Coop offered, "Drink, Cliff?"

"Yeah, thanks. A Bloody Mary's fine," he said, noting the setup on the kitchen counter—pitchers of tomato and orange juice, assorted jugs of vodka, various garnishes.

"It's chilly in here," said Stasia. Several large windows were cranked wide open. "I'm going to grab a sweater." And she drifted off to one of the bedroom wings as Coop went to work mixing drinks for Cliff and himself.

Kav wanted something stronger, but as he began crossing the great room to retrieve a bottle of Scotch from the bar, Bix stood in his way, hands on hips, saying, "You had a girl up here last week." His tone was accusing, but the impact of his delivery was diminished by his appearance—the apron made him look like a cowboy in drag.

"Yeah . . . ," Kav admitted vaguely. "So . . . ?"

Bix crossed his arms, drumming the fingers of his right hand on his left bicep.

Kav said, "And she wasn't a 'girl,' Bix. She was a thoroughly mondaine young lady." He twitched his brows. Eliciting no response, he continued, "Jeez, we cleaned up; we were careful. The housekeepers were due the next day."

With a slight shake of his head, Bix said, "I don't care about that, Kavanall. But you were in my *space*, weren't you? You parked in my space."

Kav looked dumbstruck. He seemed to be wondering, How could the old guy possibly know that? He said quietly, "I, uh, might've."

Bix raised a fist, extended the index finger, and made slow, staccato jabs in the air before his grandson's face: One. Two. Three.

Kav mumbled, "Sorry. Won't happen again."

Bix hugged him, then kissed the corner of his mouth.

Coop cleared his throat. "Can I pour you something, Bix?"

"Hell," he said with a laugh, "been sippin' all morning. Where's my glass?" He stepped to the kitchen, retrieved it from the dinner debris near the sink, raised it in a toast, and took another sip— more like a brawny slug.

Coop gave him a meaningful look. "We won't tell Stasia we saw that."

With a defiant smile, Bix lifted the glass again, raised his pinkie, and took a tiny, delicate sip.

Coop reminded him, "Your doctors wouldn't like that."

"They don't have to. They're not drinkin' it." He drank again, emptying the glass. Then he smacked it on the counter and patted his chest. "Besides," he said, "I've got my silver bullet."

Although Bix disputed Stasia's claim that "man cannot live on beef alone," she did her best to round out the meal preparations with a salad, a vegetable dish dug from the back of the freezer, and a loaf of crusty bread she'd had the foresight to bring from home that morning. She put Coop in charge of the table—"You're the one with the eye, sweets"—while Kav fussed with choosing wines, hauling far too many bottles up from the refrigerated wine cellar. Cliff's repeated offers to help were summarily refused, so he settled back on one of the tufted leather sofas, trying without success to discourage Pyrite from gnawing the toes of his buckskin shoes, doubtless wondering when someone would broach the topic of his political aspirations, a discussion of which had been Bix's ostensible purpose in summoning the clan to the mountaintop.

In an effort to ditch the dog, Cliff joined Coop at the table as he made the rounds from place setting to place setting, aligning the bottom tips of all the cutlery, using a folded business card as a ruler. The dentist told the architect, "I brought my iPhone." He drew it from a pocket. "Want to schedule that procedure?"

Could this day get any worse? Coop wasn't sure which sounded more disgusting—a "deep scaling" or a "procedure." He replied, "It's Sunday, Cliff. I don't want to bother you with that today. I was planning to call tomorrow."

"No bother at all. It all ends up here anyway." He turned the phone's display toward Coop; it glowed with the grid of a microscopic calendar. "I've got an opening on Tuesday morning, ten o'clock. It should take an hour or two. Might as well get it over."

"Might as well," Coop echoed with a grim lack of enthusiasm, feeling dry-mouthed. "Sure, sign me up."

"Done," said Cliff, tapping a few strokes on the screen.

"Pyrite!" yelled Stasia. She told the others, "He's got an olive."

Kav quipped, "Pimiento or blue cheese?"

"No," said Stasia, "a ripe olive—with a pit. He shouldn't swallow that."

Bix hustled over to the dog, bent over, and held his open hand under its mouth, commanding, "Pyrite, drop it."

The pooch eyed his master, steady and unflinching, in a battle of wills.

Bix didn't touch the dog. "Pyrite! Drop it!"

The Yorkie's maw dropped open, and out slipped a slimy, half-gnawed black olive.

"That's a good baby," said Bix, sweeping up the dog with his free hand. "*Good* little son f'bitch." Laughing, he strolled over to

Cliff, handed him the olive, and explained, "Seems to be the only command the little fella understands."

"Yes, sir. He's a clever little guy." Cliff sidestepped to the kitchen, dropped the olive in the sink, and washed his hands.

"You know, Clifford, you're welcome to call me Bix. Everyone else does, even my own family." He turned to his grandson. "Right, *Kavanall*?"

The younger man answered, "And *you* know you're welcome to call me Kav—everyone else does."

"Nope"—Bix set the dog on the floor—"I have my instructions. And I *always* do what I'm told."

"Ha!" Stasia brought an oversize salad bowl out to the table and set it down. Turning to her son, she explained, "The day you were born, Bix picked you up and said you were a cute little son f'bitch."

"It's a term of endearment," Bix said with a shrug. "But your mother put her foot down. She said, 'He has a *name*—it's Kavanall.'"

The meal was hearty, the conversation amiable, the autumn afternoon splendid. But by the time they lingered over coffee, Cliff's contemplated political career had not yet been discussed. He fidgeted in his seat; under the table, Pyrite had soaked the cap of his left shoe with drool. Bix said, "You're kinda quiet there, Clifford. Having a good time?"

He flashed a big smile. "Absolutely, sir."

"Uh-uh-uh. It's Bix."

"Yes, sir. I mean, *Bix*. It's just that . . . well, I was wondering when we might continue the conversation we began Friday morning, about . . . uh, about that open seat in the state senate."

Bix nodded. "Which nomination are you looking at— Republican or Democrat?"

Cliff gulped. "Democratic, sir. I mean, Bix."

Bix continued nodding, but said nothing.

"And given the new focus of your efforts at Emery Energy— sustainable resources, commitment to conservation, alternatives to fossil fuels—I think you'll find my party offers a good fit to help you meet those goals. And I'd be proud to represent your efforts in Sacramento."

Bix nodded. "Look, Clifford, the party labels don't really matter to me—"

"They *don't*?" Stasia interrupted with a laugh. "Since when?"

Bix continued, "The labels don't matter as much as the ideas, the loyalties, the *man*. And here you are, sharing a meal at my table, talking about honor and shared goals. Plus, you've known my grandson since college. You want my support? You got it."

"Well, uh, *thank* you, Bix," said Cliff, looking stunned by such an easy sale.

"Wow," said Stasia, "wonders never cease. An Oklahoma oil man colluding with a Democrat—what would your old pal from Wyoming say?"

"Good question!" said Bix with a laugh, thumping the table, sitting back in his chair. "But Dick's got other fish to fry right now, the whole legacy thing." Bix turned to Cliff with an eager grin. "Did you hear about the time we went huntin'?"

"We?" asked Cliff, befuddled. "Dick who?"

"Dick *Cheney.* We got pretty chummy, and a few years back, he asked me along on this weekend huntin' trip. So of course I went, and let me tell ya, there was way more drinkin' than huntin'. Only *that* time"—Bix leaned forward, craning his neck toward Cliff—"only *that* time, thank God, the son f'bitch *missed*!" Bix flopped back in his chair, choked with laughter.

"I had no idea," said Cliff. "That's amazing."

Stasia gave her husband a sidelong glance. She and Coop had heard this story, and the punch line, umpteen times. They agreed it was plausible, even likely, that Bix Emery's and Dick Cheney's paths had crossed—they knew the same people, attended the same fund-raisers, moved in the same circles—but it was anyone's guess whether they'd actually hung out together on a drunken hunting trip. Coop found it strange that Bix had always described the event as taking place at some nebulous time in the past, but had never told the story when it supposedly had happened. Asked about this, Bix had explained in a whisper, "It was all very hush-hush."

Kav said, "Congratulations, Cliffy boy. You've reeled in your first big backer. And don't worry—your little secret is safe with me."

All heads turned to Kavanall.

"Uh, Kav?" said Cliff. If looks could kill . . .

Bix crossed his arms. "Kavanall? What are you talking about?"

"Oh, just a little detail from our Ivy League days together." Kav lounged in his chair, one arm extended, swirling the last inch of wine in his glass. "Junior year, we were roommates by then. Cliff was having trouble in a class, so he bought a term paper. It saved his ass—*and* his chances of getting into dental school."

Bix turned to Cliff. "Well?"

Cliff sat upright, hands in his lap. "It was an elective I'd taken as a lark, and by the time I discovered that I was in way over my head, it was too late to drop the course. My grade point was critical if I was going to be accepted at any decent dental school, so the art history class—sixteenth-century Italian Mannerism, I think—could've sunk me. Right about then, there was an article in the school paper about this new business—it actually had an office—that had opened near campus, selling term papers. Depending on what you were willing to spend, they either recycled file copies or paid people to write new ones. You even specified what grade you wanted to get. So I bought a B." He paused before adding, "I thought an A would raise suspicions. I still don't know a damn thing about Mannerism."

The table was dead quiet for a moment. Bix asked, "Sorry you did it?"

Cliff looked him in the eye. "From an ethical standpoint, yes, extremely sorry. But from a practical standpoint, well, it solved a problem."

Bix nodded. "That's reasonable. Who knows about it?"

"Just Kav. And all of *you*, of course."

"Well, then," said Bix brightly, "your secret *is* safe." He turned to his grandson. "Right, Kavanall?"

Slowly, Kav placed his empty glass on the table. "I already said it was." Then he stood, stretching. "Cliffy? If you want to follow me, I think we should head back. We'll lose the light soon, and most people find the drive *down* to be even more treacherous than getting *up* here. Besides"—he rattled the keys in his pocket—"I've got a date tonight."

"Uh, sure." Cliff stood, folding his napkin and placing it on the table. "Could I use the rest room first?"

"Be my guest." Kav pointed the way. When Cliff had left the room, Kav walked a languid circle around the table. "Know what I think? It's a wide-open election. Maybe I should give it a try as a Republican."

Stasia sputtered with laughter. Coop choked on his coffee.

Bix grumbled, "At least it would get you off my back about the president's job at headquarters—for a while. But seriously, Kavanall, do you think you're qualified? Other than your name, why would voters send you to Sacramento?"

Stasia reminded her father, "The same voters sent Sonny Bono to *Washington*."

Kav gave her a stricken look.

"Oops," said Stasia. "Just trying to be helpful."

Coop thought Kavanall was out of his mind. Coop was his stepfather, but *he'd* never vote for the spoiled lazy-ass. And yet, Coop realized, public perception of the young man might be entirely different. Though Kav didn't, in truth, *do* much at Emery, his corporate credentials, at least on paper, would have legs, and the Emery name already had universal recognition. While the political complexion of the district was beginning to shift, it was traditionally Republican. So if Kav went for it, he could probably beat Clifford Sloan in a heartbeat.

Bix seemed to grasp the dynamics as well. "Be careful with this," he told Kavanall. "But if you get serious about it, let me know."

Kav said, "You've already promised to bankroll Cliff."

Without a moment's thought, Bix replied, "I'll buy both of you. Then I can't lose."

"Well," said Kav, adopting a breezy tone as Cliff came back to the room, "it's just an idea—something to think about." Then he and his dentist friend said their good-byes, preparing to drive back to the desert.

Bix walked them to the head of the stairs, gave Cliff a hug, wishing him luck, and kissed his grandson, grasping his arm with one hand. Then he raised the other hand, extended the index finger, and made slow, staccato jabs in the air before Kav's face. "I know what Jay Pontarelli is up to." One. Two. Three.

After the guys drove away—Bix had held Pyrite to the window like a puppet, waving the dog's paw—Coop and Stasia began stacking dishes and carrying them to the kitchen.

"Just leave everything," said Bix. "One of the girls will be in tomorrow."

"No"—Stasia hesitated—"bugs." She turned on the faucet and started rinsing plates.

With a laugh, Coop said to Bix, "You really nailed Kav earlier, about the girlfriend and the parking space." Stasia looked up from her rinsing, having not heard that conversation. Coop continued, "You've got him convinced you're psychic."

"Hell, no"—Bix waved an arm—"not psychic at all, just common sense. Once I knew he was up here, I just *assumed* there was a girl involved. But the parking space? That was only a hunch. So I accused him, and he confessed." Bix chortled at the success of his ploy.

Coop asked, "But how'd you know he was up here in the first place?"

Bix looked at his son-in-law as if he were dense, explaining, "The keypad logs."

"Ohhh," said Coop, nodding. The offices as well as their homes were equipped with security systems, and everyone was assigned separate entry codes. At the houses, it was a means of keeping track of when housekeepers, for instance, were earning their pay.

Bix added, "I check the logs every day."

Two nights earlier, in the Paradise Lounge, when Bix had let it be known he was aware that Coop and Stasia were dining with Jay Pontarelli and Kav that evening, Stasia had commented to her father, "You certainly keep your ear to the rail." She now repeated the same wry comment.

And Bix made the same reply: "It's my job."

# Chapter 4

**E**arly Monday morning, Coop phoned Teddy, asking to cancel their training session that day. Teddy asked, "Is something wrong?" In their year of working out together, it was the first time Coop had canceled on short notice.

"Just need to get a jump on things at the office," said Coop, sounding nonchalant. "Looks like a busy week."

"I have an open slot tomorrow if you want it. Seven A.M."

"Perfect. Thanks, Teddy."

But there was nothing nonchalant about Coop's desire to get to the office early that day. He knew that Austin Royce, the Emery CFO, was typically the first executive to arrive at headquarters each morning, allowing him to catch up with his work prior to the arrival of Bix and the dog, whose combined whims would consume the rest of his day. More to the point, Austin Royce was more than a glorified number cruncher and gofer; he was also an attorney and the company's chief counsel.

"Is something wrong?" asked Austin, looking up from his desk, startled to see anyone, least of all Coop, walking through his office door at that hour. Even at seven, with no one else around other than a back-room phone crew to field calls from other time zones, the CFO wore his dark business suit, complete with jacket—he was simply not a shirtsleeves kind of guy. He was a hard worker, nose to the grindstone, balding at fifty-something, a family man. On the credenza behind him, framed photos were displayed in a neat row: the wife, the daughters, a graduation, a grandchild's baptism, a boat.

Is something wrong? It was the second time in half an hour that Coop had been asked that question, and the day had barely begun. "I hope not, but maybe," he said, sitting in a chair facing Austin across the desk. "I'm not sure."

"Is Bix . . . ?" But Austin didn't finish the question. When you worked for a company led by a man nearly ninety, an unexpected visit from his family could change life as you knew it in sudden and probably unwelcome ways.

"Bix is fine"—Coop wagged a hand—"but I myself, I'm looking at a situation that might get sticky. Since anything involving me could reflect on the company, I wonder if I could impose on you for an opinion. A legal opinion."

With a nod, Austin straightened the knot of his tie. "My time is your time."

"It relates to my father's death."

Austin's brows arched momentarily. He already knew the general background; everyone in the office did.

Coop leaned forward, placing his folded hands on the desk, on top of a copy of the *Desert Sun.* At home that morning, he had been rushed and had not bothered to glance at the paper. On the front page, above the fold, he now noticed stories about casino issues and a disputed hillside development. He told Austin, "The detective who first investigated the murder is back on it, and she's been hounding me."

"In what sense, 'hounding' you? Are you talking about police harassment?"

"It hasn't gone that far, not exactly." Coop's palms felt sticky against the newsprint. Not wanting to get ink on his hands, he turned the paper over and set it aside. Below the fold, he saw the headline HANG GLIDER KILLED. Coop winced, recalling glib comments about Bat Boy, about landing in once piece. Speaking to Austin, he continued, "She wants me to volunteer a DNA sample, says it could help clear me, but I know she'd still love to nail me." He wondered, Was it the kid we saw yesterday? He looked down at the paper again and saw a locator map that detailed Highway 74 squiggling up toward Idyllwild. A photo showed a rescue crew among some rocky rubble; everything was the color of sand, except for the jolly nylon wings.

Austin asked, "What did you tell her?"

"I said I'd have to talk to a lawyer."

"Good. I'm no criminal lawyer, but that's always a prudent response. Refresh me, now. What was the timeline of the original investigation, and what were its findings?" Austin clicked a pen and poised it over a notepad.

Coop walked him through the history of the case, every excruciating detail, recalling all the particulars that had finally begun to fade, at least until Arcie Madera had shown up at the dedication ceremony four days earlier. After talking with Austin for nearly an hour, Coop concluded the story: "I was the prime suspect, really the *only* suspect, but the evidence against me was entirely circumstantial. They had zero hard proof, so there were never any charges, and Madera got stuck with a cold case hanging over her record. Now she aims to change that." Coop paused. "And in case you've been wondering all these years—no, I didn't do it."

"Well," said Austin with a soft laugh, "I can't imagine Bix would welcome you into the family if he had any doubts about that."

"If I had any doubts about what?" asked Bix as he appeared in the doorway with a broad smile. He held his hat in one hand and Pyrite in the other. "Morning, gents!"

Coop and Austin stood to greet their patriarch. Bix gave Coop a hug and gave Austin the dog. Austin set the dog on the floor near his chair, took a bowl out of a desk drawer, and twisted open a bottle of Fiji water to fill it. Pyrite flicked his tongue to take one dainty lap, then circled the room, sniffing the baseboard.

Austin asked, "Do you have a minute, Bix? Maybe we could sit down and talk about something. Seems there may be a . . . a *situation* in the works."

Bix sat. "A situation? Sounds kinda sinister." With a grin, he fingered the brim of his Stetson, suspended upside down between his knees. It looked as if he was holding a salad bowl. "What's up?" he asked.

Sitting next to him in front of the desk, Coop said, "It relates to my father's death, the unsolved murder."

Bix reached over to give his son-in-law a sympathetic pat on the knee.

Coop continued, "The detective who originally handled the case wants to stir things up again. There's talk of new forensics, of DNA."

"Can we buy him?" asked Bix, easy as pie. "Or is there anyone we can pay off to demote him? That'll keep him quiet."

"I highly doubt that. And this 'him' is a 'her.'"

"Christ," said Bix with a groan, a show of sympathy for Coop's emasculating run-in with the distaff gender. Pyrite chorused a soft whine.

Austin explained, "This detective has asked Cooper to volunteer a sample of his DNA, to be used as part of a reevaluation of the physical evidence. Cooper is reluctant, and I don't blame him. My opinion, at this point, is that he should simply stall on the request, while retaining the outside services of a top-notch criminal lawyer. I can recommend several who—"

"Nope," Bix declared flatly. "If we've got a problem, we'll circle the wagons and handle this ourselves. We're a *family* here, all of us. And I take care of my family. It's a matter of honor."

"We sincerely appreciate that," said Austin.

Bootlicker, thought Coop.

"You know," said Bix, looking at the ceiling, sounding philosophical, "success is measured lots of ways—wealth, influence, fame—but it all boils down to the same thing. Power. And once you've got hold of that power, you discover that instead of making life easier, it complicates everything. What *you've* got, everyone *else* wants. Friends become traitors. Family betrays you—bloodlines be damned—where's the loyalty, the honor?"

Coop had often noted that words like *bloodline, loyalty, honor, betrayal,* and *traitor* were known by all but seldom used in casual conversation. For Bix, however, these words were part of his everyday vocabulary. And this morning, he had managed to roll them all into a single speech.

With a grunt of disgust, Bix concluded, "There's goddamn treachery at every turn."

Add *treachery* to the list, thought Coop.

Austin said earnestly, "We'll circle those wagons, Bix."

Toady, thought Coop.

"Which brings us to another matter," said Bix. His eyes narrowed to slits as he turned to Coop, explaining, "Kavanall."

During an uncomfortable moment of silence, Coop and Austin stole a glance at each other. Coop asked Bix, "You mean, his senate idea?"

"No." He spoke the word softly, as if putting a lid on his emotions. But he built to a full head of steam when elaborating, "I know about newco, I know about PontaPower, and I know about Jay's recruiting efforts—that fucking *bastard*!"

Pyrite yipped.

Trying to defuse the tension in the room, Coop said, "It was just talk, just idle—"

"So here's the thing," Bix interrupted. "I know what Jay is up to. I understand his strategy. He wants an Emery in the front office—sure, that's part of it—but the main thing is, he wants to embarrass *me,* to humiliate *me.*"

Coop couldn't decide whether Bix was fabulously egocentric or shrewdly insightful. He said, "Jay seems to think it's 'just business.'"

"Don't kid yourself. It's all about me."

Austin ventured to ask, "Why would—?"

But Bix continued, calmer now, "So I know what needs to be done. At least, I know what would solve this particular problem." He paused, took a deep breath, then exhaled with a raspy whistle. "The president's job, here at Emery. If I give it to Kavanall, he won't give Pontarelli a second thought—*or* this Sacramento bullshit."

To Austin Royce, these words represented more than a bad idea; they threatened to dash a lifelong career goal and were doubtless the last words he expected to hear on such a fine October morning. The color drained from his face. He opened his mouth, but words escaped him, so he borrowed a slug of Fiji's finest from Pyrite's water bottle.

"Uh, Bix," said Coop, "that would be a fairly dramatic—and drastic—move. It might achieve its immediate purpose, but would it really be best for the company?"

"Hell, no," Bix answered without hesitation.

Austin found his voice: "Then perhaps you'd better sleep on that one."

Coop added, "No need to be brash. Both PontaPower and the senate idea are still in the talking stages. For all you know, Kav might be floating this stuff just to pressure you on the prez-job. If so, he seems to be succeeding. Meanwhile, he's got a pretty sweet setup right now. Why would he throw that away—to put himself in a position where he actually has to *prove* himself? I don't think so."

With arched brows and a trace of a smile, Bix stared at his son-in-law for a moment. Then he said, "Coops, you're the only one in this whole damn family with even a lick of horse sense."

"Hardly. You've proven time and again you've got plenty on the ball." Though the words sounded mealymouthed, Coop was sincere. Bix's career had spanned nearly seven decades; it wasn't dumb luck that had allowed him to build all he had built.

Bix nodded. "I'll give it some thought, about Kavanall. No rush, I guess, but in the end, I might have to promote him."

"You're the boss," said Coop, stating the simple truth.

Austin said nothing, pinching his upper lip with his lower teeth.

"Here's an idea," said Bix. "Let's do a round of golf, say, Wednesday morning. A foursome—you guys, me, and Kavanall. We can sound him out, maybe talk turkey."

With a laugh, Coop reminded him, "I'm a lousy golfer."

"Doesn't matter. It's just for fun, an excuse to get out on the course. We can play a scramble—that'll speed it along."

"You're the boss," Coop repeated, dreading the outing. He had tried to learn the game, but his swings still produced more divots than actual contact with the ball. Maybe, once they got under way and his skill level became apparent, he'd be allowed to bag his clubs, drive the cart, and keep score.

Bix told Austin, "Set up that tee time, okay? Eight o'clock Wednesday."

It was a prime tee time on short notice at the start of the season. Plans would be changed, schedules rearranged. Bix had spoken.

"Certainly," said Austin.

Bix stood; Pyrite scampered to his master's feet. Coop and Austin stood also. Bix pointed to the newspaper on the desk. "Did you read about that hang glider?"

"As a matter of fact," said Coop, "Stasia and I happened to—"

"What a jerk," said Bix, heading for the door, planting the hat on his head. "That's what you get when you take a flying leap off a mountain." He turned back, slapping one hand, hard, against the other—"Splat!" Then he walked out the door, laughing.

Pyrite yipped merrily, joining in the mirth.

When Bix was well out of earshot, Austin squared his shoulders, straightened his tie, and told Coop, voice lowered confidentially, "I could *never* work for Kavanall, and I don't care *what* name he carries—I'd be nothing but a yes-man."

But you already are, thought Coop. He asked, "How long have you worked here?"

"Twenty years, three months, twelve days." Austin grinned. "Always had a thing for numbers."

"So you have considerably more seniority than Kav does."

"God, yes. Bix brought him into the company after he graduated from college. Well, after a junket in Europe. Bix thought it would be good for Kavanall to 'see the world' a bit before settling into the nine-to-five. So he started as communications director, which he knew nothing about—then *or* now—during the October after graduation. He's been here fourteen years this month."

Though Coop had always thought of his stepson as immature, it was hard to imagine him as a young man, at school. During that same general time frame, fifteen and a half years ago, Coop had been dealing with the heady aftermath of his father's murder, which still seemed like only yesterday. And Kavanall? He'd been back east, wrapping up his junior year of sociology studies and struggling with finals while sampling the coeds of New England.

"Tempus fugit," said Austin.

Not fast enough, thought Coop.

**S**ilence is golden."

Seated at the bar in the Paradise Lounge, Coop and Stasia turned to see Bix standing behind them, holding Pyrite. "Evening, Bix," said Coop.

"Join us," said Stasia.

Coop asked, "Silence?" The bar wasn't packed, but the crowd was decent for a weeknight, and the mood was lively.

Bix took the stool to the right of his daughter and placed Pyrite on the stool to the right of himself. "Silence is golden," he repeated. "That gal with the harp's got the night off. Good. She plays that thing like she's got a broomstick up her ass."

With a laugh, Stasia said, "There's never entertainment on Monday nights."

Bix leaned close to tell her, "There's never entertainment on *any* night, not here."

Coop offered, "I do a pretty mean 'My Way.'"

"Don't you dare," said Stasia, still laughing.

"I'd appreciate it if you'd both leave Frank out of this," said Bix, dead serious. "You never met the man, so don't knock him."

"Sorry," said Coop. "Wasn't knocking anyone."

Stasia challenged her father, "And *you* never met him."

"Wanna bet?"

Without a word, the bartender appeared and served Bix a tall bourbon and Coke—his usual—and a side plate of skewered raw tenderloin. Bix plucked the cherry from the drink and gave it to Stasia, who ate it, and pulled a cube of meat from the skewer and gave it to Pyrite, who ate it. "Sorry, Coops," he said, "seems I'm out of treats."

"I'm fine," said Coop, tapping the rim of his martini glass.

Adopting a coy tone, Stasia said to her father, "I understand there might be something in the works." She sipped her martini.

"Yup," said Bix, "a golf game. I'm playing golf with your husband on Wednesday."

Stasia sputtered, then dabbed her lips with a cocktail napkin. "You're taking your life in your hands."

"Thanks," said Coop.

She continued, to her father, "But I wasn't asking about golf. I was referring to Kavanall."

"Ahhh," said Bix, nodding slowly, "your son."

"Your grandson. Are you really considering promoting him to the president's job?"

"He's got the bloodline. He's the heir apparent. What do you think of the idea?"

"Look," said Stasia, touching Bix's sleeve. "I'm his mother. I'd be thrilled for him, obviously. But you're my father, and I'd hate for you to feel you're doing this for the wrong reasons. It could create all kinds of future tensions, and frankly, I'd be caught in the middle." She squeezed Bix's hand. "I love you both."

He smiled at her for a moment and brushed her hair from her cheek with the back of his hand. Then he said to his son-in-law, who was seated at Stasia's other side, "Coops? Come here."

Coop rose from his stool and stood between Bix and Stasia, who were still seated. Pyrite moved over to Bix's lap and stared up at them. Their four noses were all within a foot of each other. With one hand on Coop's back and the other on Stasia's arm, Bix said, "You mean more to me than anyone else in the world."

Pyrite whimpered.

"You too, you little son f'bitch." The dog relaxed, nesting in Bix's lap. He continued, "So it's important that we *share* the big decisions. We're a family."

Though the words were touching, they left Coop wondering, What's the old guy up to? I'll bet he's never shared a decision in his life.

"Aw, Bix," said Stasia, "that's so sweet. I want only the best for Kav, but honestly, do you think he's qualified for a job at that level? He was never much of a student."

"At least he didn't cheat," said Bix. "Far as we know, he never bought a term paper—like some of his friends."

"If he did, he deserves a refund. His grade point was less than stellar."

The reason he didn't cheat, thought Coop, was not because he was above it, but because he simply didn't care about his grades. He knew he already had it made; there was a cushy job waiting for him in the family business.

"Let's face it," said Bix, "the prez-job at Emery is just another title. It's been vacant all these years—except on paper, *I'm* president, because corporate regulations require the position to be filled. At most companies, the president has real responsibilities, but at Emery, the job could be largely ceremonial."

"Because you're in charge," said Stasia. "You're chairman and CEO."

"Bingo."

But what about the succession? thought Coop. Bix's days were numbered. Didn't he understand that his inevitable departure would leave his entire life's legacy in the incompetent clutches of his gadabout grandson?

As if responding to Coop's thoughts, Bix said, "But I won't last forever, so whoever lands in that office—well, one day, they're gonna have a pile of work on their hands."

"No one could ever replace *you*," said Stasia.

"*Somebody's* gonna have to." Bix tossed his arms. "So it needs to be someone who's actually up to the job, someone who can take over—on the day after the funeral. Sorry to say, that's probably not Kavanall."

"Of course not," said Stasia, patting her father's hand. "I understand."

Coop suggested, "How about Austin Royce? He's been primed for that position for years. He's smart, shrewd, and loyal. He even *looks* presidential."

"Yeah, yeah, yeah," said Bix, clearly unconvinced. "Royce is a good number two, a *great* number two, so he's exactly where he belongs. If I felt he was right for the prez-job, I'd've put him there a long time ago. But I haven't." Rhetorically, he asked, "So who does that leave?"

How about your daughter? thought Coop.

Bix said to Coop, "How about *you*?"

"Huh?" asked Coop, wide-eyed. "I'm an architect . . ."

"Like I told you this morning, Coops, you're the only one in this whole damn family with even a lick of horse sense."

"B'Bix," stammered Coop, "it t'takes a whole lot more than horse sense to run an international corporation."

"Of *course* it does"—Bix slapped Coop's back—"and you've got it all. The brains, the loyalty, and you're part of the family. Plus, you know this whole 'green thing' inside and out. You can really talk that language, but I don't know beans about it. Neither does Kavanall. You could help us—and help us now, while I'm still around—to get things moving in a new direction."

No way in hell, thought Coop. He could say only "I'm, uh . . .

stunned."

Bix crossed his arms and eyed his daughter. "You've been kinda quiet, Stasia. What do you think of all this?"

She looked as stunned as Coop felt. When she finally found her voice, she blurted, "That's a *fabulous* idea!"

"Uh, Stasia . . . ," Coop began.

"Oh, sweets"—she clapped her hands around his face, gave a little growl—"listen to Bix. He's always had an uncanny instinct for this sort of thing."

Coop exhaled a tentative laugh. "I think maybe Bix was just shooting from the hip."

"Maybe," Bix allowed, "but it's something to think about. Yes sir, it is certainly something to think about."

"Oh, *yes*." Stasia kissed her father, and then, growling again, she kissed her husband.

Pyrite stirred. Bix fed him more meat.

The bartender approached them from behind the bar. "Looks like a celebration over here. Another round?"

Stasia's perfectly manicured index finger touched the rim of her glass. "I could use another, thank you."

Coop gave her a bemused look.

"What?" she asked.

"That was your second," he noted. She rarely drank that much.

"Well," she said, sitting back primly with folded hands on folded knees, "you know what they say about martinis: one's not enough, two's too many, and three's just right."

"Then I've got some catching up to do."

"That' a boy," said Bix.

They poured a stiff drink at the club, and Coop never did catch up, thinking it judicious to stop midway through his second. Not that he was driving—they would walk home, as usual—but he figured Stasia might need a bit of assistance, and besides, he wanted to have a clear head in the morning for his workout with Teddy.

Bix didn't dine with them, claiming a prior engagement, so when they toddled home after sharing a plunger-pot of dark, nutty coffee (half-caffeinated, in deference to the hour), they were alone with the palms, the crickets, and the stars.

"No," said Stasia, "I think he was *serious.*"

"Me, president?" Coop laughed. "That's crazy. It was just talk. I guarantee, come tomorrow, you won't hear another word about it."

She singsonged, "I think you're wro-ong." She slipped her hand out of his, held him by the waist, and scratched her nails against the wales of his corduroys.

"Good God," he said. "Don't tell me I'm going to get lucky tonight."

She slid a finger between his butt cheeks.

He quipped, "But we're not due till another three weeks."

"Stop that. Spontaneity is the spice of life."

"It seems," he said, stating the obvious, "you're rather turned on by the prospect of having a husband in a position of power."

"Who, me?" she squeaked. Then, with a purr, she whispered in his ear, "Power—it's the ultimate aphrodisiac."

So shortly after arriving home, keying in their entry code, and switching off a few lights, Coop got lucky. It started right there in the front hall when she slid the belt out of his cords and he slipped off his shoes. It continued on their way through the living room as she asked him to unzip the back of her dress. By the time they had closed the door to their bedroom, they were as naked as newborns, lusty as adolescents, and horned up as a pair of Rottwielers in heat. "If I'd known," said Coop, "I'd have popped a Cialis."

But he didn't need it, not that night. His call to manly duty was met with both the cooperation and the enthusiasm that the occasion deserved, and he took tenable pride in his performance. "How's that?" he whispered as they went at it.

"Smashing," she managed to say through clenched teeth. Between breaths, she added, "It's a party. An after-dinner party. A party for two."

And then, nudged by her words, Coop's mind blossomed with images of another party. With his hips on autopilot—they seemed to have a mind of their own—he recalled a birthday party, his fifth, mere months before the start of kindergarten:

They're in their new house. Cooper's mother is happy because they finally landed in the right neighborhood, but Coop isn't so sure because he hasn't met any new friends he wants to play with. "Give it time," she says. "I'm sure you'll meet just *tons* of delightful boys and girls once school starts."

But school hasn't started yet, and today is his birthday, and there's no one he wanted to invite to the party, especially that girl, the snot who lives around the corner, so his mother invited some relatives who have children, and they all had to drive from the far side of town and get all dressed up in the middle of the week, in the summer, and some of the kids are acting sort of mean about it, even though there's cake and ice cream and stuff, and his mother keeps telling them, "Just wait, just wait. There's a big surprise coming. You're going to be *thrilled*." And the other mothers are all whispering and giggling with each other.

Even though the cake has white frosting, Coop's mother promised it would be chocolate inside. His name is on top—his mom spells it out for the other kids—along with some red and blue flowers, since it's almost the Fourth of July, and five little candles. His mom lights the candles and says, "Okay, Coop, today's your big day, your *lucky* day. Think hard now, make a wish, and see if you can blow them all out at once." So Coop crunches his eyes closed, wishes for the rest of his finger to grow back while he's in bed that night, then blows hard. And just as he squeezes out a last bunch of breath to get the last candle—*Pound! Pound! Pound!*—there's this big knock at the front door.

All the kids shut up quick, like they're frozen, but the mothers are looking at each other, trying not to laugh. Then this big, deep voice outside says, "Is this where Cooper Brant lives? Is this where little Cooper saddles up his pony?"

Coop thinks he's going to get a pony.

"Yes!" shout all the children.

The door swings open, and in walks their Saturday-morning hero, Sheriff Rusty Oxhide, all decked out in boots, spurs, chaps, six-shooters, vest, badge, and a big white hat. "Dad!" yells Coop. "Rusty!" chime the kids, running to him, touching him. They're surprised to see that the shirt under his vest is bright red; on TV it looks gray.

Hands on hips, Rusty asks the little ones, "And guess who came with me."

"*Who?*" they yell.

"A p'pony?" Coop asks.

Rusty swings his hand toward the door, and in walks Miss Mimi, the beloved schoolmarm in Rusty's rough-and-tumble frontier town. The kids flock to her, screaming, hugging her. She wears a white bonnet and a big white apron. They're surprised to see that the dress under her apron is bright blue; on TV it also looks gray.

Coop steps back from the crowd and notices one of the mothers leaning to another, saying, "My, she *is* lovely. Even prettier in person."

"Isn't she, though?" With a low laugh, the other mother adds, "But I don't think they really had Negro schoolteachers back in the Wild West."

"Of *course* not—but it's good for the children."

"I suppose . . ."

Coop tugs his mother's dress. "What are they talking about? What's good for the children?"

His mom steps him aside and crouches to tell him, "They're just not used to seeing Negroes in their homes."

"But Mimi's nice."

"Yes, dear. She's wonderful."

"But Mimi's b'been to our house *lots* of times."

"Of course, dear. That's because *we're* liberal."

"Oh." When Coop's mother starts to get up, he tugs her down again, saying, "I thought we were Unitarian."

She laughs. "We're *both*, dear." She rises, returning to the other women.

"Oh."

Everyone's having a good time now, but Coop is starting to feel left out. It's his birthday, his party, but no one seems to notice. They're eating his cake, but they didn't even sing; they're too busy having fun with his dad and Mimi. And the presents were a disappointment, mostly clothes for when he starts school, which he's sure won't be anything like Miss Mimi's school on TV. But at least the inside of the cake is chocolate.

"Cooper?"

He looks up from the corner of the room, where he sits on the floor like a good little Indian with the cake in his lap.

"What's the matter, honey?" asks Mimi. "You're the star of this show."

"I dunno." He sets the plate aside and gets up. "Sometimes mom says it's tough getting old—I guess she's right."

Mimi laughs. "You're *five*. And besides, birthdays mean presents." She winks.

"Yeah. Socks and sweaters." He gives her a grin that says, Oh boy.

Fishing in the pockets of her big apron, she says, "Socks and sweaters, huh? I don't imagine they're of much interest to a rugged, adventurous young man like you. But how about . . . *this*?" And she pulls out a stuffed toy horse made of brightly colored patchwork. Its mane and tale are tufts of yellow yarn.

"A pony!" says Coop, taking the gift from her, staring into its eyes of cobalt glass.

She touches her fingers to the bottom of his chin. "Like it, honey?"

"Uh-huh." He gives an enthusiastic nod, asking, "Did you make it yourself?" On TV, whenever Mimi isn't teaching, she's sewing.

"No, sweetie, I bought it, but you know what they say: it's the thought that counts."

He squints. "What does that mean?"

"It means that even though I bought it, I love you as much as if I'd made it."

Coop locks his arms around her waist. "I love you too, Mimi."

"Oh, Cooper"—she presses his head to her belly, strokes his hair—"you're such a sweet child, every inch your father's son. Such a good boy."

"Good boy," said Stasia, interrupting the memory, wriggling beneath Coop. Groggily, she added, "Wow."

After a moment of assessing his surroundings, he asked, "How was it?" He wasn't fishing—he honestly didn't remember the climax, though there clearly had been one.

With a voluptuous stretch, she said, "Need you ask?"

"Apparently not." He rolled onto his back next to her. "I need a cigarette."

"Right," she said through a drowsy laugh. He had never smoked.

Wide awake, he lay there thinking. Perhaps a minute passed. Then he got up.

She mumbled, "Enjoy your Marlboro," and rolled onto her side, curling into a fetal ball with her face smooshed against the pillow.

Coop crossed to the door and opened it, but turned back, asking, "Did you hear about that hang glider?" But the three martinis had finally taken their toll, and Stasia's only response was a sputtering snore.

Coop found his pants in the living room and zipped into them, didn't bother with the shirt, found his loafers in the hall and stepped into them, didn't bother with the socks. He grabbed his phone from the credenza near the door, then went to the kitchen.

He switched on the lights, saw that it was well past eleven, and opened the refrigerator, craving something. It was too late for food, but he was thirsty. He'd had enough liquor for the night, and the orange juice had no appeal—too acidic. Coke, ginger ale, club soda—too gassy. Which left, of all things, milk. He was surprised to find any, surprised further that it had not expired, so he poured a glass, wondering how long it had been since he had sat down and drunk a full glass of milk. He couldn't remember the instance, not specifically, but it had surely been during his boyhood, no later than high school. Forty years. Back then, it came in cartons, not plastic jugs, and earlier still, when he was very young, he could even remember the end of the era of glass bottles, which were sealed with a cardboard tab about the size of a silver dollar; the silver dollars disappeared about the same time as the bottles. They'd had a milkman who left the bottles in an insulated box on the porch, and his mother used to wash the empties with a brush before returning them.

Late that night, in the sleek kitchen of the house Coop had designed, his glass of milk, a pure cylinder of white, looked oddly sophisticated on the countertop of polished black granite, in contrast to his memories of kids crudely blowing bubbles in their little cartons at lunch. "Always take the white milk, not the chocolate," his mother had warned him. "They use the old milk to make that. You'll throw up."

His mother wasn't the only one pushing milk. Every Saturday, Miss Mimi lectured her young charges, "Be sure to drink your milk—it helps build strong bones," and they lapped it up at recess as she served sparkling glassfuls from an ice-cold crystal pitcher. Somehow, the forces of goodwill in television land had conspired to convince young Cooper that it was no more implausible for frontier children to snack on refrigerated, sterilized dairy products than it was for them to have a black teacher in a nineteenth-century color-blind cow town.

So when he lifted the glass to his lips that night, Coop was skeptical. Although the milk was plenty cold, reasonably fresh, and perfectly presented in a Tiffany tumbler, it represented a period of his life—childhood—that still left him wondering how he'd ever lived through it. He sipped the milk, paused to taste it, and swallowed. Then he set the glass down, shrugged, and said aloud, to no one, "It's okay." The refrigerator droned in the quiet of the room.

On the counter, next to the glass, sat his phone, which he picked up and turned on. This—not cigarettes, not milk—was what had been on his mind when he excused himself from the bedroom. He scrolled through the directory, assuming he'd kept the listing over the years, just in case. And there it was: MILES, MIMI. He glanced at the clock and, in spite of the hour, sent the call.

He expected to be shunted to voice mail—or to hear the other phone ring for a while, coaxing someone out of bed—but the call was answered briskly, "Hello?" on the second ring. It was only one word, and it had been many years since Coop had heard the voice, but there was no mistaking it.

He asked, "Is this M'Mimi Miles?"

"Who *is* this?"

"Mimi, it's . . . it's C'Cooper."

She gasped. "Oh, honey! Are you all right?"

"Yes, absolutely. I'm sorry to call so late. I was afraid you'd be in bed."

"*Bed?* It's not even midnight."

"Well"—Coop laughed—"we're not getting any younger."

"You're saying I'm old?"

"I'm saying *I'm* old."

"You're fifty-*eight*," she said at once, not needing to think about the number. The conversation reminded Coop of a similar exchange they'd had at his fifth birthday party.

"Mimi, the note was kind of you. It took me by surprise, and I didn't know how to react, but you were . . . you've been on my mind lately." He thought it best not to be more specific—no point in saying he'd taken a stroll down memory lane with her that night while mounting his wife.

"Oh, honey, I know you won't believe it, but you're always on my mind."

He got to the point: "I'd like to see you sometime. A lot's been happening lately, and maybe you'll have some useful insights."

"Useful insights?" She hooted. "I'm not a philosopher, honey. I'm a has-been actress, out to pasture."

"That's hardly true."

"That's *exactly* true. But I'd love to see you. Anytime. When?"

"Uh"—Coop didn't have his calendar—"later this week." Arbitrarily, he suggested, "How about Friday evening?"

"I'll fix you supper."

"No, don't bother, please. I'll grab something after work, then drive out there around seven, if that's okay."

"Good idea, cuz I'm not a cook, either. I'm a has-been actress, out to pasture."

"You're repeating yourself."

"I'm *old*, honey—old as dirt."

# Chapter 5

Coop sipped the milk while talking to Mimi on the phone, but it was late, so they kept the conversation brief; they would have plenty of time to catch up on Friday evening. By the time Coop shut off his phone, the milk had lost its chill, as well as its nostalgic appeal, so he dumped the remaining half glass down the kitchen sink, rinsed the glass, and went to bed.

He awoke early Tuesday feeling uncommonly rested. What, he wondered, had allowed him to enjoy such a satisfying night's sleep, unfettered by dreams or by the usual vexations of his waking hours? Had it been the rush of Bix's big talk about the president's position, the unexpected gratification of impromptu sex with Stasia, the sentimental fulfillment of reconnecting with Mimi—or had it simply been the milk?

He arrived at the gym early enough to do some stretching and warm-ups, and when he finished, there were still a few minutes till his session with Teddy, so he decided to use the lavatory. On his way, passing through the locker room, he spotted someone changing, or rather, hanging a leather jacket in one of the lockers, who looked toward Coop briefly, then turned his back. But the face was familiar, one of those "faces from the gym," and so was his attire. He wore khakis, a white T-shirt, and black service shoes, the sort worn by workers, military—and cops. It was the guy, Coop realized, who'd had the shouting match with Dennis Dill on Friday.

A row of sinks with mirrors led to the toilet room, and as Coop passed by, one of the trainers, who was standing there in a towel and flip-flops, shaving, wished him a good morning and quipped, "Be sure to wash your hands."

"You bet," said Coop. The hydraulic door closed behind him as he stood alone at the row of urinals, and he was reminded again of his fifth birthday party:

When it's time for ice cream, everyone finally gets around to singing "Happy Birthday," and Coop poses for snapshots with his dad, mom, and Mimi. Sometimes the flashbulbs work; sometimes they don't. Later, they'll take the film to the drugstore. All afternoon, he's been drinking lemonade and Kool-Aid—cherry, not grape—and now he has to pee. "Don't say 'tinkle,' dear. It sounds so babyish." As he starts off toward the bathroom, his mother calls after, "Be sure to wash your hands. You don't want to get polio, do you?"

The room is suddenly real, *real* quiet.

Coop shakes his head, scared to death of getting polio.

He's seen those pictures of kids in iron lungs. It's this big metal tube they lie in. The kid's head sticks out from the end, and he has to look up into an angled mirror in order to talk to his parents. In the pictures, the parents are always dressed up, like they're going to church, and there's a nurse standing with them. On the floor, there's a ball, bat, and catcher's mitt, collecting dust, a grim reminder of happier days. Coop always wonders how the kid goes to the bathroom. Maybe the nurse helps while the parents are in church. One thing's for sure: *that* kid is plenty sorry he didn't wash his hands.

Now, in the men's room, scrubbing up, Coop marveled at the inanities parents get away with while rearing their young. Inane, but effective—half a century later, he was still washing his hands, with soap, and all he'd done was tinkle.

"You're on," said the trainer, rinsing his razor as Coop walked by. "Just saw Teddy. He's ready for you."

"Ah, let the torture begin." Coop thought he was supposed to say things like that—it was expected—but in truth, he always looked forward to his sessions.

Out on the floor, he saw Teddy in the free-weights area, checking his clipboard. As Coop drew near, they greeted each other. Then Coop asked, "What are we up to today?"

"Chest and triceps." Teddy had pulled a pair of fifty-pound dumbbells from the racks and placed them near one of the benches. "A really *mean* trainer," he said, "would always have you start with push-ups, but I assume you've done those already." Teddy flashed him an inquiring grin.

"I have," Coop answered honestly; they were part of his warm-up.

"Good. Then let's start with a basic bench press."

Coop nodded, picked up the weights, sat on the end of the bench, rocked backward to a lying position, and began the series of lifts. Though there were many dedicated bodybuilders at the gym who routinely lifted much heavier weights, the fifty-pounders represented something of a milestone to Coop. When he had started, he could barely lift half that, and he was now gaining the strength—and the confidence—to move beyond the fifties. But he still struggled some while getting into and out of position, so Teddy had recommended waiting: "This is one exercise where you've *got* to get the form right. Lose control and drop them— you can do some real damage."

Coop finished his first set, sat upright, and brought the dumbbells gently to the floor.

"Good job. So—what's new?" Teddy's routine was to begin the session immediately with the first set of the first exercise, then initiate the chitchat during the rests.

"You mean, since Saturday night?" Coop laughed, recalling the museum opening. "What a fiasco."

Teddy also laughed. "God, I couldn't believe it."

"And Bruce Rollo—talk about poise under pressure, telling everyone, 'It's only glass.' I'm surprised they didn't carry him out on a stretcher."

"Rob says it was all an act. He's *worked* with Bruce, *represented* Bruce, and believe me, the insurance claims were in the works before anyone went to bed that night."

"I forgot to mention," said Coop, standing, "it was nice to finally meet your partner. We didn't get much chance to talk, but Rob seems like a great guy."

"Thanks, he is. He thinks the world of Stasia—and was glad to meet *you*."

"Funny story," said Coop, "and I hope you won't take it the wrong way. When I first saw Rob at the museum, he was standing alone with Bruce, talking, and I assumed *they* were a couple. Stasia set me straight. So to speak."

"Meaning, Rob and *I* are a couple?"

"Right. And also meaning, Bruce Rollo is straight. He could have fooled me, but we all saw his date, and in fact—small world—I had quite a conversation with her. As for Bruce, well, that was a first. Guess I've never met a walking, talking metrosexual."

"Bruce?" said Teddy. "Not . . . *exactly.*"

Coop gave his trainer a silent, inquisitive stare.

Teddy informed him, "Bruce Rollo is bisexual."

"You know this for a fact?"

Teddy gave a slight but authoritative nod.

"Really?" Coop said nothing more, but couldn't help wondering, Does Arcie Madera have the complete picture? And if so, how does *that* work?

Coop sat on the bench again, lay back with the weights, and did a second set of reps. When he finished, he sat up, intending to explain to Teddy his connection with Arcie Madera, when he noticed in the mirror—the angled walls were lined with them and could sometimes be disorienting—the guy in khaki, who seemed to be watching him.

Coop swiveled on the bench, looking for the source of the reflected image, but when he spotted the guy, he was huffing through a set of dead lifts and did not appear to be looking in Coop's direction at all.

Teddy followed Coop's gaze, asking, "What?"

"That bruiser in the khakis—who had the run-in with Dennis Dill—you never saw him before last Friday, right?"

"Right. But I've seen him since. He was here yesterday morning, same time. Since you had to cancel, I figured I'd use the hour to do my own workout. I thought I caught him watching me. After a few minutes, he left."

Coop asked, "Your first impression—why did you think he left?"

"Because I was alone. Because you weren't with me. But that makes no sense at all. Why would *he* care?"

When Coop finished his last set of presses, Teddy said, "Let's stay on the bench." He handed Coop a barbell: "Triceps extensions."

"Huh?"

Teddy translated, "Skull crushers."

"Oh." Coop got on his back, barbell aloft, then lowered it to his head, elbows up, and lifted it again. And again.

When he finished the set, Teddy said, "Good job," and took the barbell. Rather than sitting up to chat during the minute of rest, Coop remained lying there, staring at one of the ceiling fans. Then, as if responding to some unspoken signal, he placed his hands in position just as Teddy stepped from behind to pass him the barbell again. Coop completed the second set, and after another recumbent rest with nothing spoken, he finished the third.

"Uh," said Teddy, looking around, "let's go over to the cables and do some chest flies." He led the way across the gym floor. As Coop followed, he caught a glimpse in one of the mirrors of the khaki guy, who was staring right at him.

Coop toweled some sweat from his neck while Teddy adjusted the cable arms—high and wide—and lowered the pin in the weight stack. When the machine was ready, he asked, "Remember the move? One foot forward."

Coop nodded, got in position, struggled with the first fly, as Teddy had upped the weight, but found his rhythm on the second rep and eventually made his way through twelve. Easing the cables back to their inert position, he turned to Teddy with a weak smile and blew a breath, an exhalation that sounded more like a sigh.

"How was it?" asked the trainer.

"Challenging."

"But you made it."

"I did."

Teddy hesitated. "You're not much of a Chatty Cathy this morning."

"Sorry. I've got this dentist's appointment—kinda dreading it."

"Ooh, yikes, good luck. I was afraid you might be having troubles at home."

After a momentary pause, Coop asked, "Why?"

"Gosh, sorry, I don't know. Guess I'm out of bounds."

"Not at all," Coop assured him. During their year of training together, Coop had come to understand that while Teddy rarely wasted words, the things he did say seemed highly intuitive. Coop told him, "We can talk about anything—and we *do*—I like that."

"Well," said Teddy, "it's just that last time, on Friday, you were talking about Stasia and implied that your sex life was 'off.' Then Saturday, at the museum, the two of you seemed sort of distant from each other—like you were there together, but you weren't."

With a pensive nod, Coop said, "Interesting observation."

"Just an impression."

Coop said, "I'd better, uh, take care of this"—he gestured toward the cable machine, then worked through his second set of flies.

When he finished, he told Teddy, "The damnedest thing happened last night."

Teddy's brows arched. "Is that, like, a good thing? Or a bad thing?"

"You be the judge." And Coop recounted the events leading up to Bix's off-the-wall job offer, Stasia's enthusiastic reaction to it, and the outcome of her pepped-up hormones. "I've gotta tell you," Coop concluded with a laugh, "I don't think we've *ever* had sex on a Monday."

With a nod of approval, Teddy said, "You *did* have quite a night. That all sounds pretty good to me."

Coop knew that it did sound good, or at least that it should sound good. "But . . ."

"But what?" asked Teddy. "Was the sex . . . all right?"

"Oh, *she* was happy as a clam." Coop leaned near, lowering his voice. "I came, but afterward, I couldn't even remember it—and no, I was *not* hammered."

"*Something* must've distracted you."

"I admit, my mind was elsewhere. I lacked the focus the situation deserved, and—"

"Coop," Teddy interrupted, placing a hand on his client's shoulder, "it isn't rocket science. It's sex."

"I know, I know"—Coop pulled back a step—"but it was something she said."

"Like what? 'Drive it home, big boy'? That doesn't sound quite like Stasia."

"Hardly!" Coop gave a loud laugh, fetching glances from others working out nearby. "Seriously though, she told me outright that, for her, the ultimate aphrodisiac is power."

"Lots of women feel that way." Teddy shrugged, adding, "So do lots of men."

"Point is, she was really turned on—and I mean in a primal, almost primitive sense—by the notion of mating with a man in a position of power."

"Great," said Teddy. "You've discovered her hot button."

"But that's not *me*. God knows, I grew up with my own father-issues, and she apparently has hers. But I'll never be the kind of man her father is, and I don't want to be." Coop paused before adding, "So why'd she marry me?"

Teddy paused before asking, "So why'd *you* marry *her*?"

Coop had to think about it. "You know, I honestly don't remember." Then he grabbed the cables and finished the last set of his flies.

From the far side of the gym, the guy in khaki was still watching.

Clifford Sloan, DDS, maintained a tidy practice in a quaint row of Spanish-style professional offices, replete with terra-cotta tile roofs, just off the main drag in downtown Palm Springs. A wooden sign near his door, hanging from the underside of the colonnade, bore the carved image of a single large tooth, painted the gleaming white of porcelain. It was a clean, happy molar with grooves and crannies that made it appear to wink and smile—and strong, healthy roots like chubby little legs to dance upon.

As for Cooper's roots, he feared their dancing days were over. Cliff Sloan, DDS, like prior dentists in Santa Barbara and, later, Los Angeles, had cautioned him that brushing—even Coop's finicky five-minute marathons—was simply not enough. He needed to floss. More to the point, he needed to *have flossed* since adolescence, but he had never gotten the hang of it, and the thought of forcing string between his teeth still made him cringe.

But that was a minor cringe, a baby cringe, a mere ick compared to the "procedure," the proposed remedy for his years of neglect.

Deep scaling, as he understood it, would involve multiple shots of novocaine to numb the entire mouth, then peeling back the gums to expose all of the teeth's roots, which would then be scraped of a lifetime's debris, enabling them, perhaps, to dance again—once the gums finally healed. Now, *that's* a cringe. Big time.

So it was with faint heart and queasy stomach that Coop entered the office, presented himself to the receptionist, and took a seat in the waiting room. No other chair was occupied; the remainder of that morning's schedule had been cleared for his procedure. When it was over, the others would laugh, go to lunch, or just hang around the office, gossiping, snacking on peanut brittle, while he, damp-fisted, could only await the unknown while the anesthetic petered out.

A child's shriek of agony from the labyrinth within didn't help.

"Mr. Brant?" said a perky nursette, who could not have been old enough to drive. She stood in the hallway just beyond the aquarium, which seemed to be all bubbles and no fish. "You're next!"

As she escorted him into the treatment room, he felt like Saddam being prodded to the gallows, wondering what taunts he might be forced to endure during this, his darkest hour. She instructed him to be seated, clamped his bib on, and ratcheted the chair into position, which left him feeling as vulnerable as a turtle on its back. When satisfied that he was duly submissive, she asked, "And how are *we* today?"

"Can't you just knock me out for this?"

She tittered.

"No," he assured her, "I'm not kidding."

Still the nursette tittered. She waltzed out of the room, saying, "Doctor Cliff will be right with you."

When did they start combining "Doctor" with first names? Doctor Phil? Doctor Ruth?

"Morning, Coop. Today's the day, huh?"

From his position in the chair, Coop couldn't see Doctor Cliff, as the door was behind him, but the voice sounded oddly muted, as if transmitted through a tin can. He heard the voice continue, "Time to face the music and get this taken care of." When Cliff stepped into view, Coop winced, squeaking against the hospital-green vinyl of the chair. The dentist wore not only a paper surgical mask, but also a large curved-plastic outer mask that covered most of his head like a welder's helmet. With a chortle, he clapped a hand on Coop's shoulder, asking, "How's it going?"

"I've had better days."

"Hey," Cliff babbled, "what a great time on Sunday, huh?" As he spoke, he organized an array of dental instruments on a tray that hovered near the edge of Coop's vision. He could barely see it if he stretched his neck—and he did. Each steel tool had a certain elegance, a spare, utilitarian look, precisely suited to some arcane but unthinkable purpose. While admiring their functional aesthetic, Coop felt certain they had been designed by a team of Nazi vivisectionists.

Cliff continued, "Gotta tell you, I never dreamed Bix would actually offer to support my campaign. I mean, he's a *big* ol' Republican."

"I think he's more practical than partisan," said Coop, paying little attention to their words, wishing they would just get on with it.

"It's not just the partisan thing," said Cliff, fussing with the first syringe of novocaine; in Coop's peripheral view, its needle looked like a ten-penny nail. "I mean," Cliff explained, "let's face it—in terms of political experience, I'm pretty green."

Coop said, "No greener than Kavanall."

"*What?*" Cliff's helmet snapped in Coop's direction. Through the plastic shield, through the wavy reflections of the surgical lamp, the dentist's eyes bore into his patient. "What about Kavanall?"

Oops. Coop swallowed. "I g'guess you were out of the room when Kav mentioned that he might, uh . . . take a shot at that seat as well. As a Republican."

Cliff's voice was barely audible: "Really."

"But if you ask me, it was just talk. You know Kav—he can be kind of flighty."

"Yes. Flighty." Cliff moved in with the syringe. "Okay, Coop, open wide, please." But then he backed off for a moment. "Almost forgot," he said. Then he dabbed something on Coop's gums to deaden the injection sites.

Almost forgot, thought Coop. That's what I get for using a dentist who cheated in college.

The procedure was not what Coop had expected. Much to his relief, the actual scaling, or scraping, of the roots was not done with a blade of steel, but with a tiny ultrasonic jet of water, and though the instrument probed below the gum—hence the anesthetic—it did not require peeling back the gums, as he had imagined. He kept his eyes closed restfully, watching none of it, and although the procedure was tedious, that was Cliff's problem; Coop simply zoned out, letting his mind wander. Once he grasped the rhythm of what Cliff was doing, Coop was surprised to find the sensation not painful, but quite satisfying. It felt *cleansing*.

For the hour or so that Cliff's hands were in Coop's mouth, Coop could not, of course, speak, save for the occasional "uh-huh" in response to Cliff's sporadic queries, "Doin' all right?" So when Cliff finally put away his instruments, flipped open his visor, and adjusted the chair to a sitting position, Coop was feeling almost giddily conversant, despite the numbness of his mouth; his tongue felt twice its normal thickness. "When can I eat?" he asked.

"Keep it bland this afternoon," said Cliff, "but by dinnertime, you should be able to eat anything you want."

"Really?" It sounded more like "Wee-wee?"

"Yup. Be sure to use an antiseptic mouthwash, and for God's sake, start flossing."

"I will. I promise." Christ, thought Coop, I sound like Elmer Fudd. Or Baba Wawa.

With a laugh, Cliff added, "And tell Kav to stay out of politics."

"I'll do that. I have a golf outing with him tomorrow—bright and early at the club. I doubt if he much cares how his stepdad feels about his career options, but I'll bet his grandfather's opinions will carry some weight."

"Golf," said Cliff, looking wistfully out the window, "what a great game. I didn't know you were into it."

"Trust me, I'm *not*. It was Bix's idea."

"Even so," said Cliff, still peering through the window, "sometimes it's just fun to get out there and enjoy the course."

Coop laughed. "I've heard *that* more than once."

**C**oop had cleared his calendar for the afternoon, unsure of what aftermath to expect from his procedure, but certain that it would involve no productive activity. He hadn't even planned to check in at the office, presuming he would head directly home and probably go to bed. Pulling out of the dentist's parking lot, however, he felt just fine—in fact, downright chipper, relieved beyond measure—so he decided to swing out to Emery headquarters, catch up at his desk, and see if there were any fires that required his attention.

Because he was warned his mouth would remain numb for another couple of hours, he wanted to avoid being drawn into small talk with coworkers, so he used the hall that led to the rear door to his office, tapped in his keypad code, and entered. The cool, dim room—its draperies were closed, shutting out the view of bright, bustling offices beyond a glass wall—this room, his space, was as comforting as a nest, private as a whispered secret, orderly as a monastic cell. Everything was exactly as he had left it the prior evening, except that the wastebasket had been emptied and the phone's message light was flashing. He sat at his desk, dialed up voice mail, and listened. He had two new messages.

The first began, "Hello, Mr. Brant. Arcie Madera again. Is it my imagination, or are you avoiding me?"

I'm not avoiding anyone, thought Coop. I'm stalling—on the advice of my attorney.

Madera continued, "We need to talk DNA. Again. You can make this easy, or you can make it not-so-easy." In a no-nonsense tone, she ended, "Call me, Brant."

The phone's readout indicated that the second message was internal, from Austin Royce, the CFO. It began, "Good morning, Cooper. Just wanted to keep you in the loop regarding tomorrow's golf game. I'm afraid I've had something of a minor family crisis out of town, so my wife and I will be driving up to see our daughter today. I've talked to Bix about it, and he wants to include Jay Pontarelli to round out your foursome. So I spoke to Jay, and he'll be joining you at eight. Sorry I'll have to miss it. Have fun."

Hanging up the phone, Coop said aloud, "Oh, swell."

It sounded more like "Oh, thwell."

**C**oop had already been uncomfortable anticipating Wednesday's golf outing, but switching Jay Pontarelli for Austin Royce in the foursome turned his discomfort to dread. Although both men, like Coop, were in their fifties and both routinely wore dark business suits, any similarity ended there. While Austin was a bland character—a numbers guy and a quintessential second lieutenant—he also carried himself with a certain refinement and low-key demeanor that projected a mature collegiality and no hint of menace; when Austin was present, he was always in the background. Jay, on the other hand, had never grown up and still exhibited a sophomoric bonhomie rooted in loud humor, nonstop competition, and the dark art of one-upmanship. He played to win. How, Coop wondered, could Jay's inclusion allow a duffer in the foursome to "have fun"?

Coop understood, however, that from Bix's perspective, the switch made sense. This was not just a friendly game of golf; its underlying purpose was to sound out Kavanall regarding possible career plans, to disabuse him of any notion of entering politics or PontaPower, and to keep him true-blue and loyal within the bosom of the Emery family. From Bix's perspective, Jay Pontarelli was part of the problem in a way that Austin Royce was not, so he must have welcomed Austin's need to bow out and the opportunity for Jay to step in.

When Coop arrived that morning at the staging area for the carts on the lower terrace of the Hellsgate clubhouse, he found all four sets of clubs already loaded on side-by-side carts, with Bix waiting in one of them, sitting at the wheel, Pyrite in his lap. "Morning, Coops! Great day to be out on the links, eh?"

"As good as it gets." Coop's ambiguous reply was accompanied by a forced smile.

"We should do this more often. Golf agrees with you, Coops. You look terrific."

"Thanks." Coop didn't feel terrific. He liked the clothes—trim poplin slacks, silky polo shirt, sleeveless argyle sweater for the morning chill—but the rubber-spiked shoes reminded him with every step that he didn't belong here, that he would only embarrass himself, that being a good sport about it would never begin to compensate for his jitters or mask his bone-deep deficiencies. Noting the clubs loaded on the carts, Coop asked, "Are Kav and Jay here?"

"Kavanall said he forgot something inside."

At that moment, the door swung open from the locker room, and Kav stepped out with Jay Pontarelli, both laughing. What Kav had forgotten, apparently, was eye-openers, as both he and Jay carried two large clear-plastic go-cups, one pair the color of tomato juice, the other orange, all of them garnished with the froufrou of early-morning cocktails. The colorful drinks complemented their loud outfits. Both wore shorts. Kav's shoes were an elegant cream-colored kidskin. Jay's were black, worn, and clunky, with all the charm of football shoes; his calves flexed like ropy knots as the two men walked toward the cart.

"Breakfast?" asked Kav, offering the drinks.

"Too early for me, Kavanall," said Bix.

With a chuckle, Coop shook his head.

Kav reminded them, "It's the most important meal of the day." But still there were no takers, so Kav loaded up the carts' cup holders, telling Jay, aside, "I'm sure *someone* will drink them." And they both laughed with a vigor unearned by the quip, leading Coop to assume they'd chugged a prior round indoors.

Everyone hopped into the carts, Kav sitting with Bix and Pyrite in one, Coop taking the wheel of the other. When Jay heaved his quarterback's bulk into the remaining seat, the cart listed in his direction. Bix and Coop drove the short, curving path past the NO DOGS ALLOWED sign toward the first tee.

Jay asked, "So what are the stakes today?"

"No stakes," said Bix, "just for fun. Thought we'd play a scramble."

Coop seconded, "Fine with me." Though he found golf terms confusing, he assumed Bix was referring to a game in which all the players tee off for each hole, then play subsequent shots from the best spot attained by the prior round of shots, until the ball is holed. It was a good way to move the game along more quickly, allowing golfers of different skill levels to play the course together. And for duffers like Coop, it removed a lot of pressure.

But Jay was skeptical. "Defeats the purpose of the game—why bother?" He whacked the back of his hand on Coop's shoulder, asking, "What's your handicap?"

"I've no idea, Jay. I'm truly lousy."

"Come on," Jay persisted. "On any given hole, do you come close to making a par?"

"If par is in the single digits: no."

Jay roared with laughter, assuming Coop was exaggerating.

Coop wasn't.

When they arrived at the tee, the party before them was already putting on the first green, and the party behind them had yet to assemble at their carts, so they had some breathing room. Not sure of the protocol, Coop simply asked, "Mind if I go first?" As long as he had to humiliate himself, he wanted to get it over with.

Jay gave him a be-my-guest gesture.

Coop felt on the verge of nausea as he teed up the ball, got in position, and took a few practice swings. When he finally swung for real, he knew his form was awful, and as the ball sputtered forward, he learned that his year's worth of weight training had produced no practical application to golf—not that he had expected it to. But at least he managed to hit the ball, and he managed not to dig a divot, and he managed to land the shot on the fairway, albeit only a few yards out.

"A little rusty, maybe, but decent," said Bix, nodding. With fatherly patience, he added, "Good shot, Coops."

Pyrite yipped, echoing Bix's approval.

Jay looked at Kav, rolled his eyes, and conceded, "Maybe the scramble's not a bad idea."

Bix went next. Then Kav. They were both passable, experienced golfers, but Bix's game was hampered by his years, Kav's by his go-cups. Still, they each bested Coop by a long shot, landing balls well down the fairway on a straight line to the green.

All was quiet as Jay stepped to the tee. He teed the ball high and took a practice swing, biceps bulging, thighs thick as a stud stallion's.

Please, oh please, prayed Coop. If there's a god in heaven, please let him botch this. Please, just this once.

But Jay hammered it. With an ear-splitting smack, Jay's driver, a titanium Big Bertha, sent the ball whistling skyward, arcing gracefully over the length of the fairway, then dropping and rolling to within a hundred yards of the four-hundred-yard hole.

So much for the power of prayer.

Coop joined in the hearty round of congratulations that followed, taking solace that Jay's monster drive had at least stolen the focus from his own piddling attempt. They all piled into their carts and took off down the fairway, plucking up the three deficient shots on their way to Jay's ball.

Jay marked the spot where his ball had landed. Each of them would hit a short shot from that position to the green, starting with Coop, who managed to hit his ball about halfway to the green. Of the four shots, Kav's was best, stopping on the green about twenty feet from the hole.

Coop's turn again—and he was fine now. If he found any aspect of golf enjoyable, it was putting, success at which was not dependent on raw strength. He stood squarely over the ball, turned his head sideways, gauging the distance to the hole, when a series of loud pops—shotguns—ricocheted across the course, breaking everyone's concentration.

Pyrite barked.

"Jesus Christ," said Jay, "what are they doing over there—shootin' Injuns?"

"Nah," said Bix, "coots."

Jay gave him a blank look. "Coots?"

"Sorta like ducks, every bit as dirty, but they don't have webbed feet. They like the lakes, breed there, and make a hell of a mess. The groundskeepers used to just shoot 'em, but some of the women started whining about it—felt sorry for them, thought they were cute, I guess—so now they just scare them off by shooting blanks."

"I'll be damned," said Jay, nodding. "Coots."

While lining up his putt again, Coop paused to explain, "Here in the valley, some of the newer courses are designed with an eye toward the native environment, minimizing turf, using desert landscaping for the roughs, and shunning man-made lakes. But the older courses, like this one, were designed along the traditional aesthetic, so it looks like a bit of old Scotland transplanted to the American Southwest." His point, though he didn't say it, was: if they hadn't put water where it doesn't belong, they wouldn't be dealing with coots.

Focused and intent, Coop swung the putter and smartly tapped the ball just as a few more shotgun blasts rang out, closer this time. As the ball traversed the green, the air carried a momentary whiff of gunpowder. The ball came to rest within inches of the cup.

"Hey, hey!" shouted Bix.

Pyrite yapped merrily.

Kav conceded, "Not bad, Pops."

Bix putted, then Kav—both good rolls, given the distance of the putt, but neither ended up inside Coop's.

Wordlessly, Jay Pontarelli, hot shot, set his ball on the green, preparing to out-putt the architect. Was it Coop's imagination, or had the overgrown frat-jock, Mr. PontaPower himself, broken into a sweat? Yes indeed, Coop noted, dark rings of moisture had begun to spread from beneath the arms of Jay's plum-colored polo. Shotguns popped again. "Jesus Christ," muttered Jay. Then he swung. Though his drive had been textbook-perfect, his putt was clumsy and heavy-handed at best, sending the ball well past the cup before it banked to the left, lost its inertia, and faltered to a stop.

Coop's turn. He stepped over to his own ball, the best previous putt.

Bix pulled the flag for his son-in-law, giving him a wink. "Sink it, Coops."

And with an elegant tap, Coop sank it.

"Golf," he said wistfully, "don't you *love* this game?"

**B**ack in the cart, Jay clapped a hand on Coop's shoulder, telling him, "Maybe you oughta be our designated putter."

"Perhaps," said Coop, faking a smile. He knew better than to interpret Jay's suggestion as a compliment.

While riding to the second tee, Kav asked Bix, "What happened to Austin? I thought *he* was in on this today—he set it up."

"Some sort of 'family crisis,' he told me. Something to do with his daughter, the one in college."

Jay grunted. "Ten to one she's knocked up."

Kav laughed, sputtering the cocktail he was slurping. "Glad he couldn't make it—what a stuffed shirt."

"Well," said Bix, "whatever the problem is, I hope it isn't serious. But I'm glad Jay could join us." He paused. "Because there's something we need to talk about."

Kav turned to shoot Jay a glance.

Bix added, "This involves Kavanall too."

Under his breath, Jay said, "Uh-oh . . ."

Kav suppressed a laugh, slurping his drink again.

Bix pulled up to the second tee. "Okay, Coops. You're on."

Coop found his second drive less stressful, and buoyed by his finish on the first hole, he actually made a decent shot, at least by his standards.

Bix and Kav both hit longer drives, but otherwise mediocre, by their standards.

Jay hammered another one, but it veered to the edge of the fairway, nowhere near the green. They agreed his shot was still the best of the bunch, but its position would be challenging for all of them. Coop had no delusions about sinking this one.

As they drove out onto the fairway, collecting the other three balls, shotguns fired again. Pyrite stirred as a dozen coots, gray-black, ran out of the brush, squeaking their high-pitched honk, then disappeared beyond the rise of a knoll.

The carts drove over to the fourth ball. They all got out to assess the next shot, saying nothing. Then Bix broke the silence: "Jay, you have no idea what you're getting into."

"What's that, Bix?"

"It's a damn tough business, Jay. You could lose every cent."

"Not if I have the right people."

With a steely gaze, Bix told him, "You're a damn fool. I love you, Jay, but you're a damn fool."

Kavanall put a hand on his grandfather's shoulder. "Uh, Bix, this is supposed to be 'fun' today, remember?"

Bix turned to look at the younger man. "What do you think you could possibly gain by jumping ship for PontaPower?"

"Seems you've heard quite a bit," said Kav.

"It's my job. What do you have to gain there? Hell, what do you have to *contribute* there?"

"You'd be surprised, Bix."

"Would I?"

Jay interjected, "Kav brings *plenty* to the table, Bix." He repeated, "Plenty."

Bix eyed both of them for a moment, flexing his jaw. Then he turned. Trying to sound chipper, he said, "Okay, Coops, give it your best shot."

This wouldn't be easy. There were scattered palm trees in line with the green, with a wide sand trap beyond the palms. To the left was open fairway, but going there would increase the yardage to the green. Nearby, to the right, was the rough, which was dense with brush surrounding one of the water features.

Coop asked for advice regarding which club to use, and the others agreed he should try the eight-iron, aim over the trees, and hope for the best. When he finally swung, he missed the ball altogether.

As he prepared to give it a second try, Jay said, "Nope, that's all you get."

"For God's sake," Bix grumbled, "it's just a game."

"That's fine," said Coop, "no problem," and bagged his club.

Bix's turn. He seemed flustered—doubtless still festering over PontaPower, a contentious topic he himself had broached—and his hasty swing was the worst Coop had ever seen him make.

Though he was aiming over the palms, the club nicked the edge of the ball, sending it sideways, deep into the rough.

Kav chose the easy shot, to the left, onto the open fairway.

"Aw, come on, girls," Jay taunted. "Jeez, we can do better than that."

"Then show us how," said Kav, returning to his cart, reaching for a drink.

"My pleasure." Jay set his ball, picked his club, and made a quick, neat shot over the trees, past the sand trap, and onto the green, just a few yards short of the pin.

"Very nice," said Kav as the others got into their carts.

Bix started his cart, then turned it off. "Kavanall," he said, "could you see if you can find my ball?"

"In *there*?" said his grandson, looking toward the rough. "Just leave it, Bix. I'll buy you a new ball, a new box—hell, a whole bucket."

Coop assumed Kav didn't want to soil his kidskin shoes.

Bix stared straight ahead, reminding everyone, "I didn't get what I've got by throwing away perfectly good golf balls."

There was no winning this argument, and Kav knew it, so he set down his drink, exhaled a disgruntled sigh, got out of the cart, and walked off into the brush.

When he disappeared from sight, Bix turned in his seat to tell Jay in the other cart, "Business is business; I understand that. But family is family, and you're crossing a line."

Jay considered his response for a moment, then said matter-of-factly, "Kav is a bright guy. He's frustrated. He wants to move on."

"What people *want*," said Bix, getting angry, "doesn't always matter. What matters right now—"

A single shotgun blast, very loud and very near, nipped the conversation. In Bix's lap, Pyrite stood dead still, looking toward the brush.

All heads turned. Nothing stirred, not even the coots.

After a long hesitation, Bix called, "Kavanall?"

Nothing.

Bix turned to his son-in-law. Dry-mouthed, barely audible, he said, "Coops, could you, uh . . . ?"

Coop was already out of the cart, walking toward the brush. Pyrite jumped from Bix's lap and caught up with Coop, trotting alongside.

"Kavanall?" called Coop as he entered the brush. The sun dimmed as he trod deeper into the thicket. Pyrite had to jump and scramble to keep up; his silky coat was already tangled with debris from the undergrowth. "Kav?" Coop called again. "You've got us sort of worried—"

Coop stopped short as a stagnant pond came into view; a brilliant shaft of sunlight angled down from the clearing. He saw no coots, no golf ball. But there at the water's edge lay Kavanall, spread-eagled in the mud with half his head blown away.

Pyrite dashed forward, sniffed at the body, then took a lick, tasting blood.

# Part Two

*Perpetual Motion*

It is impossible to convert heat completely into work in a cyclic process. In all
energy exchanges, if no energy enters or
leaves the system, the potential energy
of the state will always be less than that
of the initial state.

— *The second law of thermodynamics*

# Chapter 6

**R**ancho Mirage, like several of the smaller desert communities, had no police force of its own, opting to contract for those services with the Riverside County sheriff's department. When the emergency call was placed from Entrada, Cooper Brant had no reason to assume Detective Arcie Madera herself would be among the first responders. Coop had little doubt, however, that Madera would soon come calling—as soon as word got back to headquarters that it was he who had discovered the body of a shotgun victim, his own stepson.

The first responders did not include Madera, but the coroner's team was there, accompanied by a forensic pathologist and other evidence technicians, plus a phalanx of all-purpose cops. The golf course was cleared immediately, the rough and the pond were taped off as a crime scene, and the gates to the whole development were temporarily closed. The press was not admitted to the private club, but within minutes, news helicopters churned the air above it. The pristine fairway to the second hole was now a ramshackle parking lot of squad cars, ambulances, and clumsy police vans, all with lights flashing. Coop thought, Can't they at least turn those off? What's the point?

Missing much of his head, Kavanall Emery Follet was declared dead at the scene, tagged, bagged, and laid on a gurney. Word quickly spread that the shooting had been at close range, so the killing was likely not an accident—it was murder. Which forced the secure little enclave of Entrada residents to grapple with the stunning news that their long-standing record of zero violent crime had been forever shattered.

Inside the circle of yellow police tape, investigators took statements not only from Coop, but also from Jay Pontarelli and Bix Emery, who had run to the pond upon hearing Coop's cries of alarm. Coop and Jay, though badly rattled by what they had seen, were now somber, composed, and cooperative, each recounting his best recollection of the events leading up to the tragedy. Bix, on the other hand, was a mess. One of the officers attempted to question him, but he could only mumble through his sobs, "I don't know—I don't know—how can this be?" He gave the same answer over and over while squatting in the mud at the pond's edge. Pyrite squirmed in his arms as Bix attempted to wash the dog with fistfuls of water. Once Pyrite had tasted blood, they'd had difficulty keeping him away from the body, which left his coat as grisly as a slaughterhouse mop.

"Excuse me," said a female officer when one of the investigators had finished questioning Coop. "Word seems to be spreading about what happened, Mr. Brant, and your wife walked over from your home. She's just outside the police line—and distraught, of course—but there's been no public statement yet. Would you like to talk to her?" She placed her fingertips on Coop's forearm. "Or should I?"

"Thank you, officer, but I think I need to do this." It was a task beyond Coop's imagining, informing a mother of the death of her son, a son he had not fathered, a stepson who called him Pops. But there was no question—he had to do this—and to his surprise, he had no difficulty summoning the strength. Was it the call to duty, the power of adrenaline, the instinctive gravitation to the higher values of a life well led? Or was it simply the knowledge that the greater agony would be hers, not his?

The officer signaled a partner stationed at the barricade, who lifted the tape for Stasia Emery-Brant and pointed the way to Coop. She ran through the bramble, looking more frightened than grieved, meeting him halfway and holding him tight. "What happened?" she asked. "Tell me. Someone said it was Kavanall."

"Oh, Stasia"—he nodded slowly—"I'm so sorry." As she heaved a deep cry of pain, he repeated, "I'm so very sorry," cradling her head, kissing her hair.

A mechanical noise—the sound of the gurney being ratcheted to its full height—drew everyone's attention. Then the police crew stepped aside, parting, clearing a path for Kavanall's handlers as he was carted, bumping and jostling, across the thick undergrowth that circled the pond. A boxy fire-department ambulance had backed up to the police tape, its doors flung wide to receive the remains.

"I've got to see him," said Stasia, pulling away from Coop.

"*No,*" he insisted, pulling her back, "*no,*" recalling a sight that she should never see, a sight that no parent should even imagine.

As the shrouded gurney was hoisted into the truck, tears began to stream from Stasia's disbelieving eyes, and the easily summoned strength that had so surprised Coop now vanished. He could not control the bile rising in his throat, and the hand at his mouth could not stop the vomit, which spread through his fingers in gobs, falling to the ground, fouling the toes of his cleated shoes, which he would never wear again.

That afternoon, Coop and Stasia took refuge from the world at home. Stasia was in the bedroom with a doctor and a priest. The doctor had sedated her, the priest had prayed with her, and they both remained at her bedside, keeping watch over her while Coop hunkered in the kitchen, rummaging in the back of a liquor cabinet. He'd told the doctor about his bout of nausea, and the doctor had recommended that he try mixing a pastis of Pernod and water.

"Will that settle my stomach?" Coop asked.

"I guess so," said the doctor, "but frankly, you could use a drink."

Dressed in gray sweatshorts, white T-shirt, and gym socks, no shoes, he crouched in front of one of the bar cabinets, foraging behind a collection of infrequently used liqueurs, clanging bottles, in search of the Pernod. He knew it was there; they'd cooked with it once, something to do with flaming shrimp, a rare evening at home. Stasia had come across a recipe that intrigued her and had wanted to try her hand at a family dinner, so Kav and Bix had joined them, walking the short distance from their respective houses. Kav had raved about the shrimp; Bix had been polite about it. Now Kav was gone, and Bix was holed up at home— with another doctor and another priest.

Coop spotted the dark green bottle and pulled it from the cabinet. As he stood, his knees cracked. He set the bottle on the counter next to a Walgreens bag containing some half dozen flossing devices he'd picked up on his way home on Tuesday but had not yet experimented with. Screwing the cap off the Pernod, he got a strong whiff of licorice and, finding it oddly appealing, took a short swig from the bottle—Emily Post would doubtless not approve, but he was under doctor's orders.

The doctor knew his medicine. Within seconds, the flutter in Coop's stomach had calmed, so he took a glass, poured an inch or so of the bright transparent yellow cordial, and watched it turn, as if by magic, a milky pastel as he added a few ounces of ice water. As he sipped it, the phone rang—unusual, as the land line to the house had a private number that was shared with few outside the family.

It was a security guard calling from Entrada's main gate. "Mr. Brant," he said, "I'm sorry to bother you at such a difficult time, but I thought I should give you a heads-up. A police detective just arrived, asking for directions to your home."

"Is it a woman?"

"Yes, Mr. Brant. A Detective Madera."

Coop had barely hung up and was walking toward the bedroom, intending to change, when the doorbell rang. He set his glass of Pernod on the entry-hall console table and opened the front door. For a long moment, he and Madera just looked at each other, neither saying a word, as the encounter had such bizarre overtones: a day tainted by death, a cop confronting a "person of interest" now in mourning, the unannounced visit, and the unexpected sight of Coop's attire.

Madera was first to speak: "I must say, *you* look none the worse for wear."

Though the comment seemed glib, almost flippant, it carried no hint of cynicism. To the contrary, its tone sounded complimentary. Which left Coop wondering, Did she just look me up and down?

He told her, "If I'd known you were coming, I'd have dressed."

She expelled a light breath of laughter, then immediately cut it short, covering her mouth. "Sorry." She cleared her throat. "May I come in?"

"Certainly." He stepped aside, admitting her. "Stasia's resting. Let's go out back to talk." He took his glass from the console and led her through the house, pausing in the kitchen. "Would you like something to drink?"

She eyed his glass, wrinkling her nose. "What *is* that?"

He explained, then added, "The doctor suggested it. I was ill earlier."

"Hope it helps," she said, "but I'm on duty. No, thanks."

"Iced tea, maybe?"

"Sure."

He poured a tall glass for her, handed it to her with a napkin, and led her to a row of French doors leading out to the pool and terrace. Opening one of the doors, he said, "Make yourself comfortable. I'll be out in a moment."

As soon as she left, he hopped about the kitchen, one leg at a time, removing his white socks. The workout shorts and T-shirt were fine, but the socks made him feel as if he were greeting guests in his underwear. Both he and Stasia had flip-flops tucked away near the back door, as there were times when they'd be caught barefoot at that end of the house while needing to walk outside for something, and the terrace pavers could get unbearably hot under the desert sun. Coop stepped into the thongs, grabbed his drink, and went out to meet Madera.

She sat near the far edge of the terrace, in the shade of a dramatically cantilevered overhang, which framed a vista of the pool, mountains, and sky beyond. She had chosen a grouping of furniture that consisted of two upholstered loveseats facing each other over a low table. A huge red ceramic bowl sat in the middle of the table, filled with odd-sized polished steel spheres that reflected their surroundings like the old-fashioned gazing balls in grandparents' gardens.

Madera wore a pantsuit, stylish but severe, gray with black pinstripes, a far cry from her knockout little black dress at the museum. Next to her on the loveseat's striped cushion sat a small purse. Its flap was partly open, and she had removed a notebook and pen, which were placed on the table. She sipped her iced tea, watching over the rim of the glass as Coop approached from the house. Setting down the tea, she said, "It's truly remarkable."

"Uh, what is?" He sat facing her from the opposite loveseat. He assumed that what she found remarkable was the coincidence that he had now discovered the bodies of two slain family members, his father and his stepson. He thought she was looking for dots to connect. He got a glimpse of a shoulder holster and gunmetal beneath her jacket.

"It's remarkable," she repeated, "the articulation of space, the modulation of mass and void." She sat back for a moment, first studying the house, then allowing the line of the cantilever to lead her eye off to the horizon.

Huh? He shook his head—as if trying to clear cobwebs. *This,* he wondered, *this* from the woman, the crude philistine, who had described his design of Emery headquarters, the crowning achievement of his career, as "arty"?

She added, "It's so restrained, so disciplined. And yet, there's such an exuberance about it—in perfect harmony with the landscape." She sipped her tea again.

Coop slugged his Pernod.

She gave him a curious look. "Well? Can't you say 'thank you'?"

"Thank you," he obliged. Pausing to collect his thoughts, he explained, "Last Thursday at the dedication, you were considerably less enthusiastic about my work. In fact, you were dismissive—and far less eloquent. Which leaves me a bit confused. Just who *is* the real Arcie Madera?"

She flicked a wrist. "I was in cop mode that day."

"And today? I assume this isn't a social call. You've all but accused me of murdering my father, you've been hounding me for DNA, and now you show up at my door the day my stepson is killed."

"My father," she said, as if lost in her own thoughts, "he always used to tell me that harmony was the theme of his art, the *goal* of his art. 'Arcelia,' he'd say to me—and I wasn't even ten yet—he'd say, 'it takes discipline to create joy.' To a kid, that sounded nuts. I mean, fun is fun, right? But growing older, I came to realize he wasn't speaking in riddles. It's *not* a paradox—the discipline of joy, the joy of discipline."

Coop had grown up hearing similar lectures at the knee of his own father, who'd said, "Theater is *work,* Cooper, teamwork of the highest caliber, and it has the most unexpected payoff. The reward for all that effort, all that collective discipline, when you create a momentary reality through an illusion of *effortless-ness*—it's pure magic." But rather than comparing the lessons of childhood with Madera, Coop simply asked her, "Arcelia?"

"Mm-hm." She nodded. "Means 'treasure.'"

"Interesting."

"What?"

"I always assumed 'Arcie' derived from the initials R.C., as if your *real* name was something like . . . oh, maybe Rochelle Cassandra Madera."

"Rochelle!" She laughed. "Then I'd go by Rocky—too butch even for *me.*"

"Then I'm glad you ended up Arcelia." He paused before adding, "It's nice."

"Thanks." Her smile was so demure, it struck Coop as almost coquettish. Was it possible that this pretty, strong-willed deputy of the law found a trace of charm—or even attraction—in the primary suspect in an old murder case gone cold, a case that had sullied her career? She continued, "According to my mother, my father chose the name. He was the one with the poetic streak. If it had been solely up to Mom, I just *might* have been Rocky."

"You said she was a cop? I mean—sorry—a police officer?"

Arcie smirked. "Yes, she was a cop. So they were each a big influence on me."

Her mother's influence was obvious enough, but Coop asked, "Your father?"

Arcie sat back comfortably. "I'm sure it's because of his influence that I've always been attracted to creative men."

"Ah," Coop recalled, "you've said that." Then he ventured, "Like Bruce Rollo."

"Right."

Did she realize, wondered Coop, that her boyfriend also had boyfriends?

Picking up her notebook, getting down to business, she said,

"It probably won't surprise you that when your name came up in relation to your stepson's death this morning, I asked to be assigned to the case. Mind if we review what you told the officers at the scene?"

He blew a breath, not quite a sigh, not quite a whistle, as if settling his thoughts. "It's as clear as it'll ever be. Shoot." The word, as soon as he said it, struck him as inappropriate to the moment. The pinch of Arcie's brow confirmed his gaffe. He rephrased, "Ask anything you'd like."

She ran him through the sequence of events that had begun with their eight-o'clock tee time. Of particular interest was the timing of the series of gunshots heard, as well as the foursome's perception of the distance and direction of the shots. On the basis of the nine-one-one call placed from Coop's phone, which took place within a minute of the discovery, which itself was only a minute or two after the last shot was fired, they concluded that Kavanall met his fate at eight-twenty that morning, an estimate that was deemed accurate within two minutes either way.

"God knows," said Coop, "I'm no expert at this, but my gut impression was that Kav had been shot at very close range, from behind. He was so brightly dressed, it's hard to believe one of the groundskeepers would mistake him for a coot in the brush."

Madera asked, "And when you were in the cart, when all of you heard the last shotgun blast, it was a single shot, correct?"

"Yes, absolutely."

"See, here's the thing." She began paging through her notes. "When the grounds crew goes out to scare off the coots, they routinely go out in threes, which they did this morning, and they always shoot a sequence of three rapid shots, which they also did this morning—they've all given statements corroborating this. What's more, they only shoot blanks, specifically to avoid 'accidents' like this, and when they're finished, they return together to the maintenance office to check in their guns. Consistent with all of this, the maintenance logs show that the three firearms in question were back in the club's gun lockers, locked, before eight-fifteen."

"I assume you'll run ballistics."

"On shotguns? No, that's useless. The lead projectiles that kill a shotgun victim bear no markings from the barrel that fired them. The shot *casing* would, but it wasn't found—that pond is a swamp."

Coop looked her in the eye. "May I ask you a direct question? Are you trying to link this to my father's murder?" He left unspoken the implication that if the two murders were thought linked, the only apparent link would be Coop himself.

With a grin—and the slightest hint of menace—she reminded him, "You've got *enough* on your plate."

"I suppose I should be glad to hear that, given the circumstances."

"Don't kid yourself," she quickly added. "Your father's murder is still an open case, but at the moment, I have no reason to suspect you killed your stepson. For starters, I'm satisfied you were in the golf cart when it happened, so it's obvious you didn't pull the trigger. Could it have somehow been 'arranged'—a setup? Sure. But that gets far more complicated. That forces me to find a motive."

So far, so good, thought Coop. Just let it go at that. The busier she gets with Kavanall's case, the less time she'll have to dig up the past.

Because of these thoughts, or perhaps in spite of them, Coop leaned forward, elbows on knees, and asked his visitor, "Has it crossed your mind that I may be in a position to provide a few insights in that regard?"

"In what regard? Motive?" she asked with an air of indifference, looking up from her notes. But an involuntary arch of her brow betrayed more than a passing interest.

He stood. "Care to, uh . . . take a stroll?"

"All right . . . ," she said, standing, looking confused. "Why?"

He stage-whispered, "Less chance of being heard," then winked.

She rolled her eyes. "Okay, Sherlock, lead the way."

He guided her from the terrace, past the pool, and onto a paved pathway, wide enough for a golf cart, that wound its way through the compound of the three Emery houses. Reflecting on her "Sherlock" comment, Coop realized that his rationalization for the stroll—privacy and secrecy—did carry cloak-and-dagger overtones. What, he wondered, was he getting himself into? And who did he think might possibly overhear the conversation he was about to have? Stasia was in bed, drugged; Bix was likely in no better condition. And they were the very two people who had the greatest interest in bringing Kavanall's killer to justice. Still, Coop had the uneasy feeling that his opening up to Madera could be interpreted as a breach of family propriety.

He had not yet spoken as they ambled through a pass between two high knolls, when the other two homes, Bix's and Kavanall's, came into view. Parked under the porte cochere in front of Bix's house was a dog-grooming van; the air conditioner on its roof whirred in the afternoon stillness as Pyrite, Coop imagined, was pampered within, cleansed of his swamp adventure. Another van was parked at Kavanall's house near the carport that shaded his collection of several vintage roadsters—Thunderbird, Mercedes, Karmann Ghia, and a pristine two-tone pink-and-gray Nash Metropolitan convertible. The van, backed up near the front door, bore the familiar EMERY ENERGY logotype.

Madera asked, "We gonna walk, or we gonna talk?"

"Both," said Coop.

"I'm not good at taking notes while I'm walking."

"Then just listen, okay?" He took a turn on the path that led through open land, away from the houses. "My stepson was not the most likeable of men."

"Did you hate him?"

"Of course not. He didn't deserve to die. *No one* deserves to die that way."

"Someone thought he did." Madera let that observation hang between them for a moment, then continued, as if thinking aloud, "Unless this was some random, senseless killing—and the logistics don't point to that—someone had a reason, an important reason, to pull that trigger. Something substantial was at stake." She turned to Coop. "Any idea what that might be?"

It was now or never. Coop stopped walking. A pair of mockingbirds gabbed from distant palms. Under the arching October sky,

Coop told the detective, "Please understand: it's not my intention to get anyone in trouble."

"Understood. We're just talking theory now. Go on."

"I can think of two reasons why someone might have wanted Kav out of the way. In both instances, the stakes were very high."

"Hmmm." She took out her notebook. "Such as?"

"Kav was flirting with some career decisions. He was growing frustrated with his position at Emery and felt that a promotion as president was long overdue. So he was beginning to weigh two other options. On the one hand, he had an offer from Jay Pontarelli, who was in the foursome this morning, to join a start-up company that would be in direct competition with Emery. Needless to say, Bix didn't care for that idea, so he was considering handing over the president's job to Kav, even though he was clearly not qualified."

"You mentioned *two* options," said Madera.

"I don't know how serious he was—not much, I suspect—but Kav was floating the idea of running for a seat that's opening up in the state senate. Ridiculous, of course. I mean, he had the name recognition, but what else?"

Madera shrugged. "They elected Sonny Bono."

"Point is, no one ever gave Kav much credence, and with good reason, but suddenly, he seemed to have significant options."

"Interesting," said Madera, nodding, "but where are the stakes in all this? What are the motives?"

"I'm getting to that. The motives are linked—or more correctly, they're parallel. Both boil down to competition for Kav's career options. First, Kav got the idea for the senate run from a college friend of his, Clifford Sloan, who's a Palm Springs dentist. Cliff *himself* has been planning to run, and he recruited the Emerys' support. That's when Kav got the me-too idea. It stands to reason that Cliff wouldn't like that."

"Too bad," said Madera. "That's politics. It's a contest—may the best man win."

"Except: Kav's name would probably have given him an unfair advantage, and even more stinging, Kav claimed to have dirt on Cliff from their college days, something that could nip a political career in the bud—and leave Cliff feeling mortally betrayed."

Taking notes rapidly now, Madera asked, "And the *other* motive?"

"The prez-job at Emery. Up till now, Bix has held that title along with all his others, but the older he gets, the more important it becomes not only to fill the position, but to fill it with someone capable of taking over the reins and leading the company. All along, the two men who've felt they were being groomed for president were Kav, on the basis of his bloodline, and Austin Royce, on the basis of a long, loyal, and competent career as Emery's chief financial officer. Austin was supposed to be part of this morning's golf foursome—in fact, he set it up—but then he bowed out yesterday, claiming some urgent family business, and got Jay Pontarelli to fill in for him."

Madera asked, "Austin Royce—did he know Bix was considering Kavanall for the promotion?"

Coop crossed his arms. "Yes."

"And Sloan, the dentist—did he know about Kavanall's political aspirations."

"I myself let it slip, in his office yesterday. I was in for a deep scaling."

Madera looked up from her notes. "Yuck."

"Not as bad as it sounds."

She clicked her pen, closed her notes. "This helps. It's a start."

"Happy to assist. I have nothing to hide."

"Well," she conceded, looking into the sky, watching the slow travel of a jet's vapor trail, "it's not as if *you* had any plans for a senate run."

"Certainly not."

"And it's not as if *you* were in line for the president's job at Emery."

He let that one slide. "I want to emphasize, though, that I have no direct suspicion of either Austin Royce or Clifford Sloan. I know both of them, and they both seem like decent guys—more than decent. My hunch is that each is simply touched by circumstances that, on the surface, might appear to carry a whiff of suspicion."

"We'll look into it," said Madera.

He began leading her along the pathway again, retracing their steps back toward the house. As they passed between the two high berms and arrived on the deck of his and Stasia's swimming pool, he offered, "If you'd care to sit down again, I can get more tea."

"Thanks, but I need to get back."

"If there's nothing else, then, let me walk you to the car." He began leading her around the side of the house to the front.

"Actually," she said, "there is one more thing."

"Yes?" he asked, pacing alongside her.

"You still haven't returned my calls or answered my question: Are you willing to volunteer a DNA sample?"

"Sorry for being so evasive. That's not my style, but frankly, my lawyer advised me to stall you while he looks into it. He seems to have a problem with it."

"And what might that be?"

"Simple. What do I stand to gain?"

"What you stand to gain"—she halted and faced him—"is the clarification of the circumstances surrounding your father's death. You've told me you want it solved, and I'm working on it. DNA provides one of the most objective means to—"

"Objective?" he interrupted. "If you're trying to be objective, if you're not just trying to nail *me* so you can clear *your* record, then why have you gone to the trouble of assigning that undercover goon to tail me at the gym?"

"Ahhh," Madera said wistfully, "paranoia strikes deep."

"I'm not stupid. He's got 'cop' written all over him."

"Really? And what does *that* mean?"

Coop stopped himself. "It's just an instinct."

"Look, Brant, let me make this clear: I *am* an objective investigator. I am *not* prejudging you. I intend to solve both your father's death and your stepson's, wherever the evidence may lead. And I've assigned *no one* to tail you—at the gym or anywhere else. If I were out to nail you, yes, I might've done that. But I haven't."

Coop paused. "Honest?"

"Honest."

They walked the remaining distance to the curb, where she unlocked her car, an unmarked cruiser, a bland tan sedan with black steel wheels and telltale plates inscribed OFFICIAL. She got in, started the engine, and lowered her window while the air conditioning cooled the car. A police radio squawked and chattered. She turned it off.

Standing outside her window, Coop said, "Drive with care. And remember—speed kills."

She directed her gaze out the side window, then up to his face. With a trace of a grin, she told him, "Nice legs, Brant."

"Uh, if you don't mind, Detective, I don't particularly like being called Brant. It seems so—I don't know—militaristic or something."

"Ah, I see. Sorry, *Mr.* Brant."

He hesitated. "Actually, Detective, you're welcome to call me Cooper. Or Coop. Most people call me Coop."

She looked down for a moment, donned a pair of sunglasses, then looked up toward his face again. "All right, Coop. I'll do that."

"Thank you, Detective."

She did not invite him to address her otherwise.

She raised her window, put the car in gear, and drove off.

As both the priest's car and the doctor's were parked nearby, Coop was satisfied that Stasia was still being watched, was still in a pharmaceutical haze, was in no need of his presence at her bedside, so he decided to walk the grounds again, solo, pondering Madera's assurance that she was not setting a DNA trap for him, wondering if she could be trusted. He skirted the pool, passed between the two knolls, and noticed that the groomer's van had left Bix's house. Shifting his gaze to Kavanall's house, he saw the Emery truck still backed up to the front door, and to Coop's surprise, Bix was standing there in the driveway, giving directions to a couple of workers in overalls of bright green, Emery's new corporate color. Bix wore cowboy boots and a bathrobe, holding Pyrite in one arm. The dog, fresh from his spa treatment, sported a silk bow in the tuft above his brow—black ribbon, presumably in mourning for Bix's grandson.

Concerned that Bix should be resting, Coop left the path and walked toward the truck, hailing Bix with a wave from the driveway.

The older man turned. "Howdy, Coops. One hell of a day, huh?" With the back of his free hand, he wiped snot from his upper lip. His eyes were red and puffy.

"Terrible, Bix, just awful." Coop shook his head. "Uh, shouldn't you be in bed?"

"It's the middle of the afternoon. How's Stasia doing?"

"She's in *bed*."

"Oh." He turned to one of the workers, who was wheeling a desk chair out of the house and up a ramp into the truck. "*No*, for Christ's sake, not the chairs—just the desk, the files, the computers."

"Sorry, Mr. Emery." And the mover returned the chair. Another dollied out a file cabinet. Boxes brimming with office paraphernalia were scattered just inside the door.

Coop said, "You shouldn't bother with this, Bix. Stasia will sort through his things later. I'll help her."

"Thanks, Coops, but anything related to the office—that's company property."

In case Coop missed the point, Bix added, "*My* property."

# Chapter 7

At four thousand feet, Pioneertown could get plenty nippy on October evenings, and this promised to be one of those nights. Mimi Miles carried a log in from the porch, thumped the front door closed with her hip, and crossed to the stone fireplace along the back wall of the living room, where she placed the log on a pile of kindling already arranged in the grate. Unlike some of the older homes in Pioneertown, her house had central heating—"all the conveniences," Ferris Brant used to joke—so she rarely bothered building a fire, but this would be a special night.

She had already bathed, but had yet to fix her hair, and her guest would arrive within the hour. Wearing a long robe of fluffy pink chenille, she puttered about the living room in a pair of comfortable old slippers, tidying up, plumping cushions, bending over to finger-comb the fringe of a parti-colored knotted rug. When she stood erect, she pressed her fists into the small of her back, straightening her spine with a stifled grunt of pain. Her next birthday, just a few weeks off, would be her seventy-ninth, and while the years had begun to take their toll—a pill for this, a pill for that—she still radiated a beauty that echoed the past, tempered with a graceful maturity. On balance, she couldn't complain.

It was five or ten minutes past six—the clock centered on the mantel was more decorative than accurate, spinning a porcelain ballerina under a crystal dome. "Okay," she said aloud to no one but herself, "let's do *something* with this damn hair." And she left the room, closing the bedroom door behind her.

In the living room, the ballerina marked time as the light began to fade. The adobe wall to either side of the chimney had been built with whole heavy bottles set into the mortar, creating a random pattern of odd little windows. Their different shapes and colors—green, amber, cobalt, red, clear—produced a crude stained-glass effect as the sun began to slide behind the mountains that marked the edge of the property. Glowing multi-hued puddles of daylight crept across the planks of the floor, across the knotted rug, then paused at the baseboard before climbing the opposite wall.

On the mantel, propped against the stones of the chimney, a collection of framed photographs, most a half-century old, depicted frozen moments from the brief, unlikely career—and lasting loves—of actress Mimi Miles. Black-and-white publicity shots posed on the streets of Pioneertown showed her with Gene Autry, Roy Rogers, Dale Evans, Tom Mix, and a galaxy of other Western greats known more by their roles and costumes than by their names, including early television's Annie Oakley, the Cisco Kid, and Hopalong Cassidy. Prominent among the collection were two color photos. The larger was a glossy of an iconically handsome man in his mid-twenties, Sheriff Rusty Oxhide, played by Ferris Brant, waving his white hat from the saddle of a rearing palomino. The other, smaller by far, a mere snapshot yellowed by years, showed Mimi with a little boy, Cooper Brant at his fifth birthday party, who was clutching a patchwork pony, holding a smile, waiting for the burst of the flashbulb.

As the ballerina twirled, the hands of the moonish clock face suspended in the bell jar dropped modestly to the six-thirty position.

Mimi opened the door and returned to the living room lugging with both arms a sizable corrugated box, perhaps eighteen inches wide, two feet long; its aged and dusty cardboard flaps were folded shut on top. She hauled it to the front door and stooped with difficulty to place it on the floor nearby. It dropped the last two or three inches, landing with a thud that was punctuated with a metallic rattle. Straightening her body again—fists to her back again—she noted that the room was nearly dark, so she flipped a switch near the door that lit several table lamps. The one next to her easy chair had a frilly silk shade and a base resembling a dainty pink vase; the two flanking the small sofa had a Western look, with terra cotta bases and parchment shades wound with rawhide laces at their tops and bottoms.

She was still in her robe, but her hair was now in rollers, wrapped in toilet paper. She stepped to a long mirror with a maple frame sprouting coat hooks, scrutinized her face for a moment, and shrugged. Then she unwrapped her hair and removed the rollers, stuffing the tissue into one of her robe's big patch pockets, the rollers into the other. She shook her hair, then fluffed it with her fingers.

Mimi's hair had always been one of her most striking features, and over the years, its style had changed with the times. In her earlier years, it had been luminously, deeply black; all her life, it had been twisted with a tight natural curl. With shifting fashions, coupled with evolving attitudes toward race, her hairstyles had run a gauntlet of coiffure. Childhood pigtails had given way to bouffants and beehives. She'd worn her hair long and short, up and down—straightened, curled, and waved. For a brief stint in the seventies, it had been teased, frizzed, and forked as an oversize Afro; the eighties had brought an experiment with a severe pageboy style, which she had deemed an abject failure and chopped off, resulting in a recovery period with a brush cut. She had settled now on a medium-short length, worn "up," adding some wave to her curls, a style that bespoke mature dignity. At various times, she had tried dying her hair, but no more—the color had aged to a perfect salt-and-pepper, with the pepper still an inky black, the salt a radiant silver.

Looking in the mirror, Mimi frowned. "Better try a turban."

She left for the bedroom. The ballerina danced. The last winks of sunlight disappeared from the bottles in the wall as dusk turned to night.

When Mimi returned, her hair was not in a turban. She wore a matching skirt and jacket of a dark matronly tweed with a ruffled white blouse, a sparkly broach, and low, sensible pumps. A touch dressy for Pioneertown, perhaps, but this was a special night. She stepped to the middle of the room and turned to glimpse her whole figure in the mirror. "Oh, Christ," she muttered, "I look like the friggin' queen of England."

And she left for the bedroom again. The ballerina danced. The clock's minute hand crept toward the top of the hour.

**A** death in the family always turns lives upside down. Coop already knew this from the experience of both his mother's suicide and his father's murder; the sudden loss of his stepson, Kavanall, was no exception. For a day or two, life stood still and everything else was canceled as a new reality set in and a funeral was planned. Except, this time, the loss was far less personal, and he could remain more objective, even philosophical, about the tragedy. Kavanall was not, after all, his own child, and only a week ago, walking home from dinner at the club on Friday evening, he had been able to admit to his wife, without emotion or consequence, that there were times when he didn't much like Kavanall; she, with absolute candor, had acknowledged having similar feelings.

But Stasia *loved* Kavanall, naturally, as any mother would, so the death of her only child had taken the expected toll, and her pain was intensified by the knowledge that her baby was not only dead, but murdered. In a word, she was numb, and Coop now found that he mourned more for Stasia's grieving than for any loss of his own. This allowed him to be "the strong one," the loving and supporting partner who says the right words and gets things done when all else has ground to a standstill.

The night of the murder, Wednesday, Stasia had slept alone, cocooned in a down comforter and an eddy of barbiturates. Thursday, she had allowed Coop back into their bed, but had been coldly unresponsive to his touch, meant only to express consolation and commiseration. She needed time, of course, to cope with her loss, in her own way. But would she ever be able to forgive him for disliking Kavanall? Which left Coop wondering—seriously, without rancor or peevishness—if they would ever again enjoy, or even want, sex.

On Friday morning, he had considered phoning Mimi to postpone their meeting that night, but he didn't, as the trip to Pioneertown would afford him a brief but welcome respite from a world suddenly consumed with death, grieving, and arrangements. He needed a night off.

So he spent that afternoon at his office catching up at his desk, which, after two days of neglect, required considerable attention before its usual state of order was restored. As the afternoon waned and five o'clock neared, he reconsidered the evening's logistics. Earlier that week, on the phone with Mimi, she had offered to fix supper, and he had declined, saying, "I'll grab something after work, then drive out there around seven." The trip was not a long one, but it would take him into the wilds, and though he had driven it before, it had been many years, and he preferred to arrive before dark. At that time of year, the sun would set before six-fifteen, so he now decided to drive directly from his office to Pioneertown, dine there, and then meet Mimi.

As Coop's black Tesla turned off Interstate 10 and headed north along Route 62, he noted that it was the second time that week he had driven into the valley's surrounding mountains, but the two destinations, both an hour's drive, and the roads leading to them could not have been more different. On Sunday, he and Stasia had traveled the narrow hairpin curves and switchbacks to quaint and cozy Idyllwild—with its pines and jazz festivals and art galleries—perched six thousand feet in the San Jacinto Mountains, bordering the Coachella Valley to the south. This evening, Coop was heading into the high-desert foothills of the San Bernardino Mountains, bordering the valley to the north.

The route was a straight-ahead four-lane highway all the way up to Yucca Valley, where the familiar palms of the desert gave way to otherworldly Joshua trees. From there, he turned northwest on Pioneertown Road, a two-lane blacktop that would take him a few more miles up to four thousand feet. Along the way, the terrain changed markedly as the slopes of craggy, ruddy granite gave way to a vast boulder field where huge white rounded rocks—think Fred Flintsone—littered the landscape and piled into wondrous, prehistoric-looking peaks and mounds. This wasn't trendy, it wasn't chic, it wasn't Idyllwild. No, this was Pioneertown, home to some three hundred souls who remained as keepers of the legend.

The wooden road sign that whisked past Coop's windshield announced, simply, PIONEERTOWN, along with the year 1946. Anyone barreling through might miss the town entirely. The highway was its only paved street; the others were gravel or just the desert's own dirt. There was a roadhouse along the highway, but not much else—split-rail fences corralling horses, a burned-out railroad coach, a smattering of ramshackle trailers, an occasional satellite dish. The area offered a few small motels, plus a dive bar or tavern tucked away here and there.

But the principal point of interest, the town's raison d'être, was a two- or three-block stretch of dirt road running parallel to the highway. Dubbed Mane Street, it had hitching rails, not parking spaces, as no vehicles were allowed, but horses and pedestrians were. It had been built as a living, working movie set during the heyday of the Western, with original investors including Roy Rogers, Bud Abbott, Russell Hayden, and, of all people, gossip columnist Louella Parsons. Mane Street consisted of real buildings, not just façades, which, along with the surrounding terrain, were seen over the years in scores upon scores of movies and television programs. Many of the actors, especially those appearing in serials that were shot day in, day out, had homes in Pioneertown, typically of period design so that the houses could also be used as locations for filming. Mane Street still appeared in the oddball documentary or cable movie, but for the most part it was now simply a tourist attraction, with gunfights staged on weekends for the amusement of kids who never knew the genre and grandparents who did.

As a child, Coop had visited Pioneertown with his mother and watched, as the cameras rolled, his father save Miss Mimi from a bunch of bad guys in black hats—"Strangers in Town," the episode was titled. Shortly after Coop graduated from college, he drove back to Pioneertown to visit Mimi, who continued to live there long after her television days had faded. It would still be several years before Coop figured out what his mother already knew but repressed, and after that, he would see Mimi only once, not speaking, at his father's funeral, where she stood near the back of a throng of mourners.

Now, shortly after six, the sun was setting, casting a glow of rustic sepia over the town as Coop slowed the car, got his bearings, identified Mimi's street, and stopped. He knew of only one restaurant in town, the roadhouse he'd passed, so he turned around and drove back the two blocks to Pappy and Harriet's Pioneertown Palace.

The building had been a one-pump gas station when the town was founded, had later been turned into a cantina, and in the early eighties, long after Coop's last visit, had undergone its ultimate transformation into Pappy and Harriet's, now the destination that made Pioneertown more than a dot on the map. Known throughout the area, the honky-tonk hangout specialized in two things—Tex-Mex cooking, and music—drawing a motley, loyal clientele consisting of bikers, erstwhile hippies, punk rockers, New Age spiritualists, country-and-western types drawn by the local heritage, as well as an assortment of wary tourists and curiosity seekers. It was this latter group, of course, into which Coop firmly fell.

There was no missing the joint, but Coop couldn't tell where the main door was. It didn't seem to be along the main road, or even around the corner, where a few vans were parked, so he ventured into the parking lot behind, taking it slow—a clean black car and gravel not pairing well. He parked, staying clear of a prime section reserved in no uncertain terms for Harleys only.

When he got out of the car, he was immediately struck by the smell of mesquite and charred meat; a large open grill smoked from the other side of a wall of planks. The parking lot led through a kind of courtyard, an outdoor eating area with long tables, to a battered-looking slab of a door that he took to be the entrance. He hesitated before opening it. The whole setting bespoke counterculture, and while it had a reputation for being one of those places where everyone got along, Coop had the qualms of an outsider. He was, after all, something of an artist, but was he counterculture enough for this crowd? In his blazer and corduroys, probably not.

He dashed back to his car, ditched the jacket, returned to the door, and stepped inside.

It was early, so the Friday-night ruck of revelers hadn't settled in yet, but there were a few patrons scattered at the tables and at the bar in the next room. A jukebox played heavy metal, but at a background volume, while that night's band was setting up on a low makeshift stage that was little more than a raised platform. Coop could tell at a glance that he was the only one on the premises not wearing denim or leather. Not wanting to look conspicuously alone at a table, he walked over to the bar and chose one of the stools with a metal tractor seat.

"How's it goin' tonight?" asked the bartender. She was pretty, perhaps thirty, warm, friendly, and heavily tattooed.

"Great, thanks." He felt compelled to explain, "I've, uh, never been here before—heard lots of good things about the place, though."

"Glad to have you." She nodded. "Something to drink?"

He wanted a drink, all right, but this didn't look like a martini place. Besides, he wanted to have his wits about him for his rendezvous with Mimi. He also wanted to be alert and legal for his drive down the mountain later. Feeling like a total wuss, he ordered a diet Coke.

The gal served it in a Mason jar and left him with a menu, giving him a moment to absorb the jumbled milieu.

Nothing matched—not the barstools, not the tables and chairs, not even the strings of Christmas lights that hung from some, but not all, of the ceiling beams. One wall was adorned with a collection of old license plates. Cow skulls were mounted here and there like trophies. Behind the bar was a life-size bust that he learned was none other than Pappy. Among other paraphernalia displayed near the bust was an antique birdcage containing the hands of a skeleton. Another room, beyond the bar, housed several pool tables. But the detail that most captured his interest was the structure of the adobe wall behind him. It had been built with bottles set into the mortar, like odd little stained-glass windows. Multi-hued puddles of daylight crept across the planks of the floor. Where had he seen that before?

"Try the pork chop," said the bartender, noting that Coop's menu was set aside.

"It's good?"

She rolled her eyes heavenward. "It's *amazing*."

"Can't recall ever being amazed by a pork chop. Guess I'd better try it."

She gave him a thumbs-up.

During the meal—and the chop *was* amazing—Coop gabbed

with the bartender, who told him about the many bands that had played there, including some big names in a variety of musical styles. She asked, "Staying for the show tonight?"

"Sorry, can't. I'm meeting someone at seven, an old friend. Mimi Miles."

"Miss Mimi? Awww, such a cutie, what a doll. She's in here all the time—loves her jazz, loves her bourbon."

"Really? Glad to hear she still gets out and around."

While rinsing some glasses, the bartender recalled, "Long before I started working here, they say she always used to come in with Rusty Oxhide—I mean, the guy who played him on TV, remember? Everyone said they were the happiest couple in the world, even though the guy was married—to somebody else. After he died, she still kept coming in, but always, always alone. That could get some women down. But Mimi, well, she's the half-full type, grateful for what she had."

**S**hortly before seven, Coop used the men's room, labeled STUDS—the other, FILLIES—then returned to the bar to sign his check. The bartender told him, "Now that you know where we are, don't be a stranger. We're here every night except Tuesday and Wednesday. So come on back sometime—when you can *drink.*"

"I'll do that," he said with a laugh. While walking to the door, he thought of bringing Stasia next time, as it might get her mind off things, but he couldn't quite imagine her working on a rack of ribs, washing it down with a brewski from a Mason jar.

His musings were nipped as he stepped outside and noticed that the Harleys had arrived, all chrome and saddlebags. And standing in a cluster around his car were the bikers themselves, a half-dozen of them, big guys with beards and shaved heads. They turned as Coop approached, looking exceptionally preppy in a long-sleeved heather-gray cashmere polo.

"Dude!" said one of them, thumbs hooked in his belt. "Is that *electric?*"

"Sure is." Coop slowed his pace, but kept moving closer to the car.

"Far *out*!" said another. "Really hauls ass, huh?"

"Four seconds to sixty."

They all hooted, surrounding Coop and offering high fives, then trundled en masse into Pappy's.

Alone in the parking lot, Coop swaggered—à la John Wayne—the remaining few yards to his roadster.

Once in the car, he lowered the windows, popped a few breath mints, returned to the highway, and drove the couple of blocks to Roy Rogers Road. Most of the town's streets were named after its early luminaries, but Ferris Brant's short TV career didn't warrant the honorific of a namesake gravel road, nor did the supporting role played by Mimi Miles, so she ended up living on another cowboy's drag.

Coop remembered the house as being a few blocks up, near the top of the road, where it ended abruptly at the foot of a mountain. He took the hill slowly, as even Roy Rogers only got pea gravel. And then Coop's headlights fell upon it—Miss Mimi's house. As a child, he'd seen it every Saturday morning. There was no mistaking it, with its pegged-log walls and fat stone chimney. A commodious front porch ran the entire width of the house, with a railing supported by wagon wheels. Geranium vines tumbled from old wooden buckets on the stairs. Lacy-edged tieback curtains framed the little windows, glowing yellow on either side of the iron-hinged plank door.

The night was breezy, and as Coop pulled into Mimi's driveway, his lights caught a dust devil skipping across the gravel. Coop turned off the car, grabbed a box of Godivas from the passenger seat, got out, and set the chocolates on the roof while he shrugged into his blazer, straightened his collar, and brushed the wrinkles from his lap.

The front door opened. "Cooper? My God, it *is* you."

Coop remembered a similar scene every Saturday, when Miss Mimi, a beautiful black woman in her mid-twenties, would appear at her front door, sewing basket or pitcher of milk in hand, beaming an infectious smile. She always wore the same thing—a dress with a big petticoat, a full apron, a frilly bonnet—all in the small screen's varying shades of bluish gray. Now, more than fifty years later, she bore no pitcher of milk, but had the same smile, and tonight she wore a dazzling ensemble in emerald green silk, accented with the tip of a peacock feather that sprouted from the crown of her silvered hair. Though her years were apparent, she had accepted them gracefully, with a spirit and a zest that Coop rarely found in people half her age. He said, "Hello, Mimi. I'm so glad you wrote to me."

She extended her arms, "Come here, honey."

Chocolates in hand, Coop walked the short distance from his car to the porch and into her arms. "I didn't realize how much I've missed you."

"Oh, sweetie." She patted his back.

In the light from the doorway, he held her at arm's length. "You look *wonderful,* but you didn't need to get dolled up for me."

"What, *this*?" she asked with a laugh and a nonchalant wave of her hand. "It's just something I threw on."

Indoors, Coop presented Mimi with the chocolates. "Truffles," she said, "my favorite," while placing them on one of the sofa's end tables. Before settling down to talk, Coop drifted toward the fireplace and the photos propped on the mantel, when he noticed the bottles embedded in the rear wall and realized, Of course, *that's* where I saw them, right here, more than thirty years ago.

As he perused the photos, his attention was caught by the snapshot from his birthday party. Picking up the frame and peering into it, he remembered that many pictures were taken that day, but he couldn't recall having ever seen the prints. He turned to Mimi. "You know, I was thinking about this on Monday night, just before I called you. I loved that patchwork pony—my all-time favorite birthday present."

"Don't tell me you still have it." With a laugh, she sat in her easy chair. Its chintz cushions bore a riotous print of huge pink rhododendrons; their green stems and foliage blended with her dress.

"No," said Coop, also laughing, "the pony disappeared ages ago. I treasured it as a boy, but when I got too old for it, I put it away somewhere. Later, I couldn't find it."

"Wonder what happened to it . . ."

Though her musing required no response, Coop had a theory. He hesitated, then said, "When I went away to school, I think Mom got rid of it."

"Ahhh"—Mimi's head bobbed—"can't say I'd blame Peggy. Under the circumstances, I might've done the same thing. But if you want a new pony, Cooper, I'll try to find you one."

"You'll have a hard time finding one of *those*. You'd have to make it yourself."

"Ha! I could never sew worth a damn."

"You sure had us kids fooled."

"That's why it's called 'acting,' honey." She whirled one arm in a lavish Shakespearean gesture, rattling her bracelets.

Coop set down the photo, moved to the sofa, and sat facing Mimi. "Dad had such a love for theater—and such a respect for its lessons. He used to tell me, 'Own your lines, check your props, keep your focus.' Even during his academic years, he used to rehearse his lectures, almost obsessively. He would tape-record himself, reworking every line, till he felt the delivery was perfect. I understand that a kids' TV Western isn't high art, but he knew how to capture an audience. I'm surprised he gave up acting."

"A lot of people were." Mimi rested her hands in her lap. "That series could have run *years* longer, but when Ferris quit the role and headed back to grad school, the show fell apart, and that was that. He struggled with the decision, but I encouraged him, even though it meant the end of a good gig. He was brilliant, of course, and we all knew it. His love of acting was surpassed only by his love of hard science, and I mean *hard*. He told me that during college, he'd split those affections, and after graduating, he needed some time to find his true direction, his true passion. Turned out, he was in the right place at the right time for early TV. He had plenty of contacts from his acting days in school, and he just breezed into the role of Rusty Oxhide. But he never saw the series as a career. It was a lark—and a chance to bankroll some serious cash that would allow him to go back to school and work straight through his Ph.D., all while comfortably supporting his young family. Which he did. There was *nothing* that man couldn't do when he set his mind to it. And the Nobel Prize proved it."

Coop had sat listening with his arms crossed and his head lowered in thought. He looked up. "That's the first explanation I've ever heard that makes any sense at all. Thank you, Mimi."

"Don't mention it, honey." Dramatically, somewhat ominously, she added, "I'm the keeper of secrets, Crone of the Wild Frontier."

He chortled. "Then tell me, O Wise One: Why didn't Dad help set you up in another series? You were young. You had a huge following. Just because *he* ditched acting, you didn't need to."

Mimi waved both hands, fending off the question. "I'm happy here. *We* were happy here. Yes, it was an arrangement, and he led a double life. Forgive me for saying this, but your mother made it far too easy for us. She was content living on the coast and had no interest in raising you anywhere else. Even after you were grown, she found excuses not to follow Ferris out to Riverside, where his academic career was established by then. So the two households, they were really her doing, and it was an easy midweek trip for him from Riverside to Pioneertown while school was in session. Still, I always felt guilty that his time with me was stolen from you and your mother. But never doubt it, Cooper—he loved you more than life itself."

Time passed quickly—the ballerina danced—as Coop and Mimi continued to reminisce. At one point, she suggested, "Let's open the Godivas." Coop, still tasting the pork chop, readily agreed. She offered, "How about a drink? Brandy's good with chocolate."

He was tempted, but wavered, then asked, "By any chance, do you have some milk?"

"Good *boy*," she said, rising and walking toward the kitchen. On the way, she turned back, asking, "Mind lighting the fire, Cooper? Getting kinda chilly."

When she returned, bearing a tall glass of milk and a short glass of bourbon, Coop had removed his blazer and was crouched at the hearth, leaning in to fan the flames.

"Hoo-hoo!" she said, eyeing his backside. "You have grown into one *fine* specimen of a man. Have you been working out?"

He stood, feeling self-conscious. "As a m'matter of fact, I have."

"Well, whatever you're doing, honey—keep it up." She handed him the milk, studied his face for a moment, and smiled. "No kidding," she said softly, "you're every inch your father's son."

A casual listener might have found her words cliché, but when Coop heard them, they represented something of a watershed moment. He had never felt he had even begun to measure up to his father. And yet, in Mimi's eyes—in the eyes of his father's mistress—he had.

With milk and chocolates and bourbon, they continued sharing memories, but at one point, Mimi made a halting gesture and said, "Enough of the past—tell me about *your* life, your new family, your new wife. Pretty? I'll just bet!"

And Coop realized that Mimi had not heard the news of Kavanall's death two days earlier. When he told her about it—a sanitized version involving a "golfing accident" and no shotgun blasts to the head—she stepped over to the sofa and sat next to him, holding one of his hands, offering condolences.

"The funeral's tomorrow," he said. "I'm doing fine now, but I'm worried about Stasia. She doesn't even seem to want me around the house." Let alone the bedroom, he thought.

"Oh, the poor dear," said Mimi, patting Coop's hand. And they sat for a moment in respectful silence.

While Mimi had intended to shift their focus from the past to the present, the death in the present brought to mind a death in the past that had devastated both of them. After a long pause, Coop pulled a knee up onto the cushion, turning on the sofa to face Mimi. "When Dad was killed," he said, "how did you learn about it?"

She breathed a heavy sigh. "On the news. It was on TV. I was watching for it. I knew something was wrong."

"You mean you . . . *sensed* it, like a vibe?"

"No. I *knew* something had happened. I didn't see him on weekends very often; he usually went back to Santa Barbara, even after your mother died. But that Easter weekend, he stayed in Riverside, getting ready for the big presentation he was going to make on Sunday at the school. That Friday night, he drove over to see me. We had dinner, spent the night together, and when he left on Saturday morning, he said he'd stop by again late that night. It was going to be a quick visit, not overnight, because he had to get back for the Sunday-morning meeting. God, he'd been talking about that for *months*. So I fixed a late supper for us here at home, which was rare. When he didn't show up—and never called—I was sure something was wrong." She paused, suppressing a memory. "When I finally heard what happened . . ." But she couldn't finish.

For Coop, there could be no suppressing the memory, which rushed back at him—finding his father's office door open that morning, finding his father's body slumped in the chair behind his desk, finding the marks of strangulation on his neck, circled by an odd pattern of puncture wounds. A crown of thorns, he thought.

He asked Mimi, "Why all that back-and-forth on Saturday? That's a lot of driving. Why didn't he just stay with you that day?"

"He said he had an appointment that evening, and he didn't want to miss it."

With a quizzical look, Coop asked, "An appointment? On Saturday evening? Strange—what was that about?" And why, wondered Coop, had such a significant detail not previously surfaced?

"He didn't say, and I didn't ask—because I thought it involved one of his grad students. Well, a former student. Catch my drift?"

Coop shook his head, befuddled. "No."

Mimi gave him a look.

"Huh?" Coop recoiled into the corner of the sofa. "I knew for a long time that my father was cheating on his wife, but do you mean to tell me he also cheated on his mistress—with his *students*?"

"Well"—Mimi primped her hair—"I don't know that I'd phrase it *quite* that way, but remember, he was something of a god in that department."

"Jesus."

Mimi stood. "Oh, don't be such a prude."

Coop gave *her* a look.

She strolled to the fireplace, swirling her bourbon, recalling,

"All he said that morning, that Saturday, was that he was meeting in the evening with someone from Emery Oil. I assumed it had something to do with his . . . you know, the gizmo."

Stunned, Coop sat agape, asking only, "Emery?"

With a little laugh, she said, "Funny, huh? So when I saw that *you* were working there now, I thought, My, my, my, it must be one big happy family over there."

"That's one way of putting it."

"Anyway, there was a gal in his classes—real brainy, I guess—who he helped land a job at Emery, so I was just putting two and two together."

"Uh," said Coop, dancing his fingers on his knees, "do you happen to recall her name? Tessa, maybe? Tessa Irwin?"

"You know," said Mimi, finger to chin, nodding, "it's been a while, but that name *does* ring a bell."

Coop stood. "And you never talked to the *police*?"

"Oh, sure. They came snooping around right away—seems lots of people knew about me, even though Ferris thought it was this big secret. Did you say something at your mother's funeral? Anyway, the police drove out here and asked lots of questions, but I didn't tell them anything."

"Why *not*?"

"Didn't like the cop. It was a woman. She was way too big for her britches." Mimi slugged the last of her bourbon and set the glass on the mantel.

"Was it perhaps a Detective Madera?"

"Don't recall. But, yeah, it was a name like that—Spanish, Mexican, whatever."

At a loss for words, Coop stammered, "Would you, uh, care for another truffle?"

"No, honey, too late—they'll have me up all night as it is. But *thank* you for bringing them. You were always such a sweetheart." She stepped over and kissed his cheek, then stood back, snapping a finger. "Almost forgot. I've got something for *you* tonight, too. It's not all wrapped up in gold foil and fancy ribbons, but I'd like you to have it." She gestured toward the battered cardboard box near the door.

"For me?" he asked warily, eyeing the grody gift. "What is it?"

She laughed. "I'm not *sure*, exactly, but it's something to re-member your father by. He left it with me on that last morning I saw him. He was going to pick it up again later that night, so I assumed he needed it for Sunday morning."

Coop knelt on the floor next to the box, fingering its folded flaps. "If he needed it back at school, why leave it *here* Saturday?"

"He didn't say; I didn't ask. Ferris had his own way of doing things."

"That's for sure." Coop began unfolding the four flaps, cough-ing at the dust they raised. When he saw inside, he said, barely above a whisper, "I don't believe it."

"That was my reaction," said Mimi. "When he didn't show up, I took a look and thought, Jesus, that must be the gizmo."

The MacGuffin, thought Coop. He said, "The prototype."

"Yeah, the prototype," she said with an air of excitement. Then, deflating, she added, "But it's not. It's just an old office thing—a copier or whatever."

"Could you give me a hand with this?" Coop reached in to pull the device out of the box. It was a snug fit, and Mimi helped slide the box free from the bottom as Coop lifted from above. "There," he said, standing, setting the machine on the coffee table. Its streamlined shape roughly resembled that of an old Toastmaster toaster, but with its dimensions more than doubled. Rather than a chrome finish, it sported the gray-green enamel of mid-century steel office furniture. Sprouting from its narrower sides were a hand crank and an assortment of knobs and dials. Its two broader sides were hinged from the bottom, opening like clamshells that served as feeder trays for paper, in and out. In the base of the machine was a shallow metal drawer.

Mimi said, "I think it's a Ditto machine—like they used to use in schools."

"It's a mimeograph," said Coop, confounded. He slid the drawer open, saw several blank stencils and a squeegee stored there, then slid the door closed again. With the paper trays open, the machine's ink drum and printing screen were exposed. Coop tried turning the crank, but with years of neglect, the screen had turned brittle. "One thing's for sure," he said, scratching behind an ear. "That's not the water engine."

"It's a damn piece of junk," said Mimi.

Then she added, sweetly, "But I thought you'd like to have it."

Coop wasn't even sure it would fit in the Tesla, but it did, just barely—the box crunched as he forced the trunk closed. The evening had run longer than he'd expected, and it was nearly midnight before he wrapped up his reunion with Mimi, promised to stay in touch, kissed her good-bye, and departed for home.

In the dark, the route had a beauty different from the curious aesthetics of the scenery he'd noted while driving up before sunset. The cartoonish boulders, the ancient Joshua trees, the ever-changing mountain silhouettes, all were now lost in inky blackness beyond the bright cones fanning out from his headlights. Now, in the dark, the beauty of his drive sprang not from the landscape, but from the sky. Overhead, in the night, beyond the cool, thin air that barely clung to the ashen sands of the high desert, sparkled a winsome display of stars and galaxies, impossibly radiant, like some naive depiction of a mythical midnight in Bethlehem.

Then, at last, the roadway curved to reveal—ahead, through the windshield—the lights of the valley below. Coop swallowed; his ears popped. And soon, there he was, back again on the valley floor, ramping onto I-10, then off again, gliding into Palm Springs.

Entering the north end of town, he gradually decreased his speed, tamping the elation of his sprint through the wilds, cruising past several stoplights that he willed to stay green. But the next one caught him, and he braked to a stop at the crosswalk.

Though it was late, it was Friday, and the neighborhood was busy. On the corner was Tantrum, one of the area's most popular gay bars, and as the witching hour drew nigh, its patrons were pairing off, heading to their cars, ready for adventures in the wee of the night.

Coop's light was about to turn green, but just before his foot left the brake, another pair of guys sauntered into the crosswalk and passed his car. Framed in his windshield, unmistakable in the glare of his headlights, were two familiar faces. Dennis Dill, the former porn star who'd had the shouting match with the bruiser at the gym, was walking hip to hip with Bruce Rollo, the famed glass artist.

What, wondered Coop, was Arcie Madera doing at that moment?

Clearly, she wasn't doing it with Rollo.

# Chapter 8

**K**avanall hadn't set foot in a church for years, and Stasia seemed indifferent to the faith of her upbringing, especially since her long-ago divorce, attending church sometimes on Christmas Eve, rarely on Easter. Bix, however, remained a true believer, at least in name, and insisted that his grandson be buried with the full Catholic shebang. Given the circumstances of Kav's death, there could be no open casket, but the arrangements nonetheless called for a "viewing" of the white-draped coffin early Saturday morning at the funeral home, which included a receiving line for the family and the recitation of a rosary, followed by a requiem Mass at the church, replete with choir and incense, and finally the interment itself at Desert Memorial Park, just outside Palm Springs. Like a three-act opera, it would consume half the day.

Some of the mourners appeared at one installment or another, disappearing during the intervening motorcades, but Coop was present for the whole production, propping up Stasia and acting as a buffer between her and her first husband, Keith Follett, who was Kavanall's father. Stasia would have preferred not to speak to him at all—their marriage had "ended badly," she always said, putting finger-quotes around the phrase and refusing to elaborate—but in the interest of civility, their interaction at the untimely funeral of their sole offspring could not be avoided.

Which fascinated Coop. In his ten years of marriage to Stasia, he had never met Keith, had never even seen a picture. Though he rarely thought about Keith, when he did, he simply imagined him as an older version of Kavanall—willowy and effete, with crocodile loafers. At the viewing, however, when Keith introduced himself, offering his business card, Coop was surprised to discover that Keith bore little resemblance to his son. Well into his sixties, a banking executive nearing retirement, he was husky, almost portly, with close-cropped white hair and a mousy, much younger, second wife. In dress, manner, and speech, he was thoroughly unremarkable.

More surprising still, Keith bore no resemblance to Coop himself. Though Coop had never thought about it, he realized now that at some level, subliminally, he had presumed Stasia would be consistently attracted to the same type of man. But because she had married two men so utterly different, Coop was forced to wonder, If she had fallen in love with Keith, what could she possibly have seen in me?

Or, Coop also wondered, were his musings merely skewed that day by the sober dynamics of a funeral?

The viewing was tedious.

The church service was a blur.

But when the funeral party finally moved to the cemetery for the burial, Coop's mind seemed to clear, and his perception of those attending came into sharper focus—perhaps he had simply needed some fresh air. It was an early afternoon in October, a glorious day in the desert, the sort of weather that often convinced visitors to pack up and move there.

In stark contrast to the serene setting, of course, was the purpose of their gathering. A man had been killed in his prime—ruthlessly and for unknown motives—and his remains would soon be placed in the earth near those of his grandmother, Emma Emery, who had died when he was a teen, still in high school. The day she was buried, thought Coop, Kavanall would surely have been here, likely standing where I am standing now. Had that been Kavanall's first funeral, a young man's introductory glimpse at the other end of life?

At the graveside stood the priest, wearing a black cassock and lacy surplice; four acolytes (colloquially known as altar boys, but two of them were girls), one of them swaying the long chains of a censer; and six pallbearers who stood at attention, waiting to be cued to perform their last duty of the day. The only one Coop recognized was Clifford Sloan, Kav's friend, the dentist. Which forced Coop to wonder if Kavanall even *had* other friends; he could think of no others. And if Cliff had been not only Kav's best friend, but his only friend, Kav had proved how little the relationship meant by scheming to trample over his college pal's budding political aspirations.

The eulogizing and memorial speeches had taken place in church, giving the mourners a more personalized sense of who had died, but the liturgy of interment was relatively brief and strictly by the book, with the priest mechanically inserting the name of the deceased into the scripted rite, read with all the zeal of recipes recited from a cookbook: "your faithful servant, Kavanall" . . . "we beseech you to welcome Kavanall into the company of the saints" . . . "Kavanall's heavenly home" . . . and on and on.

Unseen, hiding in the branches of the cemetery's surrounding wall of tamarisks, mockingbirds laughed and gabbed.

Pyrite lolled in Bix's arms, looking up, doe-eyed, as the old man sniffled. Bix had always doted on Kavanall, but Coop suspected Bix's outpouring of generosity was motivated not so much by grandfatherly love as by his obsession with the bloodline and its perpetuation. Did Bix now blame himself, as well as Stasia, for having failed to follow the "heir and a spare" strategy?

Stasia hung on to Coop's arm as if fearing she might slide into the hole. She listened to the prayers with a blank but hard expression, a steely resolve to cry no more. Her determination, however, proved fragile, as she heaved at every mention of Kav's name.

The burial site was situated in such a way that the immediate family stood near the priest, facing the other mourners, who congregated on the opposite side of the grave. Coop found himself easily distracted from the priest's recitation, which struck him as wishful gibberish; while most other heads were bowed, he openly took stock of those who had sacrificed a shank of their Saturday to be there.

It came as no surprise that most of them were Emery staffers. Coop wasn't sure how many of Kavanall's coworkers thought of him with much affection—few, he suspected—but since Bix was there, by golly, so were they. Most of them were just faces in the crowd, like paid extras, shills, but two of them took special interest in seeing Kav laid to rest.

Back from tending to the family emergency that had prevented him from participating in Wednesday's fateful golf outing, Austin

Royce stood at the front of those gathered on the far side of the grave. As second in command at Emery, he had long lived with the uncertainty of what corporate changes might be precipitated by a death in the Emery family, but he had surely never dreamed that the Emery to exit first would be Kavanall, not Bix. In terms of Austin's prospects, this changed everything. As far as he knew, Bix had been considering only two people, himself and Kavanall, as candidates for promotion to the unfilled president's position. Coop now watched as Austin stood square-shouldered, head bowed, a poster-perfect model of dignity in grief. He was looking very presidential—like a man who knew he was sitting pretty.

Also from Emery, but standing a few rows back, was Tessa Irwin, the Emery researcher who had been fending off advances from Kavanall, an annoyance that would happen no more. Now, however, Coop saw Tessa in a different context altogether, having learned the prior evening that her devotion to his father had been more than that of a fawning grad student; she'd been bedazzled by more than his Nobel Prize. That morning she wore a simple dark dress, navy blue, with its well-tailored skirt falling just below the knees; it was the first time Coop had ever seen her not wearing a white lab coat. No question, she was a highly attractive woman, even on this grim occasion, and Coop could only imagine what she must have looked like while attending his father's seminars, when she was in her twenties. He marveled at his dad's appetites, which had transcended not only marriage vows, not only race, but also, apparently, the usual bounds of the generational divide; he would have been some forty years Tessa's senior. The term *horny old goat* sprang to mind.

". . . life everlasting," said the priest.

Another, smaller, contingent of mourners was not in the employ of Emery Energy, but associated with the company through its business and social connections. Many of these faces were familiar from the valley's robust charity circuit, for whom an A-list funeral was as much of a draw as a black-tie fund-raising gala. Photographers were present, at a discreet distance, and the moneyed mavens of culture could in fact expect to find their somber but nicely preserved faces in photos tiling the society pages in upcoming editions of the *Desert Sun* and *Palm Springs Life*. Some of these people were so familiar that their presence had become unremarkable and, God forbid, common—the antithetical consequence of the exposure they sought—but two of the luminaries from the business sector caught Coop's attention.

Garrick Bates, the software titan and founder of the arts college bearing his name, stood near the front in a pose of respectful meditation while the priest prayed on. A week earlier, at the museum opening, Bates had been lobbying to add Stasia's name—her maiden name—to the college board's letterhead. He was one of the few corporate giants in the valley whose wealth surpassed that of the Emery clan, but there were some things money couldn't buy, and the Emerys had something Bates wanted. So there he stood.

And within a few feet of him stood Jay Pontarelli, who had been in the golf cart with Coop when Kavanall was killed. Coop had never liked Jay, period. He was a blowhard, but a smart investor with an entrepreneurial spirit who had set his sights on competing with the Emery dynasty, stealing its only progeny, and rewriting the script of alternative-energy development. His audacious plan to launch newco—PontaPower, with Kavanall Emery Follet displayed front and center in the executive suite—was a scheme just big enough, a strategy just brazen enough, that it might have actually succeeded. To Coop's mind, Jay was simply bad news, and his instincts told him that Jay was somehow involved with what had happened to Kavanall. But that didn't add up, as Kav's death did not appear to be in Jay's interest. Still, thought Coop, appearances can be deceiving.

The priest said, ". . . with the angels and saints in perpetual light."

As the priest droned on, Coop's eyes continued to scan the crowd, skipping from face to face, working from the front rows to the rear, recognizing some but pausing to consider none of them until spotting, in the back, Teddy Duncan, his trainer.

Seeing him, Coop recalled his recent sessions at the gym and then instinctively, furtively surveyed the entire assembly for any sign of the bruiser in khaki, but he was nowhere. Standing next to Teddy, though, was his partner, Rob Pollard, whom Coop had met only once, at the prior Saturday's museum event. Coop felt himself smiling, as if to telegraph a greeting to the guys, thanking them for being there; he could have sworn Teddy returned the smile. Of everyone at the service whom Coop had considered, Teddy and Rob were the only ones there without obligation or motive, whose sole purpose was to express friendship and support. They both had worked with Stasia—Teddy in the gym, Rob in the local art scene—and they both adored her. Coop realized at that moment, with a measure of surprise, that he had come to think of Teddy as not only his trainer, not only his confidant, but just possibly, even though they rarely socialized, his best friend. Coop was certain Teddy had canceled Saturday sessions in order to be at the cemetery, so he was not just surrendering part of his weekend to a dreary chore; he was missing work.

Someone *not* missing work that early afternoon was Arcie Madera, also at the back of the crowd. Wearing dark, round glasses—the type in vogue among the Tonton Macoutes—she was not only in cop mode, but in bad-cop mode. Coop wondered, Are her eyes shifting behind those blackened lenses? Is she picking through the mourners, as I am, questioning whether Kavanall's killer might be among us?

And standing next to her, taller by a head, was Bruce Rollo, the glass sculptor who had not warmed her bed the prior night.

The priest concluded, ". . . through Christ, our Lord."

Some in the crowd said, "Amen," making the sign of the cross; most didn't.

The casket had been suspended over the grave on a geared contraption, and the pallbearers now surrounded it as Kavanall's remains descended into the vault. The priest recited another verse or two, sprinkling holy water with an aspergillum. Incense wafted. When the contraption was removed, the hole was covered with a rug of artificial turf, representing burial; the dirty work would be handled later by groundskeepers.

With the ritual complete, the mourners began to mingle and disperse. Some had been invited to a luncheon at the Regal Palms Hotel back in Rancho Mirage, but most would simply return to their suspended weekend activities. Bix slipped the priest a wad of bills, peeling off a few for the altar kids as well; he carried only hundreds, "smashers," as he called them. Keith Follet, father of the deceased, walked off with his young wife, saying not a word. Odd, thought Coop, though Stasia was doubtless relieved.

Floral arrangements, all white, surrounded the grave. Coop stepped forward with Stasia as she plucked a single rose, kissed it, and dropped it on the turf rug, a last farewell to her son. Then she plucked another rose, placed it in her purse, and snapped it shut with a resolute click.

Bix stepped forward, set Pyrite on the ground, dried a last tear, and followed Stasia's example of tossing a rose on the grave. He plucked a second and set it on his wife's grave, nearby. Turning to his daughter, he said, "Tough day, sweetheart. I'm so sorry," and kissed her. "Coops," he added, resting a hand on his son-in-law's shoulder, "we couldn't have gotten through this without you. Thank you, Coops—thanks for your strength." Then he fussed for a few moments collecting a neat little bouquet. Calling Pyrite, he said, "Let's go visit Frank."

Cliff Sloan left the ranks of the pallbearers and stepped over to Stasia, offering a hug and condolences; she thanked him for taking part. He then asked Cooper, aside, "Gums doing okay?"

"Think so. Hope so."

"Don't forget—call for a follow-up this week. I just want to take a quick look."

"Will do. Thanks, Cliff."

Teddy and Rob had made their way up from the back of the crowd; a few yards behind them, Coop noticed, were Arcie Madera and Bruce Rollo, getting near. Teddy and Rob embraced Stasia in a three-way hug, and her spirits seemed to lift a bit. She managed a smile, which Coop hadn't seen in three days. He told the guys, "Great to see you. Thanks so much for coming."

Teddy gripped his shoulders and looked him in the eye. "Are you doing all right?"

Coop nodded. "Yeah. It's a day-by-day thing. Sorry my schedule has been so screwed up."

"Hey. No problem. Really. Whenever you want to get back to

the routine, I'm ready for you."

As Coop gave a nod of thanks, Arcie Madera approached, followed by Bruce Rollo. Stepping close to Coop, she removed her sunglasses, saying, "It occurred to me that when I saw you Wednesday afternoon, I didn't get around to expressing my condolences. Sorry to be so thoughtless—and I'm sorry for your loss."

"Thank you, Detective, I understand. You were working that day. Today as well. And believe it or not, I appreciate it. So does Stasia."

Stasia, hearing her name, turned briefly to acknowledge the detective, then returned to her conversation with Teddy and Rob. Bruce Rollo joined them—more hugs and smiles.

Tentatively, Coop told his wife, "Seems you're in good hands for the moment. Do you mind if I step away to have a word with the detective?"

"Not at all, sweets. I'm fine."

Coop said, "Detective?" and gestured in the direction of the outdoor chapel, near the center of the grounds.

After walking some distance from the grave together, Madera said, "I noticed you weren't paying much attention to the service."

"I had other things on my mind. Besides, I'm not too keen on religion."

They walked a bit farther. She said, "I know what you mean. I lost it years ago."

"I never really had it. I was raised Unitarian. Not sure that counts." As they neared the chapel, he added, "I love churches, though. I mean, the buildings—talk about theatrics."

"Hmm." She paused, studying the chapel for a moment. "They are kind of similar, aren't they—churches and theaters? Have you ever designed one?"

"Neither. But I hope to, someday."

"You should. You'd be good at it." Then her smile dropped as her tone changed. "Mind if we talk some business, Mr. Brant?"

"Uh-uh-uh," he corrected her, "it's Coop."

She sat on a low wall at the perimeter of the open-air chapel. "All right, *Coop*."

He sat facing her, straddling the wall, about a yard away. "I assume you were watching the crowd today. I was too."

She nodded.

He asked, "Did you come to any conclusions?"

"Did you see me arrest anyone?" She grinned.

A roadrunner leapt onto the wall, saw them, and darted off.

Madera continued, "Based on our conversation Wednesday, I'm following up with Austin Royce and Cliff Sloan. I met with Royce yesterday; he was helpful, but—I don't know—there's something he'd rather not tell me. I'm still trying to sort it out. As for Sloan, I've got interviews scheduled early in the week."

"He was here this morning, one of the pallbearers."

"Ah. I wondered."

Coop leaned toward her, cocking his head. "I understand you've been to Pioneertown."

She gave him a quizzical look. "Sure, Pappy and Harriet's a few times. Who . . . ?"

He shook his head. "Fifteen years ago. Miss Mimi Miles."

Madera crossed her ankles, recalling, "Your father's, uh . . . friend."

"Yes. I decided it was time to do a little investigating of my own, so I paid her a visit last night."

Stiffly, Madera asked, "Oh, really?" Then she laughed. "Well, I certainly hope you found her more cooperative than I did."

"I did. Mimi likes me." Coop grinned. "But she didn't like you."

"*What?* She said that?"

"Not exactly, but she said you were too big for your britches. Purely in the spirit of camaraderie, I was tempted to agree with her—but I refrained."

Through pinched lips, Madera muttered, "Thank you."

"So I loosened her up with Godivas and bourbon. And guess what—she told *me* a few choice details she never shared with you."

"If you're trying to pique my interest, you've succeeded."

Coop continued, "Does the name Tessa Irwin mean anything to you?"

"In fact, it does. Talking to some people at Emery, I learned that

Kavanall was pursuing her to the point of harassment. I spoke with her by phone briefly, and I'm going to meet her Monday afternoon." Madera paused, confused. "Mimi Miles told you *that*?"

"No, Detective." Coop stood. With hands folded behind him, he paced a few steps back and forth in front of Madera, recounting, "On the day my father died, he told Mimi—and you may want to make note of this, Detective—he told Mimi that he had an important meeting that night with—and I quote—'someone from Emery.'"

"*Huh?*" Madera sat in stunned silence for a moment, then fumbled to find a pen and open her notebook.

"Not only that, but Mimi also relayed her suspicion that the meeting was with none other than Tessa, who'd been one of his grad students." Coop stopped pacing and looked Madera in the eye. "It seems Dad was boinking her."

"Why, that old goat."

"My thought exactly."

Madera tossed her arms. "This is *breakthrough* information. And you mean to tell me Mimi withheld it because she didn't *like* me?"

"Well"—Coop shrugged—"you were new on the job." He paused before adding, under his breath, "And you did come on awfully strong."

"Oh, Christ," she whined, looking up into the fronds of a palm. "Maybe I did."

Coop made a halting gesture. "Now, don't get me wrong. I'm not accusing Tessa of anything, and neither did Mimi. The Tessa angle was pure speculation, but my father did say he was meeting *someone* that night—someone from Emery."

Madera stood, collecting her thoughts, paging to the front of her notebook. "The coroner established that Ferris had been dead at least eight hours by the time police responded on Sunday morning, so we know he was killed late Saturday. You were busy tearing up the office when we arrived. There was no way of telling how long you'd been there, and no one could corroborate your alibi."

"Don't remind me," said Coop. "But as I've explained countless times before, a big project was due, and I was working late at my office Saturday night—alone."

"I wonder if Tessa will remember what *she* was doing that night."

"We have good reason to believe she was involved with my father, so news of his death surely had an impact. Even if she wasn't with him that night, she should still be able to piece together her whereabouts."

"Good point," agreed Madera. "Now, help me with this: If your father was meeting someone from Emery that night, who besides Tessa might it have been? I'm not familiar with the workings of the company, but you are."

"How handy for you." Coop sat again, thinking aloud, "Let's see. Dad had announced he'd discovered the secret to clean energy, and though everyone was skeptical, everyone was plenty interested. If he'd scheduled a meeting with someone from Emery that night, stands to reason it related to his claimed discovery. Tessa was on Emery's research team, as she is now, and she'd been a student of my father's, possibly more, so that's an obvious connection. But she was the junior member of the team then, so the meeting could've involved higher research brass; I have no idea who that might've been. At the corporate level, there's been a good deal of shuffling over the years, but at least one higher-up has remained constant—Austin Royce has been in the front office for more than twenty years. Another top exec who comes to mind is Kavanall, but at the time of Dad's death, he was still in college, three thousand miles away. As for anyone else, I need to plead ignorance, since I had no connection to the company in those days; I didn't get involved with Stasia till five years later."

Taking notes, Madera said, "Interesting." She looked up. "What about Bix?"

"What about him?"

"Could the meeting have been with him?"

"No," Coop said flatly. "Bix has 'people.' He may run the show, but he doesn't run errands like that."

"Think he *sent* someone?"

Coop shook his head. "I can't imagine that. Today, Emery is suddenly on the alternative-energy bandwagon, but back then,

Emery was oil, period. If anyone from the company had an interest in my father's research, they were working behind Bix's back.
Had he known, he would've considered it treachery, or at least
disloyalty—he can get crazy about stuff like that."

"Okay," said Madera, ticking through her notes, "I need to follow up with Tessa Irwin, Austin Royce, and Cliff Sloan."

Coop hesitated, but asked, "Have you talked to Jay Pontarelli?"

"He was in the golf foursome. He gave a statement. Why?"

Coop stood, shoved his hands into the pockets of his black
corduroys, and thought hard for an answer. "It's just instinct, I
guess. I can't find the logic, but I think Jay is wound up in this."

Madera studied Coop for a moment. "Then I'd better talk to
him." She added Pontarelli to her list.

Coop asked wryly. "Will you be talking to Mimi?"

"Yeah, seems I'm due for a follow-up visit—fifteen years later.
I'll need to get a statement regarding what your father told her
that weekend."

Gently, Coop advised, "Don't confront her. Don't challenge her.
She's one of the sweetest people in the world. Just be nice."

"Got it."

"Take her some chocolates; truffles are her favorite. And I'll
phone in advance to tell her . . . to tell her that you're . . . not so
bad."

Madera nodded, cleared her throat. "Thank you, Coop. That's
very helpful. Actually, this is *all* very helpful." She repeated,
"Thank you."

"Don't mention it, Detective."

"Coop?" She busied herself with her notes, not looking at him
while saying, "Maybe you should just call me Arcie."

Cars were now filing out of the cemetery in a slow but steady
stream. As Coop and Arcie left the chapel grounds to rejoin what
was left of the crowd, Tessa crossed their path, returning to her
car. She stopped to tell Coop, "I'm so sorry for your loss. It must
be just *awful* for Stasia. My thoughts are with both of you."

He thanked her, then said, "I don't believe you've met Detective
Arcie Madera. She's investigating what happened."

"Oh," Tessa said brightly, "we've talked on the phone. It's a pleasure, Detective." And she shook Arcie's hand, all smiles, woman to woman. "Not sure if I can be of any help, but I'll try. I'm making a big presentation at headquarters Monday morning, but once that's over"—she laughed—"I should be able to focus."

Arcie said, "Monday afternoon, we're all set. I'm looking forward to it."

"Good. Well, till then?" And she took her leave, walking the few remaining yards to her car, a powder-blue Prius, which happened to be parked alongside Bix's gunmetal-gray Hummer. Coop noticed a distinct lilt to her step, as though she didn't have a care in the world—an odd way, he thought, to leave a funeral.

As she was getting into her car, Bix appeared from the other side of the Hummer with Pyrite scampering after him. He said, "Thanks for coming, Tessa. We'll see you Monday."

"Sure thing, Bix." She closed her door, lowered the window to help cool the car, and backed up a few feet. Then she braked. "Hey, Bix?" With a glance toward the Hummer, she smiled, noting, "That's not exactly the epitome of fuel efficiency."

Picking up Pyrite, he said, "Well, we don't need to get carried away with this nonsense, do we?"

Tessa laughed, shaking her head, and pulled away.

Stepping over to Coop, Bix said, "She's a sweet girl, a good kid."

Coop thought, She's one of your senior research scientists. She's a woman of forty, an umpteen-year veteran of your company, with a brilliant mind. She's long overdue for a vice-president's spot—a classic example of the glass ceiling at Emery.

Coop said, "Bix, do you know Detective Madera? She's in charge of the investigation."

"Don't believe I've had the pleasure, but thank you, Detective, thank you so much. We appreciate all your efforts. It's been terrible, of course, just god-awful." He sounded distracted. He didn't bother shaking her hand.

She said, "We're doing everything we can, sir."

"Coops," he said, suddenly animated, "I was spending a few minutes with Frank just now, doing some thinking, some real hard thinking, when—"

"*Bix*," said Austin Royce, striding into the conversation, blotting perspiration from his balding scalp with a white handkerchief. "A reporter's been asking for you, but I said you were probably—"

"Ah!" said Bix. "There you are. I've been looking for you."

"And here I am. Happy to be needed, Bix." Royce beamed a toothy smile, striking a presidential pose, looking very eager.

Bix gave him the dog.

Then he turned to Coop, saying, "So Frank and I were thinking, Pyrite too, that maybe it's time to make some decisions and take action. With Kavanall gone—God rest his soul—I don't have the same options I used to have. Now, you know damn well there are only two men at Emery I've ever seriously considered for the president's job . . ."

Royce puffed his chest.

Pyrite's tail flipped with excitement.

Bix continued, ". . . and after seeing the way you've handled a crisis this past week, I'm more than touched; I'm impressed. You've been a pillar of strength for Stasia, and you set a fine example of a take-charge, can-do kind of attitude. That's what I call leadership, Coops. I said it before, and I'll say it again: you're the man for the job."

With a feeble laugh, Coop said, "Ever heard of the Peter principle? You'd be promoting me to my level of incompetence."

But Bix was determined, and he proceeded to explain why.

Arcie's eyes slid to Coop with a look of dismay. She jotted something in her notes.

Royce listened, deflating, as the color drained from his face.

Pyrite piddled on his arm.

# Chapter 9

Following the funeral, at a luncheon held at the mountainside Regal Palms Hotel, Coop and Stasia sat with Bix at a small round table that also included Austin Royce. A fifth chair was wedged in to accommodate Pyrite, whose snout barely reached the edge of the tablecloth. Bix finger-fed the dog morsels of bloody meat— he couldn't get enough of it. The mood in the private dining room was subdued as a pianist ran through a repertoire of comforting melodies that sounded, to Coop's ears, like maudlin old hymns. Heavy silver cutlery clattered on delicate monogrammed china as the guests forked their salmon en croûte. Taking their cues from the Emery table, they largely refrained from conversation, speaking only in whispers, which made the mawkish effect of the music all the more leaden.

Kavanall's father, Keith Follet, had been invited, along with his wife, but Stasia's tone in extending the courtesy had been so half-hearted, they had sensibly declined.

Jay Pontarelli, on the other hand, had accepted. Though Coop couldn't stand him and Stasia was indifferent, Bix still recognized him as a major investor and had insisted he be included. He now sat at the priest's table, and Coop watched as they huddled over their plates, comparing notes on the wine.

During the main course, Bix conversed a bit with Coop, but Stasia said little, alone with her thoughts. Austin Royce said nothing, stung speechless by Bix's earlier remarks about the Emery presidency.

As the salmon was being cleared for the desert course, Stasia was overcome by her memories and gave in to a crying jag. She rose, excusing herself. Coop offered, "Need some company?" But she shook her head and left the table solo.

A moment later, Pontarelli said something to the priest, got up, and strolled over to the main table. He leaned to ask Coop, "Can I have a word with you?"

"Uh . . . sure." He turned to Bix. "Excuse me, please."

Bix nodded.

Coop rose, then followed Pontarelli through a set of tall French doors of beveled glass that led out to a lofty terrace. Beyond a limestone balustrade and several stories below, hotel guests lolled around a sapphire-tiled pool, sipping pink drinks in the shade of towering date palms. Beyond the pool, a precipice gave way to the entire valley a thousand feet below.

Pontarelli slung a heavy arm over Coop's shoulder and leaned close, confiding, "What a bitch, huh?"

"I beg your pardon?"

"Death." The word wafted on warm breath scented with grace notes of salmon and a crisp pinot grigio.

"It's inevitable," said Coop. Though uncomfortable with the conversation, he took a philosophical tack, adding, "Part of life. But in Kavanall's case, his passing was anything but natural."

"That's what I *mean*—what a bitch, getting snuffed like that."

"I see your point." Coop noticed that Bix had turned in his chair to watch them through the window. He wanted to return to the table.

But Pontarelli still gripped Coop's shoulder and now led him to the edge of the terrace. With their backs to the dining room, Pontarelli gestured with his free arm toward the vista beyond, saying, "He had so much to offer."

"Kavanall?" asked Coop, incredulous. Other than his name, Coop wondered, what did he have to offer Pontarelli.

The lug nodded, saying, "I really could have used him."

"A lost opportunity." Coop was no longer conversing; he was mouthing filler. He wanted to leave.

Pontarelli glanced back over his shoulder, then spoke in Coop's ear: "Kav never had a chance. Oh, sure, I know, most guys would say he had *everything*, but when you're Bix Emery's grandson, how do you ever get a chance to prove yourself? I used to ask *myself* if it was worth it. Do you know who my dad was?"

Coop shook his head. Pontarelli—the name was vaguely familiar—transistors, maybe? But Coop wasn't listening as Jay told the story of growing up in his father's shadow; Coop was mired again in the inadequacies of his own youth. He didn't need to hear the details of Jay's struggle to forge a way for himself, to define himself. Coop had been there. And for the first time, he detected something human in Jay Pontarelli, a vein of empathy that he could tap into. Was that a tear? wondered Coop, disbelieving. He blinked away an image of the crying clown in *Pagliacci*.

Pontarelli was still talking. "Maybe Kav wasn't the brightest bulb in the box, but hey, that doesn't mean he didn't have something to offer. Right?"

"Jay"—Coop laughed—"I think you're drunk." He patted the lug's back.

Pontarelli allowed, "The wine was better than the fish."

"I really need to get back inside. Stasia isn't doing well."

"Poor thing. Give her my best, okay?"

"Sure, Jay. Thanks." He offered Pontarelli a quick handshake, left him standing at the balustrade, and returned to the dining room.

Stasia had not returned to the table. Austin Royce was mechanically spooning pomegranate sorbet to his mouth. Pyrite, with a bellyful of meat, had curled into a ball on his chair.

Bix had stepped over to the piano player and stopped the dirge. He now patted the musician's shoulder and handed him several smashers. When Bix turned to approach Coop at the table, the pianist played a slow arpeggio and began crooning about a very good year—when he was seventeen.

Coop grinned.

"What?" asked Bix.

"I thought you might pay him to liven it up."

"I was feeling sentimental." Bix paused before adding, "Kavanall died too young."

"Of course."

As Bix sat down again, he jerked his head in Pontarelli's direction, asking, "What did *he* want?"

"Just offering condolences. He was concerned about Stasia."

"Yeah?" Bix grunted. "I'll bet."

Their conversation ended.

The uneaten sorbet puddled on Coop's plate.

The piano player sang of blue-blooded girls and limousines.

**S**unday afternoon, at home in the Emery compound at Entrada, Coop was catching up with the weekend newspapers, which were spread out on a big striped ottoman in a shady area of the patio overlooking the pool. The local paper had a follow-up story about the hang glider who had plummeted to his death a week earlier. His memorial service had been held Saturday morning, about the same time as Kavanall's funeral Mass, at the top of the Palm Springs Aerial Tramway, where his ashes were scattered to the winds more than a mile and a half above the desert floor. The coverage included a large photo that showed the assembled mourners releasing multicolored balloons, which drifted over the valley before disappearing into the wild blue.

"Coops?"

Coop looked up from the paper as his father-in-law strolled into view between the two high knolls at the far side of the pool. Pyrite trotted at his heels.

"Hi, Bix." Coop stood. "Good to see you. How are you feeling?"

"Fine, fine," he said absently. Approaching, he asked, "Got a minute."

"For you? Of course. Sit down, Bix."

As they settled in chairs on opposite sides of the ottoman, Pyrite jumped into Coop's lap. Coop rubbed the dog behind its ears.

Bix asked, "How's Stasia? I think yesterday was too much for her."

Coop exhaled noisily. "I think you're right. She's back in bed. To be honest, I'm not sure when to start getting nervous about the sedatives."

Saturday night, Coop had slept with her again, but once again, she had recoiled from his touch and slept with her back to him. He had awoken once in the night to find her slumped at the vanity in her dressing room, crying. Sunday morning, she had risen late, wanted only black coffee for breakfast, said little, and looked like hell.

"Well," said Bix, "it's only been four days. She's never faced anything like this. Come to think of it, neither have I." He lifted his fingers to his mouth, choking back a nascent sob.

"I have," Coop reminded him. "When my father was killed, I felt as if part of my own life had been taken. Sorry to say, you never do get over it, not completely."

With eyes cast downward, Bix asked, "Did you see *that*?"

"Uh, what?"

"*That.*" Bix pointed to the open newspaper on the ottoman. "Can you imagine? Making that dipshit kite-boy out to be some kind of hero—that's what they call *news*?"

Coop suggested, "Perhaps the editors felt the story had a human-interest angle."

Bix wasn't listening; he was talking. More precisely, he was snarling, ranting. "While Kavanall, a goddamn pillar of this fuckin' community—an *Emery*, for Christ's sake—*he* barely gets more coverage than his paid obit."

"I'm sure the editors merely meant to protect the family's privacy."

"Don't kid yourself," said Bix with a low laugh, as if lecturing someone who was terribly naive. "This was meant to embarrass *me*." He thumped his chest.

"If you say so, Bix."

The old man gave a sharp nod.

Pyrite, lying in Coop's lap, stood, stretched, leapt over to the ottoman, and pissed on the paper.

"See?" Bix, howling with laughter, petted the dog and lifted him onto his lap. "*Good* little son f'bitch."

Coop got up, carried the paper to the edge of the terrace, and let it drain into the surrounding hedge of natal plum. Then he folded the wet pages inward and placed them next to the stack of sections that had already been read.

While Coop clapped newsprint grime from his hands, Bix sat back, explaining, "The reason I popped over, Coops—I'm wondering if you're busy tomorrow morning. Cuz if you're not, I'd like you to sit in on a meeting at headquarters. It's an update on our most important research-and-development projects."

"Tessa mentioned that." Coop sat again.

"She's doing the presentation."

Coop shrugged. "Sure, Bix, I can be there if you want." He paused in thought for a moment, then asked, "But why?"

"*Why?*" Bix laughed. "Why *not*? Coops, don't you think it's important that we start grooming you, bringing you up to speed?"

Coop raised his palms. "Bix—I'm an *architect*."

"Know what I did before I did this?"

Coop thought for a moment. "I though you *always* did oil."

Bix shook his head. "I worked in a drugstore. I was a soda jerk at a Rexall. At night, after the store closed, my buddies and I would take needles and poke holes in all the rubbers." He chortled merrily.

Pyrite panted, as if sniggering at the prank.

Coop dropped his head, holding it in one hand. "I'm not so sure I want to hear this."

"And I'd probably still be there if—"

"They don't *have* soda fountains anymore. There's not a Rexall south of Canada."

"That's not my point." Bix set Pyrite on the ground, leaned forward on his elbows, and said with slow deliberation, "There comes a time in any man's life to think *big*."

Coop eyed him askance. "Like Jay Pontarelli?"

Bix stood. "Just come to the meeting, okay?"

Coop stood, smiled. There was no point in arguing this, not at the moment. "Sure, Bix. Happy to sit in."

"That'a boy." He turned to leave.

Coop walked him around the pool. Pyrite followed.

When they reached the narrow pass between the two knolls, Bix stopped, turned to Coop, and said, "I *know* what Pontarelli is up to."

I wish I did, thought Coop.

Then Bix raised one hand, extended the index finger, and made slow, staccato jabs in the air before Coop's face.

One. Two. Three.

**M**onday's research meeting would consume a good part of the morning that Coop had intended to devote to other projects, so he decided to skip the gym again that day in order to catch up on his own work before turning his attention to Bix's harebrained campaign to lure him into the company presidency. Rising early that morning, intending to arrive at his office by seven-thirty, he sat in the kitchen before sunrise, sipping coffee and perusing the *Desert Sun*, which was spread before him on a granite countertop in the glow of an overhead light.

"Where's the fire?"

Coop turned to find Stasia standing in the kitchen doorway, clad in a silk robe—tan with black pinstripes—looking groggy but beautiful in her bare feet and night-tousled hair. He smiled. "Morning, dear. Bix asked me to attend a meeting later, so I wanted to get a jump on things at my desk."

"Oh." She crossed to the counter and poured herself a cup of coffee.

Granted, she was barely awake, but as Coop watched, he was concerned by the profound listlessness that had characterized both her mood and her actions since Kav's death. Pouring the coffee, she seemed to struggle to lift the pot; returning it clumsily to the coffeemaker, she sloshed some of the black liquid over the spout, oblivious to the spilled coffee as it hissed and crackled between the pot and the hot plate.

He found it hard to believe that only a week ago, at the club, when Bix had first broached the idea of Coop's possible presidency, Stasia had reacted with such lively enthusiasm. Hell, walking home that night, she had practically jumped his bones. Coop now wondered if the same topic might help break through her fog of ennui; he had not yet mentioned to her that Bix was continuing to float the idea.

"Damnedest thing," said Coop. "I'm embarrassed to report this, but Bix has been dropping more hints—more than hints, really—that he thinks of *me* as presidential material." Coop paused before adding, "Which is crazy, of course."

Nothing registered on Stasia's face. She did not jump Coop's bones. Her voice was devoid of emotion as she told him, simply, "You should think about it."

But he *had* thought about it. Plenty. While the job offer was an ego boost, and accepting it would bring new wealth and stature,

Coop deemed his prospects for success and satisfaction in the position to be nil.

For starters, he simply wasn't qualified. Despite Bix's dictum that he needed to "think big," Coop thought it ill advised, at fifty-eight, even to consider a career move that would demand skills so clearly at odds with those he had developed over a lifetime. He knew little about business management, let alone big-business management, and his exposure to the oil business was relatively recent, at arm's length, by marriage.

What's more, becoming president at Emery would necessitate accepting Bix as his boss. Bix, by nature, had a demanding personality, and it was challenge enough to handle him as a father-in-law; reporting to him on the job, day in, day out, would be flat-out untenable.

And finally, perhaps the most important consideration: Bix's proposal had no creative appeal. For Coop, architecture had always offered a comfortable balance between the artistic and the utilitarian; it was a tightrope he loved walking, and he walked it well. Though he had no doubt that certain business executives could raise their performance to the level of an art, he also had no doubt that he himself lacked the passion and insight to do so. He relished the challenges of the career he already had, and those challenges related to aesthetics, not spreadsheets and forecasts.

He told Stasia, "I've thought of little else."

"Then you'll figure it out," she said, not caring, staring through one of the dark windows, watching the first glimmer of dawn define the jagged silhouettes of the surrounding mountain peaks.

Did she feel, Coop wondered, that the Emery presidency had rightfully been Kavanall's all along? A week ago, she had tussled with the loyalty of a mother and the fervor of a wife. Now, however, the issue of the job was as dead as her son. It didn't matter anymore, and neither, felt Coop, did he.

He asked, "Any plans today? It might do you good to get out."
She shook her head.

"Tell you what: let's have dinner at the club tonight. We can get dressed up."

She paused before responding without enthusiasm, "Okay."

"It's a date then." He stepped to the sink and rinsed his cup.

"After dinner," she said, "I thought I might go over to Kav's and start sorting through his things."

"I'll help."

"Okay."

**W**hen Coop arrived at Emery headquarters, the sun had risen on the desert, but it was still low enough in the sky that the mountains to the west glowed orange in stark relief beneath a flawless dome of blue. He slowed at the gatehouse, waved to the guard, and drove the remaining distance to the executive parking area. As expected, there were few other cars present at that hour.

He parked the Tesla and got out to connect its charger. While dealing with the cord, he noticed, but paid no attention to, someone who left the research building and got into a car at the far end of the lot. When he finished with the cord, he began walking toward the building, then paused, remembering that the old mimeograph was still stowed in his trunk; he turned and retraced his steps to the car. Along the way, the other car, an SUV, perhaps a Jeep, drove near while exiting the lot. Coop got a quick look at the driver, who was vaguely familiar—just a face from the workplace, maybe a contractor from one of the construction sites. The SUV drove off while Coop retrieved the corrugated box from the trunk and carried it through the parking lot, through the solar garden, and into the research facility, which also housed the architectural and construction offices.

While walking the hall to the back entrance to his office, the boxed mimeograph rattled in his arms, and he thought of Mimi. Chances were good that she would soon be hearing from Arcie Madera, and Coop had promised to prime Mimi for the detective's call. That call might prove embarrassing for both women if Coop failed to get to Mimi first, so he decided to phone her as soon as he was at his desk.

He set down the box at his door, keyed in the code, held the door open with his hip, and carried the box inside. These quarters were temporary, having been designed for other purposes, and one thing his office lacked was a storeroom; in fact, there wasn't even a coat closet. Which left him standing in the middle of the space, wondering where to put a grimy old box that belonged anywhere but here. There was plenty of room, but the box was such an eyesore, he wanted it out of sight, and hiding it would be a challenge in a space so sparsely furnished.

The cabinet of flat-files had a bare upper surface, but it was six feet high, and although the box would be out of the way up there, its griminess would be all too conspicuous. Which begged the ultimate question: Just what, exactly, was he supposed to do with this piece of junk? For whatever reason, his father had kept it— and Mimi had passed it along—so Coop postponed a decision on its fate and simply placed it on the floor, around the far side of the cabinet, near the wastebasket.

He wiped his hands on a handkerchief, moved to his desk, sat, and phoned Mimi.

It was still early, and it took a few rings for her to pick up. "Hello?"

"Good morning, Mimi. It's Cooper."

"*Hi* there, honey. What a nice way to wake up, hearing your voice."

"I'm at my *desk* already." He laughed.

"You work too hard. And me? I'm just a has-been actress, out to pasture."

"Now, stop that." Dropping the jocular tone, he said, "Mimi, I just wanted to give you a heads-up. I ran into Detective Madera this weekend—the woman who questioned you after Dad died. She wants to visit you again and hear the rest of your story."

"Hmmm." Mimi mumbled, "I just *knew* I had too much to drink Friday night."

"Be *nice* to her this time. And tell her what you told me."

"I'll get in trouble."

"No you won't. I promise. And you'll find her a far more agreeable person than you did fifteen years ago."

As Coop continued buttering up Mimi for an unwanted encounter with a cop, his mind drifted back to *his* encounter—a few minutes earlier in the parking lot. The person who had left the building and driven away had looked familiar. Trying to recall more details, Coop sensed that it was not so much the guy's face as his clothing that had sparked a memory. And then, with dawning insight, Coop realized that the guy was not a contractor, not a construction worker, though he was wearing khakis and heavy black work shoes. No, it was not a face from the workplace; it was a face from the gym.

Specifically, it was the bruiser Coop had mistaken for an undercover cop.

**A**t nine that morning, Coop crossed the solar garden to the main building, where the research meeting would be held in a board room near Bix's office. He mingled outside the room with others waiting to attend, including Austin Royce and a sizable contingent of the senior research staff, all male, none of whom Coop knew. Through a glass wall looking into the board room, Coop saw Tessa Irwin setting up a laptop projector near the head of the table, a long ellipse of burnished West Indian mahogany. She was clicking through a series of charts, graphs, and photos, checking the focus. It promised to be a long meeting.

Royce stepped over to Coop, smiled politely, and asked, "Looking for someone?" His tone suggested that he meant to ask, What are *you* doing here?

Coop checked his watch. "Is this the nine-o'clock meeting?"

"Yes, but it's R and D."

"Right. Bix asked me to attend."

Royce's features pinched for an instant. "Oh."

Coop stepped him out of earshot of the others. "Just wondering—I know last week got busy for you, but were you able to study the DNA issue? The detective keeps bringing it up, still wants me to volunteer a sample."

Royce's features pinched again, then relaxed into a grin. He turned his back to the group and huddled with Coop, telling him quietly, "Yes, I've looked at all the angles, and I think you should do it."

"Really?" It was not the advice Coop had expected.

Royce nodded. "Definitely. Nothing to lose, right?"

Coop paused, smiled. "That's one point of view." He marveled at how quickly Royce had changed his advice, now that he saw Coop as a rival for the prez-job.

Royce continued, "It can't hurt to be cooperative and stay on the good side of the law, especially since Madera is working on Kavanall's case as well."

"I hear you've met."

Royce rolled his eyes, leaning close to tell Coop, "What a ball-buster. Watch out for that one."

Coop gave him a knowing nod, thinking, You don't know her at all. Her father was a sculptor. "By the way," said Coop, "I was sorry to hear of your problem last week."

Royce gave him a quizzical look. "Hm?"

Coop reminded him, "The family crisis? Something to do with your daughter?"

"Ohhh," he said with a soft laugh, "of course. Everything got overshadowed by Wednesday's tragedy—something like that puts one's minor troubles in perspective damn fast. Thank you for mentioning it, though. We got everything ironed out. It simply required a bit of face time upstate."

Coop ventured, "She's at . . . Berkeley?"

"No."

"Howdy, everyone. Mornin'!" said Bix, sweeping into the hall from his inner sanctum. He carried a tall stainless-steel travel mug of coffee in one hand; in the other arm, Pyrite. The hubbub instantly calmed as his minions parted, clearing the way for him to lead the parade into the conference room.

Tessa was ready at the far end of the table, greeting everyone as they filed in. Her laptop played background music. Coop heard someone lamenting, "It's not easy bein' green . . ." It took him a moment to realize that it was Sinatra, way out of his element, singing Kermit the Frog's big solo. Coop gave Tessa a look of wide-eyed wonder.

She laughed. "Bix asked me to play that."

Bix conceded, "I guess it wasn't Frank's finest hour, but he hit the nail smack on the head—it sure as hell *ain't* easy bein' green. Do you have any idea what this is costing me?" With a snort, he assumed his usual seat at the near end of the table, telling Tessa she could cut the music.

At prior meetings, Royce, as second in command, had always sat at Bix's right, with Kavanall at Bix's left. When Royce began setting up his notes and laptop at his usual seat, Bix said, "Let's put Coops there today. We may want to compare notes."

Stung but diplomatic, Royce replied, "Whatever you say, Bix. Um . . . where would you like me to sit?"

With a wave of his coffee mug, Bix said, "Oh, anywhere," indicating Royce should join the rank and file along the sidelines. As Royce began collecting his things to move, Bix added, "Here," and gave him the dog.

When everyone had settled in, the chair to Bix's left remained conspicuously empty. Bix said, "Let's begin with a moment of silence in respect for the memory of my dear grandson." He bowed his head.

Everyone else followed suit. Someone's intestines burbled.

Bix looked up. His glance circled the table. "Can't you say 'excuse me'?"

No one fessed up.

Bix bowed his head again, made a perfunctory sign of the cross, and then said, "Tessa? Show us what you've got." The comment drew several lascivious hoots.

She stood with a stack of agendas, brought the first copy to Bix, and began distributing the rest around the table. "Moving the research facility from Los Angeles disrupted our timetable, naturally, but that proved to be temporary. Now that we're here, we're making great progress on all fronts. I think it's safe to say we've even had a couple of breakthroughs."

"Yes, Bix"—one of her bosses piped up, clearing his throat—"I'm particularly proud of our recent efforts in the fuel-cell arena."

"Keep your pants on, Dunmire," Bix shushed him. "Let the lady talk."

"But, Bix," said the guy sitting next to Dunmire, "these days, it's not so much a matter of raw research as the funding behind it."

"Now, Max," said Bix, waving him off, "we'll get to that."

Yet another of Tessa's bosses, sitting in line with the other two, reminded everyone, "It all boils down to budgeting. It's a battle.

And where you focus your fight—where you focus your *funds*—you get your results."

Bix said, "We all know that, Sander. You've got *your* bottom line; I've got mine."

Tessa suggested, "Let's review the research. If you'll look at your agendas, you'll see that our first order of unfinished business from the last meeting was development of a comprehensive strategy of alternative-fuel introductions." She switched on the projector and began showing slides from her computer. She continued, "Our progress to date . . ."

While she spoke, Bix wrote something along the margin of his agenda, nudged Coop with his elbow, and slid the paper to him.

Coop looked down and turned the page to read it. In arthritic block letters, Bix had printed, THEY THINK I'M INTO THIS SHIT. Coop turned to him with a curious look.

"But I'm not," said Bix in a gravelly whisper. Patting his son-in-law's arm, he leaned near, adding, "It's just business, Coops. It's a game."

Dunmire, Max, and Sander took turns interrupting Tessa's presentation, reminding Bix that the progress she reported was the result of their own leadership and directives. Tessa wore her usual lab coat, looked every inch the scientist, and spoke of her research with knowledge, insight, and passion, while Dunmire, Max, and Sander wore suits, looked like bankers, and spoke of the research as simply a commodity with a price. They had doubtless begun their careers as scientists, but they had been promoted out of their realm of expertise and into the role of corporate nabobs.

Sitting there in his corduroys, taking pride in the magnificent building that lent such gravitas to these weary proceedings, Coop saw exactly what the future would hold for him if Bix succeeded in luring him into the position of yet another Emery functionary.

Dunmire said, "It's the future of energy development."

Max said, "We've risen to these challenges before."

Sander said, "All it takes is the right infusion of capital."

"Christ," said Bix, "let the little lady talk, will ya?"

And Coop understood that Stasia's blunt assessment had been no exaggeration: within Bix's company, there could be no meaningful position of authority or influence for anyone with tits.

Tessa removed her glasses and waved them toward the projection; their lenses shot two wiggling starbursts over the pie chart on the screen. "Gentlemen," she said, "there's no quick fix. Kicking the fossil-fuel habit won't be easy. It has to be a multipronged attack that explores a whole array of options—diligently and over time. Eventually we can settle on not only those alternatives that work, but those that work most efficiently. For example, cutting-edge experiments with fusion have begun to show great promise. With dedication, we can find those breakthroughs. But have no delusions; they'll be incremental. I highly doubt that our quest will end with a single big discovery—for instance, the water engine." She turned away from the screen and breathed a wistful little laugh, shaking her head.

In the quiet of the room, Pyrite's snore drifted from Austin Royce's lap.

"Ah," mumbled Bix, "the water engine."

He paused, then patted Coop's arm, adding, "Sure wish we had it."

Coop was pleased to discover that the prospect of dinner in public, even at a private club, had motivated Stasia to spend at least a few hours out of bed that day. By the time he arrived home in the evening, she was looking the best he had seen her since Kavanall's death. Her hair was just right, freshly coiffed—had she made an outing to her regular salon on El Paseo? She wore a casual but elegant ensemble of tweed slacks and a comfortable-looking shawl-collared sweater of heathery gray mohair. Best of all, her face had an unexpected radiance. Though the artistry of makeup surely played a role, Coop was reminded that her beauty had never faded; it had been temporarily marred by a depth of grief she had never before known.

"Am I okay for the club?" she asked, checking her outfit in a mirror.

"You're perfect." He meant it.

"It's not very dressy, but we'll be sorting things at Kav's, and I don't think I could handle two outfits this evening."

He repeated, "You're perfect."

Though the Hellsgate dining room was a logical choice to help her make the transition from mourning back to everyday life, the insular setting of the club offered little escape from the tragedy she sought to overcome. Everyone knew her, and from the moment she arrived with Coop, they were besieged by well-wishers whose sympathetic gestures, long faces, and shared tears served only to invoke the calamity again and again.

When they finally achieved some privacy at a corner table and their first drinks arrived, Coop said, "I'm sorry. This seemed like a good idea, but maybe I should have just cooked for you."

She offered a smile. "Now, *that* would be something worth apologizing for."

With feigned umbrage, he insisted, "I can cook."

"Uh-huh." She touched her martini glass to his. "Thank you, sweets. Thanks for dragging me out of the house."

The meal was pleasant enough, and Coop wished they could simply call it a night, walk back from the restaurant together, and take a stab at achieving a semblance of normalcy at home for the rest of the evening—a bit of reading, perhaps, or a movie, a nightcap, a fire. But Stasia had seemed determined to do some housekeeping for her deceased son, and Coop had offered to help. At worst, it would be an unpleasant task; at best, it would help Stasia begin to achieve some closure. So when she set her napkin on the table and asked, "Ready?" Coop pushed back his chair and said, "Let's do it."

As they walked back toward the Emery compound, the starry sky reminded Coop of the same walk they had taken a week earlier, when Stasia had alluded to the glass ceiling at Emery. He now said to her, "You were right about the tits."

She laughed. "What?"

"Bix's attitude toward women. That meeting this morning—Tessa ran it—sort of. I felt sorry for her."

"Hmmm." Stasia nodded, thinking, crossing her arms as they walked through the chilly night. "Tessa can take care of herself. And things are bound to change. I mean, realistically, she'll outlive Bix."

She outlived Kavanall, thought Coop.

In the carport in front of Kavanall's house, Coop noticed that the collection of vintage roadsters had recently been washed; Kav's absence would have no effect on the maintenance standards that were an expected aspect of life within the compound. Things were taken care of.

Coop had never entered Kav's house alone, but Stasia had. As they stepped to the front door, he asked her, "Know the code?" With a nod, she entered it on the keypad, used her key in the lock, and a moment later, they walked inside.

The house was well lit, looking lived-in but orderly; a computerized lighting system was programmed to welcome Kav back from lengthy travels or a night on the town, and the housekeeping staff always stuck to their schedule, regardless of whether the home had been occupied or not since its last cleaning. Standing in the living room, which seemed eerily quiet, Coop asked Stasia, "What'll become of the place?"

She shook her head. "I have no idea."

Since the house stood smack in the middle of the compound, it wouldn't be sold off to an outsider, and since there were no other Emerys in the immediate family, there was no one to whom it could be passed on. The house would probably remain, indefinitely, just as it was that night—unoccupied but regularly spruced, with the lights cycling on and off, fully furnished—but minus Kav's personal effects.

And it was the personal effects that interested Stasia that evening. She hadn't come to move furniture; she was there to go through her son's closets.

Walking to the bedroom wing, Coop glanced into Kav's office and noticed that Bix's truckers had done a thorough job of cleaning things out. Chairs, a settee, end tables, and a few lamps remained, but the desk, computer, file cabinets, and a bookcase had been removed, leaving imprints on the carpet and a room without a purpose.

Though Coop had never been in the master suite after Kav had moved in, he had designed the house and overseen its construction, so he was intimately acquainted with the lay of things as he followed Stasia into the bedroom. She had asked the staff to leave some boxes for her, and they were there. Coop noticed a small writing table near the windows, where Kav had apparently set up his laptop. The computer was gone, but its cable remained, along with the modem, in a tangle beneath the desk.

"Let's start with the bathroom," said Stasia. "That should be easiest."

Coop followed with a box, and she began going through drawers, tossing out the accumulated sundries, dried-out notions, expired prescriptions, and other etceteras that had helped pamper, cleanse, and lubricate a well-heeled life. Eyeing at least a half-dozen packs of unused dental floss—souvenirs of repeated visits to Cliff Sloan's office—Coop concluded that he and his late stepson had had at least one trait in common.

Moving to Kav's dressing room, Stasia said, "I don't know where to begin." To say that her son had enjoyed dressing well was a gross understatement. Even the term *clotheshorse* did not adequately describe Kav, who had made Beau Brummell look like a piker, and his closet proved it. Row upon row of custom-made suits, arranged by season and color, lined the walls of the dressing area and deadened the acoustics of the sizable room. Long angled shelves displayed hundreds of custom-made shoes, from sneakers to satin-bowed tuxedo pumps, all freshly polished, all perfectly shaped by cedar shoe trees. Stacks of sweaters, rows of shirts, rod after rod bearing hangers of shorts, slacks, belts, ties—it was not so much an extravagance as an embarrassment.

"Now, look," said Coop. "Lots of local charities run thrift shops. Why don't you just pick one and give them a call? They'll be more than eager to take care of the clothes."

She breathed a weary sigh. "Good idea." Then she stepped over to the built-in bureau, asking, "I don't suppose you need any cologne?"

Wryly, Coop answered, "No, thank you."

And Stasia started loading a box with bottles so numerous, Coop wondered if the bottom of the carton would give way when someone was sent to pitch it.

With the top of the bureau cleared of the bottles, there remained a lacquered wooden chest resembling an oblong cigar humidor. Raising the lid, Coop found not cigars, but a motorized velvet "arm" that rotated slowly to keep self-winding wristwatches wound. There wasn't a Timex or a Swatch among them.

Hmmm, thought Coop. The good stuff.

"I'm sure there are others," said Stasia. "We need to get into his jewelry drawers. I'd rather not leave any of it here. We can take it all home, and you're welcome to anything that appeals to you. Maybe Bix would like some of it, and then, I suppose, I'll get an appraiser for what's left and have it auctioned."

"Sounds reasonable," said Coop.

Stasia tried the top of the three built-in jewelry drawers, and as expected, they were locked. The cabinet was not, strictly speaking, a safe; it was simply intended to keep valuables out of sight and to keep staff out of temptation's way. If necessary, the single lock could be forced open, but to do so would damage the cabinet.

Stasia said, "I wonder where he kept the key."

Having designed the installation, Coop said, "I wouldn't be surprised if it's the same as the key to your own jewelry drawers. Do you have it?"

With a grin, she rattled her key ring. "Always." She chose the smallest of the bunch, and sure enough, it opened her departed son's treasure on the first try. The top drawer contained watches; the middle drawer, cuff links and rings; the bottom, less frequently used bracelets, even a few necklaces.

"Good grief," said Coop. "That's quite a haul."

"I must admit," said Stasia, "Kav liked nice things. I'd forgotten he even *had* much of this." She got a fresh box, lined the bottom with one of Kav's cashmere sweaters, and began arranging a layer of watches to take home.

Coop readied a second sweater for the layer of cuff links and rings, noting, "Styles change. Tastes change. And you can only wear so much jewelry at once."

She tisked. "You're such a *guy*."

"Thank you."

When they got to the third layer, they knelt on the floor together, facing each other over the box while removing items from the bottom drawer, bracelets first, and finally, a few necklaces. Coop pulled the last one from the back of the drawer and dangled it over the box, saying, *"Here's* an odd one."

Not that he would consider wearing any of Kav's necklaces, but this one looked downright vulgar. Most of the others were less than twenty inches long, but this was at least thirty. The others were all characterized by similarly refined designs, but this one looked crude. Though made of platinum, it was crafted to resemble, of all things, a stylized shank of barbed wire, with hook-like protrusions sprouting from the chain every couple of inches—better suited to Mr. T than Beau Brummell.

"God," said Stasia, "I haven't seen that in *years.* He used to wear that all the time when he was in college, but then he stopped."

"Like I said, styles change." Coop fingered the barbs. They weren't needle-sharp, but they came to distinct points. "Couldn't have been very comfortable."

"Well, no *wonder* he stopped wearing it," said Stasia, examining the lower end of the necklace. "This half of the clasp is missing."

"He wore it in college?" Coop asked vacantly, trying to remember something, wondering why the barbed chain in his fingers brought something to mind. And then it hit him: a crown of thorns.

Stasia was saying something, but Coop was thinking of the wounds on his father's neck fifteen Easters ago, and he interrupted her, asking, "In college, did Kavanall's spring breaks coincide with Easter?"

She shrugged. "Sometimes, I guess."

"Did he come home for spring breaks?"

"Not usually. He liked to travel whenever he could." With a wan smile, she added, "The playboy in training."

"But did he *ever* come home for Easter?"

Surprised by his tone, which seemed urgent, almost accusing, Stasia answered defensively, "Once, yes. Does it matter?"

Unwilling to share what he suspected—she would hate him for it—he reined his emotions and softened his delivery, managing a smile. "No, dear, of course it doesn't matter. But I'm curious: Do you happen to recall which year he came home?"

"Hm." She thought for a moment. "Well, it was later in college, rather than earlier. But I don't think he was a senior yet; graduation was still down the road. So that must have been his junior year."

"And he normally would have traveled?"

She nodded. "In fact, he'd already planned a week in Europe, meeting some friends in Paris, but then, boom, he decided to fly home instead. It had something to do with Cliff Sloan."

"The dentist?" Coop pocketed the chain.

"His roommate. Cliff wasn't from a moneyed family, and he couldn't afford those big trips, so Kav decided to spend time with him here. They drove down to Tijuana for a long Easter weekend." Stasia stopped speaking, lifting a hand to her mouth.

Coop asked, "What?"

She got teary. "Something happened. When Kav got back, he'd been beaten up, badly. I was hysterical, but he tried to make light of it—something about call girls and tequila." With a heave, she began to cry. "Awww, my baby. How my baby suffered."

Coop moved the box aside and pulled Stasia close to him.

But she pushed him away.

"And *you*"—she spat the words—"you didn't even *like* him."

# Chapter 10

Later, while getting ready for bed, Coop told Stasia, "I'm feeling sort of wired. Maybe I should sleep in the other room tonight—wouldn't want to keep you awake." She offered no objection, so Coop padded down the hall to one of the spare bedrooms, wondering if their conjugal bed was now forever off-limits.

He woke early on Tuesday, placed his cell phone in the pocket of his robe, got the coffee brewing, and stepped out to the terrace by the pool. The tops of the tallest palms glowed yellow with the day's first shafts of sunlight, which stirred mockingbirds from their slumber and coaxed them into song. Coop glanced at the Roman numerals on the face of his new watch, a classic Cartier tank—used, but in mint condition—and decided to wait a few minutes, till seven.

He returned briefly to the kitchen, poured a mug of coffee, took the morning paper, and settled again by the pool, skimming headlines. At a minute or two past seven, he switched on his phone, checked the home number on the card Arcie Madera had given him, and placed the call.

She apparently checked the caller ID. "Ever heard of office hours? What's wrong?"

He responded brightly, "And a pleasant good morning to you too, Detective."

She took a deep breath. "Sorry. Good morning, Brant."

"It's Coop."

"Whatever. What's up?"

"Oh, nothing much. Just thought you'd like to know I've discovered what may be a crucial piece of evidence in one of your cases."

"*Have* you, now?" She laughed.

"Yup." It wasn't much of a response, but something in its delivery gave her pause.

She asked, "Which case, the old one or the new one?"

With no trace of levity, he answered, "The old one."

"I'm listening . . ."

"Can we meet somewhere? I'd rather—"

"Sure. I'm busy this morning, driving over to visit Mimi Miles in Pioneertown, but anytime after that is fine."

"How about lunch?" Even to Coop's ears, the suggestion sounded a tad too eager, and he had to remind himself he wasn't making a date. "I could drive over and meet you when you're finished. Maybe Pappy and Harriet's?"

"That'll work. High noon?"

"High noon. And oh, Arcie? Don't forget the chocolates; Mimi likes truffles."

"*Yes,* Coop, I already have them." Then she covered the phone for a moment, speaking to someone who was in the room with her.

And Coop realized, with a measure of dismay, that she had woken up with Bruce Rollo that morning. But that, of course, was none of Coop's business.

When Coop arrived at his office, punched in his code, and opened the back-hall door with his key, the cooled air within the dimly lit room carried a whiff of peppery pine, which he recognized as one of the cleaning products used by the overnight custodial staff. He switched on the lights, set a small leather portfolio on his desk, and noticed that the usual contents of the glass desktop had been slightly rearranged during cleaning. After realigning the askew items, he sat and checked his voice mail. While taking notes—there was nothing of urgency—he noticed a yellow Post-it protruding from a flap of the mimeograph box, which remained where he had placed it, near the wastebasket, which had been emptied.

Curious, he rose, stepped over to the cabinet of flat-files, crouched near the box, and read the note left by the cleaning staff, which asked, simply, TRASH?

Plucking the note from the box, he returned to his desk, picked a marker from the pencil tray, and paused to consider his response. The mimeograph was old and worthless. Mimi had examined it, and so had he. Though they had shared an initial reaction that the machine might have been Ferris Brant's fabled prototype, it clearly was not. Even fifteen years ago, it was a piece of outdated office junk, yet Ferris had found reason to squirrel it away with his mistress on the day he died. Though he'd surely had his reasons, they would never be known. The only thing Coop knew with certainty was that the machine was a mimeograph, not a water engine, and it was cluttering the otherwise immaculate surroundings of his office.

He uncapped the marker and printed in neat block letters, just beneath the query, YES! Then he added his signature and returned the note to the box, sticking it on the flap where he had found it.

For the next few hours, Coop busied himself with issues that seemed suddenly mundane—work orders, spec sheets, code compliance, impact studies. These paled in comparison to the weightier issues of murder and motive that had seized his attention when Arcie Madera reappeared twelve days ago; their weight had snowballed ever since. At his desk, he kept checking the Cartier on his wrist, a reminder of the grim—and deadly—irony that his father and his stepson were linked, but how? This question crowded out all others as he waited for eleven o'clock, when he could leave for his lunch meeting with Arcie and reveal his stunning new suspicions about Kavanall.

A few minutes past eleven, he wrapped up a phone call with one of the construction foremen, saying, "Sorry, gotta cut this short. Bix is waiting on the other line." He wasn't, but it worked like a charm, and a minute later Coop was headed out the door and crossing the parking lot.

As he unlocked his car and tossed his portfolio onto the passenger seat, he noticed Jay Pontarelli getting out of a car parked in one of the visitors' spaces. Jay had spotted Coop and now hailed him, striding across the asphalt, looking hulkier than ever in a stretch-fabric business suit; its vest clung to his abs like a corset.

Shit, thought Coop, smiling.

Drawing near, Jay joshed, "Early lunch? Must be nice."

"Meeting. Need to run, Jay." Coop started getting into his car.

"Hold on, hold on"—Jay waved him out. "I need to talk to

you."

Coop stood with his hand on the door. "Okay."

Jay hesitated. Averting Coop's gaze, he asked, "This . . . Detective Madera. How well do you know her?"

"She investigated my father's death, years ago, and now Kav's." Dryly, he added, "I guess it's what you'd call a 'professional' relationship—she handles *all* the murders in my family."

Jay clamped a hand on Coop's shoulder. "She's been asking me questions." His features twisted with a wry expression.

"You were there in one of the golf carts when Kav was killed. She took statements from all of us."

Bix's Hummer drove into view and pulled into the parking lot. Jay said, "But she came back for a follow-up interview. She found out about newco."

"That's common knowledge by now, Jay."

"Maybe"—he bobbed his head—"but get this: she didn't say it, but I think she feels there might be some connection between newco and what happened to Kav."

Coop crossed his arms. "Is there?"

Taken aback for a moment, Jay removed his hand from Coop's shoulder. Then, with a big laugh, he cuffed Coop's shoulder, saying, "Well, *no*. Of course not!"

Coop joined in the laughter. "Of course not."

Bix lowered his window to watch them as he pulled into his parking spot.

"So anyway"—Jay huddled with Coop, affecting a confidential tone—"she's a tough one. If you can, steer clear of her."

"Well"—Coop nodded slowly—"she's not the sort of person I'd ask out to lunch."

Jay aped the slow nod, giving Coop a thumbs-up.

As Coop drove away, he saw Jay trot over to Bix, and then the two of them walked toward the main building, Pyrite skipping at their heels.

Along the route to Pioneertown, Coop hardly noticed the heavy midday traffic on the interstate, the dramatic change of scenery as he took the state highway up to Yucca Valley, or the thinning, cooler air as he turned for the steep last leg of his journey along Pioneertown Road. The purpose of today's trip wasn't sight-seeing, nor was it colored by the nostalgia he'd felt four days earlier while tracing the same route on the way to his reunion with Mimi. Today his purpose was altogether different, and he was meeting a cop for lunch—the same cop Jay Pontarelli had just warned him to avoid, the same cop who had suspected, but had never proved, that Coop had killed his father. Today, finally, he meant to rid himself of those suspicions, and nestled inside his portfolio was the missing piece of physical evidence that could help him do it.

But most of all, as he drove along, he pondered the sheer irony that lurked within the solution to his dilemma. Fifteen years ago, the fallout of the suspicions hanging over him had further eroded and ultimately ended his first marriage; now, as he was on the verge of clearing his name by helping to identify his father's kill-er, he knew he risked the future of his second marriage.

Immersed in these thoughts, he missed the timbered road sign as he entered Pioneertown and zipped past Pappy and Harriet's. He might have missed the town altogether—a blink could do it—but he happened to catch a glimpse of the honky-tonk's rustic façade shrinking in his rearview mirror, so he braked for a U-turn and took it slow going back, just in case there was a tough female cop watching.

But he didn't see her. In fact, he saw no other cars at all, either on the main road or along the side of the restaurant. It was nearly high noon, and the entire town seemed, in a word, dead.

Coop pulled onto the side road and then into the rear park-ing lot, taking the gravel at a crawl. He parked near the back entrance—still the only car in sight—got out, stretched, and was beginning to feel creeped out. But then it clicked. He realized he had not stumbled into one of those chainsaw scenarios as the last man standing; rather, it was a Tuesday, and the bartender had mentioned during his previous visit that Pappy and Harriet's was closed that day.

His cell phone rang. Looking at the readout, he grinned. "Hello?"

"Are you feeling watched?"

"No," he said nonchalantly, wondering where the hell she was.

"I clocked you at seventy."

"Add it to my rap."

Gravel crunched from the far side of the restaurant as Arcie's tan cruiser backed slowly into view. Making eye contact with Coop, she could easily have continued their conversation from the car's open window, but she still spoke on the phone: "Change of plans. Follow me."

"Yes, ma'am."

When Coop was back in his car, Arcie pulled past him and drove to the highway, turning toward the far side of town. Coop followed, and as the road curved sharply to the right, he realized they were leaving town already. It was a matter of only a few blocks, but Coop was now in territory previously unexplored by him.

They hadn't gone far, perhaps another quarter mile, when Arcie signaled and led him into the parking area of a run-down establishment with a weathered sign spanning the driveway: MOSEY ON INNE. The gratuitous *e* tacked onto the word *inn* bothered Coop far more than the mangy hound barking from the end of a chain. Toward the rear of the property, in a sandy clearing among the Joshua trees, lurked a little motel of six or eight units—straight out of a bad movie, thought Coop—while up near the road was a saloon that also served as the motel office, identified in neon, dark by day, as LOUNGE. Near the mailbox, a small sign hanging from eye hooks informed would-be guests, VACANCY. I'll just bet, thought Coop.

A pickup and a motorcycle were parked at the roadhouse; back by the motel, nothing. Arcie parked near the bar entrance; Coop, next to her. He got out of the Tesla—in these surroundings, it might as well have been a vehicle from Mars—and retrieved the portfolio before locking the car with a beep. Arcie asked, "Afraid someone will steal it?"

"Just habit."

She allowed, "A good habit," and locked the cruiser after hefting from the floor of the backseat a bulging old briefcase, the type that closes with a strap.

Coop followed her inside and found the roadhouse to have a look similar to that of Pappy and Harriet's, though this place was much smaller, without the stage area for live music. "Hi there, Sarge!" said the bartender, a big guy with red hair, a beard, and of all things, a beret; he didn't look or sound French. With a broad gesture encompassing the empty premises, he added, "Anywhere you want."

"Thanks, Gus." And Arcie led Coop to a small room near the back, an enclosed porch with a couple of small tables set up for games, backgammon on one, chess on the other. She set her brief-case on the floor near the backgammon table and sat, asking Gus, "Mind if we move this?"

"I'll get it," he said, moving the game board to the other table. "Drinks, Sarge?"

"Sorry, on duty. Coop?"

"Sorry, driving." He gave her a wink, then set his portfolio on the floor, leaning it against the leg of his chair.

"Diet Coke?" she asked with a shrug.

Coop nodded.

She told Gus, "And a couple of menus, please."

"Sure thing, Sarge."

When Gus left, Coop paused before asking, "Are you actually a police sergeant?"

She laughed softly. "No. My rank is detective."

"Ah." Then he added, "I knew that. And Gus isn't French."

"In fact, he is. It's Gustave. If he's offering the poached oysters au Muscadet, try them."

"Well," said Coop, feigning interest, "October does have an $r$ in it," but he wasn't sure he believed her.

She leaned back, crossing her arms. The rickety chair creaked. "Now, what's this about your father's murder?"

He leaned forward a few inches and lowered his voice. "It happened last night. I stumbled onto something that might well be a crucial piece of evidence pointing to Dad's killer. If I'm right, it would be explosive. What's more, it suggests that Dad's murder and Kavanall's might be linked."

Her brows arched. "You have my undivided attention."

Just then, Gus arrived with the sodas and menus.

Arcie asked him, "Oysters today?"

He shook his head. "Not till Thursday—truck from the coast. Besides, drinking Coke with them? Watching that would be a dagger to my heart."

"You're such a softy."

"I am, Sarge. Your best bet today, burgers. Couple of big ones, medium-rare? Nice thick slice of Camembert?"

Coop nodded. His mouth watered.

"Sure," said Arcie, "sounds good. And, Gus? My friend and I are discussing some police business. I know you're not busy, but if anyone comes in, could you seat them well away from us?"

He gave the slightest nod. With a conspiratorial grin, he said, "Private dining." Then he stepped out for a moment and returned with a folding screen, closing off the doorway to the porch.

When he moved off to the kitchen, Arcie said to Coop, "Tell me what you found."

"Let's back up a moment." He scooted the chair closer to the table and leaned on his elbows. "On the Easter morning when Dad's murder was discovered, when you arrested me, I was the only person at the crime scene other than the police, correct?"

"Correct."

"I saw things the public never saw; I know details of how Dad died that were never published. Is it safe to say that other than the police—and the killer—I'm the only person who got a good look at the wounds on Dad's neck?"

She nodded. "He died of asphyxiation from the strangling, but that ring of puncture wounds—talk about a sickening twist. They seemed to leave a message. They always left me wondering if the murder was connected to some occult ritual."

"I know what you mean. A crown of thorns, that's what kept going through my mind. But then, last night, in the most unexpected place, I discovered something that seems to provide some answers—but it raises a ton of new questions."

"Okay, where is it? *What* is it?"

Coop reached to the floor, unzipped the portfolio, removed

the necklace, and placed it full length in the center of the table between them.

Arcie's eyes widened as she studied it, unblinking. She expelled a low whistle, then asked, barely above a whisper, "Where in hell did you get this?"

Coop sat back, telling her flatly, "It was Kavanall's."

She closed her eyes, absorbing the impact of his words. "How do I know you didn't have this all along?"

"Ask Stasia. She was with me last night when we found it in the back of Kav's locked jewelry cabinet. She has no idea of its significance, so she has no motive to lie about it. When she learns the truth, I don't know how she's going to handle it, and frankly, I'd rather she learn it from you than from me. So if you need to verify where the necklace came from, just ask Stasia."

Arcie now had her notebook on the table next to the necklace. Flipping back through its pages, she asked, "Didn't you tell me Kavanall was still in college, three thousand miles away, when your father was killed?"

"Yes, but here's the update: The murder coincided with his spring break. He normally traveled during those vacations and had planned to go to Europe that year, but according to Stasia, he canceled the trip and came home instead. He told her he was going to Mexico for a long Easter weekend, and when he came back, she said he was badly beaten up."

Nodding, Arcie struggled to keep up with her note-taking. She said, "I now have Mimi's statement on record that your father was meeting 'someone from Emery' that night, so this is starting to fit. But what was Kavanall's purpose? Why did he change plans and come home that spring?"

"According to Stasia, he wanted to spend the time with Cliff Sloan."

Arcie's eyes shot to Coop's.

"Yes," he told her, "Cliff Sloan, the dentist, who was Kav's college roommate. The story goes, they were planning to meet in Tijuana."

"*Tijuana?* What for?"

"Well, duh—hookers!"

"Oh." She sat back, fingers to chin. "Clearly, the Tijuana story was a cover. Kavanall's real purpose, apparently, was to meet your father in Riverside. But they didn't even know each other, right? So let's say Kavanall had been sent there. He was on a mission."

"Which means," said Coop, leaning back, whirling a hand, "that Tessa Irwin or Austin Royce may have been involved. They were there at the time, early in their careers at Emery, and may have recognized an opportunity to make their mark." Coop also considered what roles Dunmire, Max, and Sander—Tessa's weaselly higher-ups—might have played.

"Interesting you should mention Tessa and Austin," said Arcie. While speaking, she took a stiff brown-paper evidence bag from her briefcase and slid the necklace into it. "I've met with both of them now, and I've done some follow-up. A few unexpected details have emerged."

"Anything you can share?" Coop twitched a brow.

A rap on the doorjamb interrupted them. "Are we getting hungry?" asked Gus, folding the screen back with one hand, carrying a tray with the other.

Arcie said, "That smells wonderful, Gus—as usual," and cleared the table of her notes.

Gus served them, asking, "Sure I can't tempt you with a small glass of Bordeaux? Perfect with the beef and the cheese."

"I'm fine," said Arcie.

Coop looked stricken.

She laughed. With a flick of her hand, she told him, "Oh, go ahead."

Coop nodded to Gus, who was back in a flash with a generous pour of velvety purple wine served in a claret glass.

They tasted the burgers and cooed their approval to Gus, who left, folding the screen closed behind them. After a few bites, Coop reminded Arcie, "Tessa and Austin?"

"Mmm"—she swallowed, dabbing her lips with a napkin—"it's poor procedure, to say the least, sharing details of an investigation with a layman, let alone a potential suspect."

Coop set down his burger and raised both hands in a don't-shoot gesture.

"But," she continued, "I think it's safe to say you've graduated to the status of an informant. Or even a collaborator."

"You mean, like, a sidekick?" He sipped his wine. "Like Pancho to Cisco? Or Tonto to the Lone Ranger?"

She sputtered. "Seems you've got a serious case of B-Westerns on the brain. Must be the locale."

"Must be, Sarge."

She set her napkin on the table. "Look, Coop, I had my doubts at first, but it seems you're playing it straight with me, and I appreciate that."

"Yup, pardner, I'm a square shooter."

"Would you let up on the cowboy crap?"

He mimed zipping his lip.

"I may have a screw loose"—she twirled a finger at her temple—"but I'd like to brainstorm some of my findings with you." She paused, laughed softly, and added, "Must be the elevation."

"Must be, Arcie."

"So here's the dope. First, Austin Royce. I told you on Saturday I had a vibe that he was reluctant to tell me something. His story about the family crisis was so vague, it left me thinking it was probably a cover for something else."

"I know what you mean," said Coop. "I talked with him briefly yesterday, and when I offered a few words of support regarding his 'problem,' he didn't understand what I was talking about. I had to remind him of the crisis with his daughter."

Arcie nibbled the end of a French fry, then set it down. "Turns out, he *is* hiding something. We ran a check of credit-card transactions. It seems his wife did fly to San Francisco on Tuesday evening, returning this past weekend. But Austin wasn't with her. He left a credit trail at home in the valley on Tuesday night and again on Wednesday afternoon, but there were *no* transactions to pinpoint his whereabouts on Wednesday morning. Clearly, he lied about his reason for bowing out of the golf game." Arcie lifted another French fry to her lips, concluding, "What we don't know is: Why?"

Coop smeared an index finger through a gob of melted

Camembert on his plate, then licked it. "So Austin's not in the clear. What about Tessa?"

Arcie sat back, taking a breather from the hearty lunch. "I met with her yesterday afternoon. She was relieved to be finished with her R-and-D meeting that morning, and I also sensed, as I had at the funeral, she was relieved to have Kavanall out of her hair. I needed to question her about her relationships with both Kavanall and your father, and boy, I got more than I bargained for on both scores."

"Really? In the office, she's been fairly tight-lipped about personal matters. She tends to stick to business."

"Well, she was ready to talk yesterday. We're both women, both in our forties, both working in male-dominated professions—she must've felt there was a bond. In fact, she thanked me for the opportunity to 'unload,' as she put it. I was with her for two hours." Arcie fanned the pages of her collected notes.

"Was Mimi's hunch correct? Was Tessa involved with my father?"

Arcie nodded. "She was."

"And how about the meeting with 'someone from Emery'? Mimi thought it was Tessa; I think it was Kavanall."

"Tessa wasn't with your father anytime that weekend. She'd started working at Emery a year or so earlier, so she splurged and took her first big vacation, a spring cruise with a few girl-friends. We were discussing this in her office, and she had a framed snapshot right there on her desk. It showed her toasting her friends with mai tais as they passed through the Panama Canal on Easter morning; the camera had stamped the date in the corner of the picture."

"How convenient for her."

"Exactly. It seemed way too coincidental that she happened to have a photo at hand as evidence of her whereabouts on a significant date fifteen years ago. She offered to provide further documentation of the trip, and I'll check it out, but somehow I couldn't help thinking she had booked the trip specifically to be able to *prove* she was anywhere but Riverside that weekend. She claimed the trip was wonderful; when I asked her casually if she's done much cruising since, she said she keeps wanting to, but that Easter trip was her first and only cruise."

"Intriguing, to say the least." Coop had finished his hamburger and sat hunkered over the table, swirling his wine.

"You bet, but there's even more to this story—the Kavanall angle. He didn't begin his career at Emery until a year and a half after your father's death, but Tessa first met him nearly three years earlier, during the summer when she started the job. Kavanall was back from school for a while, and they met at the corporate picnic, which I understand is a big deal every year for the top staffers."

"It's dreadful," said Coop, "but I always go with Stasia."

"Well, Kavanall certainly enjoyed it, at least that year." Arcie paused for effect, then dropped the bomb: "He managed to get Tessa pregnant."

Coop set the wine aside. "Huh?"

Arcie nodded. "And get this: he insisted on an abortion."

"He was a sweetheart, through and through."

"The procedure didn't go well."

With an elbow propped on the table, Coop rested his head in his hand. "Uh-oh."

"She got an infection, which damn near killed her. It rendered her sterile—and required a complete hysterectomy to prevent its spread."

"Jesus. No *wonder* she wasn't interested in his recent advances." And no wonder, he thought, she seems glad to be rid of him.

Gus rapped at the doorway. "Can I get you anything?"

"No, thank you," said Arcie. "We've finished."

He entered. Eyeing the empty plates, he joked, "You didn't like it." They assured him otherwise, and he cleared the table, except for their drinks.

When he was gone, Arcie reached into her briefcase and pulled out a thick, worn folder, which she placed on the table. "Earlier," she said, "you speculated that Kavanall's murder might be linked to your father's. If we're looking at Tessa, that theory seems logical enough, but you voiced that opinion before I gave you the rundown on Tessa. Why? What's fueling your speculation?"

Coop thought for a moment. "Let me answer that question in the form of another: When word got around that the investigation of my dad's death was being reopened, did someone feel that Kavanall's very existence was a threat?"

She weighed his words, nodding. "Stated another way: We have strong reason to believe Kavanall killed your father. We also have reason to believe their meeting that night was instigated by someone other than Kavanall. And *that* person couldn't risk having Kavanall's involvement discovered, because it could lead back to him."

"Or her," Coop noted. "But yes, that's the gist of it." He raised his glass and finished a last sip of wine.

"I want to show you something," she said, placing the folder in her lap. "Since I needed to go back to square one with Mimi this morning, I brought along your father's file. Turns out, I had no use for it at Mimi's, but I do now. You may find these disturbing; they're photos from the crime scene."

"Thanks for the warning, but I was there. I'll be all right."

She retrieved the evidence bag from her briefcase and slid the necklace onto the table. Then she fingered through the file and pulled out a picture, placing it near the necklace. "These are the wounds on your father's neck." It was a close-up showing a tape measure held alongside the row of puncture wounds. Arcie took a ruler from her briefcase and measured the distance between the barbs on the necklace. "Looks right on the money," she said.

Coop agreed.

She took out another photo and showed it to him. "You saw your father's body that morning, but I doubt if you saw this. It was found inside his shirt and had caught in his waistband." Pictured was an extreme close-up of a small metal object. "We determined it was part of a jewelry clasp, platinum."

Coop peered at the photo, then at the end of the necklace. "No doubt about it—it's like the missing piece of a puzzle."

"And lab testing should nail it. Obviously, after fifteen years, there's no telling who's handled this"—she slid the necklace back into the bag—"and if Kavanall was smart, he thoroughly washed it. Still, with all its crevices and barbs, there's a reasonable chance we can link it to the crime through DNA testing. We already have your father's sample and Kavanall's; it would be helpful to have yours."

"Okay, Arcie, I trust you. You've got it. But . . ." He hesitated. "What?"

Sheepishly, Coop asked, "Will it hurt?"

"No," she told him, suppressing a laugh, "it's just a swab inside the cheek. Tell you what: We've got a lab in Indio as well as Riverside. Indio is closer for you. I'll set it up, and you can go in whenever it's convenient."

He agreed with a nod.

She cleared the table and searched for another photo. "Here's something else you probably didn't notice." She put the picture on the table. "There was a tall bookcase in your father's office, and this is the view from above, shot from a ladder. You'll notice there's quite a bit of office equipment stored up there, probably old stuff that wasn't being used. Everything was dusty; it had been there quite a while. But one of the techs noticed a clean rectangle in the dust up there where something had recently been removed. Do you have any idea what that might have been? We've wondered all along if perhaps the assailant took it."

"Wow," said Coop, picking up the photo. But he didn't need to examine it. "I know exactly what was there. And Dad's killer didn't take it; Dad himself removed it." Coop explained how Ferris had given a mimeograph machine to Mimi and how Mimi had recently passed it along to him. "It's in my office right now. I've gone over it a couple of times, and it's not the MacGuffin."

She looked up from her notes. "The what?"

Pausing to chuckle, he then explained, "Dad referred to his prototype as the MacGuffin. It's a term popularized by Hitchcock to describe the object that drives the action of a plot. It might be the missing diamond or a treasure map or a roll of microfilm. In *The Maltese Falcon,* it was the statue of the bird. But it doesn't always have to be a physical object; it might be top-secret information or a scientific formula. George Lucas simply called it the object of everybody's search. Well, everybody's been searching for the elusive water engine for centuries, and Dad claimed he found it.

At first glance, the machine he left with Mimi looked promising, but trust me, it's not the prototype; it's worthless. I've decided to throw it out."

Arcie scrunched her brows. "Don't do that. We'd like to take a look at it."

"Sure. No problem." It was Tuesday. His office had been cleaned Monday night, and it would not be cleaned again until Wednesday night.

"Great." Arcie returned the evidence bag to her briefcase. "MacGuffin or no MacGuffin, I think it's safe to conclude we now have Ferris Brant's murder weapon."

Thinking of something, Coop expelled a quiet laugh.

"What?" asked Arcie.

"My stepson killed my father. It's downright operatic."

Arcie smirked. "It's almost Oedipal."

# Chapter 11

When Coop arrived back in the valley that afternoon and turned onto I-10, he opted to skip the exit that would have led to his office at Emery headquarters and, instead, kept driving east, some twenty miles to Indio. At the county law complex—a sizable campus consisting of a jail, courthouse, and sheriff's substation, collectively dubbed the "justice center"—he managed to find its forensics lab, which Arcie had alerted to expect him. He was out and on his way in five minutes.

Since he was now considerably closer to his home in Rancho Mirage than to his office on the far side of Palm Springs, he decided there was no pressing business that required his attention, and by four o'clock he had passed through the main gate at Entrada, skirted the golf course where Kav had been killed, and was pulling into the garage of the house he had designed.

Stasia had scrawled a note in the kitchen: I'M OUT. DON'T WAIT FOR ME. It gave no indication of her whereabouts. As the afternoon waned and the western sky warmed with the glow of sunset, Coop considered phoning his wife to double check about dinner, but not wanting to appear overprotective, he didn't call. Though he felt a measure of concern—it was unlike her to do this—he chose to interpret her absence as a sign of continued recovery. She was doubtless in the company of friends, most likely a group of women from one of her charity committees.

After sunset, he fixed himself a cocktail and, when that was finished, dressed for dinner. Though he had slept in a guestroom the previous night and would probably do so again that night, he had not otherwise moved out of the main bedroom, where he continued to use his bath and dressing quarters. He put on his favorite Armani tie—not necessary, as it was "just the club"—but forced to dine alone that evening, he was determined to look his best and make the most of it. Leaving the master suite, he glanced into Stasia's dark dressing room, then switched off the rest of the lights behind him.

When Coop arrived in the main lobby at Hellsgate, the maître d' greeted him with an unctuous good-evening.

"Thank you, Richard. I wonder if Bix happens to be dining alone." Though Coop had no desire to be caught one-on-one with his father-in-law, he felt it would be even more awkward to end up at separate tables, solo.

"No, Mr. Brant, I believe Mr. Emery had other plans. Your usual table?"

"Actually, Mrs. Brant won't be joining me, so I thought I'd eat at the bar."

"Very good, sir." Richard bobbed his head, walked Coop to the other side of the lobby, and held open for him the door to the Paradise Lounge.

The harpist began a slow, florid rendition of "Heaven's Just a Sin Away."

**D**inner was uneventful, and except for a bit of gabbing with the bartender, Coop was left alone with his thoughts while eating.

Coop still found himself alone when he returned to the house and Stasia was not there. He caught up on some reading for a couple of hours, had a splash of cognac, and then, around eleven, decided to get ready for bed.

Wearing a pair of linen lounge shorts, he stood brushing his teeth in his bathroom when he heard the peck of Stasia's heels on the stone floor of the hallway, approaching the master suite. He rinsed his mouth and stepped out into the bedroom as she entered. "Well, good evening, dear." He smiled. "I was getting a little worried."

"Why?" she asked, tossing her handbag onto a little upholstered bench near the door to her dressing room. She unfastened a wide patent-leather belt that cinched the waist of her dress, then dropped it on the bench as well.

He moved over to her and offered a kiss; she deflected it to the corner of her mouth, barely pecking back. He said, "I didn't think you'd be out so late."

"I didn't expect to be. Garrick Bates phoned and suggested

meeting for a drink. He wanted to talk about that board position. It got long, so we decided to have dinner."

"Well, then, you were in good hands." Coop stepped away, toward the bathroom.

"What's that supposed to mean?"

He turned, feeling accused of something. "Nothing—hope you had a good time. Will you be joining his board at the college?"

She gave a listless shrug.

"For whatever it's worth, I think you should do it."

"Why? The board is purely advisory; it doesn't make any decisions or *run* anything. Sound familiar?"

Coop understood her point: Garrick Bates ran his business interests the same way Bix Emery ran his. Even though Bates's board position was little more than window dressing, at least he had offered it; Bix, on the other hand, had *no* women on his board, not even his own daughter. It was a worthy distinction, but Coop sensed Stasia was in no mood to hear it. He said, "It's your decision. You've got a lot to offer."

"Other than my name?"

"*Yes.*" He moved a single step in her direction. "You're capable of so much more than you realize."

"I'm lazy?"

"*No.*" He moved another step closer. "I'm saying you don't give yourself enough credit."

She wasn't listening. "And don't forget, my name's not what it used to be. As you've been only too eager to point out"— she turned and walked toward her dressing room—"I've been hyphenated."

There could be no reasonable response to that comment, no lighthearted rebuttal or soothing reassurance, so Coop tossed his arms and returned to his bathroom.

As he struggled with a flosser, cringing each time it popped between two teeth, he wondered how things had degenerated so quickly. The downward slope, he had discovered, was not only slippery, but steep. Last time, fifteen years ago with Cheryl, the breakup had developed over many months. It had taken her nearly a year to plant the hate in their daughter, Clio, before asking Coop to get out.

"Uh, Coop?"

He turned, surprised by the hesitation in Stasia's voice, the softness. Smiling at the sight of her, he asked, "Yes?"

She fiddled with the tasseled sash of her long silk robe. "About your sleeping in the other room . . ."

"Yes?"

"It might make sense to move your things into that bathroom as well."

"Oh."

"It might make things a bit easier."

"If that's what you want, Stasia."

"Easier for both of us."

**W**hen Coop awoke Wednesday morning in a guest bedroom and showered in a guest bath, he felt as if his world had been upended. He had missed a week's worth of training sessions with Teddy, but today he intended to reestablish his regular schedule at IronLand. Grateful for an excuse to get out of the house early, he was eager to return to a groove that made his life feel normal.

By the time he pulled into the parking lot at the gym, the sun was shining, the world was gearing up for a busy midweek workday, and IronLand looked crowded. While walking from his car to the building, Coop scanned the parking lot for Jeeps. He saw at least a half dozen and laughed at his paranoia. When he had seen—or *thought* he had seen—the khaki guy at Emery headquarters, his vehicle had looked something like a Jeep, but Coop wasn't sure, nor was he sure of the color, except that it was dark. That Wednesday morning at the gym, there were SUVs at every turn, and many were dark. Not much to go on.

Inside, he changed, with no sinister encounters in the locker room, only a few hellos from familiar faces. After strolling out to the exercise floor near the ab machines, he grunted through his warm-up routine, including crunches on a Swiss ball, then hopped onto a treadmill, burning a few extra calories while waiting for Teddy.

Though Coop had steered clear of gyms since the time he left high school until he connected with Teddy a year ago, he had been a weekend runner most of his life. He had never run a race or pushed his endurance beyond a few miles, but he'd always enjoyed being active and had found that the solitude of running cleared his mind, inducing a Zen-like clarity of thought that verged, at times, on euphoria. In recent years, when his knees and feet had begun to resist the rigors of a long run, he'd side-stepped the temptation to seek remedy in painkillers and simply scaled back his routine, replacing the run with a brisk, steep walk on the treadmill. Though many complained about the monotony of the machine, Coop found he liked it—zoning out could make an hour's exercise pass very quickly—plus, it had kept him fit through middle age, primed for the real work that would not begin until retaining Teddy.

"Welcome back."

Coop hadn't been on the treadmill ten minutes, but he had already slipped into the zone and wasn't sure how long Teddy had been standing there. "Thanks," said Coop, slowing the belt and stepping off. "It's good to be back."

"Let's see"—Teddy checked his clipboard—"legs and back today."

"Really?" Coop rarely questioned Teddy's choice of routine, but he noted, "We hardly ever work on legs."

"Yours are already in great shape."

"I hear that now and then." Coop thought of Arcie's comment the prior Wednesday, during her visit to the house after Kavanall's death.

Teddy continued, "Legs respond best to practical training, like running or tennis, but since you've missed a few sessions, let's try the machines."

"You're the boss." Though it didn't seem Coop would be hefting any free weights that morning, out of habit he pulled on his lifting gloves and secured their Velcro closures while following Teddy across the gym floor.

They stopped at one of the leg-press machines. Teddy loaded the weights as Coop got in position, lying on his back. The first set proved difficult. When Coop finished, Teddy said, "We'll stretch the hamstrings at the end of the workout."

"Good. It's been a while. That always helps." Rather than hoisting himself out of and back into the machine for each rest, Coop simply stayed put, staring at the ceiling. Unable to look around the gym, he asked Teddy, "Any sign of our friend lately—that bruiser who had the dustup with Dennis Dill?"

"Nope. Once you started missing your regular sessions, he seemed to lose all interest in the place."

"Hmmm." Coop struggled through the second set of presses. During the rest, after catching his breath, he said to Teddy, "I happened to see Dennis Dill the other night."

"You mean, at the museum opening? I saw him too."

"No, no. After that. Last Friday, late, at Tantrum."

Teddy's face came into view, grinning, as he crouched next to Coop, asking, "And what were *you* doing at Tantrum?"

Coop laughed. "Nothing. I wasn't there. I was driving home and ended up stopped at a light as the bar was letting out. He was leaving with Bruce Rollo."

"See? Told you: Bruce isn't straight."

"No, I guess not." Coop hesitated, then asked, "Do you know how I can get in touch with Dennis? I'd like to talk to him."

"About Bruce Rollo?"

"No. About his encounter with that bruiser."

"Sure, I know how to reach him." Teddy leaned near, adding, "But he'll charge you by the hour."

"An hour will be plenty."

When Coop managed to finish his third set of presses, Teddy said, "Good job. Now let's do some leg curls." He led Coop over to another machine, adjusted its seat, and asked Coop to sit, legs extended. When the pins were adjusted in the weight stacks, Coop began the first set, drawing his feet down and beneath him, working against the resistance of the pads at his ankles.

During the rest, Coop could now easily look about the gym, as he was seated at about eye level with Teddy, whose face was pinched in an expression of concern. The trainer asked, "How's Stasia doing?"

Coop thought, Where to begin? He said, "It's been a rough

week. For both of us."

"I'm really sorry. Didn't mean to pry."

"No," Coop assured him, "I'm glad you asked. Not just glad—grateful. There's really no one else I can talk to about this." With a soft laugh, he added, "Jeez, that sounded kinda pathetic."

"Not at all. Look, your legs are fine. I think you can afford to skip some of these"—he indicated the clipboard. "Do you want to take a few minutes to sit down and talk?"

Coop nodded, then got up from the machine. "My legs are *fine*?"

"Yeah."

"Earlier, you said they were in *great* shape."

"Oops. Your legs look *fab*-ulous!"

"That's better," said Coop, flexing his calves as he followed his trainer to the gym's front desk, which was also set up as a juice-and-smoothie bar.

Teddy signaled one of the guys behind the bar, who responded with a thumbs-up and set to work blending something. Then Teddy led Coop to one of the trendy brushed-aluminum café tables arranged in a quieter lounge area, elevated a few steps to overlook the main floor. Sitting with Coop, scooting his chair close to the table, Teddy asked, "Now, what's this about Stasia?"

"Her son's death really hit her—badly."

"Of course."

"And a few nights before it happened, we had a frank discussion about Kavanall. I assured her that I'd always respected him, but at her prompting, I made what could be perceived as a passive admission that I didn't like him."

"Uh-oh. Was she upset?"

Coop leaned over the table, shaking his head. "Not at *all*. In fact, she volunteered that even though she loved him, there were times when she *herself* didn't much like him."

Teddy's eyes drifted to the ceiling. "I'll bet I know where *this* is headed."

"You guessed it: now that Kavanall is gone, her memory of that conversation—colored by maternal instincts—is highly selective, and suddenly, I'm the bad guy."

Teddy turned as someone from the bar brought him a smoothie in a tall plastic cup, along with a smaller second cup, empty. Teddy thanked him, and he retreated to the bar. Then Teddy poured a large clod of the stuff into the extra cup and passed it to Coop, saying, "See what you think."

Upon first tasting it, Coop thought he might gag, but he managed to swallow it and forced a smile. "What's in this?"

Noting Coop's expression, Teddy grinned. "Don't ask."

It was brownish, with hints of peanut butter, coffee, and God only knew what else, but whatever it was, Teddy, who had the far more enviable physique, seemed to like it, so Coop reasoned that it could do no harm and just might, in fact, be worth acquiring a taste for. Downing a second sip, he found it more palatable.

Teddy prompted him, "So suddenly, in Stasia's eyes, you're the bad guy."

"Right. Not that she *blames* me for what happened, but she blames me for not sharing her grief. And the irony is, she doesn't understand that I *am* grieving, in spite of something—something awful—that I've since discovered about Kavanall."

"Something?" With the side of his hand, Teddy rubbed a chocolaty smear from his lips. "Like what?"

"I just can't go into it right now, even with you, Teddy. Sorry."

"Okay, I understand."

"Actually, you don't. But when *she* learns this, and eventually she'll have to, it's going to challenge every loving memory she ever had of her son. I'm afraid it might overwhelm her—which won't help a marriage that already seems to be falling apart."

Teddy slumped back in his chair, saying quietly, "Christ, Coop. I'm so sorry."

"And the hell of it is—" Coop stopped himself, winced, then said quietly, with his eyes closed, "I'm not even sure it's a marriage worth saving."

Teddy exhaled a noisy breath, not quite a sigh, not quite a groan. "Last week when we talked about Stasia, you said you couldn't remember why you married her."

"I still don't."

"Well, then, how did you meet?"

"Back then, Emery was headquartered in Los Angeles, and my architecture practice—what was left of it—still had its office in Santa Barbara, not far from there. Out of the blue, I got a call one day from a secretary at Emery, asking if I'd care to submit a competing proposal for a corporate conference center they wanted to build on the coast. I needed the work, and the project sounded plenty interesting, but I couldn't imagine why they would approach me, as my practice had been almost entirely residential—and it was common knowledge, at least within the profession, that my career was on the skids. When I asked her, 'Why me?' she said she'd been given a list of a half-dozen architects to approach, and she was simply the contact person. She asked if I'd like to schedule an initial meeting to review the parameters of the project.

"I jumped at it, naturally. When I arrived for the meeting and the secretary took me into the conference room, I was surprised to come face-to-face with Stasia—daughter of Mr. Big himself. She explained that her father had given her the project of vetting the design process, which made sense, given her history of involvement in the arts. We enjoyed working together, and when I finally submitted the proposal, she loved it. More important, so did Bix, who asked to meet me, and over dinner that night, he awarded me the job.

"Once the project was under way, Stasia's role in it ended, but by then we were friends, both divorced in recent years, and one thing led to another. When we started talking marriage, I was sure Bix would be a problem, but as it turned out, he was all for it. I was stunned."

Finishing his story, Coop sat back, shaking his head. He drank more of the brown glop, still confounded by the turn of events that had landed him within the innermost circle of the Emery dynasty.

Teddy asked him, "Why were you stunned? By anyone's measure, you're an intelligent, good-looking, and talented man. Why did you think Bix wouldn't approve?"

"Have you forgotten?" Coop leaned forward on one elbow. "My career was tanking—and my first wife had dumped me—

because there was still a cloud of suspicion trailing me from my father's murder." Summing up his reasoning, Coop said, "Under those circumstances, I wouldn't want *my* daughter to marry me."

Teddy laughed. "I wouldn't advise that, either."

Coop shared the laugh. "You know what I meant."

"Yeah, I follow." Teddy crossed his arms, thinking for a moment, then said, "Bix is obviously a smart guy. Insightful. He knew how to read you, and he had faith in you. I mean, he would never let his daughter marry someone he suspected of murder."

Coop mirrored Teddy's pose, arms crossed, thinking. He recalled that Austin Royce had made a similar comment nine days earlier in his office. Coop had been telling him about the DNA request from Detective Madera and had mentioned, as an aside, "In case you've been wondering all these years—no, I didn't do it." And Royce had responded, "I can't imagine Bix would welcome you into the family if he had any doubts about that."

Teddy finished his smoothie. "Feeling better?"

"The talk helped. Not sure about the muscle brew"—he suppressed a belch—"but thanks."

**B**efore returning to the main workout floor, they trashed their plastic cups, and Teddy directed Coop to a display along the back wall where several dozen merchants, tradesmen, and professionals, mostly gay, tendered their business cards in a Lucite rack. "Here you go," said Teddy, plucking one of the cards and handing it to Coop.

Dennis Dill's business card was classically black-on-white, tasteful, and above all, discreet. Beneath his name, a single line of engraved type listed his offerings in inventively vague terms: MODELING, LIFE COUNSELING, PERSONAL SERVICES.

Coop slipped the card into the pocket of his workout shorts and followed Teddy to resume their session with some back exercises, beginning with a seated cable row.

When their hour was up, after the hamstring stretches, Coop showered, changed, grabbed his gym bag, and carried it from the locker room toward the building's entrance, ready for the office. He had transferred Dennis Dill's card from his shorts to his corduroys, intending to phone him from the car. But Coop paused near the smoothie bar. His car had a hands-free interface with the phone he carried—well-intentioned technology, but an imperfect means of conducting a conversation that would likely require both subtlety and delicacy—so he detoured to the same café table where he had earlier talked to Teddy. Then he retrieved the card, took a seat, switched the phone on, and placed the call.

On the fourth ring, just when Coop assumed he would be transferred to voice mail, a man answered, "Good morning. This is Dennis."

"Good morning, Dennis. This is Cooper Brant. You don't know me, but I'm a client of Teddy Duncan's at IronLand."

"Cooper Brant . . . ," repeated the voice on the line. "Oh! The architect? Yes, I remember you from the gym." Practically purring, he added, "Of course."

"Uh, this is a little awkward."

"Tut-tut, now. No need for that, not with me. What can I do for you, Cooper?"

Coop explained that he wanted to spend some time talking to Dennis, perhaps for an hour the following morning. They agreed on the rate, two hundred dollars, and Dennis gave directions to his home, concluding, "Don't worry about a thing—I'm *very* discreet," which left Coop at a momentary loss for words. Dennis added, "You *are* married, aren't you?"

"Yes, b'but perhaps I d'didn't make my intentions entirely clear. I really do just want to talk."

Dennis laughed. "Sure, doll. We can play it that way, if you like. I'll see you tomorrow morning at eleven." He hung up with a smooch.

Coop noted the meeting on his calendar, where he found a reminder to schedule a follow-up visit with Cliff Sloan, who wanted to have a quick look at his gums. Cliff had said it would take less than five minutes, "so I can work you in anytime; just let me know when to expect you." Now that Coop had managed a couple of flossings, he felt ready, almost eager, to bare his gums, so he thought he might pop in today—before lunch, while his mouth was still presentable.

He punched in Cliff's number, and on the first ring, the call was answered by voice mail: "Thank you for phoning the dental offices of Dr. Clifford Sloan. We are closed on Wednesdays in order to accommodate the needs of those patients who can see us only on weekends. Please call back tomorrow, or simply leave a message after the tone, and we'll look forward to serving your needs." *Beep.*

Crap, thought Coop. He would not be able to see Cliff before lunch today—or tomorrow, for that matter, as his morning was tightly booked, including his session with Dennis Dill. Responding to the beep, Coop identified himself, said that Cliff had asked him to come in anytime, and concluded, "I'll probably drop in tomorrow, Thursday, in the early afternoon, say one-thirty. Thank you." And he hung up.

He marked his calendar, stood, and began to leave. He had not moved three steps, however, when he thought of something and halted. By now he had stored Arcie Madera's various numbers in his phone's directory; he pulled up her cell listing and placed the call. Moments later, he said to her voice mail, "Arcie, it's Coop. This may mean nothing, but I thought I should pass it along. I just found out that Cliff Sloan's office is closed on Wednesdays. Nothing unusual in that—lots of doctors and dentists swap Wednesdays for Saturdays. But at the risk of stating the obvious: Kavanall was killed on a Wednesday morning, and now we know where Cliff *wasn't*."

Within a half hour, Coop arrived at Emery headquarters, waved to the guard at the gate, and followed the winding entry road back to the executive parking lot. Getting out of the car, he took his portfolio, stowed his gym bag in the trunk, and set the alarm. Instinctively, he scanned the area for Jeeps—and bruisers in khaki—as he walked from the lot, through the solar garden, and toward the research building. He spotted no one at all, nothing suspicious, not even a dark-colored SUV, which left him chiding himself for his paranoia as he entered the building and took the back hall to his office.

While standing at his private entrance, however, and tapping in his security code, he was overcome with a sense of foreboding, triggered by both a smell and a noise. It was the barest whiff of something from a nearby research lab that brought to mind a long-ago neighbor's toy chemistry set. And at that moment, down the hall, a drinking fountain's condenser switched off with a quiet thud. The sequence—the whiff followed by the thud—transported him to a similar experience, fifteen years prior, walking the hall of a deserted campus building in Riverside, approaching his father's office.

Coop unlocked the door to his own office, opened it slowly, switched on the lights, and discovered that his foreboding had sprung not from paranoia, but prescience. His pristine quarters, his refuge from a messy world, had been ransacked.

Drawers from the taboret next to his glass-topped desk and from the credenza behind it had been flung on the floor, their contents strewn about. Files gaped open with their folders rifled, flung everywhere. His computer was missing its guts, the CPU. Even the tall cabinet of flat-files had been pillaged, with years' worth of plans, schematics, renderings, and elevations now trampled on the floor like so much garbage. Next to the cabinet, near the wastebasket, the boxed mimeograph, identified as trash, remained untouched. Coop squatted, removed and crumpled the Post-it, then stood, lifted the box in his arms, and set it out of the way, overhead, on top of the tall cabinet.

As Coop turned to his desk and saw its chair shoved aside, his mind flashed with the image of his father slumped in a desk chair, one leg kicked forward, arms drooping to either side, head lolled backward, mouth and eyes open. Just behind Coop's chair, on the wall above the credenza, hung the framed color photo, now askew, showing Sheriff Rusty Oxhide waving his white hat from the saddle of a rearing palomino. He'd been the TV idol of millions of kids, and although he was little Cooper's dad, he was still bigger than life.

Coop stepped over to the desk, lifted the phone, and called security.

Within a minute, a quartet of Emery guards rushed into Coop's office, weapons drawn. One of them asked, "Are you all right, sir?"

"No," he answered dryly, "but physically, I'm fine. Whoever did this is long gone."

Holstering his gun, another noted, "No signs of forced entry."

Coop said, "The door was locked when I arrived just now, and the security code had been set." He also pointed out how the curtains were still drawn against the glass wall to the outer offices, and the communicating door was locked.

"Anything of value missing?"

Coop shrugged, indicating the general disarray. "The computer."

One of them took notes and another took pictures as Coop tried to assess if anything other than the computer had been taken.

A minute or so later, the director of security, who wore a blazer with a badge, walked through the door with Bix; the others snapped to attention. Pyrite brought up the rear, halting in his tracks as he assessed the shambles with a low, quizzical whine.

"Jesus, Coops," said Bix, stepping forward to give his son-in-law a hug, "what the hell happened here?"

"Not a clue."

Bix squeezed Coop's shoulders. "I'll get a cleaning crew in here right away. We'll get you fixed up."

"Thanks, Bix, but I need to pick through this on my own. What has me most worried is the computer. I had a lot of recent work stored in it."

The director said, "You needn't worry about that, Mr. Brant. Your computer backs up nightly to the corporate mainframe."

"It does?" Technically, Coop was not a company employee, but an outside contractor with an on-site office. He was relieved to know his work had been saved, but dismayed to realize his every keystroke had been archived.

"Have you noticed any suspicious activity lately?"

"In fact, I have." Coop related his various encounters with the guy in khaki, most recently two days earlier, right there at Emery headquarters. "At first I thought it was an undercover cop, but now, I highly doubt it."

"One thing's for sure," said the director. "Whoever did this was someone with access. We seem to have a problem, and it's internal."

Coop thought, Austin Royce is internal, a heartbeat away from Bix. And Tessa Irwin is internal, just across the hall. Coop walked Bix a few steps from the others, saying, "I need to share some thoughts with you, but not here, not now. This is pretty sensitive."

Bix nodded, pausing to think. "Today's no good. I'm driving over to San Diego later for a meeting tomorrow morning. On the way back, I thought I'd stop at Questover—wanna try that recipe I found. So tell you what: come up to the cabin tomorrow around four, and we can have a good long talk, just us. Can it wait that long?"

"Sure. Meanwhile"—Coop breathed a disgusted sigh—"I've got my work cut out for me right here. Christ, what a mess."

Bix hugged him. "Don't fret, Coops. We'll get to the bottom of this." Then he turned to his security director, looking steamed. He barked, *"Right?"*

The guy in the blazer winced. "Absolutely, sir."

Pyrite yapped.

# Chapter 12

**S**tasia asked, "Why did you marry me?"

It was Thursday morning. Coop had stepped outdoors with his coffee and newspapers to begin his day in the solitude of sunrise by the pool. He'd slept alone and fitfully—no surprise—and now he needed to enjoy at least the illusion of serenity for a few minutes before leaving for the office, where he would continue his efforts to dig out of yesterday's mess. Absorbed in his thoughts, he hadn't even heard Stasia walk out from the house, coffee in hand.

He said, "That's quite an opening line."

"Sorry. Good morning." She sat on the opposite love seat, facing him over the low table where the papers were spread out. She wore rumpled silk pajamas, frosty mint green; he was dressed for the office in his favorite corduroys, bottle green.

He said, "Good morning. Sleep well?"

She shook her head. "The pills ran out." She slurped the coffee.

"There's probably a reason they give you only a week's worth."

"God, it's been a week now, hasn't it?" She ran the fingers of one hand through her hair. "It seems like forever since Kav died; at the same time, it seems like yesterday."

"Without the pills, your focus should improve."

She grinned. "Not sure I want it to." She frowned. "The thoughts, the dreams, the questions—what a night. I woke up on the wrong side of the bed. Literally."

"Miss having me there?"

"Honestly?" She gave him a sheepish look. "No. I'm so sorry, Coop. You've never been less than wonderful, but suddenly, something's missing—or rather, something seems to be coming to a head, something I can't quite put my finger on. Last night, lying there in the dark, I just couldn't shake the question: Why *did* you marry me?"

Coop closed his eyes. He'd been tussling with the same question of late and found the answer every bit as confusing and evasive as Stasia now did. He opened his eyes and told her, "I loved you. I still do, of course."

She nodded.

But he wondered if he meant it. Was it love, or was it simply a matter of habit, of comfort? And even that was slipping away. Lately, their marriage had been anything but comfortable.

She said, "When we met, everything just seemed to, I don't know . . . *fit.*"

Smiling, Coop recalled, "It did, didn't it? We seemed so right for each other, so *ready* for each other. I couldn't believe how lucky I was. I hadn't felt that way in years—since before Dad died." Coop's brow wrinkled in thought.

"What?"

"May I turn the question around on you?" He leaned forward, asking, "Stasia, why did *you* marry *me*?"

She set down her coffee and slowly whirled her hand, thinking. "Love, of course."

"No cheating. That was my answer."

She sputtered a little laugh.

"But think about it," he said. "We weren't kids. We'd both been through the mill already. When we were drawn to each other, it wasn't puppy love; it wasn't infatuation. Like you said, it felt as if everything just *fit,* and very quickly. Which is great. But that alone isn't generally enough reason for two mature, independent adults to say 'I do.' So if it wasn't just the fit, and it wasn't infatuation, what did you see in me that made you want to marry me?"

She lowered her head into her hands and said, barely above a whisper, "I don't know, Coop." After a long pause, she looked up again. "Truth is, Bix sort of railroaded it."

It was the least plausible explanation for his marriage that Coop had ever expected to hear. He asked, "B'B'*Bix*?"

"He felt you were right for me. And you know Bix—Father knows best."

"I'm stunned. And I *was* stunned—when he approved of the marriage."

"Approved of it? He *suggested* it—long before you did."

Coop's face wrinkled with a queasy thought. Then he voiced it: "The competition for the conference center. I was really proud of that work. Did I win the job fair and square?"

"You deserve to be proud of it. The design is magnificent."

"But was it the *best*?"

"Sweets"—she leaned forward, elbows on knees—"it was the *only*."

He flinched. It suddenly made sense, but he had never once allowed himself to consider the possibility. "I was told a half-dozen architects were competing."

"So was I, at first. But yours were the only plans submitted."

Coop fell back in his seat.

Stasia explained, "Those were the boom years. I assumed the other guys were busy."

"Well, crap." Coop thought he might cry. "That job was the beginning of my renaissance, professionally. My rise from the ashes. It was my very best effort, and I won it by *default*?"

"Don't put such a dorty spin on it, sweets." She rose. "More coffee?"

"Uh, sure," he said vacantly. As Stasia stepped into the house, Coop thought, Dorty? You'd be dorty, too, if you'd just learned your career was a sham. You'd be more than dorty—*plenty* dorty—if you'd just discovered that your marriage had been arranged by a manipulative, micromanaging gasbag with too much money, a flair for the perverse, and no sense of boundaries whatever.

"Thank you, dear," he said sweetly when Stasia padded back from the kitchen and poured his coffee. Droplets spattered in the low-angled sunlight. The cup steamed in the cool morning air.

"I was thinking," she said, refilling her own cup and sitting again, "it almost feels like a pattern."

"Hm?" He blew across the surface of the cup and sipped from it.

"Well, I guess it takes more than two to make a pattern—two marriages. One is long ended; the other, let's face it, is winding down."

"Is it? It doesn't have to. We could work on it."

She sighed. "That takes a good amount of will, Coop. I just don't think I have it."

"I'm sorry."

"Don't be. It's not as if we ended up throwing things at each other. And in the beginning, there was no infatuation; you said so yourself. Start to finish, there's been very little passion. Whatever kept it going, it just seems to be gone."

"Good grief," he said. "This sounds like 'Can't we be friends?'"

"Can't we?"

"Well, of *course,* but shouldn't we at least—"

"You know," she interrupted, "when Keith and I got married, we were probably too young. That marriage didn't get off to a good start, but then Kavanall came along, and everything settled down. We were a family; we had a purpose. Bix doted on Kav and treated Keith like a son. Everything was fine; it was stable. I assumed it was rock-solid. But then"—Stasia's expression hardened—"out of the blue, something went wrong."

"What happened, Stasia?"

She stiffened. "It ended badly."

"I *know.* That's what you always say. But you can tell *me.* Did he hurt you?"

She laughed. "You mean, did he hit me? *Keith?* Heavens no! He just sort of flaked out. Male menopause, midlife crisis—whatever you want to call that, he had it bad. I mean, for Christ sake, he was a *banker,* about as bland as they come. And suddenly, one day, he drops this big-ass bomb that he's been seeing someone, he wants out, he needs a new life. It was just *so* unlike him, so unexpected. And to this day, I don't believe there even *was* some 'other woman.' That new wife of his? She came along years later."

"Refresh me," said Coop. "When did the two of you break up?"

Stasia paused, recalling, "It was a year or two before you and I got married."

Coop nodded, putting it in perspective: "A year or two after my own divorce."

Wryly, Stasia noted, "Must've been a bug or something going around."

Coop put in a few hours at the office that morning, sorting through his scattered files, trying to restore some sense of order to his work space, trashing any paperwork that should have been pitched anyway, and assessing what might have been taken other than the computer; as far as he could tell, that was the only item missing. By midmorning, an Emery tech had replaced the CPU, reinstalled all his software, reconnected him to the company mainframe, and restored all his backed-up directories. Coop said to the tech, "Amazing." But he thought, Alarming. My every keystroke *has* been archived. When they're backed up, are they also reviewed?

Shortly after ten-thirty, Coop checked the cash in his wallet and left the office to drive into Palm Springs for his appointment with Dennis Dill. He lived in the Las Palmas area, an upscale old neighborhood near the north end of town where many of the homes could legitimately be described as estates, occupying sizable tracts of walled land. During the town's golden years, many of these had been getaways for Hollywood royalty. Some still were, but others had been converted to inns or "party houses" for catered events.

Dennis Dill lived in one of these converted properties, occupying a coach house that overlooked a well-manicured courtyard and garden, a grand old elliptical pool, and the main house beyond. A bit of Versailles, thought Coop as he walked through the gate and rang the doorbell, hidden within a cluster of vines exactly where Dennis had told him to find it.

"Is that you, Cooper?" said a voice, approaching from around the corner of the coach house. "Oh, my—yes, of course," said Dennis as his bleached-blond mop of hair popped into view. He was perhaps fifty, nice looking for his years, with good muscle tone maintained at the gym. Except for a slight paunch at the belly, he had kept generally lean, and it was easy to believe that in prior years he'd had the right stuff for a career in adult videos. As to his other assets, he left little to doubt, having donned a pair of saffron silk harem pants that displayed a conspicuous bulge that Coop judged impossibly plump. Dennis also wore beaded Balinese sandals—so easy to slip out of—and a sheer chiffon vest of shocking fuchsia that revealed a glint of bling in one of his nipples. He glanced at his watch, a vintage Mickey Mouse with a yellow nylon strap, saying, "Right on time. I like that."

"It's my nickel," Coop reminded him. "Why waste it?"

Dennis looked taken aback for a moment, then burst into loud laughter. "My *God*, you're a wit!" With a lavish rolling of both arms, the sort of hoo-ha fit for a sultan, he asked in a deep, deep voice, "Won't you follow me?" and led Coop around to the main terrace and through the open French doors of his living room in the coach house.

Despite Dennis's theatrics and over-the-top costuming, Coop found the setting, the building, and its interior thoroughly charming. The main room had a polished tile floor with a small round dining table centered near the open doors and looking out over the pool. A graceful old chandelier of tin and crystal hung over the table, suspended from the two-story ceiling. A loft, apparently the sleeping quarters, divided the high back wall, accessible by a winding stairway of wrought iron. Throughout, the furnishings were tasteful and comfortable, mostly French antiques, both classic and provincial. Coop nodded his approval. "Did you decorate it yourself?"

Dennis primped. "Of course, doll. Can I get you something to drink? Cocktail maybe?" He checked his watch again. "It's five *somewhere*."

"Some water would be great, thanks."

"Comin' right up!" And Dennis whisked into the galley kitchen. Rattling ice, he called to Coop, "I thought we might start with a bit of massage, see how that goes, then take it from there."

Coop stepped to the kitchen doorway, saying, "Honest, I just want to talk."

Dennis met him in the doorway and handed him the glass, winking. "Okay, big boy"—he ran his finger down the length of Coop's necktie—"I'll talk you up."

Coop stepped backward into the living room. "M'Maybe we should sit down."

Dennis followed him into the room. Gesturing, he suggested, "How about the daybed?" It was piled with cushions and big enough for two.

Coop countered, "How about the table?"

"Dreary, dreary, dreary"—Dennis wagged his head—"but you're the customer."

That's better, thought Coop, as they each took a seat, across from each other, at the little dining table. It was less than three feet in diameter, and though it was surrounded by four chairs, it would have been a tight squeeze for four diners. For two, for talk, it was perfect.

Dennis folded his hands on the cheery chintz tablecloth. "What's on your mind, Cooper? Let me guess: life with the wife just ain't what it used to be."

"In fact, it's not." Coop sipped his water. "But that's not why I'm here. I've got something entirely different on my mind."

"Ooh!" said Dennis, intrigued beyond measure. "Shall I set up the sling?"

Coop leaned forward. "Just *listen*, okay? This gets kind of complicated, but I'm interested in that guy who yelled at you at the gym a couple of weeks ago. It was a Friday morning."

"Well, he was *certainly* interested in you."

Wearily, Coop responded, "I know, I know. It seems we keep crossing paths, and it can't be coincidence. Frankly, I think he's stalking me, and I'm not sure what to do about it."

"Simple," said Dennis, flicking a wrist. "If you're hot for each other, just ask for his number."

"I'm *not* hot for him, and I highly doubt he's hot for *me*. I don't think he's gay."

"I tend to agree. Did you notice? He called me a faggot."

"I did notice. I thought it was crude."

"Thank you," said Dennis with a curt nod. "No gay man would ever shout a word like that in public." Dennis paused. "Unless he's a closet case." With a shudder, he added, "Or a Republican. Or a Republican closet case. Or a closet Republican."

Coop rolled his eyes. "Can I assume, then, that you don't know him?"

"Never saw him before in my life."

"Can I ask you to think back and tell me exactly what happened that morning?"

"You were there. You saw it all."

"I was on the T-bar with my butt in the air."

"Oh, honey. That Teddy is a beast—an unmitigated *beast.*"

Coop smirked. "I've only got an hour, Dennis. Tell me what happened."

"Well"—Dennis sat back, crossing his arms—"I was there at IronLand, doing my routine with the free weights, gabbing with some friends. And we noticed this, this . . . *man.* I mean, talk about butch! I'm not usually into that, but this guy, well, he had a certain rugged, animal appeal, just oozing all that badness. James, one of my friends, dared me to go over and ask for his number. I've never exactly been shy, so I waltzed over and said, 'You're new here, aren't you?'

"But he wouldn't even look at me. He just kept pumping away, and that's when I noticed he was looking at *you;* he wouldn't take his eyes off you. I started to tell him he was barking up the wrong tree, when he finally turned to me and asked—loud—what the hell my problem was. 'Well,' I said, kinda huffy, 'that doesn't seem very sociable. Since you're new here, we'll let it go this time, but if you want my advice, mister, I think a bit of attitude adjustment is in order.'

"He didn't hear a word of it, or at least he pretended not to, because he was far too busy—watching you again. So I tapped him on the shoulder and said, 'Yoo-hoo. Are you listening? That guy is married. I mean, to a woman, a real woman." But instead of thanking me for these insights, he shot up from the seat of the chest-press machine and yelled in my face to keep my hands off him. He was at least six inches taller than I'd realized and built like a brick water closet—I *loathe* scatological metaphors—so I backed off fast.

"By now, James and the boys were laughing. What could I do? What could I say? Well, I swaggered back over to them and explained, 'We had a nice chat, but he's just not into me.'"

Coop asked, "And you never saw him before that?'

Dennis shook his head. "Or since."

"I have."

"So," Dennis continued, "let's just say my gaydar was out of kilter that morning. I assumed he was into this rough-and-tumble dominance scene, but it never crossed my mind he might be to-tally straight. Usually, if there's a closet issue, I can sense it from the start, and it requires a more finessed approach. Same thing with bisexuals."

Which, for Coop, brought to mind Bruce Rollo. He said to Dennis, "I've known many gay friends over the years, but at least to my knowledge, no bisexuals. Some of my gay friends insist that bisexuality doesn't even exist, that it's a myth or a cop-out."

Dennis nodded. "If you're half-gay, you're gay. Like being half-black. I used to feel that way myself, but I've come to figure that if anyone should try to keep an open mind, Lord knows, it's *moi.* And the truth is, I've actually known a handful of them—genu-ine, well-adjusted bisexuals who swing both ways, enjoy it, and don't agonize over it."

"Such as"—Coop hesitated—"Bruce Rollo?"

Dennis arched his brows.

Coop said, "I happened to see you last Friday night. I was driv-ing home late, and you were leaving Tantrum together."

"Ah." Dennis laughed. "You had me thinking you were clairvoyant."

"Hardly." Coop laughed as well. After a pause, he nudged, "So you do know Bruce?"

"Mm-hmm." Dennis examined his nails, explaining, "We met shortly after he moved here for his gig at the college. He's a friend, not a client, but we do like to play now and then. I have to give him credit—he's up-front about everything. I'm well aware he's involved with a woman. She's a cop."

"A sheriff's detective, actually," said Coop. "She was with him at the museum opening. Did you see her?"

"I met her. She's truly lovely—has a bit of an edge, but I like that. If I had any interest in women, *that* way, I'd be attracted to her myself. So I'm glad they found each other." Offhandedly, Dennis added, "But of course it won't last."

It was now Coop's brows that arched. "Oh?"

"Well, think about it: I know Bruce has strong feelings for her. Maybe he loves her, maybe not. But it's not in the cards that he could ever fully *commit* to her. I mean, he can't just flip a switch and decide he's not attracted to men anymore; that will always be part of who he is. Plus, there's simply the matter of logistics. Bruce is a *visiting* professor at the school. That gig's not open-ended. When it's over, he's gone."

Outside, beyond the French doors, a tiered fountain trickled at the far end of the oval pool. A pair of finches splashed in the lower basin. Though Coop had been discomfited by the prospects of spending an hour in the private quarters of a paid escort—a sex worker—he now felt oddly at ease with Dennis, who had brought unexpected clarity to an issue that had been nagging at Coop just below the level of full consciousness. Bruce Rollo's bisexuality was suddenly transformed from a hazy, lingering threat into a harmless detail, perhaps even a benign omen.

Though Coop now had all the information—and more—that he had hoped to glean from Dennis, he felt no rush to leave and found himself enjoying a discussion that drifted through various areas of common interest, from cars to conservation to mid-century design. Coop learned that Dennis had studied architecture when he began college, then transferred into photography and filmmaking. Who'd have guessed?

At a lull in their pleasant chatter, Dennis checked Mickey. "You still have some time left. In fact, I'd be happy to throw in a few extra minutes if there's anything you'd like to . . . explore. Heaven knows, I'd like to."

"I'm sure you're just being nice. But thank you, Dennis."

Dennis gave him an odd look that verged on concern. "Just being *nice*? Get real." He studied Coop for a moment, then smiled. "Shucks, with your preppy little shoes and your little knit tie and your jolly green *corduroys*, for God sake—you're awfully cute. I mean, more than cute. You're adorable, Cooper."

Coop could not recall that anyone had ever said that, and in fact, he'd always judged himself a far cry from adorable. It could simply have been a flirtatious exaggeration from Dennis, and yet, he had couched the comment in an invitation to intimacy—off the clock, no less—so Coop chose to interpret the flattery as sincere. Not knowing how to react, he masked the confusion on his face by taking a drink of water; then he set the glass on the table.

Dennis walked his fingers across the tablecloth, moved the glass from Coop's hand, and took Coop's fingers into his own. "Awww," he clucked, "an owie." Holding the stub of Coop's ring finger, he asked, "What happened here?"

"I was a baby. Accident in my crib."

"It's like a strange but mesmerizing . . . *flaw*." Dennis smiled. With both hands, he gently pulled Coop's hand toward his face, taking a closer look. "It's your mark. It makes you special and unique." He drew it closer. "Know what?" he asked quietly. "It's pretty damn hot." Grinning, Dennis kissed the stub, then drew it into his mouth.

When Dennis whirled his tongue around it, Coop withdrew his hand.

He cleared his throat. "You said two hundred, right?"

"Stay awhile. There's time."

"Thanks, but no. I need to be going."

It was shortly past noon when Coop left Dennis Dill's and drove out of the Las Palmas neighborhood, which abutted the downtown area of Palm Springs. Because he was expected at one-thirty at Cliff Sloan's office, which was also downtown, there was no point in returning to Emery headquarters, and he decided to find somewhere to have lunch right there along the main drag, Palm Canyon Drive. While the street offered a wide array of trendy little restaurants, any one of which would be suitable for a light midday meal, he made his choice not on the basis of cuisine or location, but on his recollection that one of them had a particularly tidy men's room where he could lock the door behind him and have some privacy at the sink.

He needed to brush and floss. In anticipation of those duties, he had loaded his zippered portfolio with the appropriate supplies, and while waiting for his check to arrive, after the Cobb salad had been cleared, he slipped into the men's room and went to work, opening wide to banish every last vestige of bacon, avocado, and blue cheese; the cracked peppercorns proved a special challenge, requiring a second pass. By the time he finished, a line had formed; he ducked the dirty looks as he unlocked the door and returned to his table with the portfolio tucked under his arm.

One of the standees muttered to another, "What the hell was he doing in there—having a baby?"

When Coop returned to the car, he popped a breath mint, checked his phone for messages, and finding none, drove the few blocks to the Spanish-style strip mall where Clifford Sloan, DDS, maintained his snug suite of offices. Coop pulled in near the hanging sign with the happy, dancing molar. Two or three other cars were parked nearby, but the vast majority of spaces was empty. It looked like a slow afternoon. Good. Coop hoped to get in and out quickly, as he had barely made a dent in the ravaged files at his office.

He presented himself to the receptionist and took a seat across from the aquarium—still plenty of bubbles, still no fish, at least none that he could see. After waiting five minutes, he had heard nothing at all, save the bubbles, from the labyrinth within—no chatter, no drilling, no footsteps, no children's cries, no plumbing. He checked his Cartier; it was just one-thirty.

"Mr. Brant?"

The voice startled him. Had he dozed? He looked up to find the nursette, improbably young and curiously small, standing near the fish tank.

"This way, please." She led him into the same room where his procedure had been performed, then asked him to be seated, clamped on his bib, and lowered the back of the chair till Coop was nearly parallel to the floor.

"This really isn't a full-blown exam," said Coop. "Cliff just wants a quick look."

The nursette tittered as if he were an imbecile speaking absolute gibberish. She moved to the door, said, "Doctor Cliff will be right with you," and disappeared.

A moment later, the door opened again. Coop said, "Hi there, Cliff," though he couldn't see him from the chair.

"Jesus Christ." The door closed again. Cliff scooted a stool over to the chair and sat, telling Coop in an agitated whisper, "There was a *detective* here this morning—a *police* detective—and she seemed to think I killed Kav!" Cliff wore neither the surgical mask nor the plastic helmet today; the strain from his encounter that morning was apparent in his face.

Looking up at him, Coop asked, "She *said* that?"

"Not in so many words." Cliff adjusted Coop's chair so they could converse face-to-face. "But she scared the crap out me. She gave me the shakes—just look." He leveled a hand before Coop's face, and it was indeed shaking.

Coop's only thought: Glad I'm not here for a procedure.

Cliff continued, "I mean, the *questions* she asked—she wanted to know where I *was* on the morning Kav was killed."

"Uh, where were you?"

"Golfing! It was Wednesday. I've got a regular foursome with another dentist and a couple of doctors. We rotate clubs; that morning we were at Thunderbird."

"I assume the other guys will back you up."

"Of course. And the club will have a record of our tee time."

"Great," said Coop. "You're in the clear."

Calmer now, Cliff asked, "Think so?"

"Sure." After a pause, Coop added, "Unless you hired a hit man."

Cliff went ashen. "That's not funny."

"Did she happen to ask you about the time during college when you and Kav planned an Easter vacation in Mexico?"

"She did, in fact." Cliff planted his hands on his hips. "How'd she know about *that*?"

With an innocent shrug, Coop noted, "She's a detective."

"I mean, that was what—fifteen years ago? We were juniors in college. That's ancient history. It has nothing to do with Kav's death. Why even bring it up?"

"Maybe she was trying to establish the depth of your friendship, which works in your favor, by the way."

"Hmmm." Cliff weighed Coop's words, conceding, "That's a good point."

"Fill me in, Cliff. How did that Easter trip come about? How did you and Kav come to be friends?"

Cliff stood, explaining, "Back then, Kav and his family lived in Los Angeles; I grew up here in the valley. Even though they were out here quite often, that's not how we met. For dorm assign-ments, the college tried to pair up incoming freshmen who might have some common background, and from the opposite coast, it must have appeared we were neighbors. So we ended up as roommates, and the friendship lasted. We'd hang out sometimes over the summer while we were both home, but for the shorter breaks, Kav usually traveled. I couldn't; I was already in debt for tuition."

Coop said, "But for spring break of your junior year, Kav changed his plans."

"Right. He was planning a week in Europe—Paris, I think—but decided to come home instead. Since we were both going to be around, he suggested we drive down to Tijuana late Saturday night, then spend a couple of days there over the long Easter weekend."

"Why Tijuana?"

Cliff gave Coop a look.

"Oh. That's what I thought."

Cliff continued, "At first, the plan was to meet down there, but I was having trouble with my car, a real wreck. Kav offered to drive over from L.A. and pick me up so we could ride down to-gether. He said it was no problem because he had some sort of meeting to take care of on Saturday, between here and L.A."

"Where, do you know?"

"Riverside or maybe Redlands, over there somewhere. He said it should wrap up by early evening, and he told me to be ready to go by eight o'clock. Well, he didn't arrive till nearly midnight, and brother, was he a mess. He was bloody, his clothes were torn, and he had multiple bruises on his face and arms. What really grossed me out, though, were his hands—the palms were, like, *shredded*. I wanted to take him to an emergency room, but he wouldn't hear of it. And he didn't want to stay at my place because my parents would ask too many questions. So I got a motel room for him, did the best I could to patch him up, and after a couple days' rest, he headed home. Needless to say, we never got to Tijuana."

"How did he explain what happened to him?"

Cliff sat on the stool again, leaning close to tell Coop, "He said he'd stopped for a quickie with a hooker, and things got out of hand. I didn't buy it. I mean, what was she—a truck driver? But that's the only explanation I ever got."

Coop could think of another explanation, but he didn't voice it.

Cliff said, "Okay, now, let's take a look," and lowered Coop's chair into position. He donned a pair of magnifying glasses, squeaked into his latex gloves, picked up a little round dental mirror, and said, "Open, please."

Coop said, "Everything feels fine," then opened wide.

"Mm-hm." Cliff poked around with the mirror. "Nice. Very nice. Good work."

Coop smiled, tasting latex on his lips.

"Hmmm." Cliff grabbed another instrument. "Let me just . . ." And he scraped something from between two of the molars. He wiped the pick on Coop's bib, then went in again to remove something else. After three or four such incursions, he quipped, "Cobb salad?"

Within a minute, Coop was out of the chair. Cliff patted his back, saying, "Big improvement. Keep up the flossing."

"Don't worry—I've learned my lesson." Coop moved to the door and was about to open it when he turned and said, "I didn't realize you'd been such a caring friend to Kavanall. I'm sorry for your loss, Cliff."

"Thank you."

"And I guess Kav had a streak of kindness as well, which I never fully appreciated."

"How so?"

"Well," said Coop, "it was good of Kav to change his plans for you."

Cliff looked thoroughly confused. "When?"

"When he came home for Easter vacation."

Cliff laughed. "He didn't change his plans for *me*. Are you kidding?"

"Stasia said he canceled his trip in order to spend the time with you."

"Oh, please. That may be what he told his mother, but it's not what he told me."

Coop held his breath for a moment, then asked, "What did he tell you?"

"Kav canceled his trip because Bix asked him to come home for some special project—said it would be valuable experience for his future career in the company. Kav didn't want to do it, preferring to spend the week in Paris. So Bix sweetened the deal: if Kav would come home for Easter, Bix would send him to Europe for the entire summer after graduation."

Cliff crossed his arms, concluding, "And that's exactly what happened."

# Chapter 13

When Coop had suggested a private meeting with Bix—the prior morning, after discovering his office had been ransacked—his purpose had been to take Bix into his confidence and to share his evolving, but highly sensitive, theories that either Austin Royce or Tessa Irwin might have had a hand in Kavanall's death. Now, late Thursday afternoon, as Coop started his way up the steep, winding route to Idyllwild for his four-o'clock powwow at Questover, Coop was suddenly more focused on the death of his father than on the death of his stepson.

Clearly, there was a link, and as the puzzle began to take shape, piece by piece, Coop struggled to make sense of the mounting evidence that the missing link was none other than Bix himself. The extent of his involvement and the exact role he had played, these were mysteries yet to be solved, but Coop now found it likely that Bix held the key to untangling the entire convoluted scenario.

Since Coop had requested the meeting, the agenda was his to alter as needed. Bix didn't know that his purpose had changed; Bix didn't know that Coop's intent was no longer to confide in him, but to probe him. So driving up the mountainside, taking switchback after harrowing switchback, Coop revised his thinking and planned his new approach. He smiled at the recollection of his father's stock advice: own your lines, check your props, keep your focus.

But before Coop could decide on a precise plan of action, he wanted additional confirmation that Bix had somehow engineered his marriage to Stasia; if it was true, that likely represented the point of merger where events of the distant past would eventually be linked to the events of a week ago. When Stasia had dropped the bombshell that morning, she was not, by any objective measure, in the most lucid state of mind, having spent a sleepless night of withdrawal from a week of medicated numbness. Still, her revelations, however outlandish and unexpected, made sense. With a bit of backup, they could help lay the whole foundation for understanding what made Bix tick. With a flash of insight, Coop thought of the one person who could lend some added perspective to the setup for Stasia's second marriage.

A road sign alerted him to the scenic overlook, just beyond the next turn. Traffic was heavy in both directions that afternoon, and he needed a break from the knuckle-blanching grip that had guided the Tesla along the ever-changing precipice, pulling it back from the brink, curve after curve. He signaled and braked, causing the cars behind him to back up at his bumper as he waited for a gap in the oncoming stream of vehicles barreling downward. When at last he had an opening and turned, the cars he had stopped blasted onward, bats out of hell.

The parking area for the overlook was deserted; everyone was far too rushed for sight-seeing that afternoon. Coop got out of the car and strolled over to the spot where he and Stasia, two Sundays earlier, had seen the hang glider launch his final flight. Along the rough-hewn railing that separated the telescopes from the vast beyond, an impromptu memorial had been left by friends—inscribed photos, wilted flowers, deflated Mylar balloons, jars of burned-out candles, a few teddy bears.

Coop checked his cell phone; service could be spotty up here in the mountains, but standing at the edge of the lookout, he had no problem grabbing a signal from the valley below. Then he checked his wallet, found the business card that Stasia's first husband, Keith Follet, had given him at Kav's funeral, and placed a call to the Indian Wells office of the private-banking center where Keith was president. When the receptionist answered and Coop asked to speak to him, she said he was just stepping out of the office. Banker's hours, thought Coop; it was just past three-thirty. The receptionist continued, "Let me see if I can catch him. Who's calling, please?"

Several moments later, Keith was on the line, sounding winded. "What a surprise, Cooper. How can I help you?"

"This is somewhat personal. Can you talk?"

Keith hesitated. "Sure. Hold on." Coop heard him leave the

phone, close a door, and return. "How's Stasia doing?"

"Not well, but she seemed marginally better this morning. We managed a rational conversation for once. No mood swings. No tears."

"Good."

"Yes, good," said Coop. "Except, she feels our marriage is over. And frankly, I'm inclined to agree with her."

Keith paused before saying, "You weren't kidding—that *is* 'somewhat personal.'"

"Yes, but I can't help feeling you may be able to relate to our situation."

"Really? How?"

"This morning, Stasia painted a pretty clear picture of the circumstances that brought her and me together. There were a few choice details I'd never heard before. It seems our Cupid wore a Stetson and cowboy boots."

"Ahhh." Keith waited for Coop to continue, but Coop was silent. Keith said, "He can be fairly intrusive, can't he? I'm sorry, Cooper."

"Stasia's story didn't end there. What I found *most* intriguing were the circumstances that surrounded the end of *your* marriage."

Keith said, with a note of defensiveness, "It was all perfectly civil."

"So I understand. But according to Stasia, your departure came out of the blue. You told her you were involved with someone else, but she never believed you. She was confused then, and is still confused now, about why you wanted out. I, however, have an inkling."

"That was *so* long ago," said Keith. "It's over. Why dredge it up?"

Coop replied with another question: "How was Bix as a father-in-law? What did you think of him?"

"Well," said Keith, "he could be a challenge. I hardly need to tell *you*, though: there are advantages to being part of that family, so you just make it work. You chalk off his intrusiveness to his age or his genius or his eccentricity or *whatever*. Point is, when you buy into that family, you buy into Bix. And on balance, he's an all-right guy. He always treated me well."

"As long as you did what you were told, correct?"

"There was . . . an *element* of that, sure. You know Bix—he can be very persuasive."

"Are you sitting down, Keith? Cuz I need to ask you something point-blank." Coop paused for effect. "Did Bix pay you to leave his daughter?"

After a moment of stunned silence, Keith said, "I *ought* to be insulted by that question." But he didn't sound insulted. In fact, he laughed.

Then he added, "I could *never* admit to a thing like that."

But he didn't deny it, either.

**S**hortly after four, Coop rounded the last bend of the side road that led up to Questover, the overblown, woodsy "cabin" he had built at Bix's bidding. Just as he was about to pass under the timbered sign spanning the driveway, he braked abruptly for a truck that was leaving the property; then he backed up a few yards to let it pass. It was a tradesman's van, deepest maroon, immaculate, with a whisper of gold lettering on the side that said, simply, MOUNTAINVIEW SECURITY, but nothing else—no description of services, not even a phone number. The truck had one too many antennas, plus something on the roof that resembled a gunner's turret, minus the muzzle. Coop shook his head, laughing, wondering, What the hell?

He drove under the sign, noted that Bix's Hummer was already parked in the reserved space near the front door, then took the winding drive around the house down to the lower level, where he parked in the clearing among the unearthly manzanita trees and primordial pines.

Tapping his code into the keypad, he opened the back door, stepped inside, and called, "It's me, Bix!" Music was playing—Sinatra, of course—a goofy, up-tempo Latin-style number about the zillion tons of coffee in Brazil. At the sound of Coop's voice, Pyrite skittered to the railing of the balcony above, sticking his snout between the spindles to yap a cheery greeting.

Then Bix appeared behind the dog, doing a jaunty little dance step, one hand on his hip, the other raised high, holding a paring knife, which he wagged in time to the samba beat. He wore a long white apron, smeared bloody red. "Howdy, Coops! Come on up."

As Coop climbed the stairs, feeling he'd been transported to an alternate universe, Frank dittied something about a politician's daughter who was accused of drinking water. In Brazil, apparently, the offense warranted a fifty-dollar fine. At the top of the stairs, alarmed by Bix's appearance and recalling the truck in the driveway, Coop asked, bug-eyed, "What happened?"

"Huh?"

Speechless, Coop ran his hands down his torso, alluding to Bix's gory apron.

"That recipe I told you about? Manzanita jam? I've discovered something: it ain't easy. Wanna give me a hand?" And he cha-cha'd over to the kitchen's big center island, beckoning Coop to follow with swirls of his knife.

Bix had always been an enthusiastic, adventurous, and inquisitive cook—all the more so because he didn't have to clean up after himself. But to Coop's eyes, the state of the kitchen that afternoon went well beyond messy, even for Bix. He had managed to gather a sizable pile of the sticky little manzanita berries—brick red, the size of baby peas—and was in the process of cleaning them on the green granite countertop. But many had already scattered to the floor and had been mashed underfoot. Something was bubbling on the stove top; another pot had boiled over, leaving a syrupy puddle around the burners. The berries had an earthy smell that reminded Coop of leaves and twigs. And there was something in the oven. Judging by the innards near the sink—gizzards and such—Coop guessed a whole chicken was roasting.

Pyrite plopped in front of the oven and went to work gnawing at the stray berries that had clotted in the long guard hairs around his paws.

Coop tossed his jacket aside, rolled up his sleeves, grabbed a knife, and joined Bix at the counter, helping with the daunting task of cleaning the berries, which involved removing their tough, sappy little stems and scraping off the dirt that had bonded to them where they had fallen to the ground.

"I don't know, Coops"—Bix shook his head—"maybe this wasn't such a bright idea. I tried boiling a bunch of them as is. Figured the crap might just float to the top." He jerked his head over his shoulder, toward the stove. "Didn't work."

Frank sang about dating a girl, a Brazilian, who smelled like a percolator.

Coop asked, "What was that truck I saw leaving—trouble with one of the keypads?"

"Nah. They were just here for the monthly sweep."

Coop placed a single clean berry in a tidy pile he had started; like the coffee beans in Brazil, there were billions to go. He asked, "Sweep?"

"A routine precaution. Better safe than sorry, Coops. We don't live like other people; you need to learn that. What we have, they want. They might try to rob us blind, but they'll never steal my privacy."

"You think the place might be . . . *bugged* or something?"

"Not if you keep on top of it. But you'd be surprised."

"I guess I would be." Coop was familiar with monthly exterminator service and monthly window cleaning, but a monthly spyware sweep?

Frank sang of the things you couldn't get in Brazil: cherry soda, tea, tomato juice, even potato juice. Down there, everyone drank only coffee; in fact, they put *coffee* in their coffee. When the song had played for the third or fourth time, Coop asked, "Heard enough of that?"

Bix laughed. "Sure, Coops. Sorry." He punched a button on a remote control and plunged the room into silence, noting, "They don't make 'em like they used to."

Deadpan, Coop agreed, "They sure don't."

After a long, tedious session of fussing with the berries—and speaking of little else—Bix said, "Let's cook this slop and see what we've got." It didn't look promising. The experimental pot, the one with debris in it, had reduced to a syrup but had not gelled. The color was brown, not red, and the smell was even earthier than that of the raw berries. But a tentative taste from the tip of a spoon offered hope. Bix clicked his tongue in his mouth. "Might be good on ice cream."

"Do you have any?"

"No."

While Bix began a fresh pot with the clean berries, adding sugar and water, Coop set to work at the sink, scrubbing the residue from his hands, which felt like pine pitch and was every bit as stubborn. From the kitchen window, he noted that the sun had disappeared behind the surrounding mountains, throwing the grounds into deep shadow. Within an hour, the sky would be black. While drying his hands with a dish towel, Coop walked around the room, switching on lights.

Bix banged a lid on the pot, announcing, "Cocktail time—and I think we deserve it."

"Nothing for me, Bix," said Coop. "I've got that drive ahead of me, and I've never done it in the dark."

Bix turned to him and said flatly, "I don't like to drink alone."

"Yes, sir." Coop grinned. "Whatever you're having is fine. But make it a short one."

"That'a boy." Bix poured a couple of bourbon and Cokes, big ones, and Coop noticed that the Coke was little more than a splash. Bix said, "Want a cherry in it? Don't have any!" He howled a laugh; Pyrite joined him.

"That's fine, Bix, no problem."

Bix handed Coop the drinks. "You get us settled wherever you want, and we can talk. I just want to slice up some cheese first—something to nibble on."

"Good idea." Coop took the drinks to the seating area of the great room and set them on a low table that was centered squarely before the huge hearth of the stone fireplace. A pair of sofas faced each other over the table—a good setup for a serious conversation.

Bix fussed in the kitchen, checking the chicken in the oven; when he opened the door, the room took on the hearty scent of sage stuffing. Then he rummaged in the refrigerator for a wedge of cheddar, which he set about slicing on the counter. He said, "I'm all ears, Coops. A little curious, too. What did you want to talk about? You said it was sensitive?"

"It is." Coop sat in the middle of the sofa that faced the kitchen. "Yesterday in my office, your security guy called the break-in 'internal,' said it was someone with access."

Bix walked over from the kitchen, carrying a plate of cheese; Pyrite followed. Setting the cheese in the center of the table, Bix said, "That has me worried, all right. Any ideas?" He sat facing Coop from the other sofa. "Oops, first things first." He raised his glass. "Cheers, Coops."

Coop returned the toast, and they both took a first sip. The tumblers contained practically straight bourbon. Coop winced; Bix smacked his lips. Then Bix repeated, "Any ideas?"

Coop nodded, setting down his glass and reaching for a cube of cheese. "Several. Now, these are just theories, mind you. Possibilities. I'm not accusing anyone."

"Understood." Bix took a handful of the cheese cubes and popped one into his mouth. Another dropped. Pyrite was on it before it hit the floor. Bix commanded, "Pyrite, drop it!"

Oh brother, thought Coop. This'll be a test of wills.

The dog looked Bix in the eye—the picture of defiance—but didn't swallow.

Slowly, with a hint of menace, Bix said, "Pyrite? I told you: *drop* it."

The dog's jaw moved. Then it opened.

Bix snatched the cheese away. "Good little son f'bitch, you'll get your treats later."

Pyrite jumped into his lap.

Coop continued, "Remember that guy I was telling you about, the one who seemed to be stalking me?"

A look of concern crossed Bix's face. "That sounds kinda sinister, Coops. Are you sure you're not imagining this?"

Coop played along. "Possibly, but something tells me he's the one who trashed my office. Granted, he's not 'internal,' but I'll bet someone else, someone with access, put him up to it. The question, of course, is why?"

Bix quickly added, "And who?" He took a slug of his drink, swallowed, and asked, "Who within my company could have put this thug up to it?"

Well, thought Coop, could it have been *you*? For the sake of discussion, he suggested, "How about Austin Royce?"

*"Austin?"* Bix broke out in a belly laugh. Pyrite moved from his lap to the seat cushion. Bix said, "That milquetoast? You think he's capable of cloak-and-dagger stuff?"

"When people are motivated, they get plenty capable. Think about it, Bix: Austin has wanted the prez-job for years. He thought it was his due. Two days before Kav was killed, he heard you talking about promoting Kav in order to keep him out of Pontarelli's company. On the morning Kav was killed, Austin was mysteriously called out of town. Then, at Kav's funeral, he heard you offer the job to me. And now *I'm* starting to feel like a victim." Coop sipped his drink, then stood and walked with it toward the kitchen.

"Need something?" asked Bix.

"Just some ice." Coop checked to make sure Bix wasn't watching, then stepped to the sink, slid most of his bourbon down the drain, topped it up with Coke and water, and added a few ice cubes.

"I have to admit," said Bix, "I hadn't thought of Austin that way—the timing and all. The way you put it seems to make sense, but I just can't see Austin lurking in the bushes on the second fairway with a shotgun. He wouldn't have the guts."

Coop returned, sitting across from Bix again. "This is purely hypothetical"—in fact, Coop himself didn't believe it—"but Austin could have hired someone, a hit man. That thug, for instance."

"Sure," said Bix, swirling his finger in his drink, "anyone could've hired anyone. That doesn't tell us much. And besides"— Bix paused, leaning forward—"why would Austin risk getting involved neck-deep with this? I don't think he would, not when he was with a headhunter that morning."

Coop was taking a sip of his pretend cocktail, but choked on it. "Huh?"

Bix set down his glass and crossed his arms. "Austin wasn't tending to any 'family crisis' last Wednesday. He went to L.A. to talk to an executive recruiter. Guess he saw the prez-job slipping through his fingers and decided to cover his ass."

"How do *you* know where he was?"

Bix grinned, reminding Coop, "It's my job." He stood, carrying his glass to the kitchen for a refill, muttering, "Kavanall thought he could do it; Austin thinks he can do it. But they're both wrong." He smacked the glass on the counter and turned to Coop, shouting, "I *am* my company! Anyone else would just drive it into the ground."

Coop noted, "You've offered the job to me."

Instantly calm, Bix said, "And I still want you to have it. You're different, Coops. You're like a son to me, the son I never had."

Coop thought, You might want to rethink that after you hear about the conversation your daughter and I had this morning. Coop said, "I'm not qualified, Bix. I'd only be a disappointment. The man for the job is Austin Royce."

"Bah." Bix sloshed bourbon into his glass. "Austin Royce is an incompetent, lazy bastard. Hell, he's not even much of a dog-sitter. And you've opened my eyes to something else, Coops. He's devious. I can't afford treachery in the ranks. Next week, he's out."

Coop stood. "Uh, Bix . . . don't be rash."

"He needs to go. It's good to clean house now and then. Fresh blood, that's what I need. That's why I need *you*. But I've gotta tell you, Coops: from this moment on, you're to stay clear of Jay Pontarelli."

"What are you *talking* about?"

Bix smirked. "I *know* what he's up to."

"I wish *I* did."

"Oh, don't play dumb—you're too smart for that. I've seen you two talking, more than once. I know what he's after."

Coop stepped over to Bix. "*Me?* You think he's after *me?*"

Bix stared into Coop's eyes for an uncomfortably long moment. Then he explained, quietly and deliberately, "He's after your father's prototype. He wants to run me out of business with it."

"In all d'due respect, Bix, that's . . . d'delusional."

Bix wasn't listening. He said, "Jay thought Kavanall had the prototype."

"Why would he think that?"

"And now," said Bix, "he thinks *you* have it."

Coop froze. With his mind in a dizzying spin, he steadied himself against the edge of the counter. Though tempted to ask Bix, Do *you* think I have it?, he reined his emotions and said vacantly, "I should be going. Stasia may need me." His thoughts were on the mimeograph, still stowed—he hoped—atop the flat-file cabinet in his office. Arcie Madera had asked to have a look at it.

Bix offered, "Another drink before you leave? One for the road?"

"No, thanks." Coop managed a laugh. "You know me—a real lightweight. Besides, I'm not sure about dinner plans." It was dark by now, and Coop expected Bix to suggest, Why don't you stay? There's a bird in the oven.

But he didn't, saving Coop the awkwardness of declining. Instead, Bix said, "Well, be sure to give Stasia a kiss for me." Then he clapped his arms around Coop in a parting hug and sent him out into the night.

The sky was brilliant with a riotous display of stars, but as soon as Coop passed through the village and turned onto the highway, he felt overwhelmed by the blackness that consumed the sheer wall of rock and pines rising from the inner edge of the road. At its outer edge, the land disappeared, as if a bottomless sea of ink. As he began the descent, the sporadic streetlights petered out altogether, with only the center line and the occasional reflectors on posts to guide him. Unlike that afternoon, there were now very few other cars on the road. Coop reasoned, Of *course* there's no traffic—who'd be nuts enough to try this drive at night?

Now and then, at the outer turn of a switchback, he glimpsed the twinkle of headlights approaching from below—far, far below—or the reflection in his mirrors of other cars beginning the descent, above and behind him. But there weren't many. Twenty minutes into the trip, he could count on one hand the oncoming vehicles he had passed; none had passed him from behind.

One, however, was getting closer. Coop paid it little heed, as he was absorbed not only with the precarious task of driving, but with the perplexing outcome of his meeting with Bix. Coop marveled at the old man's readiness to fabricate plots of conspiracy against himself—the spyware sweeps, the snap decision to fire his second in command, and above all, his absurd notion that

Jay Pontarelli was now trying to lure Coop into competing with the Emery family's business. These imaginings went well beyond the bounds of idiosyncrasy or cantankerousness; these were the irrational ravings of a wealthy, coddled, insulated—Coop barely dared to think the word—madman.

And before Coop knew it, the other guy, behind him, was riding his bumper.

Then, the brights. From Coop's road-hugging position in the sleek little Tesla, the vehicle lurching behind him might as well have been a Mack truck; its lights were mounted high enough to blast directly through Coop's rear window. But as he began to discern features of the other vehicle's grill, he realized it was not a truck at all. It was a Jeep, it was dark, probably black, and it was trying to run him off the road.

When Coop grasped what was happening, his first instinct was to call for help, but his phone's interface was flashing NO SIGNAL on the dashboard. He squinted, trying to see the roadway beyond the glare in his mirror. The curves came faster and faster as he tried to gain some distance from the crude black-pipe utility bumper that had already nudged him once or twice. No question, his roadster was capable of outracing the Jeep—but *here*?

On a straightaway leading into the next switchback, the Jeep pulled into the inner lane, next to Coop, trying to force him, inch by inch, to the edge of the outer lane, beyond which the lights of the valley shimmered four thousand feet below. As the Jeep scraped his door, Coop stole a look at the driver and confirmed it was the thug from the gym. As Coop weighed his options, none of which were good, a car appeared several hundred feet ahead in the oncoming lane of the curve, forcing the Jeep to back off; the wild honking of the other car crescendoed as it passed, then disappeared in the night.

Seconds later, Coop passed a sign for the scenic overlook and, once again, weighed his options. If he kept driving, he knew the odds of returning safely to the valley floor were stacked against him. If he stopped at the overlook, the thug would surely do the same. Then what? Was he in fact the very person who had killed Kavanall? Was the shotgun in the Jeep? At least, Coop reasoned, if he stopped, he would change the whole dynamic of the pursuit—and he just might be able to catch a cell signal and sound the alarm.

As Coop rounded the curve approaching the overlook, he didn't signal; he didn't even bother slowing down. He just jerked the wheel and fishtailed into the parking area, spraying gravel. And there, chatting over coffee, were two highway patrolmen, one on a motorcycle, the other in a squad car. Out on the roadway, the Jeep hit the brakes and started backing up, but quickly reassessed the scene and took off again down the mountain.

Both patrolmen rushed to Coop's car.

Coop opened his door. "Thank God," he said as he started to get out.

One of them ordered, "*Remain* in your vehicle, sir."

The other asked, "What seems to be the problem?"

Catching his breath, trembling, Coop said, "*Problem?* That g'guy tried to run me off the road."

"Could you identify the vehicle?"

"You saw it. It was a black Jeep!"

"Did you happen to catch the license number?"

"No."

"Is that liquor on your breath, sir? It smells like whisky."

"It's bourbon. I had a sip or two—nearly an hour ago." With rising agitation, he insisted, "I am not drunk!"

The two patrolmen shared a skeptical glance. One of them suggested, "Then maybe the *other* guy's a drunk."

"No. He was in full control, and he knew exactly what he was doing." Coop gripped the wheel, calmed himself. "Listen to me: Fifteen years ago, my father was murdered. A little over a week ago, my stepson was murdered."

One of the cops asked, "The name of your stepson?"

"Kavanall Emery Follet."

The cops looked at each other.

"And here's the pisser." Coop paused.

"What?" asked the other cop.

"Apparently, I'm next."

# Part Three

## *Absolute Zero*

As temperature approaches absolute zero, all processes cease, and the entropy of the system approaches a constant minimum.

— *The third law of thermodynamics*

# Chapter 14

**A** battery of field sobriety tests, including breathalyzer, to which Coop readily submitted, convinced the patrolmen that he was not a drunk driver, and when he produced Arcie Madera's card, which included private numbers jotted by hand, they began to take seriously his claims of an evolving pattern of deadly intent. By then, though, the black Jeep had descended the mountain and disappeared in the valley, and without a license number, there was little chance of apprehending the thug driving it.

One of the patrolmen asked, "Do you feel you need police protection, Mr. Brant?"

Had it actually come to that? Coop said, "I hope not. But frankly, what scares me is the drive down the mountain. I'm pretty frazzled by all this."

"I don't blame you," said the other patrolman, the one with the squad car. "Tell you what. I was about to drive down anyway. Why don't you follow me? I'll take it slow; just stay on my tail. No one will bother you."

"Great idea. Thank you, Officer. I should be fine once we get to the bottom."

The drive was uneventful—in fact, Coop found himself wishing the officer would pick it up. When at last they rolled into Palm Desert at the bottom of the long rise through the foothills and stopped for the light at El Paseo, the cruiser signaled, turned right, and disappeared from sight.

Sitting at the light, itching to go, Coop considered phoning Arcie, but he wanted to check on the mimeograph before reporting to her, and he assumed the Highway Patrol would keep her in the loop—if they had not already done so. When the light turned green, he gunned it, heading north across the valley to catch the interstate. With the time lost at the overlook, it was now nearly eight o'clock. A few minutes later, he merged onto the westbound lanes of I-10, which would take him out toward Emery headquarters. The steady thrum of the freeway traffic had a calming effect, almost hypnotic, which allowed him to consider that evening's events with a clearer head.

Someone had tried to kill him. In all probability, the thug in the Jeep was not working alone, driven by his own motives, but had been assigned the task by someone else—someone who had a habit of pulling strings and making things happen. Although Coop had requested the private meeting with Bix, it was Bix who had suggested having it at Questover. Once Coop had arrived, Bix had tried to liquor him up, later sending him out into the night with no offer of dinner. Was the whole thing a setup? Had the whole thing been staged to punish Coop for imagined flirtations with Jay Pontarelli?

Just that night, Bix had explained his spyware sweeps as a "routine precaution." Was he now taking preemptive action to keep Coop from jumping ship and joining the competition? Bix had also acknowledged—bragged about—his intrusive meddling and information gathering, which he justified with his stock response, "It's my job." He'd once considered it his job to dispose of his first son-in-law; had he now set his sights on his second?

As Coop left the freeway and headed into the wilds, he perceived his father-in-law in an entirely new light, and the image that emerged was frightening. Had Bix arranged the murder of his own grandson, the sole descendant who could perpetuate his beloved bloodline? What sort of mental contortions could drive a man to reach such a decision? Was he evil to the core? Or just old, addled, and psychotic?

His name flashed by in huge stainless steel letters on a wall of stacked stone: EMERY ENERGY. Coop braked as he neared the main gate. Waving to the guard, he wondered if his comings and goings were being noted. Probably so. Were they also being reported directly to Bix? Anything was possible.

At that hour, the executive parking lot was empty. He pulled into a space near the buildings, trotted through the pathways of the solar garden, which looked grimly uninviting in the dark, and ducked inside the research facility, where the bright lighting of the lobby and halls looked sterile and off-putting. Had *he* designed all this? Or were his perceptions merely skewed by his frame of mind?

As far as he could tell, there was no one around; even the re-search labs, where inquiring minds frequently tinkered into the night, were dark. He paced through the back hallway, arrived at the private entrance to his office, and tapped his code into the keypad; that, too, was being recorded somewhere. Unlocking the door, he inched it open, then slipped inside and closed it.

Standing there in the dark, he wondered, Why all the stealth? It's not as if I don't *belong* here—this is my own goddamn office.

Even so, he was reluctant to switch on the bright overhead light-ing, so he stepped over to his desk and turned on a single lamp. Its halogen bulb glared on the glass desktop, projecting onto the ceiling shadowed silhouettes of his telephone, pencil tray, and keyboard. The surroundings of the room lurched into view from the darkness. There was still filing to be sifted through—it would takes weeks—but compared to the shambles of Wednesday, to-night his office seemed to be in order, with no signs of further intrusion. On top of the tall cabinet of flat-files, the corrugated box given to him by Mimi remained exactly where he had left it. The racing of his pulse began to ease.

Since Coop had been away from the office since morning, he thought he should check both voice mail and e-mail for messages, but reconsidered. His computer and his phone passed through company cables, and he had no doubt there would now be height-ened interest in anything he had to communicate. Besides, he was not there to catch up at his desk. He was on a mission—well, an errand—to retrieve the mimeograph. Arcie had asked to see it, and while it was clearly not the elusive prototype conjured by Bix that very evening, Coop wanted to get it off Emery property and into her hands.

The ventilation was not running at that moment, and the room was eerily quiet—so quiet that Coop could hear his footfalls on the carpeting as he crossed from his desk to the flat-files. He reached overhead for the edge of the box and began to pull it from the top of the cabinet. As it passed the point of equilibrium and angled down toward his forehead, he heard something: within the box, within the machine, something small slid from the far end and came to rest, mere inches from his head, with a gentle but distinct tick that sounded like plastic hitting metal.

"Holy crap," he muttered.

Coop had examined the mimeograph on Mimi's coffee table the night she had given it to him, and he recalled a long, shallow drawer in the base of the machine, where he had found a supply of waxy paper stencils and a rubber-bladed squeegee, neither of which would make the sound he just heard. He and Mimi had missed something.

Coop lowered the box to the floor, knelt next to it, and opened the flaps. Reaching inside with both arms, he pulled the mimeograph free, then pushed the box aside and set the machine on the carpet. Sitting back on his heels, he slid the supply drawer open. And there, resting against the front edge of the metal drawer, was the small object that had slid from the back—a clear plastic case containing an audio cassette, identical to the hundreds of others used by Ferris Brant to rehearse and refine his lectures.

Picking up the cassette, Coop rose to his feet, then moved to the desk, where he examined the tape in the light of the lamp. Along the spine of the case, he recognized at once his father's clear, confident block-style backhand: THE MACGUFFIN.

The inscription was followed by a date in late March, fifteen years prior.

**S**tricken numb and momentarily breathless, Coop slipped the cassette into a pocket of his sport coat, then packed the mimeograph in its box, marveling that he had been on the verge of trashing it—the object, apparently, of everyone's quest. He switched off the lamp, carried the box into the hall, gave a furtive look in both directions, then closed the door without logging out on the keypad.

Taking the box to the car, he could barely restrain himself from running; should someone notice him, he did not want to appear hurried. When he stowed the mimeograph in his trunk, he took care to nudge the lid closed without crunching the box as he had done in Pioneertown.

Coop got into the car and pulled out of the parking lot. He wasn't sure where to go or what to do next, but he had to get away from headquarters. As he approached the main gate, the guard leaned from his window and signaled for Coop to stop.

"Yes?" he asked, looking up from the roadster.

"Finished for the night, Mr. Brant?"

"I think so, yes. Why?"

"You didn't punch out, sir."

Coop thumped his forehead. "Guess I forgot. Could you log me out?"

"Happy to. Have a good evening, sir."

Coop thanked him with nod, then tore off into the night.

With a glance at his high-tech dashboard, he confirmed what he already knew: though his car was equipped with gadgets galore, it could not play an audio cassette. Though that particular recording format was still in limited use in educational settings and for dictation, its heyday as an entertainment medium had long passed. He recalled having a boom box that could play cassettes—it also had a folding hatch for CDs—but he hadn't seen the thing since making the move from the coast; it was long gone. Driving back to the interstate, he patted the tape in his pocket, wondering, How the hell do I play this?

Glancing at the dashboard again, he noticed that the car's electrical charge was beginning to run low. It had been a long day, with far more driving than was typical for him, much of it in the mountains. He needed to recharge, and the best place to do it was in his home garage. If he planned to do more driving that night, he would have to use another car—which gave him an idea.

He zipped onto the interstate, then off again in Rancho Mirage, and ticked away the few remaining miles to Entrada, which he entered from one of the unmanned side gates, using the transponder clipped to his car's visor. Within a minute or two, he was inside his garage in the Emery compound, connecting the Tesla's charging cable.

It was after nine now. Stasia's car, a Jaguar convertible, was gone. A third car, a beefy new sedan they rarely used, was available but of course had no tape player. Coop, however, had other options. He took the transponder from his car's visor and slipped it into his shirt pocket. He took the box from the trunk and set it in a dark corner just outside the garage. Then he closed the garage door and took off at a jog, heading around the back of the house.

Rounding the pool and ducking between to two knolls, he

planned to check if any of Kavanall's vintage roadsters had a tape player. All of the cars dated from *before* the cassette era, but he thought there was a good chance at least one of the four had had an aftermarket player installed. If so, it would be unremarkable for him to borrow the car. While Kav was still alive, he had encouraged the whole family to drive any of them at will, which helped keep the collection in better running condition. Coop had often complied, taking all of the cars for brief weekend spins. In his mind's eye, he could visualize a black slot added to one of the dashboards, wedged in among the frenzy of chrome knobs and buttons.

Kav's house came into view, with the cars displayed in their antique glory under spotlights from the carport's ceiling. Coop's trot halted as he ducked to take a look inside the Thunderbird, which had a radio, but no tape player. Then the Mercedes—nope. Then the Karmann Ghia—strike three. Which left only the Nash Metropolitan—and behold, there was the slot, just the right size, not for an eight-track, not for CDs, but designed to play the cassette that rattled in Coop's pocket.

He checked in the glove box, where, because there was no history of theft within the guarded walls of Entrada, Kav had always made a spare key available. "Bingo," said Coop, tossing the key in his palm.

Then he paused to think for a moment. He assumed the transponders issued to Entrada residents were assigned to specific cars. Because they worked electronically, he thought it probable their use was recorded somewhere, meaning that someone with access—or someone with clout, like Bix—could keep tabs on the comings and goings of anyone he pleased. If those logs were to show that Coop *left* Entrada that night, and someone aimed to find him, he would be all too conspicuous in a rare-as-hen's-teeth black Tesla roadster. No less distinctive would be a pristine two-tone pink-and-gray Metropolitan convertible, but even that would blend into the scenery if the car being sought was a Tesla. The game wouldn't last long, as the ruse could quickly be discovered, but at least it would buy him some time.

And how did he plan to spend that time? He had no idea what

the rest of the night might hold, but he knew there were two things he must accomplish: first, go somewhere and listen to his father's tape, and second, report his findings to Arcie.

He reached into the Metropolitan, removed the transponder from its visor, and tossed it into a clump of lantana, replacing it with the transponder from his pocket. Then he got into the car, started it—it balked at first, but seemed fine—and checked to see if the tape player was working. When he switched it on, an Abba tune jangled, "Money, money, money . . . ," full blast. He switched it off and pulled out from under the carport.

Though he assumed Bix was not at home—he'd had a bird in the oven—Coop drove at a crawl through the compound without headlights, returning to his own garage. As the Metropolitan's engine idled with a sputter, he hopped out of the car, retrieved the boxed mimeograph, set it in the passenger's seat, and then drove away, headlights on, exiting Entrada via the same unmanned side gate where he had entered. Somewhere, he reasoned, a computer blipped, recording that his Tesla had left the grounds. Coop grinned.

As soon as he reached the highway, he was tempted to play his father's cassette, which presumably held answers to fifteen years of doubt and speculation. But the wind noise in the open car was considerable, and traffic along the interstate, even at that hour, was heavy, so he opted to wait. He would find a place, somewhere secluded, where he could stop the car and listen to the tape with his full attention.

He kept driving west, and somewhere in the wilds, beyond the exit that led to Emery headquarters and beyond the exit that led to Pioneertown, he left the freeway and headed toward the vast energy farms in the San Gorgonio Pass, where thousands of towering wind turbines whirled their giant blades in the constant flow of air that streamed in from the coast, backed up at the mountains, and gained speed as it blew into the valley, pinched between the San Bernardinos to the north and the San Jacintos to the south.

He zigzagged from one narrow utility road to another until he found himself removed from the lights and the noise of the freeway, until he found himself utterly alone in the scrub of the desert. The road, which deteriorated to a potted, unpaved access drive, ended at the base of a windmill, and there he stopped. His lights shone bright against the white shaft of the turbine, which rose three hundred feet—thirty stories—dwarfing the tiny car. Coop switched off the lights and killed the engine. He looked up into the sky, where majestic blades whooshed in the night air, carving circles in the starlight.

And there, at last, he ejected the Abba tape and tossed it out to the snakes and the scorpions; something rustled in the brush where the tape landed. Coop then retrieved his father's cassette from the pocket of his jacket and slid it into the player. The mechanism swallowed it, engaged the tape, and began to play. Coop slumped in his seat, staring into the breezy heavens as he heard his father tapping the microphone, clearing his throat. Then he spoke:

"Ferris Brant. Easter lecture. Revision nine.

"Gentlemen—*and* esteemed ladies—good morning. Thank you for taking time out of your busy schedules to meet with me here today, especially on such short notice—on Easter, no less. I'm truly humbled by your interest in my research.

"But you wouldn't be here if you didn't already understand the implications of this quest, which are indeed far-reaching, not only for business interests such as oil and transportation, but also for government, defense, and society as a whole. The stakes could not be higher.

"The water engine. We've all heard of it; we've all laughed at it. But the idea is so powerful, it has remained the goal of an elusive search persisting for centuries. On the one hand, science has told us that, even in theory, energy cannot be extracted from water, which matches no definition of 'fuel,' at least as we've known it. On the other hand, advocates of the idea insist that it is the idea *itself* that fuels the imagination and inspires the research.

"I ask you: Who, a century ago, would have thought moon landings could ever become a practical reality? Who, in our own lifetime, grew up thinking that such advances as nuclear medicine, genetic imprinting, or even computer networks were anything more than the stuff of science fiction? And yet, because those goals existed in theory, they were pursued until the science caught up with the idea. Again and again, skeptics have been proven wrong.

"Here, today, you see before you a draped object, not very big, but capable of changing our destiny. Alongside it, two everyday items: a kitchen funnel and a beaker of water. I assure you, it's plain old $H_2O$, a lowly draft of Riverside's finest. Later, I'll drink a bit of it, and I'll gladly share it with anyone who volunteers to corroborate my claim that the beaker does not contain rocket fuel.

"As to the drapery, I admit that it's an overtly theatrical touch. By employing it, I know I risk painting myself as a magician, preparing to pull a rabbit—perhaps the Easter Bunny himself—from a hat. The true purpose of the drapery, however, is not to keep you in suspense, but to allow me to forewarn you that appearances can be deceiving.

"With that said, and without further ado: *Voilà!*

"I know, I know. You're thinking, That piece of junk? Why, that's nothing but an old duplicating machine.

"Well, yes, it *was,* but I found it provided a handy framework—a surrogate chassis, if you will—for the development of a groundbreaking technology and the presentation of a revolutionary idea. Soon, as promised, I will open our unassuming prototype and provide a complete demonstration.

"Before proceeding, however, it's important to understand the theoretical basis of this discovery. This gets kind of complicated, but we need to confront the technicalities head-on. So let's begin by reviewing the laws of thermodynamics, in order.

"First . . . ."

With the blades of a thousand wind turbines stirring the starry sky, Coop listened as his father articulated the scientific foundation of his idea. With a jet streaking miles overhead, its roar but a whisper, Coop listened as his father detailed the pros and cons, mostly cons, of extracting energy from water. With a chorus of crickets and wind and distant diesels sounding from the depths of the desert night, Coop listened as his father's demonstration of the prototype led logically, point by point, to an inventive theory of energy production that could indeed change the world. And with the lecture's conclusion, Coop finally understood—with no trace of the rancor of generational rivalry that had festered since boyhood—the extent of his father's genius.

The tape, which had taken no more than twenty minutes to play, ended. Coop switched it off and, still slumped in the seat, expelled a long sigh. As his voice drifted to the sky and disappeared in the darkness, he felt both rested and faint, both fulfilled and drained, both enlightened and perplexed. But he could now predict exactly how this protracted and painful episode of his fractured life would at last play out. He was determined that the wrongs of the past fifteen years would soon be resolved.

Sitting upright, he straightened his jacket and took out his phone. Though it was nearly ten o'clock, it was time to call Arcie.

She answered on the first ring. "Cooper? Where the hell have you been? I've been trying to reach you."

"I've been busy."

"Yeah. I got a call from the Highway Patrol." Lightening her tone, she asked, almost playfully, "Just what *have* you been up to?"

"I may have solved another murder for you—Kavanall's. Interested?"

She seemed at a momentary loss for words.

Coop continued, "I thought so. Plus, it seems I've located my father's missing prototype, complete with a rehearsal tape of the lecture he was planning. Thought you might like to have it. Busy?"

"Where are you?"

"Um"—he glanced about—"in the middle of nowhere. Are you in Riverside tonight?" He wondered if she guessed the subtext of his question: Are you spending the night with Bruce Rollo in Palm Springs?

"Yes," she said, "but I can meet you there."

He suggested, "How about Pioneertown? Not too far for either of us—I'm halfway there now—and we'll need some privacy."

"I'll call Gus and ask him to hold that back room for us. Maybe he'll keep the kitchen open. I worked late at my desk and haven't eaten much. Hungry?"

"Starved." Other than a few cubes of cheese with Bix, Coop's only meal that day had been the Cobb salad—no wonder he felt faint. He asked, "Do you happen to have a standard-size cassette player?"

"I keep an old one in the car for recording notes."

"Bring it."

From the middle of nowhere, Coop managed to find his way back to the interstate, then breezed up Route 62 to Yucca Valley and made the last hop over to Pioneertown. Pappy and Harriet's was open, and it was packed; even from the road, it was noisy.

Infinitely more promising, at least for the purpose of a confidential tête-à-tête, was the Mosey On Inne. As Coop pulled off the road and into the parking area, he noted that, as before, there were no cars at the little motel; as before, the VACANCY sign was posted on the mailbox; as before, a pickup and a motorcycle were parked at the roadhouse. Tonight, the neon LOUNGE sign was lit, and there were a couple of other cars near its entrance, but not Arcie's tan cruiser, which came as no surprise, as Coop had expected to arrive first.

Though he did not feel he had been followed that night, by a Jeep or anything else, he recalled Bix's comment about routine precautions—"better safe than sorry"—so he drove the Metropolitan back to the rear of the property and parked in the sandy clearing among the Joshua trees, in front of the farthest motel room. He got out of the car, took the box from the passenger seat, and carried it across the gravel lot to the roadhouse.

As he entered, Gus greeted him, "Hello, my friend! I've been expecting you," and immediately ushered him through the main room, where a few other patrons nursed drinks at their tables, then back to the enclosed porch, where the folding screen had been placed in the doorway and the backgammon table had been set for two. As Coop set his box on the other game table, Gus said, "Sarge tells me she's hungry. Wants the oysters au Muscadet. They're nice and fresh. Will you join her?"

"Absolutely. Thanks, Gus."

"Diet Coke?" Gus laughed.

Coop gave a weary laugh as well. "I could really use a martini."

Gus gave an approving nod. "Gin?"

"Of course."

"Hendrick's—slice of cucumber?"

"Better yet."

As Gus turned to leave, Coop asked, "Do you have a tablecloth or something?" The Mosey On Inne was not a white-linen sort of place. "I've brought this for the detective"—he gestured toward the box—"it's sort of a surprise."

Gus nodded. "I'll find something."

When he returned with Coop's martini, Gus also had a piece of folded fabric under his arm. He served the martini, which looked perfectly prepared, then unfurled the fabric smartly, explaining, "I've been replacing the curtains in the rooms. This was left over." It was a lovely silk foulard.

Coop thanked him and, tasting the drink, complimented him. When Gus left and closed the screen, Coop removed the mimeograph from the box, set the box aside, set the machine on the second table, and draped it with the silk. Then he returned to his martini at the backgammon table. As he waited, he smelled something wonderful cooking.

Within a quarter hour, he heard someone arrive. Gus said, "Yes, yes—he's here," and brought Arcie back to the porch. Coop stood as they entered and was surprised when she greeted him with a subdued but spontaneous hug.

"I was worried something happened," she said. "Didn't see your car." She had a tote bag, presumably containing the tape recorder, which she set on the floor near the table.

Coop explained about switching cars and parking in back. As he spoke, Arcie eyed his martini. When he finished, she told Gus,

"I'll have what *he's* having, please."

"Sure thing, Sarge. And the oysters are almost ready." He left.

Coop seated her at the table, then sat across from her. He slid his martini an inch in her direction. "Taste?"

"Thanks, Coop." She smiled, then sipped. "That's really nice—with the cucumber."

"It's gotten warm, though. May need another."

She turned to look at the draped object. "Is that 'it'? Looks mysterious."

"You don't know the half of it."

"So, then." She sat back. "Tell me about your day."

Where to begin? In order: Coop said Stasia had revealed that their marriage had been railroaded by Bix and that she now wanted out. He detailed Dennis Dill's account of his run-in with the thug. Coop then explained Cliff Sloan's theory that Kavanall had been working for Bix on the Easter in question. And finally, Coop recounted how he'd been nearly run off a mountain road by the thug, then nearly arrested for drunk driving.

"My, my, my," said Arcie, "you really *have* been busy."

"But none of that holds a candle to what happened during my meeting with Bix. I have strong reason to suspect that the thug reports to *him*."

Gus interrupted with a rap on the doorjamb, then moved the screen aside and entered with a tray. He brought them not one martini, but two, plus water, bread, and a huge platter of the poached oysters, still bubbling from their finish in the broiler, blanketed with a foamy Muscadet sabayon sauce. Coop found the aroma nothing short of orgasmic. He quipped, "You know what they say about oysters."

"Oh, puh-*leeze*," said Arcie. "Don't be so obvious."

They toasted Gus, who smiled and left. After sampling the first of the oysters with rapturous groans of approval, they resumed their conversation.

"What happened with Bix?" Arcie dropped her oyster shell into a spare bowl.

"Plenty. I'm still trying to sort it all out, but here's the corker: at a very tense moment while Bix was on a rant about Jay Pontarelli starting up the competing business, he said to me, 'Jay thought Kavanall had the prototype, and now he thinks *you* have it.'"

She glanced at the silk drapery. "Do you?"

"*Yes*. But Jay never knew squat about the prototype; that's just one of Bix's wild conspiracy theories. Point is, how did *Bix* associate Kavanall with the prototype in the first place? Easy: *he* sent Kav to my father's office to get it."

"And now"—Arcie connected the dots—"*he* thinks you have it."

"Correct. And the crazy thing is, he's right, though I didn't figure it out till tonight." Coop then recounted how he'd found the tape in the mimeograph and later listened to it, just before phoning her.

"Intriguing, to say the least." She dropped another shell into the bowl. "But something's not adding up. The guy who tried to run you off the road—you suspect Bix put him up to it. But if Bix thinks you have the prototype, why would he do that?"

"Because in his eyes I'm guilty of the same mortal sin as Kavanall—conspiring to compete against him with Pontarelli. As far as the prototype is concerned, Bix still wants it, all right, but he figures that if *he* can't have it, no one can—especially Pontarelli."

Arcie dabbed her lips with her napkin, then set it in her lap. She paused before asking, "You honestly think Bix was capable of putting a hit on his own grandson?"

"A week ago, Arcie, I'd have said it was unthinkable. But I know far more about the man now than I did then. Just for starters, I've learned he was willing to sacrifice his own daughter's life—figuratively—to an elaborate scheme. Might he also have sacrificed his grandson's life—literally—to the same scheme? I'm beginning to think so. It's all starting to fit. For instance, in the last few days, two people, Austin Royce and my trainer, Teddy, have made essentially the same observation: that Bix would never have let his daughter marry me if he'd had any suspicion that I'd killed my father. Let's face it—plenty of other people suspected me. So the only explanation for Bix's total *lack* of suspicion would be his knowledge of the actual killer."

Arcie shook her head as if to clear her thoughts. "Wow. Either the booze is kicking in, or you're beginning to make sense."

He smirked. Tossing away another oyster shell, he checked his watch. "Dinner at midnight—how very chic."

"It's getting late. Gonna show me the gizmo?"

"The MacGuffin? That's dessert. Eat your oysters."

**W**hen the oysters were gone, they lingered in conversation, even after Gus had cleared the table and brought a final round of drinks—a splash of Armagnac in two large snifters, which he said would give their meal the proper finish. Their talk centered mainly on the revelations of Coop's day, but also drifted into more personal matters.

"Do you recall Dennis Dill?" Coop asked Arcie. "He said he's met you."

She grinned, nodding. "Not exactly my type. But, yes, he's friends with Bruce."

"Dennis likes you." Coop hesitated. "But he says that you and Bruce . . . well, he doesn't think it'll last."

"Doesn't he? And why's that?"

By now, Coop was in too deep to back out, so he forged onward: "Look, I'm sorry if this is out of line, but are you aware that Bruce Rollo is bisexual?"

"I've heard rumors to that effect—from Bruce himself. He's been perfectly open about it."

"Great. Great." Coop paused again. "But how does that work? With Bruce."

"It's pretty basic, really—like a plug in a socket. He seems to have the hang of it."

Coop laughed. He leaned forward, splaying the fingers of both hands around the base of the snifter. "I *mean*," he said, "how does that work—in terms of commitment?"

She leaned forward, elbows on the table. "Bruce is a wonderful man. As I've said before, I'm drawn to his creative streak. But 'commitment'? I don't kid myself; I know he isn't Mr. Right."

"So he's Mr. Right-Now, as they say?"

She didn't answer. Instead, she set her glass aside and looked at Coop's hands. Then she gently tapped his truncated ring finger.

"How'd that happen?"

"You and Dennis Dill have more in common than you realize. He asked me the same question this morning."

"And what'd you tell him?"

"I was a baby—don't even remember it happening. It was an accident in my crib."

"Ahhh." She nodded, then laughed quietly.

"What?"

"Well, I didn't think it was a *football* injury."

Gus popped in and announced last call, asking, "One more?"

They declined. Coop noted, "I've passed one breathalyzer tonight—wouldn't bet on two." So Gus left to take orders from the other patrons, whose voices drifted through the closed screen.

Arcie checked her watch. "All right, Mr. Brant, time for show-and-tell."

He rose, stepped around her to the other table, and slowly lifted the piece of silk, saying, "Behold."

She stared at it. "You were right. It *is* a piece of junk."

"Uh-uh-uh," he clucked, wagging an index finger. "Bring your tape player?"

"Right here." She lifted her tote from the floor and unloaded her notebook, a microphone, a headset, an AC adapter, and the battery-operated machine. As Coop plugged it in near the table, she asked, "Bring the tape?"

He handed it over from the pocket of his jacket, suggesting, "Maybe you should use the headphones. I've already heard this, but no one else needs to." He jerked his head toward the main room, where the voices of stragglers could still be heard.

She nodded, donned the headset, put the tape in the machine, and pressed PLAY.

**W**hile Arcie listened, Coop paced, swirling his Armagnac, sipping. She sat without expression, writing notes. Now and then, she caught his eye and arched her brows. As the tape ran on, Coop kept glancing at his watch, and when nearly twenty minutes had passed, he sat facing her again with his fingers cradling the snifter.

Finally, she sat back, switched off the machine, and removed the headset. "No doubt about it—that's your father, and that's his prototype."

Coop leaned forward, asking quietly, "So you understand the magnitude of this?"

"Yes."

"Which means, we need to act fast. Or I could be a dead man."

"Or . . ." She leaned forward.

"What?"

She stroked the stub of his ring finger.

Then she whispered, "Or . . . you could be a very wealthy man."

# Chapter 15

It was true, what they say about oysters.

Sometime before six on a Friday morning in October, the sun had not yet risen—it would not inch up from the surrounding peaks and begin to warm the high desert for another hour—but the eastern sky was already rimmed with the first gray glow of dawn. To the west, a fat half-moon lolled cold and white atop a pile of prehistoric boulders, wrapping up its night, ready to sink from view.

In a corral down the road, a horse coughed. A few small, hungry birds were up and at it, pecking through the scrub in search of dropped seeds. A dog awoke, yawned, and stretched, rattling its chain.

In a sandy clearing among the Joshua trees, dew sparkled on the porch railing of the little motel. Only its end unit, the one farthest from the road, had its lovely new foulard curtains closed to the outside world. Parked directly in front of it was a two-tone Nash Metropolitan convertible with its top down. Next to it, twice as long but not half as stylish, was an unmarked police cruiser, bland and tan. They were parked so close, they almost rubbed fenders.

With the click of a lock, the door opened from the motel room. Cooper Brant stepped outside with a corrugated-cardboard box. He pulled the door closed behind him, then carried the box to the Metropolitan and placed it in the passenger seat, which was wet with dew.

Bad enough, he thought, to be wearing the same clothes as yesterday. Under the circumstances, he could handle that, but he preferred not to start the day sitting in damp bottle-green corduroys, so he opened the car's trunk, hoping to find a towel or a rag. Better yet, he found a chamois, which he used to dry off the driver's seat and wipe down the windshield.

He returned the chamois to the trunk and was about to close it, but stopped.

He stepped over to the tan sedan and stretched over the hood to clean its windshield. When he was finished, he paused to leave a handprint in the dew on the driver's window; two of the five digits looked like thumbs.

After putting away the chamois, he got into his car and fired up its little engine, wondering how long it would take for the heater to kick in.

Gravel crunched under his tires as he backed into the parking lot, then passed by the roadhouse, recalling those oysters.

An hour or so into his drive, Coop thought of something, pulled off the road, took out his phone, and placed a call. A voice answered, "Hey there, Coop. What's up?" It was Teddy Duncan, Coop's trainer, waiting for him at IronLand.

"I feel like such an idiot," said Coop. "Things have been crazy lately. It's no excuse, but when I got up this morning, I lost track of what day it was."

Teddy laughed. "Late night?"

"It was. In fact, I was out of town."

"Where are you now?"

"Uh . . . here and there."

With evident concern, Teddy asked, "Is everything all right?"

Choosing his words with care, Coop answered, "It's tremendously complicated."

"You mean, with Stasia?"

"That's part of it. Look, Teddy. I'm just not sure about these next few days. I want to get back on our regular schedule—more than you'll know—but I'm sort of at the brink of something, and things could go either way."

"Coop," said Teddy with an uncomfortable laugh, "you're scaring me now."

"Gosh—no—it's nothing for you to worry about—not at all."

"If you say so, Coop. Good." But Teddy sounded skeptical.

"So let's leave it this way: I'm planning on Monday morning, and I'm looking forward to it."

"Deal. Think you might bring me up to date?"

"Trust me, Teddy—you'll get an earful."

**C**oop waited till ten that morning to place the next call. When the secretary answered, he said, "Connie, it's Cooper. Is Bix in?"

"Mr. Brant! Mr. Emery has been so concerned. I'll put you right through—and I do hope nothing's wrong."

Seconds later, Bix was on the line: "You've got us all in a panic, Coops. Everything okay?"

"I'm fine, Bix. A little shook up from last night, but otherwise okay."

"Stasia said you never came home."

"I dropped off the car, but had to get out of there. I don't think I was followed."

"What the devil are you *talking* about? Where are you?"

"I'd rather not say, Bix—God only knows who might be listening. You won't believe this, but after I left Questover last night, someone tried to kill me, tried to force me off the road—at four thousand feet."

Bix paused. "Are you sure it wasn't just some crazy driver?"

"He knew what he was doing. He was obviously working for someone. And I think I know who."

Flatly, Bix asked, "Who?"

"Jay Pontarelli. You really opened my eyes yesterday. At first I didn't buy your theory—I thought you were being paranoid—but all of a sudden, the stakes have gotten much higher. You were right. Jay thinks I've got the prototype of the water engine."

"That doesn't make sense, Coops. If Jay thinks that, why would he try to kill you?"

"Because"—Coop paused for effect—"he doesn't want me to sell it to *you*."

Bix said nothing.

Coop continued, "Jay must figure, if *he* can't have it, no one can. And suddenly, I'm a marked man."

"Hmmm," said Bix, "there's a certain logic to that."

Coop thought, I'll just *bet* it makes sense to you. He said, "So if, in fact, I had the prototype, I'd be nuts to hang on to it."

Bix cleared his throat. When he spoke, his tone was that of a harried parent, losing patience. "All right, Coops, this game has been going on long enough. Fifteen years. One question: Do you have it?"

"Believe it or not, yes, I do. I myself didn't believe it—till last night."

"What the hell does last night have to do with it?"

"Details later. We need to talk some business first. I've been reconsidering your offer of the prez-job. Apparently I have more to contribute to the company than I realized. Together, we could put the Emery name on my father's water engine—and then the game is over for a long, long time."

"I'll need to *see* it. I trust you, Coops, but this is too big for farting around."

"Of course. So here's what I propose: this afternoon, let's meet, just the two of us, at Questover, and—"

"All the way up *there* again?"

"Hear me out. We're looking at the deal of the decade, maybe the deal of the century. We need privacy and security. Questover is secluded, and you just had the place swept yesterday. I have the prototype; it's with me right now. I'll bring it, and I'll demonstrate it. It comes with complete instructions—in a tape from my father."

"No kidding . . ." Bix was mulling something.

"No kidding. We're two reasonable men, Bix, and we share a common goal. I'm ready to talk terms."

With a low laugh, Bix said, "You're smarter than I gave you credit for."

"I'll take that as a compliment—coming from you."

"Okay. I can be there by two."

Coop paused to consider. "I *think* that'll work. Sure, I'll try to be there by then."

"And be alone, hear me? It's just us—man to man."

"Yes, sir."

After they said good-bye, Coop pocketed his phone. He stood with his rump perched on the doorsill of the Metropolitan, parked in the clearing behind and below Questover, where a housekeeping crew had been toiling since eight to cleanse the kitchen of

Bix's experiment with manzanita jam. The rear doors of their van were flung wide, revealing an extensive arsenal of sprays, powders, mops, scrubbers and scouring implements, all of which were conscripted into service that morning.

The crew wrapped up their duties around eleven-thirty, with the kitchen looking magazine-worthy. One of the women asked Coop, "Can I fix you some lunch before we leave, Mr. Brant?"

"No, thank you, Irma. I'll manage on my own." He tinkered in the main room at the big coffee table in front of the fireplace, where he had placed the cardboard box.

"Very good, sir. Then we'll be on our way."

"I'll be in and out, so don't bother locking up. I'll log you out later."

"Yes, sir. Thank you, sir. Have a pleasant day."

Coop waved a cheery good-bye as they trundled down the stairs and out the back door. No one paused to touch the keypad before loading up the van and driving away. Coop grinned. Anyone trying to check on his whereabouts would have no idea that he'd already arrived for the meeting at two.

He cleared everything from the top of the coffee table, then covered it with several layers of old newspapers. Lifting the mimeograph from its box, he decided that he and Bix would sit as they had the night before, with Coop facing the kitchen; he placed the mimeograph near his side of the coffee table.

Shortly after noon, he removed his sport coat, carried it down the hall to one of the guest rooms, and left it there, returning with a portable cassette player, which he set on the coffee table, away from the mimeograph. The tape was in his shirt pocket.

Moving to the kitchen, he rummaged in a cupboard and found a plastic funnel. Then he opened the refrigerator and browsed its contents, removing, first, a bottle from Pyrite's stock of Fiji water and, second, a plastic-wrapped plate of the leftovers from Bix's roasted bird.

The water, still sealed, was for the demonstration that would follow.

The chicken was for lunch.

**A**t home in the compound at Entrada, Stasia picked at her lunch, a cold pasta salad dressed with pesto, hearts of palm, and a sweet salsa of chunky fresh tomatoes. She forked one more noodle to her mouth, ate it, then dumped the rest of the plate into the sink and switched on the disposal, which sucked away the oily mélange—extra-virgin—with a hungry slurp.

She put the plate in the dishwasher, closed its door with a thud, lifted a glass of chilled chardonnay from the counter, and carried it back to the master bedroom suite, where the boxes she'd called for had arrived.

Coop had already cleared his things out of his bathroom. Now Stasia began the task of clearing his closet. With the wine in one hand and a box in the other, she entered his dressing room, assessed its contents, and decided to begin with the pants. Kneeling on the floor, she set the wine on the carpet and took the first pair of corduroys from the bottom row of hangers. It was a black pair, fine-waled, perhaps the same pair he'd worn at their wedding.

She folded the pants carefully, placed them in the bottom of the box, then brushed the tips of her fingers across the corduroy's downy nap.

Her nails left parallel trails along the thigh.

**B**y one-thirty, at Questover, Coop was ready and waiting. He sat in the center of the sofa, within reach of Ferris Brant's prototype, which was now draped with a checked gingham tablecloth, red and white, the sort found in pizza places. Funnel, bottled water, and tape player were also at hand. He recalled his father's advice: Own your lines. Check your props. Keep your focus.

Remembering something, he went down to the back door and punched in the cleaning crew's exit code.

When he returned upstairs, he ducked into the guest room and flossed his teeth. Bix's old bird had been a gristly one.

**A**round two o'clock, out on the road, a chrome-laden Hummer, gunmetal gray, climbed the last few hundred feet of elevation beyond Idyllwild. Inside, Bix gripped the steering wheel with one hand; his other hand held it loosely while tapping out the rhythm as Sinatra sang "Old Devil Moon." Pyrite got up from Bix's lap, stepped onto the center console, stretched, and then moved to the passenger seat, settling against someone's khaki-clad leg.

The rider said, "Give me your phone."

Bix passed it over. A block or so short of Questover, not yet visible around the next bend, Bix pulled to the side of the road, stopped, and turned off the music. "I wonder if he's here. Christ, I'm not even sure if the damn cleaning crew's left yet."

"You'll find out soon enough." The rider finished punching a number into the phone and returned it to Bix. "That's all set; just press 'send.' If you decide you want me to come in and finish things up for you, find an excuse to make the call. You can say anything you want on the phone. The only thing I'll be listening for is 'It's a go.' After that, there's no stopping me. Once you've said it, check your watch; I'll come through the door in exactly three minutes. Got it?"

"Got it." Bix nodded, rehearsing, "It's a go."

"And for God's sake, when you enter the house, be sure to leave the door unlocked. I don't want to be left standing there ringing the bell like the damn Avon lady. Got it?"

"*Yes*, Zimmer, I won't lock you out. Now, scram. I need to get up there—alone."

Zimmer tousled Pyrite's ruff, opened the door, and stepped down to the road. His heavy black service shoes beat a quick, quiet path into the surrounding pines.

Bix shifted the Hummer into low gear and climbed the remaining distance to Questover. Passing under the sign, he cruised the last few yards to his parking space near the front door, then killed the engine. He got out, lifted Pyrite out—"that's right, you little son f'bitch, we're here"—and set him on the ground.

The dog scampered over to a low hedge of boxwood and peed on it.

"Good boy. Come on now, sweet pea."

Pyrite returned to Bix's heels as the old man walked up to the front door.

Inside, Coop stepped out from the guest room, shrugging into his sport coat. He closed the door behind him, and while returning through the hall to the great room, he heard the Hummer arrive, heard its engine stop, heard Pyrite's yapping as a key rattled the lock. When the door opened, Bix stood there for a moment, tapping his code into the keypad, which bleeped beneath his fingers. Then he called, "Anybody home?"

"Hi there, Bix," said Coop, stepping forward, checking his watch. "Right on time. Just got here myself."

"Hi, Coops." Bix came inside, closing the door. "Where have you *been*?"

But Coop didn't answer. Instead, he backed off a pace and crossed his arms. "I thought we agreed to come *alone* today."

Caught off guard, Bix responded dumbly, "Huh?"

"This meeting is highly confidential, but you brought some company." Coop paused, then laughed. "Pyrite."

"Ha!" Bix slapped his leg. "That little son f'bitch hears everything, but you can trust him—he never talks."

The dog barked, then started sniffing his way around the room. The kitchen typically commanded his highest level of interest, but recently cleansed, it had a residual antiseptic tang that afternoon, which sent the dog skittering down the hall, where he disappeared among the guest rooms. Coop called, "Here, Pyrite," and the dog returned, settling on one of the sofas, the one where Bix would sit.

Bix looked in that direction. The checked tablecloth caught his attention. "What've you got there?"

Coop grinned.

Bix stroked his chin, then suggested, "How 'bout a drink?"

"No," Coop said decisively, "we need clear heads for this. Sit down. Let's talk." And he led his father-in-law to the coffee table, where they resumed their positions of the previous night—Coop near the prototype, Bix across from him, next to Pyrite. Coop said, "It's real. It works."

"Show me."

"Appearances can be deceiving, so first a few words of explanation—from the inventor himself." Coop took the cassette from his pocket and passed it to Bix, saying, "That's Dad's writing on the side. I'd know it anywhere."

Bix fingered the tape, looked at it, passed it back. "You've had this all along, haven't you?"

"Truth is, I've had it only a week, and I didn't figure out what it was till last night."

"Yeah, right." Bix winked.

Coop put the tape in the machine and began playing it. He told Bix, "I think you'll know his voice."

The tape began, "Ferris Brant. Easter lecture. Revision nine. Gentlemen—"

"Hell," said Bix, nodding, "anyone over fifty would recognize *that* voice."

Coop tapped his lips with an index finger, encouraging Bix to listen.

Ferris lectured, "You wouldn't be here if you didn't already understand the implications of this quest . . . . The water engine. We've all heard of it; we've all laughed at it . . . . Again and again, skeptics have been proven wrong. Here, today, you see before you a draped object . . ."

When Ferris spoke of the beaker of plain water, Coop twisted the cap off the bottle of Fiji water, drank a slug as proof of its contents, and offered it to Bix, who declined, wagging his hand.

Ferris continued, "With that said, and without further ado: *Voilà!*"

Coop lifted the checkered tablecloth and dropped it aside.

Bix crossed his arms. "Christ, what *is* that—some shitty old Ditto machine?"

Coop said, "It's a mimeograph."

Ferris explained, "I found it provided a handy framework—a surrogate chassis, if you will—for the development of a ground-breaking technology . . ."

Bix nodded, reconsidering, listening.

Prior to the promised demonstration of the prototype, when Ferris began reviewing the laws of thermodynamics, Coop stopped the tape. "I think we can skip this part—it's pretty dry—

and pick it up later."

Bix lifted a hand. "Hold on, Coops. No question—that's Ferris Brant talking, all right, and I guess that contraption must be his invention. I wish you'd let me in on this sooner, but I'm glad you finally came to your senses." He leaned forward, elbows on knees, asking, "What do you want?"

Coop paused, thinking. "The president's position, I could actually make something of that—if it came with a measure of independence and authority."

"What else?"

"Well, I hardly need to tell you what this technology could be worth to the company. I mean, how do you even begin to measure it?"

Bix nodded. "Yup, I imagine we're into seven figures—*well* into seven figures."

Coop gave him a look.

Bix conceded, "Maybe eight."

"Maybe nine," said Coop.

Bix laughed. "You're fuckin' nuts."

"Jay Pontarelli didn't think so. That's what *he* offered me. But I told him I'd rather keep it in the family."

"I'm touched." With a snort, Bix added, "Do you have any idea how long it took me to make my first hundred million?"

With a cowboy twang, Coop answered, "A whole lot longer than it just took me, I reckon."

Bix stared him down for a long moment, jaw flexing. Then he pulled out his phone. "Austin Royce is waiting for my call."

"I thought you were going to fire him."

"Next week. I figured he might be useful today—to help me settle this with you. He knows why I'm here." Bix pressed a button on his phone.

Coop asked, "There's a contract written up? Just fill in the blanks?"

"Something like that." Then Bix said into the phone, "Austin, I'm sitting here with Coops, and we've come to terms—hell of a lot steeper than I thought. Nine figures. Yes, I'm serious. Not a lump sum, of course. It'll have to be a package—salary, signing bonus, stock options, percent of profits on the device, the usual ball of wax. Work out the details, and just make it happen. Point is: it's a go." Bix checked his watch.

Instinctively, Coop checked his as well; the second hand swept past the twelve at exactly two-fifteen. Coop thought, It's a go? Odd phraseology from Bix.

Then Bix repeated it: "That's right, it's a go." He checked his watch again. "Thanks, Austin. I'll be back in touch later." He clicked off and pocketed the phone.

"So," said Coop, "it seems we're partners."

"You better believe it. Joined at the hip."

"Will you level with me about a few things?"

"Anything you want. Shoot."

"Last night, you said that Jay Pontarelli thought Kavanall had the prototype. Did you think so too?"

"I wasn't sure."

"What I'm driving at"—Coop hesitated, exhaling heavily— "and I've come to think of you as a father, Bix, but what I really need to know is this: Was it you who sent Kav to Riverside the night my father was killed?"

Bix sat without speaking for a moment, looking at Coop, looking *through* Coop, as if considering the weight of the question. "All right," he said with a nod, "since you already seem to know it, there's no point denying it. Yes, I sent Kav to Riverside, but I didn't send him to kill your dad. I sent him there to make a preemptive offer on the technology. Your dad laughed at him and threatened to expose the 'shady tactics' of Emery Oil during his speech the next morning. They argued. Then they fought, and things got out of hand. Stupid bastard—I mean Kavanall, not your father." Bix glanced at his watch.

Coop did the same; one minute had passed. He said, "But you *doted* on Kavanall."

"Doted on him? I couldn't stand him—the flake—but he had me by the balls, since we both had a part in what happened that night. Your father told him he gave the water engine to someone for safekeeping, but I couldn't afford to believe *anybody*. If the contraption even existed, I figured either Kavanall took it or your dad gave it to you." Reflecting briefly, Bix added, "Back then, I wanted to buy it and bury it. Now, I want to build it. How times have changed."

"So you covered your bases," said Coop. "You brought me into the family and kept us all at the compound."

Bix grinned. "*Now* you're catching on—keep your friends close, but keep your enemies closer."

It was news to Coop that he was Bix's enemy.

"And it worked," said Bix. He gestured toward the mimeograph. "There it is."

Though Coop was loath to admit it, the old guy's contorted logic almost made sense. He said, "There's no delicate way to put this, but something tells me you killed your own grandson."

"You saw me sitting in the golf cart when it happened. That's called 'plausible deniability'—a dear old friend taught me about that during a weekend huntin' trip." Bix checked the time again. Another minute had passed since his phone call.

Coop allowed, "You may have been in the cart . . ."

Bix shrugged. "I call the shots. Always have. It's my job—and I'm damn good at it. On the second fairway that day, I muffed the ball and sent Kavanall into the rough. That was the signal that I'd made up my mind. He'd just talked about having 'plenty' to contribute to PontaPower. He was taunting me, and he paid for that mistake. Plus, I thought he was holding out on me—with the water engine. Turns out, he wasn't. Turns out, you were."

"Is that why I almost had an 'accident' on the way home last night?"

"That was then, Coops, and this is now." Bix checked his watch.

So did Coop. Some two and a half minutes had passed—very nearly three.

Bix chuckled, sitting back. "Do you honestly think I'll let you walk away from here knowing the things I just told you? And do you honestly think I'd pay that kind of money for something that might not even work? If it does work, great, I'll have it; if not, too bad, nothing lost. Either way, Coops, you're simply out of the picture now."

"Am I?" Coop pinched his cheeks. "Seems I'm sitting right

here."

"Cute. Did you honestly think I'd be dumb enough to come up here alone?"

Coop countered, "Did *you* honestly think I didn't think you wouldn't?"

Bix cocked his head. "You kinda lost me there. What?"

"Did you honestly think . . ." And instead of finishing the question, Coop raised his hand to the lapel of his jacket and flipped it over briefly, revealing the small black bud of a microphone. Its wire disappeared inside the coat.

Bix froze where he sat, eyes fixed on the mike. When Coop dropped his hand and the lapel flipped back, Bix checked his watch, then turned his head for a quick look at the front door. He started to say something.

But Coop spoke over him: "As long as you've spent all that money today, you're entitled to see what you bought, don't you think?"

With panic evident on his face, Bix stammered something.

Coop continued, "So you're going to get the full demonstration, the one that got preempted fifteen Easters ago." He fast-forwarded the cassette, which squeaked and squealed. Watching the tape counter, he said, "Right about here." He then punched the PLAY button and turned up the volume.

Ferris Brant was saying, ". . . time to get down to business. It's the moment you've all been waiting for. First, let me just drop open these side trays . . ."

As Ferris spoke, Coop took the role of his father's stand-in, demonstrating with the items right there on the coffee table. He opened both of the mimeograph's paper trays. He wedged the plastic funnel into a crevice near the top of the machine. He uncapped the water bottle, tasting it again, then poured about half of it into the funnel. Ferris laughed softly, noting, "This part's sort of messy." Water started to leak from the bottom of the machine, blackened by residual ink from its innards. As Ferris spoke, Coop followed along and slowly turned the side crank, which resisted at first, since the mesh of the transfer screen had grown brittle over so many years of disuse. As instructed by the tape, Coop emptied the remaining water into the funnel, cranking faster. An inky mess now flowed from the turning drum as the screen it-self began to shred. It flopped and slapped with each turn of the crank, oozing onto the table. The cranking stopped. "As you may have guessed by now," said Ferris, laughing heartily, "I've called you here this morning to make a point."

Bix's face had reddened. Slowly, deliberately, he said through a low growl, "Why, you *son* of a bitch."

Pyrite pricked his ears. Accustomed to hearing the phrase spo-ken as a term of endearment, but confused by its present tone, the dog got up from where he lay, standing on the cushion next to Bix, tilting his head in a manner that asked, What's up?

Affably, Coop asked Bix, "Would you just listen?" He once again flashed the old man a peek at his lapel bug. "There's more."

The tape played on: ". . . hope you'll forgive me for interrupt-ing your plans, but it was crucial that we face these issues as a group, united in purpose . . ."

Bix checked his watch. So did Coop; it was now more than six minutes since Bix had placed the call. He turned, trembling, to look at the door again.

Coop raised his brows in an expression that asked, Expecting someone?

". . . if a powerful consortium of energy interests such as you could find the commitment in your hearts, in your guts, to kick the fossil-fuel habit . . ."

Bix's angry, reddened face suddenly flushed. With a wild look in his eyes, he wrapped both arms around his chest. His mouth opened to emit a powerless gasp. When he tried to stand, he couldn't. Sitting at the edge of the sofa, he grappled inside his shirt and withdrew the chain around his neck, from which hung his silver bullet. Coop had never seen Bix's chain before; it was identical to the stylized platinum barbed-wire necklace that had garroted Ferris Brant.

". . . there is no single silver bullet. The solution consists of many answers, which we need to begin exploring *now*, today, not in the rush of some future crisis . . ."

Bix struggled to unscrew the bullet-shaped locket. When he

finally had it open, he fumbled the nitro pill—round and white, like a tiny aspirin—which fell from his fingers. Pyrite sprang from the cushion and snatched the pill before it hit the floor. Bix croaked, barely audible, "Drop it, Pyrite."

". . . with dedication and foresight, we can develop a whole array of alternatives . . ."

While the tape continued playing, Coop said, "And you know the real irony, Bix? One of your own employees, Tessa Irwin, delivered the very same message this past Monday at your R-and-D meeting. She'd already heard the lecture, back in her graduate seminars. Dad's goal was simply to get the message out of the classroom and deliver it to those who could implement it fastest. Today, everyone understands what he was preaching, but fifteen years ago, it was visionary, even radical."

Struggling for breath, Bix mouthed, "Drop it, Pyrite." With a spasm of pain, one leg kicked, nearly hitting the dog.

Pyrite ducked under the table, then reappeared at Coop's ankle.

"Turns out," said Coop, "Dad's vision was not only radical, but dangerous. Two people died. Lives were ruined. Fifteen years, wasted; a valuable head start, lost. And all along, who was in the background, pulling the strings?"

Writhing, Bix slipped to the floor.

Coop commanded, "Pyrite. Drop it."

The pill landed near the tip of Coop's shoe.

Bix stretched out his hand, but his reach was short by a yard.

". . . so again I must apologize for the admittedly unorthodox method I contrived to assemble you this morning . . ."

Down the hall, a guest-room door burst open, and into the great room rushed Arcie, with a headset looped around her neck, along with a squad of police personnel—two plainclothesmen and two in uniform. She yelled to Coop, "Someone said, 'Drop it.' Is there a weapon?"

"No," he assured her, standing. "Bix must be having a heart attack. He had a nitroglycerin tablet, but dropped it."

Two of the officers had already moved Bix to an open area of the floor, administering CPR. Another was calling for medical backup, but it would be slow in arriving, given the remote location. In the background, the lecture tape continued to play.

Coop explained to Arcie, "And the dog grabbed the pill."

"Good God," she said, crouching to look at Pyrite, fingering his chin. "Hope it doesn't kill the little fella."

"He'll be all right."

". . . while preparing for this lecture. Among friends and colleagues, I often spoke of my secret prototype as the Mac-Guffin . . ."

The CPR did not seem to be going well.

Coop said to Arcie, "Bix kept checking his watch. I think he was expecting company."

Arcie nodded. "Good thing we had the front of the house staked out. He was armed, all right—but not anymore."

One of the CPR guys said, "I think we're losing him."

"Losing him?" said the other. "I think he's gone."

Arcie stepped to Coop, put an arm around him, and leaned her head on his shoulder.

As Coop pulled Arcie into a full hug, his father's lecture drew to a close:

". . . dates back to the 1960s. Two legendary filmmakers, Alfred Hitchcock and François Truffaut, sat down for a series of taped interviews, and the plot device of MacGuffins was discussed at length. Though the master of suspense frequently used them, he didn't much like them. 'So you see,' concluded Hitchcock, 'a MacGuffin is nothing at all.'"

# Chapter 16

Five months after Bix Emery died—nearly sixteen years after Ferris Brant's death—Cooper Brant, son-in-law of the former, son of the latter, discovered his favorite pair of corduroys, bottle green, stowed in a box mislabeled BATH TOWELS. His wife, Stasia Emery-Brant, had already begun packing his things on the day her father was to die—not out of spite, not out of eagerness to send her husband away, but rather with a clearheaded recognition of a new reality and with a resolve to face the inevitable.

That afternoon, learning of her father's death, which followed her son's by only nine days, Stasia slipped into an emotional tailspin, but Coop was relieved to observe that the setback would prove both minor and temporary. That very evening, when he broke the news that Kavanall had died on Bix's orders, he witnessed a remarkable transformation in Stasia. Within a matter of hours, her grief gave way to disbelief, then denial, which in turn was supplanted by acceptance. And by the next morning, she was voicing a healthy determination to exact revenge on the old bastard.

"But he's already dead," Coop reminded her.

Though patricide was no longer an option, Stasia had devised another, a fate Bix would consider worse than death: his legacy would be soiled, his wishes would not be followed, and there would soon be a woman at the helm of Emery Energy. Stasia now owned all of the company's family-held stock, more than Bix himself had controlled, so she could structure things any way she damn pleased. That would begin the next Monday. Meanwhile, on Saturday, the day after Bix died, Stasia seemed preoccupied by her creative juices, by the plan to reinvent both herself and her father's company, so she busied herself with absentminded make-work, packing her husband's things—and that's how Coop's green corduroys, worn the day before, got boxed with the extra towels.

The actual separation, which took place a few days later, was wholly amicable. Coop and Stasia took off their rings, and Coop moved out of their house in the Emery compound. Stasia even suggested that he should move into one of the two unoccupied houses—Kavanall's or Bix's—but such an arrangement, while friendly, struck Coop as entirely too close for comfort.

He'd long had a dream to design and build his own house, not as part of a family compound and not subject to the stylistic whims of others, but as a pure expression of his own aesthetic philosophy. That could wait; that was a process requiring study and deliberation, and there would be plenty of time for it later. For the time being, he simply needed a place to live, so he found an existing house on the other side of town, which he judged un-remarkable, but it had "good bones." No gates, no guards, no bubble. When he moved in, he considered the setup temporary and left a number of unopened cartons stacked in the garage.

Arcie Madera visited frequently, sometimes spending the night. By December, two months after Bix died, Bruce Rollo was out of the picture entirely, having accepted a new teaching gig—in Italy. In January, *Architectural Record* devoted its cover story to the new Emery headquarters, declaring it "iconic" and its architect "a fer-tile creative talent who, with one masterful stroke, has entered the top ranks of American design." On the evening when Arcie first read the article, she said, "Wow, talk about an early valen-tine," and reminded Coop of her attraction to creative men. By February fourteenth, Coop could afford to be highly selective in accepting future projects, and he and Arcie, sipping champagne, began discussing the possibility of a life together.

But they agreed it was unseemly to start making plans while, technically, he was still married. Though the divorce was un-contested, the lawyers kept finding snags, given the size and complexity of the estate to be settled. By the time all the *t*'s were crossed, it was March, and Coop was scheduled to ink his final signatures on a Thursday morning in Stasia's office at company headquarters.

He awoke alone at home that day—five months after Bix had died. It was not a gym morning with Teddy, so Coop could take his time getting out of the house. He lingered in a robe on the patio, finishing his coffee and the papers. There was a front-page story about Mason Zimmer, the hit man, which was big news locally. He'd been a part-time security officer at Entrada, which explained both why Coop had thought he looked familiar and why Coop had mistaken him for an undercover cop. Zimmer did indeed have a black Jeep registered in his name, and he had been golfing on an employee's pass the morning Kavanall was killed. Topping it off, a shotgun was found in his golf bag, stored in a security-office locker. Open and shut. But additional legal maneuverings had again postponed the trial, and it seemed a plea bargain was in the works. He might get off with less than life, no parole. Whatever the sentence, thought Coop, the arrest and conviction would look good for Arcie. What's more, the earlier case in Riverside was no longer an unsolved blemish on her record, and Coop frequently enjoyed reminding her that befriending him had been a boost to her career.

After rinsing out the coffeemaker, he walked to the bathroom to begin his ablutions and, finding no fresh towels, recalled the unopened boxes in storage. So he stepped out to the garage, found the box of towels, and noticed, next to it on the floor, the corrugated box containing the old mimeograph. He had an idea, laughed, and put the machine in his car. Then he opened the box of towels and found his pet pair of cords.

He'd been wondering for months what had happened to them. He shook them out, found them clean and reasonably unwrinkled, and decided to wear them that day.

It was a perfect spring morning in the desert, the sort of brilliant, dry day with cool air and penetrating sunlight that made snowbirds ask, Why would we ever leave this? As Coop drove past the block-long sign of stacked stone and stainless steel, braking the Tesla at the Emery gatehouse, he reminded himself that his soon-to-be-final divorce would not spell the end of his presence there. The campus was far from complete, and with his newfound recognition from the *Record,* Stasia had been quick to mention, "You signed on for the whole deal—and I can't imagine anyone else finishing it." After waving to the guard, Coop followed the winding drive back to the executive parking lot. He got out of the car and retrieved the boxed mimeograph from the trunk, then carried it through the solar garden to the main building.

The facility had been brand new when Bix had died, and nothing had changed—not visually, at least—but Coop sensed, walking through the doors and along the main corridor, that the atmosphere of the place had been refreshed and enlivened. News of Bix's death had sent the company stock plummeting at first, but as the effects of Stasia's takeover began to be felt, confidence in the company and its future soared. First-quarter profits, to be announced in a few weeks, would leave skeptical stockholders both surprised and pleased.

There was a whole new lineup in the front offices. Austin Royce, the CFO who had yearned for the presidency, had been elevated even further, to chief executive officer. Borrowing a page from Bix's playbook—"keep your friends close, but keep your enemies closer"—Stasia had recruited Jay Pontarelli as president, making an offer he couldn't refuse and stopping PontaPower cold in its fledgling tracks. Perhaps most important, Stasia felt a genuine commitment to the alternative-energy goals to which Bix had merely paid lip service, and one of her first executive actions was to promote Tessa Irwin as corporate vice president for research. Tessa's higher-ups —Dunmire, Max, and Sander—were offered early-retirement packages, which they went for like hungry dogs snapping at raw meat.

But the biggest change, front and center, was within the inner sanctum. On the glass wall outside the reception room, elegant gold-leaf lettering announced, simply, ANASTASIA EMERY-BRANT, and beneath it, in contrast to her father's litany of power, a single title, CHAIRMAN. A worker in a jumpsuit stepped through the door several paces ahead of Coop. He carried a small tray of tools, including a razor knife, which he set on the carpet, inside the window, near the gold-leaf lettering. It seemed Stasia's name was about to be shortened.

The two secretaries from the previous dynasty remained. Connie said, "Go right on in, Mr. Brant. She's expecting you."

As Coop entered the holy of holies, Pyrite yapped, rushing to sniff Coop's feet.

He set down the box, patted the dog, and stepped over to greet his wife, who got up from her chair behind the biggest desk in the building, looking every inch the titan.

"Hi, sweets," she said with a smile. They kissed.

Coop crossed his arms, nodding. "I think you've found your calling. You belonged in this office a long time ago."

With a soft laugh, she noted, "You were the only one who knew it. You had more faith in me than I had in myself." Eyeing the ratty old box, she asked, "What's *that*?"

"My dad's MacGuffin. I thought Tessa might like to have it—they could put it on a pedestal in the research lab with a big sign, 'Water engine, keep the faith,' or whatever."

"Most thoughtful. I'll see that she gets it."

Coop noticed a series of papers lined up along the edge of Stasia's desk, along with a pen. He asked, "So then, that's it? End of an era?"

With a wan smile, she echoed, "End of an era."

Everything was in order, and she had already done her signing. It took Coop only a minute or two to add his signature to all the documents.

When he was finished, she asked, "Plans for the weekend?"

"I'll be with Arcie. Saturday we're driving over to Pioneertown to visit Mimi. Sunday we'll visit Arcie's mother—I've never met her."

"Ah. Well, I hope it goes well, sweets. Give Arcie my best."

"Thanks, I will. She's meeting me for lunch today. Care to join us?"

"I would, truly, but there's just too much going on here." As they started moving toward the door together, Stasia said, "Not to bring up a sore subject, but I understand they've finally installed Bix's headstone; I really dragged my feet coming up with an inscription. If you're interested, check it out."

"I'll do that. It's such a nice day, I'll head over there after lunch."

As a thought occurred to Stasia, she smiled. "Would you care to take Pyrite?"

The dog yapped.

She continued, "He used to go with Bix a lot to visit Mom's grave, but I rarely have time enough to get out with him."

"I'd be happy to take custody for a few hours."

Stasia got the leash, and Coop crouched to attach it. Then they walked out to the reception area and kissed good-bye.

Coop said, "I'll have Pyrite back by two." He led the dog to the door, then turned, telling Stasia, "And good luck. Have a speedy recovery from your procedure."

She gave him a quizzical look.

He jerked his head toward the guy kneeling with a razor blade at the window, explaining, "Your hyphenectomy."

"Oh, *you*," she said, sputtering with laughter.

Then she blew him a kiss.

**F**aded little flags, plus offerings of coins and cigarettes, decorated the flat, unassuming headstone of Frank Sinatra's grave. Above his name, engraved for the ages: THE BEST IS YET TO COME.

"Over here, Pyrite!" called Coop.

The dog abandoned nosing the cigarette butts and trotted across the quiet drive, then pranced through another section of graves to the row of plots reserved for the Emery family, where Coop and Arcie stood holding hands, eyes cast to the ground. Half a year ago, only one of these plots had been occupied—by the first in the clan to die in California, Emma Emery: DEVOTED WIFE, LOVING MOTHER. She alone had staked out this turf for two decades, but now the neighborhood was getting crowded.

To Emma's left, three spots away, lay Kavanall. Above his name and dates: LOST TOO SOON. Coop wondered about the two intervening vacancies. One of them, clearly, was meant for Stasia, but the other? Perhaps Kavanall's father? Or some future husband of Stasia's? Of one thing Coop was certain—he would never lie there.

And tucked in next to Emma, to her right, was Bix himself, with a line of raised letters across the top of his newly installed bronze plaque: IT'S MY JOB. Arcie's brows pinched. "Odd inscription," she said to Coop.

"Stasia struggled with it. I can only imagine what she *wanted* to say."

Stasia had not even allowed Bix to be buried within the church—no last rites, no funeral Mass, no graveside service. Urged by Bix's longtime pastor to reconsider these decisions, Stasia had been adamant: "He was a believer, and he died with murder on his soul, which ought to seal the deal—but I'm taking no chances he might cop a reprieve. No priests allowed."

Arcie shook her head. "What a shame for a family to fall apart like that."

Coop reminded her, "They took part of mine with them."

She squeezed his hand tighter. "I know, Coop. I'm sorry."

He exhaled a breathy sigh. His mood lightened. He asked, "Ready?"

"Sure."

He reached into a pocket of his green corduroys and pulled out his keys. As he turned to leave, Pyrite dived toward his shoes.

"Hold on," said Arcie. "The dog's got something in his mouth—it fell out of your pocket."

"Really?" Coop hunkered down to investigate. "Pyrite. Drop it."

"It looked like an aspirin, maybe."

Coop repeated, "*Drop* it."

Pyrite obeyed. A little white pill fell into Coop's hand.

"Nah," said Coop, "can't be an aspirin—way too small." And with the middle finger of his other hand, he flicked the pill out of his palm. It shot toward Bix's headstone, bounced off the polished bronze, and landed in the grass beyond, about a yard away—still out of reach.

Coop turned and began walking Arcie to the car. He asked, "Busy later?"

"Not after five."

"Care to spend the night?"

"Try and stop me." She wrapped her arm around Coop's

waist, hooking a finger through one of his belt loops. Glancing behind, where Pyrite tarried near the graves, she called, "Come on, precious."

"Were you talking to me?" asked Coop. "Or the dog?"

Arcie smirked.

Pyrite yapped, skipping to their heels.

❏